THE RETURN OF
THE DWARVES
BOOK 2

Also by Markus Heitz

THE DWARVES

The War of the Dwarves
The Revenge of the Dwarves
The Fate of the Dwarves
The Triumph of the Dwarves
The Return of the Dwarves Book 1

LEGENDS OF THE ÄLFAR

Righteous Fury
Devastating Hate
Dark Paths
Raging Storm

DOORS

Doors: Twilight
Doors: Field of Blood
Doors: Colony

Oneiros
AERA: The Return of the Ancient Gods
The Dark Lands

THE RETURN OF THE DWARVES

BOOK II

MARKUS HEITZ

Translated by Sheelagh Alabaster

Arcadia

First published in Great Britain in 2024 by

Arcadia
An imprint of
Quercus Editions Limited
Carmelite House
50 Victoria Embankment
London EC4Y 0DZ

An Hachette UK company

The authorised representative in the EEA is Hachette Ireland, 8 Castlecourt Centre,
Castleknock Road, Castleknock, Dublin 15, D15 YF6A, Ireland

Cover design: Guter Punkt, München / Anke Koopmann
Cover illustrations: Elm Haßfurth / elmstreet.org
Translation: Sheelagh Alabaster

Die Rückkehr der Zwerge II was originally published in German in 2021 by
Verlagsgruppe Droemer Knaur GmbH & Co. KG, Munich, Germany.

A CIP catalogue record for this book is available
from the British Library

PB ISBN 978-1-52942-489-8
EBOOK ISBN 978-1-52942-490-4

1

Typeset by Jouve (UK), Milton Keynes

Printed and bound in Great Britain by Clays Ltd, Elcograf S.p.A.

Papers used by Arcadia are from well-managed
forests and other responsible sources.

I

Girdlegard

Northern United Great Kingdom of Gauragon
Foothills of the Grey Mountains
Platinshine
1023 P.Q. (7514th solar cycle in old reckoning), autumn

From his position up on the roof of the fortified house, Barbandor Steelgold from the clan of the Royal Water Drinkers was proudly appraising the progress of the current stage of the rebuilding works. As the lone sentry keeping watch over the devastated town this had been his vantage point until eventually other dwarves arrived in Platinshine ready to build the town anew.

On all sides the sounds of hammering and clattering could be heard. Cranes were being worked by sheer muscle power, heaving wooden beams, piles of stones or stacks of roof shingles. Heavy stone blocks were being placed in the breaches in the town's double walls, and then cemented into position, thus ensuring the burned-out settlement was no longer vulnerable to attack. Foremen issued loud instructions to labourers and machine operators. Elsewhere, bagpipe and flageolet music entertained the workforce, encouraging them in their efforts and improving everyone's mood as they toiled and sweated in the last warm rays of the sun.

By winter we'll have broken the back of the work. Barbandor had been elected councillor because of his services to the town. He had accepted the responsibility with pride and delight, and now, over his outer clothing and chainmail tunic, he wore the embroidered white sash of office, making it clear to the townspeople that he was the person to bring their worries and queries to.

All in all the town now had about one thousand souls again sheltering within the walls. Life was returning, filling the dark-haired Fifthling with immense satisfaction.

Platinshine had been badly damaged by fire in the white dragon's disastrous visitation, following the town's refusal to pay Ûra the tribute she demanded, and there was a considerable amount of repair work to be embarked on. But it was the loss of all the original inhabitants that was far more grievous.

Barbandor's brown eyes turned again to gaze over at the Grey Mountains. Since the recent changes wrought by Tungdil Goldhand's secret plan, the rocky landscape had become almost unrecognisable. Cartographers would have a lifetime's work ahead of them, making the necessary alterations to the old maps. Barbandor rubbed his plaited beard and played with its decorative white gold clip while he surveyed the mountain range. The outline of the peaks was no longer the same and none of the extant records concerning the tunnels, corridors and shafts were of any use at all now.

But these changes meant that Girdlegard was now safe and secure against incursion.

All five previously open access points in the mountains had been permanently destroyed by means of carefully planned rockfalls and collapses. Where the new entrances were located was known only to Goldhand.

He will announce it as soon as the Brown Mountains have been liberated, I presume. Barbandor shut his eyes, relishing the warmth of the sun on his lined and scarred face. More than a few extra furrows had been acquired in recent orbits, created by his exploits and by anxiety. *Let us hope victory against Brigantia will soon be ours.*

'Hey there, Master Steelgold!' The shout came loud and clear over the noise of construction. 'Come down off your roof, will you? Otherwise I'll be thinking you are your own statue, standing up there, Councillor!'

Barbandor opened his eyes and searched the lanes and alleys below to see who was calling him. About fifteen paces diagonally beneath there stood a young blonde dwarf girl dressed in a simple woollen garment and a leather mantle over it against the autumn chill. She was holding a bundle in both hands. The fabric was stretched, indicating the contents were a considerable weight.

'What is it?' he called down to her.

'I've found something I need to show you.' She pointed to the fortified house and hurried over. 'Meet you in your office.'

What is this all about? Barbandor knew the young dwarf woman. Her name was Gyndala Tenderfist of the clan of the Gold Finders. She was originally from Forgeburg, near the lava fields. It was one of the eastern settlements keeping an eye on the movements of the fire-eater orcs. *I don't suppose she'll have come just to bring me something to eat.*

He went down through the hatchway and took the stairs leading from the attic to his sparsely furnished official workplace. There had been no time to arrange any decoration apart from the banner with the town's coat of arms.

Gyndala placed the tightly wrapped bundle on the table. She wore her long blonde hair braided. Her light-coloured eyes shone with eager impatience. 'This is for you,' she announced.

'Very thoughtful of you.' Barbandor stepped closer and tried to guess what the bundle contained, going only by its bumpy shape. 'But I suppose it's not really a gift.'

'No. I found it in the burned-out house that used to belong to the healer. In the cellar.' Gyndala opened the jute bag. 'There wasn't much left.'

Barbandor had at first feared she might be presenting him with some of the mortal remains of Master Goldspark, but the contents of the bundle actually proved to be a random collection of charred objects that it took him some time to identify. 'Those are orc things.'

'From *those* orcs killed outside the Platinshine gates by the town's catapults,' Gyndala went on enthusiastically. She laid the items out carefully as if they were some kind of treasure she was displaying. 'The fire has damaged them badly but you can still see that they're totally different from the kind of belongings the lava field beasts we've been plagued with would normally have.'

Barbandor lifted two metal discs and studied them, rubbing off the rust. He opened two leather bags that gave off an intriguing smell of roasted herbs; then he picked up a dagger and knocked the dirt off it, revealing high-quality steel underneath.

'Indeed. Very different, Gyndala. I agree with you,' he murmured as he examined the items.

'I was struck by the craftsmanship,' she said excitedly. 'It cannot compare with our own metalwork, of course. But it's definitely as good as anything that humans might produce.' She picked out an engraved clasp that must once have fastened a garment. 'And look at the filigree work here. Amazing, for orcs, don't you think?'

This find substantiated Barbandor's idea that these beasts had come in from the Outer Lands in order to hunt for dwarves and to try to find Tungdil Goldhand's wooden chest with his journal in it. Together with his friend he had thoroughly spoiled their little game on the banks of the Towan that time. 'Quite clever work. If their intellect is similarly advanced then I'm mighty glad the mountain passageways through to Girdlegard are closed now.'

'Yes, it's more peaceful, apart from the siege going on in the Brown Mountains. But that's a long way away. When I left Forgeburg it seemed like the fire eaters had all gone.' Gyndala sat down and rested her chin on her hand while she investigated the various pieces. As she sniffed at what was left of the herbs, the pale fluff on her plump cheeks shimmered in the autumn sunshine.

Barbandor had heard about the orc groups in the east of the foothills. While Platinshine had had to deal with the salt sea orcs, the fire-eater beasts had tried to establish a reputation as flameproof raiders, by settling in small villages and outposts on islands high above the lakes of liquid fire. Forgeburg had always managed to control these orcs if they strayed too near to areas inhabited by dwarves or humans.

'I thought you'd wiped them out?' he said.

'No. As soon as they see they're losing, they retreat off to one of the larger islands in the lava. Or they hide out in caves filled with fumes that are noxious for us so we can't pursue them.' Gyndala put the brooch down. 'Just wait. It won't be long before the pig-faces attack again. But if they do, my big brother will sort them out and no mistake. Their weird frilly ears will be trembling and their rotten teeth will be falling out, by Vraccas!'

'How is it you're so sure the fire eaters will be attacking again?'

'Winter's on its way. They'll need supplies.' Gyndala rolled a few dried fibres into a small ball and stared at it. 'I wonder what *that* is.'

'Healing herbs, I suppose. Or tobacco, maybe, for chewing?' *I like a good chew of tobacco myself. I hope that's the only thing we've got in common.* Barbandor weighed the metal discs in his hand. They would have been part of scale or lamellar armour. Something was not right, his gut was telling him. 'They're too heavy,' he muttered, suddenly understanding.

'Too heavy?'

'I'm thinking back to the armoured orc that came out of the Towan. I assumed he'd arrived, like the four dozen others, swept down the river from the Outer Lands, but . . .' Barbandor furrowed his brow. 'But in armour like this they'd never have made it in the river all the way to us.'

'They survived the Emerald Falls. So why couldn't they have managed to shoot the rapids . . .' Gyndala paused. 'By the Eternal Smith! You are right. Not even a pig-face can swim hundreds of miles in an icy river where there's strong currents and rocks and undertows.'

Barbandor stared at the small metal plates he was holding in his tough calloused hands. *I made a dangerous error.* He chucked them down on the table with the rest of the things and made for the door. 'Thank you for bringing me what you found. You've no idea how much you've helped me to make sense of things.'

'You're welcome.' Gyndala looked at him, full of curiosity. 'Where are you off to?'

'I'm going to check the works. At the outside wall,' he said, grabbing his heavy battle weapon with its elaborately engraved steel axe head, and settling it in its holster over his shoulder. 'See you later. Meet you in the Green Barrel. First round's on me.'

'I'll hold you to that,' she called after him.

Well, two-thirds of what I said was true, so I wasn't actually lying. Barbandor did not want the dwarf girl coming with him. He must make good his mistake without putting Platinshine's inhabitants in a state of panic. The shock from recent events still sat too deep, so as leader of the council and in his capacity in charge of the town's defences he must conduct his own enquiries.

Barbandor hurried through the streets and alleyways, handing out praise to the labouring workers as he went. He inspected the repairs to the double rampart of the town defences and then he left Platinshine on the road that led out to the Towan river and to Smallwater.

He was glad that no one stopped to ask him what he was going to the humans' village for. This way he would not need to tell a lie.

As he made his way quickly through the shelter of a little wood towards the river and the Emerald Falls, the truth occurred to him. It was as if dragon scales had fallen from his eyes. It was obvious. *Why didn't I realise?* The weight of the armour and the fact that the beast spoke in the vernacular. In the Outer Lands Girdlegard's common tongue was hardly ever used. And certainly not by orcs.

He gave himself the excuse that the dragon Ûra had attacked them that very evening and he had himself been injured. After that he had been preoccupied with trying to protect Platinshine and then he had gone off with Goïmron and his friends in search of Goldhand. *Why would I have bothered thinking about those dead orcs?*

Barbandor reached the pool at the foot of the Emerald Falls, where he was greeted by rolling clouds of spray, throwing up the occasional red and yellow leaf. Autumn had made the colours of the surrounding trees strikingly attractive and the air was full of the smell of damp moss and fungi.

He looked up at the top of the waterfall. *If the orcs didn't fall from up there* – and he scanned the cascading white and green curtain of water – *then they must have emerged further down.*

He walked forward cautiously, his upturned axe to hand as a support as he made his way over the slippery stones.

Whether there would still be the slightest trace now, after half a cycle had passed, was a moot point, he thought. No more orcs had appeared in the meantime. Neither on the building site in Platinshine nor elsewhere in Smallwater, the village that was now being rebuilt by the humans.

Ûra's attack on our settlement maybe kept them from raiding us. Barbandor climbed across the lowest of the boulders and got within forty paces of the edge of the waterfall. *Every creature is frightened of the Falls.* He was drenched in the spray, soaked through in a matter of heartbeats, and he had to wipe the moisture away from his eyes several times. The going was treacherous and he picked his path with the utmost care. *But now the dragon is dead. The orcs might well want to take advantage of the circumstances, and the fact that the Brown Mountains are under siege. They may try to return.*

Barbandor had never discounted the threat of Elria's curse. Suspiciously he eyed the frothing pool into which the powerful emerald waters plunged. The basin appeared bottomless and was in all likelihood keen to pull any unsuspecting dwarf to a watery grave at the instigation of the goddess Elria. *May Vraccas keep me safe.*

To aid concentration he kept a little ball of chewing tobacco in his cheek. Cinnamon and mint together with the sharp taste of tobacco enlivened his thinking.

At the side of the main river that the Towan had merged with, Barbandor climbed up the rocks, step by careful step, then he replaced his axe in its holster on his back and, continuously soaked by the curtain of water, edged up the vertical wall, pulling himself up with cold wet fingers.

At a height of approximately twenty paces he noticed a naturally formed ledge going off to one side behind the cascade. The carved marking on the stone was, however, certainly not natural in origin. He did not recognise the rune but he was sure it had been made relatively recently, as it had only the thinnest of moss layers over it.

As I thought! Barbandor quickly moved on to the ledge and took tiny steps along. He was approaching the waterfall itself and through the first section of the cascade and the cloud of spray he could make out a darker shape that might indicate a large niche or a cave opening.

Barbandor was undecided.

He had no evidence that there were orcs hiding behind the waterfall. But if there were any and they caught him there would be a fight with an uncertain outcome. *I have no idea how many there might be.*

His curiosity got the better of him. In his capacity as councillor responsible for defence it was his duty to make sure.

The water showed its true force. Even the margins of the Emerald Falls plunged down on to him with such power that it felt as though he was being pelted with stones. His fingertips gripped the crevices in the stone with all the strength he could muster. His boot soles kept slipping.

I shan't make it over to that shadow shape. His neck, shoulders and back muscles were killing him and he could hardly breathe. *Elria has devised a method to drown me while I'm standing upright! I'll have to tackle this another way entirely.* Just as he was about to give up and turn back, his right hand lost its grip on the rock.

His fingers grasped thin air and his upper body arched back outwards. The full force of the waterfall hit him mercilessly now and the combined weight of the heavy axe and his chainmail tunic was overwhelming.

The power of the cascade washed Barbandor off the ledge as if he were dirt to be swept away. He swallowed icy water and choked, which made him take more into his lungs.

His fall halted dramatically as something caught hold of his ankle and he struggled, upside down, in the noisy rush of the

Emerald cataract. Gasping for air, he felt himself pulled upwards and grabbed by strong hands that then threw him down on to a hard surface.

His eyes were full of water and he vomited, bringing up water and the remains of his stomach contents. Wavering torchlight shone on him and he became aware of the vague impression of several pairs of high boots. Judging by the size of the footwear, the boots must belong to orcs.

Looped round his foot was a rope the beasts had caught him with mid-fall, saving him from toppling down into the plunge pool. *But their intentions were most probably not friendly.*

After a final spasm he wiped his eyes and glanced around. He did not bother with grabbing his battleaxe. They would have run him through before he could have retrieved the weapon from its holder. They had only to tug at the rope to make him trip and fall.

Three muscular orcs stood less than one pace away from him. Apart from the boots they were wearing simple leather loin protectors decorated with burned-in patterns, and belts across their chests with long daggers attached. Two of them had dark grey skin, while the third had skin of a striking night blue. Their limbs and torsos bore colourful tattooed designs; the dark blue orc's ornately intertwined decorations were done exclusively in bright white, which made them stand out.

After a short exchange of words that Barbandor could not follow, one of the grey orcs made his way along the ledge and disappeared in the mist, moving as if it were the easiest thing in the world.

The blue-skinned orc pulled Barbandor along with a tug on the rope and dragged him into a side cave where the thunderous noise of the waterfall was somewhat reduced in volume.

'Let us talk, groundling,' he began, speaking in the common tongue of Girdlegard but with a heavy accent. He crouched down. Barbandor saw his strong canine teeth were painted to look like the fangs of a wolf. The other teeth had been dyed black. 'Did you come here on your own?'

The dwarf sat up and tried to loosen the rope but a deep growl from the orc made him change his mind. 'You are worried you will all be killed.'

'I am concerned about quite other things that you know nothing of,' came the amused response.

'I shall be missed. My people will come looking for me. They'll follow the signs I left. You and your beasts—'

The orc laughed quietly. His long, curved fingernails were clean, as was the dark mane of hair on his head. Several strands had gold thread twisted round them. The general impression was of an orc that was well groomed – or maybe the waterfall had washed him clean. 'A designation I've not heard before.'

'Are you from the Outer Lands?'

'What are the Outer Lands?'

'It's on the far side of the Grey Mountains.' Barbandor felt his strength returning. He would wait for an opportunity and then attack. At the first sign that the beast's guard was down . . . 'I have never come across an orc like you before.'

'Then enjoy the sight of me as long as you can.' The orc surveyed him. 'What is your name?'

'Child of the Smith.'

'You do not wish to tell me what you are called? Do you fear your name being used? A taboo?' The orc grinned. 'My name is Borkon Gràc Hâl and I am not afraid who knows it. I am not afraid of any curse. Nor am I afraid of you.'

Barbandor was astonished by the civilised tone of their conversation. This was a spectacularly different type of encounter from the last time he had met one of their kind.

A loud shout was heard coming from the larger cave. Getting to his feet, Borkon turned his head, his mouth open to reply.

This will be my chance! Barbandor grabbed his axe with both hands and used the muscles in his shoulder to add leverage. The blade tip whistled through the air and hit the orc in the centre of the chest, slicing through his strong muscles. There was the crack of bone under the skin. Borkon stepped back under the impact, his head whirled round and his watery green eyes focused furiously on his dwarf attacker. He took hold of the axe head in his right hand and yanked it out of his flesh, releasing a stream of blue-black blood. The cut sealed itself immediately. The severed bits of bone fused again with a crunch, regaining their original shape.

Barbandor pulled on the axe shaft but the orc's grip held it as fast as any metal statue might have done. 'What in Vraccas' name are you?' *Is he one of the Undead? Has the curse of the Dead Land come back to visit itself on us in the shape of a new demon?*

'An orc. Granted, not the usual type, but an orc all the same.' Borkon suddenly released his hold on the axe head, making the dwarf nearly lose his balance and fall over backwards. 'Try that once more and –'

'Spare me your threats.' Barbandor's heart was beating fast as he retrieved his weapon, eyeing as he did so the dark blood sticking to the blade. 'I am a Child of the Smith. It is in my nature to root out and kill monsters like you.'

One of the grey-skinned orcs came in and dumped Gyndala, dripping wet, on the stone floor. Bleeding from two injuries on her neck and shoulder, she sat up, gasping. 'I'm sorry, Barbandor,' she said, in obvious discomfort. 'But I just had to follow you. I guessed that you –'

'Be quiet. Silence. Both of you,' Borkon commanded, turning to exchange words with his fellow orc in a throaty, harsh tongue.

'Gyndala, by Vraccas!' Barbandor whispered, concerned for her. 'Look what you've got yourself into.'

'I didn't want you to confront the pig-faces on your own. I—'

Borkon delivered her a kick, toppling her forward so her forehead slammed into the stone. She collapsed, unconscious.

'You are in luck, groundling. Thanks to her, you shall live.'

The grey-skinned orc grabbed her wet braided hair and yanked her head back, snapping her neck.

No! It had happened so fast that Barbandor had not been able to intervene. But as he sprang forward with an angry shout, intent on avenging Gyndala's death, Borkon reared up in front of him. With one hand he lifted the dwarf up by the neck and with the other he took hold of the axe.

While this was happening, the grey orc severed Gyndala's head from her shoulders with his knife, and everywhere was soon spattered in a mixture of her red blood and the water on the floor. Then he took off one of her shoes, came over to Barbandor and cut off a thick dark strand of his beard together with its distinctive white-gold clip.

Holding the dripping skull, the boot and the lock of beard hair, the grey orc turned and went out of the cave. The other grey orc came in and lifted the dead dwarf girl's corpse by the belt of her light-coloured dress, carrying her as if she were a bag. Her arms and legs hung down and blood poured from the neck stump.

'What are you doing?' Barbandor groaned in horror.

'The groundlings will find your girlfriend's skull and your beard hair in Smallwater. We can quickly use the boot to lay the tracks and it'll all add up. Those greedy humans must have killed you both because they did not want to hand over their loot,' Borkon explained. 'Nobody will think of looking for you here, behind the Emerald Falls. And if they do, by then the ledge will have disappeared.' He picked up the engraved metal weapon without putting the dwarf down. His arm showed no sign of a quiver under the weight. He pasted blood from the blade across Barbandor's brow and drew a sign with his finger. 'You will be my guest. A special feast in your honour will be served very soon.'

The grey-skinned orc laughed and shook Gyndala's decapitated corpse to make it seem as if it were still alive.

Caught in a steely pincer grip, Barbandor was running out of air and near to passing out.

'You will now answer my questions,' he heard Borkon's voice say as if from a great distance. 'I have any number of things to ask you.'

Just before he lost consciousness, Barbandor realised that the orc had been addressing him in the dwarves' own language.

The ancient form of that tongue.

Girdlegard

In the Brown Mountains
Brigantia
1023 P.Q. (7514th solar cycle in old reckoning), autumn

Doria Rodana de Psalí sat at the table next to her aprendisa Chòldunja and studied the brown-haired Brigantian facing them. His robe was an individually tailored affair in a sandy beige, its cut reminiscent of the älfar form of dress; the zabitay insignia was prominent on the high collar. *What does he intend to do with us?* She reckoned his age to be similar to her own, in the mid-twenties. His unshaven stubble gave him a slightly older appearance and his forehead bore a decorative branded scar whose design was derived from the Berengart crest.

A simple repast was on the board before them; they had what they needed. *Apart from their liberty.* Upon their arrival in the fortress the zabitay had assigned them these two chambers and warned them not to leave their rooms under any circumstances. He was fully aware of who it was he had brought with him to Brigantia after the battle – and he knew the women were both being sought in Girdlegard. Rodana could not work out whether he was trying to protect them or whether this was for his own benefit.

They were supplied with simple, fresh clothing that fitted reasonably well. This was unusual in itself, given the puppeteer's sylph-like proportions. They were given an opportunity to wash. Had the situation been different, Rodana and Chòldunja might well have felt content with their comfortable accommodation. But their lives were still in danger.

The man was reading some notes he had brought with him and the expression on his face indicated his anxiety. It seemed the news was not good.

Chòldunja poured tea for her mistress and then for herself. The golden liquid steaming in the shallow dishes exuded a herbal aroma. The sixteen-year-old's hair, which was dyed part brown and part black, had been fastened back in a bun, concealing its generous length.

Rodana cleared her throat. 'What is to happen now, zabitay?'

'My brother commanded me to kill you and your apprentice as soon as I found you,' he answered, leafing through the various bits of paper. Then he looked up. His voice was harsh, a hoarse whisper that held only a hint of how musical it must once have been. The scar on his throat showed that an injury had caused the change in his vocal cords. 'I am Klaey Berengart, the youngest brother of the Omuthan, and I am the zabitay commanding the aerial cavalry division.' He placed all the papers on the table and pointed to an empty dish, which Chòldunja filled with tea. 'You both saved my life. I have preserved yours by affording you refuge here in Brigantia. Girdlegard wants you dead.' He lifted the tea to his lips. 'This is what all my spies are telling me.'

'You've sent out spies to enquire about us?' Rodana asked in a mocking tone. She brushed a chin-length strand of blonde hair back behind her ear, emphasising her high cheekbones and her dark lips. 'What an honour for us.'

But Klaey remained serious. 'By sparing you now I am saving your lives for a second time. And thus endangering my own, since I am disobeying a direct command from the Omuthan,' he explained. 'So you are doubly in my debt.'

'Thank you for doing the calculations for me.' Rodana had already suspected that the hospitality granted the two outcasts would not be unconditional. 'What do you expect from us in return?'

Klaey's bright-blue gaze turned to Chòldunja. 'My brother made a mistake when he ordered your death. I shall convince him of his error. You *have to* help our side in the current siege.' A light smile formed. 'You will be helping to protect your own life if you do, ragana. Set one foot outside the walls and you will be captured and executed.' He pointed to the door. 'The same thing will happen in Brigantia itself, too, until I can persuade my brother to change his mind.'

'Do you speak of the same brother that you recently set alight with liquid fire?' Rodana doubted that the star of the zabitay of the Flying Cavalry Division, as he had put it, would still be high in the firmament of the family hierarchy.

'That was the work of a magus, whose powers I had totally underestimated,' Klaey replied, frowning. 'But I shall be avenged. With your assistance, ragana.'

'But I—' Chòldunja began.

'We will gladly do our part,' Rodana interrupted her apprentice's protest, before it cost them their lives. 'You have seen what she is capable of. Think of that ball of fire she destroyed the orcs and the riders with.'

'That's exactly what I'm relying on. Although I thought at first . . . Anyway, that doesn't matter. Now I know that it was the ragana's work.' Klaey put down his tea. 'We are being besieged by, among others, that famulus that calls himself a magus. He has several artefacts at his disposal from the Chamber of Wonders. And there's a groundling who knows about magic, too.'

'What?' Chòldunja blurted out, laughing at this. Rodana thought she was pretending to be so surprised. 'No, that can't be true. There are stories, that once upon a time –'

'I saw it happen. And experienced it myself. *He* is the reason that my incendiaries missed their target and set my brother's tent on fire instead.' Klaey's right hand was clenched, the knuckles turning white. 'I took note of his face. I knew exactly who he was. He was one of the group with Goldhand that we met to negotiate with immediately before the battle.' He coughed to clear his throat. 'I shall speak with the Omuthan and then you will be able to move freely in Brigantia.' He got up and made for the door. 'You are never to leave your accommodation. Not until you hear from me.' And then he was gone.

Hardly had the door closed behind the departing zabitay before Chòldunja crumpled. 'Mistress, how could you?'

'What? How could I lie to save our lives?'

'No! I mean how could you let him believe that I am still in possession of my special powers?'

'How much do you think we are worth in his eyes if he finds out the magus has now got your moor diamond dangling from his neck chain and that without it you can't do anything at all?' Rodana put her arm round her downcast aprendisa's shoulders. 'Or if he learns it wasn't us who wiped out the Gauragon cavalry with a fireball?'

'We'll be worth less than nothing,' Chòldunja admitted in a small voice.

'As high a value a woman can represent for a man who does not consider her his equal. And he is in no need of us as mistresses. He has plenty who are willing to do whatever he wants, because of his name. And we are being hunted in Brigantia. All of this makes lying essential. Continuous lying if we must.' Rodana gave the young girl a kiss on the top of her head. 'But for the time being we are safe, here in these rooms.'

'Safe, that is, until the Omuthan decides to demand a display of my arts.' Chòldunja buried her face in her hands. 'O spirits of the swamps, stand by me!'

Rodana sighed and embraced the sobbing girl again. 'They are sure to.' She stroked her hair and her shoulders. *Even if there isn't a swamp for miles and miles.*

After a while the young woman calmed down, and she wiped away the salty drops from her hot cheeks. 'Thank you, Mistress.' She sniffed and snuffled and drank some tea. 'It's awful. There's me desperate not to be a ragana anymore and I run away from home but the diamond puts me – and you – in such danger. I am so very sorry, Mistress. I should have—'

'It is what it is. Let us face up to the situation. Only the gods can undo past events.' Rodana took some deep breaths. 'What does the loss of the moor diamond mean for you?'

'It is bound to my person. It gave me power and I gave it strength. Without it I lose my energy, orbit by orbit. I shall become too weak to do anything much . . . It could take up to a whole cycle.' Chòldunja's face grew pale. 'If I don't get it back, I might . . . even . . . die.'

'Chòldunja!' Rodana exclaimed, horrified.

'It's not definite. But it might happen.' The juvenile apprentice sipped the warm tea. 'Either that or I manage to retrieve it.'

She hesitated. 'Or else I find an adequate substitute jewel I can bind myself to.'

'Oh, so there is hope! What else would you need, apart from the gemstone itself?' The fear and concern in Rodana's face turned to determination and confidence. 'We're in the realm of the Fourthlings, here, remember. Where else would we be in a better position to find a suitable jewel? Or does it absolutely have to be a moor diamond?'

'No, it doesn't. Any pure diamond of the first water might do. But . . .' Chòldunja dropped her head and her voice was hard to make out. 'The ritual for binding a stone to oneself is cruel. Cruel for me. And for the victim.'

Rodana understood. 'A ragana has to consume an infant,' she murmured, going pale. That sunlight shaft of hope, that there might be a way out, disappeared abruptly.

'And incorporate the soul of the baby, yes. Into myself and into the gemstone . . . That's how the union is made.' Chòldunja was close to tears again and her lips were quivering. 'I ran away from home, so I would never have to do that, Mistress! And now I might be forced to do that very thing, in order to save us both.' She looked at Rodana helplessly. 'And even then, my powers are minimal. I'm only at the beginning stage of the training. The Omuthan is sure to have me executed if I can't defeat the besieging army.'

Rodana took her hand and pressed it. 'We'll think of something. No newborn child will have to die. And nor will we.'

'You sound so sure.'

'I am sure.' Why this was, Rodana could not have said. However much she might smile and feign optimism, their situation was perilous in the extreme.

Klaey had seldom felt as nervous as he did now. He had kissed his lucky charm three times already to give himself confidence.

In long loping strides he made his way along to the chambers where the Omuthan was being treated by a team of Brigantia's best healers. Klaey had been refused access to his severely injured brother so far, for fear the visit might over-excite the patient. In his present state of health any strain on the Omuthan's heart had to be avoided.

I shan't let them turn me away this time. It was vital that Klaey be able to speak to his eldest brother personally, in order to explain the series of events that had led to the accident high above the battlefield, and to stress that it had not been his fault. *A dwarf with a magic spell. Who would have thought it?* He was convinced he had recognised the misbegotten culprit who had cast a spell in the form of a blast of wind that had swept him out of the saddle. That had been the start of the misfortune ending with defeat in the battle and with the disappearance of Deathwing.

Knowing his brother, Klaey was sure Orweyn would not be content with issuing a stark verbal reprimand. The tent, several commanding officers and some of the Berengart siblings had been caught in the inferno and had gone up in flames when Klaey's firepots missed their intended target. Sooner or later, the death sentence would come.

I'm not having that. Klaey turned the corner towards his brother's suite of rooms. The walls of the corridor still held remnants of the original dwarf-craft decoration, amended and changed in the course of decades of Berengart occupation of the fortress. The ruling family had a liking for geometric patterns and floral designs. *I don't care if I do get him over-excited. He must listen to what I've got to say before he gets a chance to issue a death warrant. He has to hear the truth.*

Noticing another of his brothers conversing with servants at the door to the apartment, he slowed his steps. Kawutan was in full Brigantian ceremonial military dress and Ilenis, his wife, was in red court attire, as if she were going to an official reception or had just come from one. *Why are they here?*

At nearly thirty-eight, Kawutan was the fourth oldest brother and always got on well with Orweyn. When they were standing next to each other they were so alike, they could almost be mistaken for twins. The family brand on his brow was creased with furrows.

'Klaey! Good to see you,' said Ilenis in greeting, seeing him approach. She alerted her spouse and the servants. The brunette beauty looked amazing and her smile was a dream, a gift she had passed on to her four daughters.

The murmured discussion stopped and they all turned to Klaey.

'Glad to find you both here. Are you going in to see Orweyn?' Klaey concealed his uneasiness. The swift motion as Kawutan put his left hand behind his back as if hiding something did not escape him. 'Is he any better? What do the healers think?'

'We've just been in. The burns are proving difficult to treat. It's because clothing and skin are fused together. The healers are wondering how he can be helped if they are to avoid amputation,' Kawutan replied. He made a distinguished figure in his dark-green uniform with his medals, badges of honour and the ornamental braid. A sabre hung at his side.

Why is he carrying a weapon? 'But he is conscious, isn't he?'

'He is. And he is busy issuing orders.' The smile flashing on to his clean-shaven face looked as believable as a glass hammer and about as dependable.

'That's good. So I can go in.'

But Kawutan placed his right hand flat on Klaey's chest. 'Some of the orders he gave concern yourself, little brother.'

'Aha?'

'He does not want to see you.'

Klaey clicked his tongue impatiently. *As I feared.* 'What

happened was not my fault. It was a magus attacking me. He threw Deathwing off course. The ropes tore and—'

'Whatever,' said Kawutan, breaking in. 'He said you would try to talk your way out of it and told us all not to believe you. It was your mistake. You are the murderer of Finsal, Ulenia and Dovulin. You burned our brothers and sisters. And several of the zabitays.' Slowly, he brought his left hand forward – and triumphantly showed Klaey the Omuthan Seal. 'He has appointed me, as the eldest surviving sibling, to be interim ruler over Brigantia. And my considered view is that we need to arrest you. You will be held in prison until Orweyn regains his strength and can decide your fate. I shall not be attempting to judge your case myself.'

You miserable jumped-up little cuss! If the other siblings had not died he would never have been considered for the temporary post as regent. Orweyn thought him a second-rate figure. *Everyone knows that.* But this made no difference. If you held the seal, you held the power.

'It was the magus!'

'Do you have witnesses?'

'How is anyone else going to have had a chance to see what was happening in the thick of a raging battle?'

'Then the decision is final.' Kawutan looked him up and down. 'You will be taken to the dungeons, but your needs will be met. You will lack no comforts.'

With smooth grace Ilenis slipped her arm through her husband's. 'Think of how it will look to people,' she said, sounding reasonable. 'The Berengart dynasty must show a united front, don't you agree? Particularly given the terrible events during the battle. I think Klaey's explanation makes sense. Everybody will be able to understand.' Her gaze darted back and forth between the two, so different, brothers. 'Tell everyone. Put the blame for the tragedy on the army that's besieging us and our forces are bound to fight with renewed vigour and passion.'

Kawutan gave her a kiss on the cheek. 'Your advice is good, my dear wife.'

'As usual,' she agreed with a charming smile, stroking his arm and his chest. 'Let's leave everything else up to the Omuthan to decide when he is well again. But for now we need to avoid any hint of estrangement in the family. The Berengarts must stay strong!'

'I agree,' Klaey chipped in swiftly. He was grateful that Ilenis had spoken up. 'So can we keep to my version?'

'Agreed.' Kawutan smiled at his attractive spouse. 'We shall place all the blame on that magus.'

'Well, it *was* him.'

'That's as maybe.' His brother pointed to the door to the royal bedchamber. 'But you still won't be permitted to see him. You will respect this restriction. Or else I shall have to have you arrested for some other matter and kept under guard.'

'But–'

'Have you understood what I said?' Kawutan raised his hand, the one with the royal signet ring, as if he were holding a whip for subduing some wild animal and directing it back into its cage. 'I am not saying this as your brother but as your Omuthan.'

Interim Omuthan. Klaey sketched a bow. His brother moved off.

'It would be nice to meet for a game of cards some time,' Ilenis suggested brightly, embracing Klaey. Her fingers traced his sides down to the level of his waist, pulling him close for a moment. The warmth of her body came through the fabric and revived sweet memories. 'Like we used to so often in the past.'

'Yes. Of course. Let's catch up.' Klaey breathed a kiss on to her cheek and released her. 'Thank you for your advice.'

The meaning of the glance Ilenis gave him back over her shoulder as she left was clear. His brother had no inkling of how these card games normally ended. With only winners, no losers.

Klaey congratulated himself on his splendid relationship with his sister-in-law. She had ensured he would not be imprisoned. She had not been acting totally unselfishly in that regard. He would be given the opportunity to demonstrate his gratitude. An extensive opportunity.

Kawutan halted. 'It occurs to me we should make an example to our people. The fact of its having been a mistake doesn't obviate the need for punishment. It would have been your duty to stop the firepots falling, somehow or other. Or you could have sacrificed your own life to save the Omuthan.'

Klaey wanted to yell at his brother and punch him on the nose, but he forced himself to feign agreement. 'Of course. What penalty do you envisage?'

Kawutan turned his head, while Ilenis slipped her arm in his once more. 'Has your flight-mare turned up?'

'No.'

'In that case you are demoted to being a simple junior banner officer again. That's until you find something else to fly with.' Kawutan looked smug. 'No flight-mare, no rank. Quite simple. Demotion until further notice.' He raised his hand in salute, letting his ring of office flash in the lamplight. 'Good luck finding another flight-mare. Or whatever else you would like to ride. How about a tiny dragon? Or you could tie some pigeon wings to a pony?' He laughed as he turned the corner into the next corridor, his wife at his side.

'Stupid idiot.' Klaey plucked the zabitay insignia from his shoulder and handed it to one of the servants, who pretended to have no idea what had just happened. Now Klaey was more keen than ever to show Ilenis his undying gratitude. *Just wait till Orweyn is back to being Omuthan . . .!*

Initially, Klaey did not return to his own quarters. He needed time. He liked to walk around while he was thinking.

Kawutan was far too stupid to realise how useful a ragana might be, and might even insist on her being executed. On the other hand, he appeared not to know about all Orweyn's orders. For this reason he chose to tell neither Kawutan nor Ilenis about his new enforced guests. This way he would be able to find out more about the powers of the moor-witch, who had eradicated Gauragon's lancers with a fireball. Just like a dragon.

Klaey slowed down. *What if Chòldunja has planned this? Did she plan to smuggle herself in through my intercession? What if she wants to harm Brigantia from within?* The idea did not please him at all.

As he wandered through the corridors he considered his options. He had to come up with a way of keeping the ragana under his control. With her powers she would find it easy to bring death and destruction to the fortress. *A poison. Something that could make her obedient.* The longer he thought about it the stranger he found the behaviour of the two young women. *Why did Rodana and Chòldunja follow me instead of using magic to get away? Were there too many soldiers at Two-Stream Hill for the ragana's witchcraft?*

Before he realised which way he was walking, he found himself in the vast conference chamber that Orweyn used for strategy meetings with his zabitays. Maps and charts hung on the walls, and on the table there was a scale model showing the fortifications and the whole valley. The enemy encampments, the positions of the siege engines, everything was represented here, down to the tiniest detail, as if it were some game painstakingly constructed for very careful children to play with.

Kawutan is not up to the office he has taken on. The attackers will come up with some clever ploy and he'll be too stupid to notice. They've got so many experienced people on their side. And they've got the knowledge the dwarves bring. Klaey studied the drawings and then touched the throwing arm of one of the model war-wolf catapults. A little stone was hurled against the wall, clicking against the model ramparts, only to be deflected and roll back across the table. *Orweyn has to get back to us as soon as ever it is possible. Or we will be lost. Even the ragana witch won't be able to prevent that, I fear.*

'Greetings from Dsôn Khamateion,' said a woman's lilting voice out of the darkness. The illumination in the hall dimmed, as if it were frightened of the sound.

Klaey jerked upright. This made the scars on his neck and abdomen hurt, as if they were recalling how they had been inflicted. However hard he peered into the dark shadows, he could not see anyone who could have spoken.

'Perhaps you should take your greetings to present to my brother Kawutan,' he croaked in response. 'He is our Omuthan at present. Until Orweyn recovers.'

'I have not come to talk to him, but to put a proposition to you,' the blackness murmured.

'Show yourself.'

'I don't feel like it. It's a question of my words here, not my physical form.' The älfar concealed themself in the ink-black dark. 'I suggest, in the name of the Ganyeios, that you be appointed the Omuthan, Klaey Berengart. Not as an interim arrangement, but permanently.'

Klaey knew who he was dealing with here. Somewhere in the room, hidden in the darkness she had created, was Ascatoîa. 'How would that come about?'

'If one thing comes to another. An injured person dies. A brother suffers an accident. A sister walking up on the ramparts is fatally struck by an arrow.' The älfar woman listed the possibilities in mild tones. 'Unfortunate events can occur. No one will suspect you. You won't be anywhere near when these things happen.'

'And the reward?'

'The recompense would be that you, as the Omuthan, would enter a pact with the Ganyeios and you would follow the orders he gives you. What with his wisdom, our power and the military arts of Dsôn Khamateion, Brigantia would break the siege and destroy the enemy forces. And then we would unite to take over Girdlegard.'

'So Brigantia would be nothing but a kind of administrator for the älfar?'

'No. We are generous. You would get half. You'll get the eastern part and we'll keep the west.'

'What about the dragons?'

'They won't be a threat. Our ships now in the Inland Sea are equipped with weapons that can shoot down any dragon.' Ascatoîa laughed quietly. 'You don't have to decide straight away. It's not easy, being the last of the ruling Berengarts. But think on. The longer you hesitate, the more likely it is that the walls will fall.'

'And with them, presumably Dsôn Khamateion, too.'

'I don't think the groundling folk and their friends can defeat our empire. And if they do, we'll take off and start again elsewhere. But Brigantia will remain completely cut off. There's no retreat possible. You have your backs up against walls of rock. Literally.' The älfar woman seemed to purr seductively as she spoke. 'The Ganyeios will not be making this offer a second time. I shall return for your answer in seven orbits.'

Klaey listened out intently for any sound of retreating steps. 'And if I decide sooner?'

Silence.

'I say yes!' he called out. 'I'm saying yes to your proposal!'

But there was nothing but silence surrounding him.

Girdlegard

Brigantia, in the Brown Mountains
1023 P.Q. (7514th solar cycle in old reckoning), late autumn

Goïmron stepped out of the large conference tent pitched on the artificial hill. He needed some fresh air. The warmth inside had been making him drowsy. He had a thick mantle over his shirt, tunic and hose and a fur hat on his head of short black curls.

While delegates and commanders from all the Girdlegard realms were engaged in a lively discussion of tactics with Mostro and the leaders of the dwarf tribes, the rest of the camp lay quiet. Not a note of music. No singing anywhere. All the fighting men and women and dwarf warriors were resting, eating or sleeping, preparing for the coming assault they would be launching on the morrow.

Here and there a small brazier fire could be spotted among the wood and canvas shelters. The larger yurts might still have lamps burning. But most of the humans, dwarves, elves and meldriths were in the land of dreams by now.

I hope their dreams are sweet. Goïmron looked up to the crow's nest where the lookouts were keeping watch up in the giddy heights, gathering information about movements on the far side of the walls; Brigantia's defenders were readying themselves for the expected onslaught. They had spread tarpaulins and lengths of cloth above alleyways and courtyards, but the constant heavy rain of recent orbits had caused the fabric to rip in places, allowing glimpses of the activity within. The commanders were not feeling complacent about what the lookouts reported. Brigantia was well prepared. They had people, creatures and weaponry in plentiful supply. And the defensive walls had been strengthened and improved over the course of recent cycles.

Goïmron gave a heavy sigh. Rodana was over there somewhere in the midst of all that cruelty, death and destruction. He would have given anything to be able to speak to her. He needed to know what had happened to her, and what she was doing now, this very moment. But between her and him there were a good hundred paces of distance, studded with danger, terrible adversaries and so many misunderstandings. *I should get up on to the top platform and let the wind clear my head.*

He heard footsteps squelching in the mud behind him as someone approached. Metal clinked against metal. 'That stupid old fool,' Gata snapped crossly. 'He should never have turned down the black-eye's offer.' The blonde dwarf warrior was standing next to him, wearing the white wolfskin mantle that had once belonged to her father. She had discarded the mourning ribbon long ago. 'The pig-faces could have swung themselves over the ramparts and have taken all the arrows.'

Goïmron wondered how often he would have to hear her opinion on this. The Thirdling queen had no idea that it had not been Tungdil Goldhand making that key decision. He, Goïmron, had been the one to reject Mòndarcai's offer of a pact. *Me, entirely on my own.*

It did not reassure him in the slightest that Goldhand, once his senses had been restored, had neither confirmed nor denied authorship of the decision. And Gata's intense disapproval of the move increased his vague feeling that he had made a big mistake.

'Who knows?' he said, hoping she would drop the subject.

'Well, we'll never know, will we? I doubt our black-eye friend is ever going to come back to repeat his proposal to us.' Gata turned to look at the mighty walls, where many braziers and lamps were burning up on the high battlements. It looked as if hundreds of demons were staring over towards them, ready to attack by dead of night 'By Lorimbur! If anyone had ever said that I'd actually be admiring something the Fourthlings had made and not laughing at it and calling it arty-farty elfish twaddle, I'd never have believed it.'

Goïmron cleared his throat. The night air of autumn turned his breath to a white cloud in the darkness and he could feel the damp on the clean-shaven skin of his face. The dark sideburns did not warm his cheeks at all.

'Oh, no! I didn't mean it like that.' She rushed to amend the impression her words had made.

'I know what you meant.' He looked at the six huge war-wolf catapults encircling the fortifications, by sunshine or starshine continually shelling the walls with stones and boulders. The artillery crews were changed at regular intervals to avoid any halt to the bombardment, but so far they had made no progress. They had made no breach, no matter where the attack was aimed. Pieces fell off the walls here and there but there was a protective layer to the stonework that absorbed the impacts to a great extent. Apart from a couple of little towers and most of the decorative borders, the walls had sustained very little damage. The ramparts had proved as impregnable as its original constructors had intended. 'So we're going ahead with an assault on the walkways?'

Gata nodded grimly. 'We're making no headway with getting through the walls, so we'll have to get over them.'

'What news from the mining operation?'

'The Fourthlings ... your ancestors, of course, knew what they were doing when they built this fortress and they put traps in everywhere they could. We've lost quite a number of workers already. And, of course, alarms were set off each time. But eventually they should manage to gain access' – Gata pointed over to the large conference tent – 'but that lot are all against the idea of being patient. They think we can't afford to wait, after those two autumn storms, and given the powers of the ragana. She is stronger than expected. It's making the famulus nervous.'

Goïmron recalled the violent storms that had swept through the camps, causing a great deal of destruction. 'I really don't think the storms were the work of the ragana.' The mighty gusts of wind had nearly toppled the huge war-wolf machines, and had dragged smaller catapults and sling devices off their stands, hurling them against the walls and breaking them up. Shelters had had to be completely rebuilt, and there had been many casualties needing medical attention and quite a few bodies had been buried in the stark hinterland. 'She no longer has her diamond and she doesn't represent a viable threat.'

'You're wrong there! Those raging windstorms did not occur naturally.'

'She's a *moor*-witch. You see any swamps round here?'

'Take a closer look. After all that rain the whole camp is a marsh. That's what made Chòldunja powerful. She might have found another gemstone to make up for the loss of her diamond. Who knows how many infants she's been eating?'

'She's really only a child herself. There's no way she's got the power to control the elements.' Goïmron gave up trying to convince Gata to change her mind on this. Mostro's constant rants directed against the young aprendisa had been effective. There was no countering the influence of those speeches. Goïmron chose instead to try to change the subject. 'Where's Vanéra? Didn't she say she'd be coming?'

'The Esteemed Maga sent two wagons full of artefacts from her Chamber of Wonders, along with a whole list of excuses why she had to remain behind in Rhuta.' Gata sounded bitter. 'We're stuck with the would-be magus and a load of magic thingamabobs – but no one knows if they're going to be any use.'

'Nobody knows.'

'That doesn't make it any better, does it?' Gata looked at the war wolf on the outer right-hand edge of the siege works. 'Good we've got that one working again. The carpenters were busy on it for eight orbits to sort out the storm damage. I agree with Mostro on this: the longer we wait, the stronger the ragana's power will grow. And winter's on its way earlier than usual. There'll be no shelter from the icy cold in the north-east. We'll be ten paces deep in snow and there'll be drifts in places twice as high as that. Our troops won't be able to cope with that kind of weather.'

'Do you think tomorrow's attack might work?' If there was really going to be the amount of snow that the girl warrior was predicting, Goïmron thought it would be better to wait until winter set in and then they could build siege ramps up to the walls with the ice and snow. *But there'll be no takers for my idea.*

'It's not a question of *thinking*. It's a matter of planning. The arrangements have been made and the artefacts have been distributed to the various units.'

'But I'm asking your opinion.' Goïmron held up a hand to ward off her next argument. 'Don't go on about Mòndarcai again.'

'My opinion? I think that we'll lose a lot of good people tomorrow because this is not the perfect plan of attack. Nor has it been perfectly prepared,' Gata replied. 'But it could work. I'll spare you the details. You are not a dwarf of the warring variety, Goïmron.'

'Yes, I know: I'm a gem cutter. Dealing with the sort of arty-farty stuff that elves like.' This time the battle preparations would not depend on his being to hand for one of Goldhand's speeches, so he was at liberty to decide for himself what his part in the coming attack should be. It had already been agreed that the ancient hero should remain behind on the commanding hill, sitting on a throne, far enough away from the action but able to serve as an inspiration to the troops.

Goïmron had never been a natural-born warrior, it was safe to say. His claim to fighting fame was restricted to his skill with darts and dartboard. And he could be handy with a sling in one-to-one combat. He would not be taking part in the fighting. He took a sideways glance up at the lookout post. The platforms had been extended until the whole thing reminded one of a huge tree with horizontal branches. *I could do something useful from up there on the crow's nest.* His hand slid into the bag he carried over his shoulder. This was where the sea sapphire was, in its dragon-shaped frame. *I could work in secret. Everyone else can concentrate on what the famulus is doing.*

'You're no longer just a gem specialist. You have brought harmony and unity between the dwarf tribes, such as had not been seen in Girdlegard for a thousand cycles.' Gata gave him a friendly shove. 'And you very nearly put paid to old Goldhand's plans with the mountain passageways. No one could ever match that achievement.'

Despite the misery he felt, Goïmron had to laugh. His friend joined her laughter to his own. 'We'll toast the victory together tomorrow.' His eyes found the brooch she wore on the collar revers of the military garb she wore under her armour. 'Just so I don't die not knowing, can you tell me what that brooch is? You always wear it.'

'This?' Gata stroked it with her thumb. 'A souvenir. It belonged to a forebear of mine.'

'Yes?'

'The last chancellor of my own clan. There are drawings of him wearing this. A gift from the elves to show their gratitude. It got lost when he died but my father came across it by chance outside the eastern fortress. He handed it on to me because he wasn't keen on it for himself. He thought it a bit spooky.'

Goïmron took a closer look but came to no conclusions. 'What do the symbols mean? They aren't dwarf runes. At least, none that I'm familiar with.'

'I don't know and not even Telìnâs could tell me. But it gives me a good feeling. Just knowing that one of my ancestors wore it – so I feel connected.' Gata smiled and caressed the brooch once more with her thumb. 'As soon as we've won our battle and peace has been restored, I'm going to take it to the experts in Enaiko, the City of Knowledge. Someone there is bound to be able to tell me what it means.'

'It's sure to be something wonderful.' Goïmron was delighted with his idea about viewing the progress of the forthcoming battle from up in the crow's nest. From the lookout platform he could use his gemstone wizardry to influence events. He needed to identify a good target for his magic powers. 'Tell me, is there, do you think, a weak spot anywhere on the walls?'

Gata made an exaggeratedly theatrical gesture towards the mighty fortifications. 'Can you spot a little crack somewhere that I might've missed?'

'No.'

'Then there's your answer.' Gata sighed. 'Apart from the two small towers we demolished, there was nothing doing. I think we'd have needed to hurl boulders the size of a three-storey building if we'd wanted to make a breach in that stonework. And by the time someone comes up with a design for a war wolf of suitable dimensions, then actually gets it constructed by the carpenters, and the counterweight devices calculated for and set up, well, we'll be long gone. We'll have died of old age. The elves, too. Even Goldhand.' She glanced at him in surprise. 'How come you're asking that?'

'I wanted to have a bit of hope, I suppose.' Goïmron pointed over to the conference tent. 'Should we go back in, do you think? Get warmed up? They'll have made a fresh hot punch – no rum or brandy in it today.' He turned round casually at the lookout post. His decision was made. *That is where I'll work from.*

'Oh, and before I forget: Brûgar's been looking for you for ages today.'

Goïmron remembered with a guilty start what the bald-headed warrior with the blue pointed beard had promised him following the battle of Two-Stream Hill. *He was determined to find evidence and prove I'm a magus.* Goïmron had hoped that Brûgar was going to let well alone. 'What does he want?'

'He said there was something he needed to talk to you about. Private stuff.' She looked concerned. 'Have you guys had an argument?'

'No!' he shot out, far too quickly.

'Do you owe him money? Promised him a beer, have you? Or tobacco, maybe? You'd be playing with fire there,' she continued with a broad grin. 'He takes his pipes and tobacco deadly seriously.'

'What? No, nothing like that.' Goïmron had to laugh at the thought of delivering two great big barrels of Best Black tobacco to Brûgar's quarters. 'Who knows what bee he's got in his bonnet. Whatever it is, it can wait till after the battle, I'm sure.'

'Do you reckon? I'd hate it if one of you copped it and then came back as a ghost because you hadn't settled things first.'

Goïmron gave her a playful shove, and immediately regretted it when his elbow struck the hard metal armour under her wolfskin. The nerve to his hand went numb. 'Nobody's going to die.'

'Oh, yes, they will. Lots of us will.' Spontaneously Gata leaned over to kiss him full on the mouth. Soft and warm, and neither over-long nor too intimate. 'And *that's* something I didn't want to leave unsettled. You wouldn't like it if I came back to haunt you, would you? I hope that's not the kind of thing Brûgar had in mind. He'd be tough to have as a rival.' She blushed and hurried off towards the conference tent so as not to have to listen to what he said in response.

Goïmron could still feel the touch of her lips on his own.

Could hear her words echoing in his head.

It brought a smile to his face.

I'm going to make sure that neither of us dies tomorrow. He followed swiftly in Gata's wake, back to the warmth where the aroma of hot spiced punch filled the airless tent. *After the battle I'll have a tankard of the real stuff.* He went to stand next to Goldhand, who seemed to have nodded off, while the commanding officers and Mostro were grouped round the campaign plan, shifting figures around and arguing about which units should do what in the coming offensive. *Vraccas, I beseech you. Be at our sides and grant us a victory without too great a loss to our troops.*

The Doulia? Mm. I'd say they were helpful men and women who take their children along with them when they volunteer for service. All for the greater glory of their god Doul.

And by the way, Doul is one of the few divinities who came to Girdlegard and stayed. But he is only worshipped within a certain caste.

Strange, that, isn't it?

Excerpt from
Reflections of a Thoughtful Woman
(anon)

II

Girdlegard

The Brown Mountains
Brigantia
1023 P.Q. (7514th solar cycle in old reckoning), late autumn

'Goïmron!'

At the sound of his own name, he struggled to open his heavy eyelids and found himself looking at a dwarf's scarf-swathed face topped by a fur cap. Ice and hoar-frost crystals sparkled in the dark beard.

'Yes?' he responded in a mild voice, as he concentrated on gathering his senses.

'What are you doing up here in the crow's nest?'

With difficulty he pulled himself up to sitting and checked to see if his arms still worked. His limbs felt frozen stiff and his chilled muscles were in revolt as he attempted to move. 'What am I doing? I'm waiting for the fighting to start.' He rubbed his eyes. 'I didn't want to miss anything so I climbed up here before dawn—'

'But the battle's already under way!' Astonished, the scout interrupted him.

By all the demons of Tion! Goïmron leaped clumsily to his feet and looked out over the edge of the platform. He had taken up his position here in secret but then he must have fallen asleep. *How could that have happened?*

The daystar had already risen over the tops of the mountains and the icy slopes were glittering in the sun's rays.

Putting his eye to the spyglass he took from his bag, he swept the instrument from side to side. 'How goes the day?' he asked. Without the protection of the low wall, the wintry gusts cut into his face and blew straight through the mantle he had thrown round his shoulders. Up here, one hundred paces above the ground, the wind whistled icily round his ears.

'It's not looking good. Tough going.' The scout hung around next to him, looking bemused. 'We've been trying to make out their troop movements but as soon as the fighting started this awful fog rolled in. If you ask me, it's the ragana's work.'

Goïmron bit his tongue so as not to contradict the soldier. Mostro had got to everyone with his wild tirades, in which he had been describing Chòldunja, the young aprendisa, as a terrifying and fully fledged witch. *Using fear as a motivator.* Goïmron was getting next to nothing from using his spyglass.

A heavy grey mist, rolling down to the fortress from the glittering mountainsides, had filled the whole fortified edifice right up to the top of the battlements. Tendrils of hazy vapour were issuing out through the holes designed for pouring out boiling pitch and red-hot cinders on to would-be invaders, and the curls of mist from the battlements sank to join the billowing carpet of fog below. Vague movements could be detected at ground level as figures ran back and forth. Their own gigantic war-wolf catapults were only seen as huge outlines like giants lying on their sides, raising an arm every so often with a violent jerk to hurl large stones.

'It looks like the whole fortress is up in the clouds,' Goïmron muttered. He stared through the spyglass, desperately seeking an opportunity to put his magic powers to work.

There were long siege ladders propped up against the battlements in places. But the defenders were ready and busy shoving the ladders away with long staves, or were emptying buckets full of stones, or shooting arrows and crossbow bolts to hail down on to the attacking forces below even before Goïmron could get any magic organised.

'We can't get any information through to the troops. The fog is too thick,' the scout told him. 'Even if we had any actual facts to let them know about. We can't see a thing.' He handed Goïmron a mug of steaming tea, and brought his scarf down from his face so he could be understood better. 'Here you are. It'll warm you up. You must be frozen stiff if you've been sleeping up here for a full three sandglasses.'

Goïmron stretched out a hand to take the cup. He kept watching the walls. *Maybe I could get the mist to lift. That would help our cause.*

At that very moment there was a dazzling flash in the middle of the clouds of fog. Iridescent stars hissed upwards and exploded against the ramparts. Sparks shot up and disappeared in the sky.

'There! At last!' Goïmron moved his spyglass eagerly over to where Mostro had surely just hit home.

The soldier at his side gave an unhappy snort of laughter. 'No, that hasn't worked.'

'What do you mean?'

'It'll be some stupid useless artefact again. It's been like this ever since the fighting started.' The dwarf with the hoar-frosted beard looked morose. 'There'll be whooshing and some sparks and some stinks, then some animal noises or some orchestra playing or loud laughter like from a giant or some damn fool flock of coloured birds or a cloud of soap bubbles. Oh, and just now it rained a load of toffees on to the enemy walkways. I suppose the Brigantians were supposed to be defeated by having their teeth go rotten.'

Oh, no, that's not what we needed. Goïmron could imagine his friend's face. Brûgar had never had a good word to say for magic and now he would find all his contempt was justified. Anything that might be halfway useful in a conventional battle was worth nothing in a siege.

'Earlier, there was some kind of stuffed beast that had come alive,' the bearded soldier went on, blowing on his tea to cool it. 'Sounds like someone must be injured, judging by the screams.'

'Well, that's something.' Goïmron thought back to his own experience in the Chamber of Wonders when the drinx had come alive and nearly killed him. 'These creatures can be very dangerous, as soon as—'

'But the injuries were all on our side. Not the Brigantians,' the soldier said with a sigh.

By Vraccas. Enough. Goïmron put his mug down. He slipped his hand into his pocket and grasped the sea sapphire. *Let the fog disperse!*

IT'S TOO FAR AWAY. Goïmron heard the gemstone's response in his head. AND THERE'S TOO MUCH OF IT.

How about a strong wind, then. Is that possible?

AS LONG AS THE FOG IS STILL ROLLING DOWN FROM THE MOUNTAINS THERE'S NOT MUCH POINT. THEY SHOULD BREAK OFF THE ATTACK. THE LOSSES ARE UNNECESSARY AND IT'S GOING NOWHERE.

Goïmron agreed with the suggestion. It made sense to him. He turned to the lookout to ask: 'Can we give the signal to retreat? With a bugle call? The offensive is getting nowhere in this pea-souper.'

'We've got several signal horns set up that I'm sure they'd be able to hear down at the foot of the walls. But it's not up to us to decide on the orders.' The bearded dwarf went on, 'It's only the full assembly of commanders who can do that. Or Tungdil Goldhand.'

Goïmron was already stowing the spyglass away and moving over to the narrow ladder. 'I'll go and ask him. It's only Brigantia that's gaining anything from our attack.' He started to make his way down the hundred-pace ladder, rung by rung, which was no easy task given the icy chill and the hefty gusts of wind. It needed all his concentration.

The Fieldmarshals' Hill was not far. That was where the most legendary of all the dwarves was waiting in an open-sided octagonal tent, warmed by braziers. Waiting to be informed of the first victory. That news would not be brought to him today. Neither the famulus nor the artefacts had come up to expectations on that front.

And they won't, either. Not on this orbit. Goïmron jumped down the last few rungs and raced up the hill in the fog, heading for the outline of the yurt, whose canvas walls had been rolled up to allow a good view of the battle. A good view, that is, had there not been such a thick curtain of fog obscuring events. The warm glow of the lamps and braziers showed him which way to go.

There were several hissings and howlings from the direction of the ramparts when some artefact or other was set off at the front line of attack – the effect would have gone down well at a fairground or a popular celebratory reception. But as it was, the magic was dissipating uselessly, having no impact on the mighty fortifications. The Brigantian forces up on the battlements or posted behind the arrow-slits were neither distracted nor impressed, so no advantage could be gained.

Goïmron was surprised, once he could see into the conference tent, to note that Mostro was there with Goldhand. The famulus had retreated from the perilous area at the foot of the walls. *And he's abandoned our people to their fate.*

'What are you doing here, Famulus?' he called out. 'Shouldn't you be with the troops to support their efforts?'

Mostro, extravagantly dressed in a blue and gold robe, with a mantle of black sable fur over his shoulders, made a deprecatory gesture. 'No point. The ragana has been using her despicable powers and has beaten us with fog and phantasms and trickery.' He ran his hand through his wavy blond hair to check his appearance was in order and looked at the ancient dwarf sat waiting in his upholstered armchair, wrapped in warm blankets. 'She has even altered the way Vanéra's artefacts work. To Tion with the moor-witch!'

'But all this time you've had her diamond hanging round your neck. How on earth can she do any magic?' Goïmron objected.

'She'll have found herself some new gemstone. There'll be plenty of precious jewels for her in the Fourthlings' old realm.' Mostro glared at him suspiciously and stroked his pointed black beard. 'Are you on the side of that child-eater? Are you standing up for her?'

'No. But I don't think she's got anything to do with what's been happening.'

'You know nothing at all about magic and wizardry, Master Chiselcut. You can leave it to me when it comes to assessing the situation. Given my knowledge and experience I see myself more as a magus, rather than a famulus. Please amend the form of address you use for me.' The famulus stretched his hands out towards one of the braziers. 'How long shall we keep trying? Maybe we'll have made a breach in three or four runs of the sandglass.'

Goïmron looked at Goldhand, who was silently watching the undulating carpet of fog, as if he were searching in it for an answer. Wearing his polished armour and a fur-trimmed cloak, with his silver beard and hair, and with one hand on the handle of his war-hammer, he was the very picture of a High King, without actually being one. His restrained elegance was much more convincing than Mostro's arrogant appearance. 'I think we should call off the attack.'

'Oh? So that's what you think?' the self-styled magus snapped. 'So you know what our losses are, do you? They'll be hardly worth mentioning.'

'So far we have lost one thousand, four hundred good soldiers.' The answer had come from the mouth of Telìnâs, who had quietly entered the tent. His elegant armour showed several dents and bloodstains from the injured fighters. He did not seem hurt himself. 'I have come to ask you in the name of my commander to order that the retreat be sounded, Master Goldhand.' He sank on to one knee. 'There is no point in continuing to attack the walls. Even our elf-eyes cannot locate a target properly in this fog. And death is raining down on us from the battlements.'

'No,' Mostro declared coolly. 'Let's keep it up for another two courses of the sandglass.'

'What kind of a cold-hearted creature are you? Every grain of sand that falls in the glass means another valuable life sacrificed,' Telìnâs snapped back. 'All for nothing.'

'Make more of an effort, *Master*—' Mostro got no further. The elf had made an incredible leap over to his side and dealt him a shove that sent him nearly colliding with the brazier. With the same hand Telìnâs prevented the young man actually falling into the flames, by grabbing him by the collar. 'That's how swiftly death hits you,' he warned. 'You are standing a long, long way from the action, Famulus Mostro. It's easy for you to demand more effort.'

Mostro pulled himself free, red-faced with anger. 'How dare you lay a finger on me?'

'Since you're asking me: it was completely intentional,' the elf responded calmly. 'Goïmron, get up on the crow's nest, will you? And let the lookout give the signal for retreat. It was a mistake to pursue the attack without sufficient preparation and with this lack of visibility,' said Goldhand soberly. 'I shall set my seal on the written order for you.' He turned his head slowly to confront the famulus. 'You are to return this instant to the front line at the walls and use your powers to ensure there are no more casualties.'

Mostro went pale as suddenly as he had previously gone red. 'How am I supposed to manage that?'

'You describe yourself as a magus and you have been supplied with the gemstones you asked for. Employ whatever you can that will work. And make haste. You bear the responsibility for the initial failure.' The significance of Goldhand's dismissive gesture was unmistakeable. 'You promised powerful magic. We have seen no sign of any. I'm sure you don't want people calling you boastful, do you? Or even calling you a liar.'

Mostro clamped his jaws shut in defiance and hurried out into the grey vapour that hung full of shrill whistles and odd animal sounds along with the clatter of projectiles.

'My thanks, Master Goldhand.' Telìnâs bowed his head to the aged dwarf.

'We should have remained resolute and not have given in to the urgings of the famulus,' said Goldhand, criticising his own actions. 'I shall ascribe the numbers of fallen and the wounded to my own misjudgement. I should have realised what a difference the mist would make.'

Goïmron was keen to expound on this, but first he must carry out Goldhand's command and race back to the crow's nest to get the troops to retreat. He went over to the desk and wrote out the order, placing a blob of sealing wax under the words for Goldhand to press with the seal on his ring. 'Don't be too hard on yourself. I'll be back soon.' And off he ran.

As he ran he fumed about the part Mostro had played in the disaster. The fatal mixture of his arrogance and overestimation of his own abilities, together with his lack of understanding and his drive to take centre stage had combined to create the catastrophe that was this orbit's failed attack. As far as the famulus was concerned the casualties were only names and numbers, fallen in the attempt to take the fortress.

He has no real feeling for the reality of the situation. The dead are not just items on a list but sons and daughters to be mourned and missed. Goïmron almost wished that Goldhand might have trouble with his faculties again at the next strategy meeting, so that he could make the requisite decisions himself.

Like he had done with the rejection of Mòndarcai's pact. *He might have provided a few thousand orcs but they'd not have brought us victory as things stand.*

He had finally climbed the hundred-pace-high ladder and handed over the order. At once the long trumpets sounded out, recalling the attacking force from their positions all along the walls. They were to regroup in the encampment and see to getting the wounded treated.

But, as if the fog wanted to prove to Goïmron that the ragana was certainly involved, the swathes of mist dissolved into light drizzle while the massed Girdlegard troops withdrew and made their way back to camp. Now they were all clearly visible.

The Brigantians took advantage of the opportunity and opened a barrage with every weapon at their disposal already set up on walkways and platforms round the ramparts. Spears, crossbow bolts, arrows and metal balls swished through the air, provoking muffled screams as they rained down on the retreating figures in the plain. The number of casualties rose considerably.

I've got to deflect their aim. Goïmron clasped the jewel in its dragon-shaped fitting.

WE'RE TOO FAR AWAY. THERE'S NOT ENOUGH ENERGY FOR THIS. SORRY AND ALL. IT'S DOWN TO YOU, said the sapphire. YOU'VE GOT TO PRACTISE MORE, MY FRIEND. I REGRET I CAN'T DO ANY MORE FOR YOUR PEOPLE.

'There! They've removed the tarpaulins so they can use the catapults at the back,' the dwarf at Goïmron's side said in horror, lifting his spyglass. 'Quick! Get as good a look at the weapons as you can,' he shouted to the other lookouts. 'Note the shape and then draw a sketch of them.' Goïmron did not need to be told twice. Using his spyglass for the task meant that he felt less helpless. The guilt and uselessness had been taking an acid hold of him. *This is a thousand times better than watching our people being slaughtered.* Conscientiously he made his observations up on the crow's nest, noticing every detail he could about the weaponry that had so far been concealed behind the reinforced walls. He looked up and down the alleyways and the staircases behind the ramparts, until . . .

What, in Vraccas' name, have they got THERE?

Goïmron's hand stopped in mid-movement.

The lenses showed him a pack of peculiar creatures that had taken up positions on the platforms at the rear and were having, it appeared, a little nap, untroubled by all the noise and the turmoil all about them. They looked like outsize wolves, with black hides that shimmered like armour. Even if they seemed to be dozing quietly while the catapults did their work, their ears were pricked upright and they were listening. They were aware of what was happening. When one of them opened his long muzzle in a yawn, multiple rows of sharp blue-white teeth became visible. *And those long talons of theirs will cut straight through chainmail and armour!* Goïmron took out some paper and charcoal, noting down the details of the creatures' appearance. The males seemed to be the larger ones in the pack.

As if in response to some command all the heads in the pack shot up, eyes open wide and the same bright bluish-white as their fangs. Then the creatures in the pack leaped up and raced off, vanishing down a staircase in the corner.

'Did you see those beasts, too?' Goïmron asked the dwarf at his side.

'Which ones do you mean?'

So you didn't. There were no dogs like that, whatever they were, in Girdlegard. *They must be from the Outer Lands. But when could they have arrived in Brigantia?* Goïmron studied his sketch again before picking up his spyglass once more to observe what was happening on the other side of the Brigantian walls.

While dwarves, humans, elves and meldriths were retreating to the safety of their encampment, where the healers were ready to attend to the wounded, the Brigantians were busy erecting new canvas screens to cover what they wanted concealed.

As if from a powerful lantern, bright yellow light suddenly flooded out of one of the narrow alleyways directly behind the nearest section of the ramparts. The Brigantian defenders in the roadway scattered to avoid being touched by the glow. *Another surprise.* Goïmron wished his spyglass lens had greater magnification.

I'LL DO MY BEST, said the stone. HURRY. I SHAN'T BE ABLE TO KEEP THIS UP FOR LONG.

The polished lens of the viewing scope shimmered and the image of the inside of the Brigantian citadel tripled in size, detail and focus. *Why didn't I think of that before?*

SOMETIMES THE SIMPLEST IDEAS TAKE TIME TO OCCUR TO ONE, MY FRIEND.

Goïmron's heart stopped in horror.

A creature in a silver suit of armour was stomping along the narrow cobbled passageway. The people moved smartly out of its way, pressing themselves back into the walls to let it pass.

Its size, in comparison with those standing nearby, showed

up as about three paces in height and it was broad in the beam. It carried a variety of weapons on its back and by its sides. The closed visor of the helmet had the form of a demon's ugly face and all around its head there was a wreath of deadly spikes. The bright yellow light that Goïmron had first noticed was issuing from the helmet's eye-slits and was burning a path free in front.

Goïmron had not been able to work out the significance of the pack of wolf-like creatures but at the sight of this creature he knew immediately what legendary being it was. *It's an acront! But . . . why are his eyes sending out that yellow light? Aren't they supposed to be purple? And what's he doing on the side of the Brigantians?*

The acront immediately vanished through an archway and the yellow light was gone.

'I saw that, too,' whispered the awestruck lookout at his side. 'Vraccas preserve us.'

Goïmron grabbed the sketches he had made and hurried off. Now he really did need Tungdil Goldhand's advice.

Girdlegard

United Great Kingdom of Gauragon
Province of Grasslands
1023 P.Q. (7514th solar cycle in old reckoning), late autumn

The stolen black flight-mare on which Stémna had fled the battle scene responded to pressure from its rider's thighs and directions from the reins because it instinctively realised that otherwise it was doomed. The glowing orange feather she held at its neck leaked out a fraction of the explosive power contained therein. Without this ever-present threat the

one-time Voice of the White Dragon would have been unceremoniously unseated.

'I know you hate me,' Stémna murmured to the black steed.
She flew south on its back, leaving far behind her the devastated region the Omuthan's troops had ravaged and scorched,
rather than allow the victorious dwarf-tribe forces any joy of
the territory. 'But life's like that. Sometimes we just have to
obey even if we don't want to.'

Stémna's wish, to meet her mistress's killer on the battlefield, had not been granted. After the fighting she had circled
the Fourthling fortress at a safe height and had flown round the
Brown Mountains, but to no avail. She had found not a trace of
Mòndarcai. As she knew the unlikely älf did not belong to Dsôn
Khamateion, she did not risk the dangerous journey there to
try to discover him.

Now the search would begin in earnest.

Rumour had it that the salt sea orcs and the Kràg Tahuum
beasts had formed an alliance under Mòndarcai's leadership.
Sooner or later Stémna was sure to come across him somewhere
in the castle complex. She must be patient and find a good place
to wait – wait and watch. In the course of the journey she had
managed to purloin some warm, inconspicuous clothing. At
this altitude and at this speed the air, especially at night, cut
like the icy winds of deepest winter. Her round hat with its
orange plumes was of limited use against the cold. But at the
moment the afternoon sun was making things bearable.

The black stallion snorted and headed lower without being
told to do so.

'What's the matter? Tired?' She was enjoying this form of
travel and had come to appreciate how regal and invulnerable
her mistress the dragon must have felt, speeding through the
upper air – until the unlucky orbit on which her death was
caused by the treachery of Ardin, the blue dragon that had

defected to Mòndarcai's side in order to attack Ûra. 'Not yet. This is not a good place to rest.'

But the steed continued its descent, spreading out its wings to reduce speed; the wind whistled through the plumage on the wings. Beneath them there ran a small stream that it must have spotted and aimed for in the hope of a drink.

'All right. If you must, but be quick.' Stémna did not remove the glowing feather she was holding against the stallion's neck. If she did, the animal, magically transformed by the älfar, would not hesitate for an instant to sink its vicious teeth into her flesh and tear her to pieces. 'We've got to get past the Land-bolt and then carry on to the south-west.'

Stémna did not intend to fly over the top of the ridge that was eight thousand paces high, even if Ardin was no longer in residence up there. The blue dragon had paid for its treachery with its life. Flying at those heights would not suit her, she knew; she would have a problem getting enough breath in that thin air. And the flight-mare would be sure to take advantage if she showed any weakness. She would not give the stallion an opportunity like that.

The flight-mare swept gracefully downwards, slowing and drifting at about a dozen paces above the ground as if it were afraid to let its hooves meet the floor.

'What are you up to?' Stémna applied the glowing feather and let it heat up, causing a smell of burnt horse-hair. 'Don't you try to —'

With a whirring sound, two arrows whizzed close by, narrowly missing her face and shoulder.

'What the —! Curses! Up, up! Quick!' Stémna yelled, pulling her head down.

But the flight-mare snorted furiously and leaned directly into the next barrage. A sharp tip pierced its front foot and three further arrows struck Stémna in the leg and her side. The next time the creature turned abruptly, she was thrown off, such was the drain on her strength caused by the pain.

Neighing wildly, the stallion shot up over her, flying random loops and dodging the missiles that followed.

Stémna fell through the half-bare branches of a tinder tree. The dried leaves and twigs broke her fall, tore at her clothing and whipped at her until she ended up in a soft bush, surrounded by red and gold foliage.

The wretched animal did that on purpose. Groaning with pain, she sat up and pulled the two arrows out of her leg. Judging by the shape of the arrow tips, these were the kind normally used for hunting. *So it's not soldiers.* The third arrow was in her side, stuck sideways. All she could do was to break off the feathered shaft. She knew it would not be wise to pull out the whole arrow as that could cause dangerous blood loss. *This demon's brood of a flying horse wanted to get rid of me at any cost and did not baulk at the risk of getting injured itself.*

Gritting her teeth, she pushed herself up to standing, using the trunk of the tree for support. She pressed herself against the bark and listened out.

'. . . fell down over there . . .' came a man's excited voice from further inside the woods.

'What kind of thing was it?' another voice asked.

'It was that flight-mare everyone's talking about. Except it was a woman riding it, not an älf,' said a third. 'Hey, look over there! That must be something of hers!'

Stémna did her best to keep her breathing quiet despite the pain. *Come any closer and I'll set you alight.* Putting her hand to her head, she was horrified to find her hat with its powerful magic plumes had gone. *In the name of a thousand demons!*

The rustle of approaching steps told her the men were close by.

She searched around for a hiding place in the grove. Autumn

had taken most of the foliage, so it would be difficult to conceal herself in spite of the camouflage colours of her dress and her sheepskin coat.

At some distance she noticed a hollow tree. *I ought to be able to make it.* She shuffled over, limping badly, holding her side and looking out for danger.

'Look! Blood!' one of the men called out excitedly.

'I've picked up her tracks,' said another.

Moaning, Stémna crouched down behind a greenberry bush. It was another thirty paces or so over to the hiding place she'd decided on. *And I'd be laying them a fine trail to follow.* She looked down at the gashes in her leg, now bleeding freely. *Perhaps . . .*

'Got you!' said someone behind you. She was kicked then hit over the head. Everything went black.

When Stémna opened her eyes again she saw, by the evening light, the ruins of a burned-out village now being restored. Scaffolding, beams and blocks of limestone were piled up in front of the charred shells of buildings.

She found herself upright and tied to a wooden pole, hands tethered behind her back and her feet on a pile of dry branches. *I'm to be burned at the stake.*

Surrounding her at the village crossroads there must have been about fifty men, women and children in ragged clothing, all staring at her and crowing with delight or shouting out their anger. Some held flaming torches.

'Look! The Voice of the Dragon has woken up,' an elderly woman cried out, laughing, her voice full of hatred. 'Good! That means you'll be aware of every instant when we burn you alive!'

The others cheered and hurled stones and filth at Stémna, much of it striking her in the face. The stink of faeces and rotten food stung in her nasal passages.

'We know exactly who you are,' the woman went on, as she was handed a flaming torch by one of the men. Part of the old crone's face showed terrible scars from the burns she must recently have received. Her sparse grey hair revealed livid bald patches on the skull. 'I can see from your expression that you don't remember. This is Richcrumb. You came here and visited devastation on us a few orbits ago, burning down our entire village to warn the surrounding settlements what happens if they refuse to pay the tribute.'

'Ûra is dead now and that's what's going to happen to you!' shouted one of the men, before bending down to pick up a stone to throw at her chest. The impact on her breastbone caused her great pain.

'You will suffer the same death that you brought to so many of us,' the older woman announced with satisfaction. 'We've brought all the kindling and soaked the branches so that they take longer to burn. It'll roast you to a turn. You will feel all the heat. You'll feel the flames burning through the soles of your feet, through your clothing, and eating away at your skin, you'll have your pretty blonde hair flare up round your head when it catches fire.'

Stémna was desperately trying to think what she could do. The ropes at her wrists were too tight for her to loosen, however much she struggled against them. She was firmly fixed to the stake.

I have failed utterly. She had always reckoned things might end this way after the death of her dragon mistress. Some time, she thought, after she'd been able to do away with the murderous älf. But not now. Not so horribly quickly. Not without her revenge. Not without having exacted justice. *A miserable pitiful failure.*

Stémna's pride forbade her any attempt to talk her way out of the situation with a tissue of lies. These people here would never believe her. 'I should have made sure you burned the same way,' she spat out.

The older woman stepped forward, the burn marks scarring her face very visible. 'Then someone else would have taken my place.' She slowly lowered the firebrand and the twigs and tinder caught. The little flames crackled their way to the top of the pile, sending up clouds of smoke. The damp wood was reluctant to blaze, just as the old crone had promised. 'We want you to suffer. We are exacting the same punishment as you and that white demon of yours doled out to our people. This is for all the victims. And for all their loved ones. For everyone you have hurt.'

The smoke stung her eyes and made her cough. Kept fully awake by the stabbing pain from the arrow wounds in her leg and in her side, she would be aware of every tortured instant of her death. 'If you're wanting to hear me beg for mercy you'll be disappointed.' She spoke the words with difficulty. 'I did what I considered the right thing.'

'It is enough for us to know that you will die in terrible pain,' the woman said with contempt. 'We're not expecting anything else from you.' She spat in Stémna's face. 'Follow your mistress into death.'

There were renewed cheers from the villagers as the pile of branches burned more strongly.

A wall of heat swept up to Stémna. At first she found this pleasantly warm, given the autumn chill in the air. But only at first. The pungent blue swathes of smoke increased, making breathing almost impossible and causing her to choke and cough. She could hardly see anything, as the combination of smoke and weakness from blood loss impaired her vision.

'Let's burn this thing along with you.' A man stepped forward through the fog and hurled a light-coloured round object into the pyre. 'Hated, just like yourself. Burning, just like you.'

Stémna did not at first see what it was he had thrown, but

when she had blinked the tears out of her eyes she saw what it was. *My hat!*

The flames had already reached the soft white felt of the brim and the fabric started to roll up in the heat. Before Stémna had properly gathered her thoughts, she saw a huge tongue of flame dart out of the crown to touch the remaining plumes fastened into the hatband.

The resulting detonation was of such overwhelming power that it threw her, tied as she was, together with the stake, straight up into the air, surrounded by orange-coloured clouds that darkened and fell on everything they could consume. Screams and yells of horror resounded on all sides, turning to roars and relentless sobbing.

Stémna had landed face down on the earth in a state of confusion, her hands still fastened behind her back, but the stake had come free. She could hardly move. Terrible pain sped through her entire body.

The glow of the fire spread. There was a smell of singed hair and burning flesh as the villagers succumbed to the flames. The blaze took hold of the wooden scaffolding round the Richcrumb houses the people had been trying to rebuild. The explosion had caused several of the buildings to collapse completely. Orange flames licked at the scattered corpses, burning them through to the bones. Stonework had burst under the pressure waves and immense heat. Some of the dead were already nothing but a pile of ash in the shape of a human.

Stémna took deep breaths and tried to battle the exhaustion that was overcoming the pain. If she gave in to the drowsiness she would never wake up again. *But it's vital I survive. I want to destroy that älf. I . . .*

Someone turned her over on to her back. 'That's her.' She was aware of a vague face floating over her, a light splodge with holes for eyes, mouth and nose. 'She's still alive.'

'Finish it off,' Stémna said scornfully. 'But your homeland will never—'

She was interrupted: 'We are not from Richcrumb.' A second flesh-coloured shape swam into her field of vision. 'We could leave you here, Stémna. Or we could rescue you. That's as long as you promise to change your ways. If you abjure your old life and become one of us. With all the consequences. Because, in reality, you always did belong to our kind.'

'What . . . what by all . . .?' she stammered, utterly confused.

'You have always been a slave. Ûra's slave. We are doulia. We volunteer to be slaves, just like you,' the female voice of one of the pale face-shapes above her explained. 'Swear you will never return to your current way of life and come and join our community. Dedicate yourself, along with us, to the greater task. With all the powers you possess and which we have just witnessed.'

'Or we can just leave you here. To die. In your previous existence,' said a faceless man. Stémna could hardly grasp what they were saying, but she knew she was lost if she was not helped. And then she would never manage to track down and destroy her mistress's murderer. In the service of her mission of revenge she was willing to swear allegiance to any divinity on offer.

'I vow to become a doulia,' she said, finding it difficult to speak smoothly.

'With everything this entails? To become one of us from now on?' the man continued in a friendly tone.

'With everything. With anything at all, for shit's sake,' she gasped out, tasting blood in her mouth.

'I don't know, Enes,' said the woman suspiciously. 'Was that really a valid vow? I think she should say the whole thing properly. Or else let her die. That oath might have been a lie.'

'No! No! Really. I mean it. I'm deadly serious,' she groaned, coughing again. 'Please. I want to become a doulia. One of you. Just like you were saying. I swear it on my life!'

'We'll accept that for now,' Enes decided. 'We'll put it to her again when she's recovered. Till then, she's one of us. A doulia.'

At this, Stémna was lifted up by gentle hands and carried carefully away. Her relief was so great that she burst into tears.

Once upon a time a young maiden walked into the Wonder Zone without noticing where she was going.

As she walked along she collected small souvenirs of her journey, including three magic nuts. When she got back to her hovel of a cottage she heaved a sigh and wished she had a sackful of gold. And lo and behold, one appeared. The first of the three nuts had conjured it up for her.

The girl cried out in surprise, 'Well, I'll be kissed by an orc!' – and lo and behold, an orc arrived. This was the work of the second nut.

And the orc kissed the girl. And then it ate her up.

But the third magic nut is still lying up there on the blood-stained floorboards of her humble cottage.

You might find it one day.

Short fairy tale from Ribasturian

III

Girdlegard

In the Brown Mountains
Brigantia
1023 P.Q. (7514th solar cycle in old reckoning), winter

Goïmron observed the others' faces; some of the attendees had gone slightly red. It might have been the enthusiastic discussion causing this, or maybe the heat in the tent. Or the alcohol. Yet again the seconded representatives from the humans, dwarves, elves and meldriths had assembled in the large conference marquee tent.

Following the two noteworthy and disturbing discoveries that Goïmron had made from the high crow's nest observation post, the debate this time was not about making a further attempt to storm the walls before the onset of winter. They were discussing the significance of the sketches he had made.

And what the consequences would be.

Goïmron was seated at the side of the regally attired Goldhand, who had immediately recognised the wolf-like creatures the gemstone specialist had spotted while watching from the high platform. They were narshân beasts.

The aged dwarf knew them well, having come across them during his time in the Black Abyss. He had even once kept a narshân pack himself, using them for carrying messages.

Peerless in any skirmish, they were never defeated. As well as their armoured hides and the claws sharp enough to slice through metal, they possessed iron-hard fangs often coated with poisonous material.

'But what is one of the acronta doing here in Brigantia's random collection of creatures and oddments? They've got throat-cutting brigands, monsters and all sorts of other scum. Didn't all the Towers That Walk die out?' Gata, who had not wanted to dispense with her full armour even for this official strategy meeting, looked round the circle of representatives from the various factions. 'Shouldn't the acront be actually attacking them? In all the old stories we heard about the acronta, they and the black-eyes were always locked in a deadly feud. And Dsôn Khamateion, as everyone knows, is an ally of Brigantia.'

'And the eyes of an acront shine purple, not yellow,' Goldhand pointed out firmly. 'That's what concerns me most. Something has happened to change the acronta.' That there was something odd going on behind the fortress ramparts was obvious to the assembled company. New questions were emerging. So far no one had come up with any credible theories. There would be no chance of solving the puzzle from over here on this side of the walls. Of this Goïmron was convinced. *What we need is a spy on the inside.* His thoughts turned to Rodana again. If he could somehow manage to make contact with her, their military prospects would be greatly improved. *Maybe with magic?*

'In the present circumstances there will be no further attempts to storm the fortress,' said Telìnâs, who was wearing a flowing robe in green and brown tones, adorned with the sash indicating his rank within the fîndaii, the elite imperial guard unit. In front of him on the table was the folded paper version of an acront he had made while listening to the others. The model stood one finger-length in height. 'Whereas we've been lacking the necessary military force to storm the walls success-fully, our opponents seem to have acquired new allies for themselves. This is not a good combination.'

'There never used to be any narshâns in Brigantia. And they've never had any acronta till now,' said Bendoïn Feinunz, muttering to himself. As former high commander of all the border fortresses, he knew the enemy better than anyone else. At present he was in charge of all the Fourthling forces. 'We would certainly have got word of it before now if that had been the case.'

'And they've only just turned up. Where have they come from? The access passage through from the north-east is closed, just as Master Goldhand planned. Or, is it?' Mostro made no attempt to disguise a scornful hint of recrimination in his words. The extravagant gown he wore was intended to create the impression of his being of higher status than all the others in the tent.

'So you think there may be a fault, a gap in the demolished approach passages? And that these creatures might have come through that way?' Goldhand shook his head, his long white hair sweeping across his shoulders. 'That way through has been completely closed off. I would put my hand in the nearest fire to vouch for that, I'm so sure.'

Gata looked sceptical. 'And why would they want to come to Brigantia, anyway? What would entice them to come to an insignificant realm already on its last legs and currently under siege by vastly superior numbers?'

'Who knows what the Omuthan might have promised them in return for their assistance?' the famulus retorted. 'There could well be a continuous stream of them surging through to Brigantia. They'd then have all the extra reinforcements that we do not have available to us.'

'Ooh, to think of it! If only we had a teensy little bit of magic to help us out,' Hargorina said cuttingly. 'But instead of proper magic we get silly kids' stuff: toys and fireworks and creatures that only inflict damage on our own ranks. Berengart does not need any new troops to withstand our attack and send us packing.' She jutted her chin. 'All that magical power we were promised – more powerful, we were told, than anything witnessed in the battle on Two-Stream Hill. I've yet to see any of that.'

'It's all the ragana's doing. She's blocking my magic energy,' Mostro snapped sharply back at the sturdily built red-haired dwarf commander. 'You and Master Feinunz haven't even managed to get a single siege ladder up to the battlements with your people on it. How should–'

'That's enough,' said Goldhand. The participants all fell silent out of respect. 'We shall have to admit we have lost the winter for any attack on the Brown Mountains. For that reason, we must focus on what is to come.' He looked at the famulus. 'You will have realised what I'm referring to, Master Mostro?'

That's quite neat, Goïmron thought, *the way he's avoided using the form of address Mostro has been insisting on. He didn't call him Magus.*

'You're talking about the day after tomorrow, then?' The famulus pursed his lips crossly and pushed his fingers through his artfully dressed hair as if to calm its waves and curls. 'Tomorrow being the final orbit of the current solar cycle.'

That's all we needed! Goïmron had quite overlooked the vital importance of this impending date in the calendar. In the coming night the 1023rd cycle would end – and thus, with it, any magic power that was not embedded in a particular person or bound by spell to a specific artefact.

Somewhere within Girdlegard a new Wonder Zone would come into being in the next three orbits, making a source of new energy available to those with certain magical gifts.

It worked to supply magi and the like with what they needed, in the same way as a spring provided refreshment with life-giving water. The annual search for the renewed magic source had been a ritual for many cycles now.

But no one knew exactly where the new force would bubble up.

A fundamental question indeed in their present difficulties.

'You're expecting the Brigantians to make a sortie on that very orbit, Master Goldhand?' Telìnâs studied the scale model of the fortress and the ring of besieging army positions. A tiny work of paper sculpture art was being formed in his hands. 'The ragana will be needing a new power source, too, won't she?'

'We can discount her entirely. Chòldunja has lost her moor diamond. It's hanging round Mostro's neck,' Goïmron cut in. He had had enough of hearing the young woman scapegoated for the failings of the famulus. 'If I understand correctly, it won't be easy for her to find a replacement. So she is in no position to do any witchcraft at all. The fog wasn't her doing and she wasn't responsible for any of the other things the famulus has messed up.'

Mostro leaped to his feet in fury. 'That is monstrous. Outrageous!' he shouted, red in the face.

'It's the truth, and you know it, Master Mostro.' Goïmron refused to let himself be intimidated. He had kept quiet for far too long. Here, among the assembled commanders, his opinion was respected. 'The Brigantians won't be risking a sortie that's totally reliant on Chòldunja's help. But who knows what else they have up their sleeves, over there behind the walls?' He pointed at the self-styled magus, who was being forcibly restrained by Telìnâs. The elf was holding him back with one hand to stop him launching himself at Goïmron. 'But *you* will certainly be in need of new magic energy. So we should let you have some of the troops and send you off to roam the land and seek out the new Wonder Zone.'

'Is that something you have experience with, Master Mostro?' Goldhand asked. 'You are practically a magus in your own right, and you must know various magic formulae. Will you be able to locate the new magic source?'

Every pair of eyes in the tent turned to the dark-blond young man in the pretentious costume.

'The Esteemed Maga Vanéra trained me well,' he replied, carefully skirting round the implied doubt as to his abilities.

'Meaning?' Goïmron pressed. He was sick of the constant evasiveness of this self-important human.

'Meaning that I have studied some of the relevant spells,' he said, changing tack. 'You've all seen what I can do on the battle-field. On Two-Stream Hill. And here.'

'So that's a no,' Gata summed up, adding a heartfelt dwarf oath. With her left hand she indicated the map of Girdlegard on display next to the model of the fortress. 'Fine. Quite an area to search. The new magic source could be absolutely anywhere.'

'Not so fast. I have already done some preparatory research.' Mostro pointed to some faint graphite markings on the paper. 'Those are the places where the sources have been located in the past fifty cycles,' he explained. 'To find out about further back than that I'd have to go to archives, but they are held very far away from the mountains. Anyway' – and he indicated a town in Khalteran and one in Sinterich – 'There have been a couple of repeat events. So my suggestion would be to work across the area from east to west in the hope the source might turn up again for the third time in one of those locations. Let us send out scouts to reconnoitre. They can go there and keep their eyes open for clues.'

'There haven't ever been any triple occurrences recorded, have there?' Goïmron wanted to know.

'Yes, once. In a silver pine forest to the east of Silândur,'

Telìnâs responded, putting a paper narshân next to his little acront. 'Never since that, though.'

Goïmron considered the possibilities. Given the number of important personages in the meeting it was not really his place to speak out. He was only a gem cutter. On the other hand, he was a gemstone magus and would be the only one of them not about to lose his magic power at the end of the cycle in two orbits' time – thanks to his natural talents and to the sea sapphire that no one else had the slightest inkling about. *It's not an unlucky stone as far as I'm concerned.* 'Might it not be a good idea to get Vanéra to join our efforts at the siege? She could bring a whole load of extra artefacts. She can't cast any spells, of course,' he said, referring to the famulus. 'Whereas Mostro, for example, won't be capable of any wizardry at all without refreshing his magic energies.'

'I agree,' said Gata, turning to address Mostro. 'We'll give you some of our best soldiers to help you. Until you can manage to provide your own magic protection, that is, Master Famulus.'

'And the rest of us will hold the fort, so to speak, here at the siege,' added Goldhand. 'We need to ensure the Brigantians' own magicians – if, indeed they have any—'

'Apart from the moor-witch,' murmured Mostro.

'If we can prevent them sending out any magicians they may have to try and locate the new magic source to refresh their powers; that would represent a strategic advantage for us. Our next onslaught on the walls will be successful,' the ancient dwarf hero concluded his proposal. 'We will be in urgent need of your specialised knowledge, Master Mostro! Otherwise we'll be losing troops all the time. We'd be attacking the walls entirely fruitlessly, just giving the Brigantians more time. If we're not careful we'll find they've recouped strength sufficiently to attempt an attack on us.'

'Or maybe the älfar will come crawling out of the shadows.

Or that weird black-eyes with his whole army of pig-faces will turn up again,' the disgruntled black-bearded Bendoïn contributed. 'How do we handle him?'

'We are speaking of a deadly warrior who managed to remove the threat of the dragon Ûra.' Telìnâs put his finger on the icon marking Kràg Tahuum. 'I'm not going to go so far as to say that Mòndarcai is more dangerous than the combined forces of Brigantia, but if he turns against us, we're lost.'

'How many orcs are we talking about here, do you think?' Goïmron asked everyone.

'We can only hazard a guess for the salt sea orcs. No one's ever been able to get far enough into their hostile territory to find out. Probably an army of less than eight or ten thousand, I'd say.' This was the view of the Gauragon commander.

'Kràg Tahuum is surrounded by a huge defence ditch a hundred paces deep. The whole place measures a thousand by a thousand paces and it goes up to tremendous heights with all its buildings and towers. The citadel there can house at least two or three thousand trained fighters, along with the rest of their tribes.' Telìnâs placed a coin over the sign for the fort. 'They know what they're doing when it comes to defence. Less effective, I'd say, going out on to the field of battle.'

Goïmron had to admire the young elf's assured composure. He had benefitted greatly from his promotion to the Elf Empress's guard. *It sounds as if he must have been to Kràg Tahuum.*

'The fact the orc tribes are uniting is extremely dangerous for us. But winter is not their preferred season. They'll want to stay inside their walls, or be back home in the salt plains,' said Hargorina. 'Come the spring they'll be a real threat. Especially if they have that clever black-eyes commanding them.'

'But by then the Brown Mountains will be in our hands,' Mostro predicted confidently. He had recovered from the criticism the others had heaped on him and his arrogance was back. 'I solemnly vow to all of you I'll provide you with a breach in the walls as soon as I get back here with renewed magical powers.'

Goldhand nodded slowly. 'This all sounds like the right way to proceed. To this end, we shall announce throughout Girdle-gard that it is vital that *we* be the ones to locate the new Magic Source. Every man, woman and child must keep their eyes peeled and report any findings to their nearest authority figure, so that news gets to us with all possible speed.'

'There are bound to be lots of false positives, I expect,' said Mostro. 'Lay people will find it hard to distinguish between genuine magic phenomena and incidents that are merely odd.'

'Of course. But better too many reports than let the black-eyes or Mòndarcai's beasts get there first.' Gata took a deep breath and seemed on the point of adding something, but after a glance at Goïmron she closed her mouth again.

He guessed that the Thirdling queen had been about to criti-cise the fact that Mòndarcai's offer of a pact had been rejected. *I'm glad she didn't.*

'There is no spell to help you locate the magic source?' he enquired.

'What a question! Without the magic powers it is hardly going to be an option, is it?' Mostro responded condescendingly. 'You should think before you make any more suggestions, Master Chiselcut.'

'Or an artefact that could show which way to go?'

'No.'

'And no special formula that could be pronounced *before* the magic runs out?' Goïmron thought it illogical that finding the new source of power should depend purely on chance.

Mostro stroked his pointed beard. 'My dear Master Chiselcut. For hundreds of cycles magically gifted people have been confronted with exactly *this very problem*. Did you really think nobody's ever thought about these matters before?'

'Sometimes the most obvious solutions are the last ones we think of.' Goïmron directed his gaze once more to the map of Girdlegard. There was still something worrying him. 'What do we do if this time the new area can't be found? What if no one finds it at all?'

There came no answer.

Not even after a long wait.

Everyone in the conference tent knew that in that case all the Girdlegard troops besieging Brigantia would find themselves in extreme peril. There were orcs and älfar waiting for an opportunity to seize power. Then there was the matter of the älfar fleet of ships with their blood-red sails, together with their Undarimar allies. A war on multiple fronts would test the combined forces of humans, dwarves, elves and meldriths to the limit of their endurance. Test them to destruction.

Goïmron became acutely aware of how the commanders' confidence and courage were ebbing away, following these words of his. *I should have kept my opinion to myself.*

The entrance opened.

Dressed in a long mantle against the chill, the srgàlàh Sònuk stepped in, preceded by a gust of icy air and a slight smell of smoke. He was holding a short-handled spear with an unusually long, broad blade at its tip. 'I humbly beg the indulgence of the honourable assembly. Please excuse my tardiness.' He inclined head and shoulders respectfully to the noble gathering. With his conspicuously impressive canine head on the muscular human body he clearly stood out from the other members of the unusual alliance. 'I was investigating a fissure in the rock near the north side of the camp, where I had noticed a suspicious scent. It could have indicated that Brigantians were planning to make a sortie with a band of assassins.'

Goïmron liked the srgālàh very much. But at the same time he did wonder what Sònuk was doing here at the commanders' meeting. Normally he preferred to keep away from official gatherings of this nature.

'Very praiseworthy, my friend. But we are dealing with different concerns here,' said Mostro, remonstrating firmly with him, albeit in a soft voice.

'I heard about that. It's a matter of the Wonder Zone, I understand.' Sònuk grinned, revealing fangs the length of one's finger, which always made his smile appear slightly threatening. 'That's why I'm here.' With the forefinger of his left hand he tapped the end of his long snout, which ended in a golden leathery nose. 'I'll be able to sniff it out for you.'

Klaey wandered through the southernmost part of the tunnel that had, until very recently, led to the other end of the Fourthling dwarf realm. He was astonished by what had occurred a few orbits earlier and wanted to see the extent of the destruction with his own eyes. No more than a third of the original tunnel had survived. The rest had collapsed, cutting Brigantia off entirely from the north-east. There had been no warning.

Klaey was surprised at the number of unknown creatures walking about down here and the different faces he came across. They must have come through from the Outer Lands just before the passageway caved in. *But what for? What are they after?*

'You're a long way from the fortress,' he heard Kawutan say, reproachfully, at his back. 'As a junior banner officer cadet your task is surely to check the supplies. Instead you're on a little outing, are you?'

Klaey rolled his eyes before turning round. Since the älf female had not appeared again after making her seductive offer, he was still going to have to deal with Kawutan's arrogance and Orweyn's prolonged absence.

'I'm not on an outing. I'm checking to see whether parts of the side passages can be saved,' he lied. His voice was still a croak. 'I take my task extremely seriously. The siege will be a long one.'

Dressed in full armour, his brother Kawutan was equipped for battle, with a unit of five guards to protect him. His spouse Ilenis followed, accompanied by her domestic staff and a number of doulia slaves walking five or six paces behind. They were distributing alms to the needy homeless folk who had narrowly escaped the destruction and were now sheltering in nooks and crannies along the way. Ilenis was wearing an expensive white dress and a silken cloak, which made the scene even stranger.

'And did you find anything?' Kawutan wanted to know.

'No. Most of the side tunnels have caved in as well.' Klaey threw Ilenis a swift glance, which she answered with a secret smile. 'And what about you?'

'I'm gathering my own impressions of the scale of the disaster.'

Klaey could hear he was not telling the truth. *Two liars here and each one thinks he can fool the other.* 'That's praiseworthy of you. And how is our good brother Orweyn doing?'

'Improving.'

'Has he been told what's happened?'

Kawutan shook his head. 'It might impede his recovery, the healers decided.' All the time he was looking around discreetly, as if he did not want Klaey to notice. 'You won't be able to go and see him, though.'

'Does that instruction come from the healers?'

'It comes from me. Our elder brother should decide for himself, as soon as he is capable of it, whether or not he wishes to receive you. I am unwilling to pre-empt his verdict.' Kawutan gestured towards the tunnel leading south. 'Get yourself back to the fortress and start checking your lists, banner officer cadet. I think we have enough supplies in reserve to see us through three cycles. The besieging armies will have bitten off more than they can chew.'

'Of course, noble Temporary Omuthan.' Klaey made an exaggeratedly deep bow to his brother. 'Shall I keep anything special aside for you? A certain type of beer? Drugs?'

His mention of his brother's particular tendency to over-indulgence caused the accompanying soldiers some amusement, which they were at pains to conceal.

'Let me have a think about that,' said Kawutan. 'Ah yes, I know – why don't you find us a flying night-mare? That would be great, if you can manage it.' Kawutan swept past, pretending to examine the many cracks in the ten-pace-high ceiling of the broad tunnel. 'And try not to lose the next one.'

Klaey strolled over to Ilenis and greeted her with an embrace. She stroked the nape of his neck discreetly. 'What is the idiot doing?'

The woman in her mid-forties laughed. 'Is it so obvious that he didn't come here to inspect the tunnels?'

'He knows absolutely nothing about mining and he's got no one with him who'd be able to advise. If he fancies a little trip with his wife I can imagine there are many nicer places to go where he wouldn't be having to take a bodyguard along.' Klaey folded his arms and watched Kawutan. 'I noticed there was an acront in silver armour in the fortress. And some black armoured wolves with shiny white eyes and fangs. They're from the Outer Lands. Did my brother summon them?'

Ilenis laughed outright. 'No. Not Kawutan. It was Orweyn. He called them in even before the Brigantian army attacked Gauragon. He was afraid he might run out of soldiers on his victory campaign, so he sent messengers to the Outer Lands to get volunteers.'

'An acront? Acronta would never agree to collaborate with us, let alone work with the älfar.' Klaey leaned against the attractive woman.

Ilenis did not show how intimately the pair of them were really acquainted. She kept her hands to herself. 'Quite a marvel, don't you think?'

'So they must have turned up at the very last moment, coming through the tunnel just ahead of its collapsing.'

'I assume so.'

'If they were recruited they'll be demanding their wages soon.' Klaey thought this might be why his brother had come here with five bodyguards, wearing full armour and carrying weapons. *Not enough for a proper fight, but he'll be wanting to give a show of strength. We can't afford to have these creatures and people at our backs as potential enemies while we're under siege.* 'Do these mercenaries share a leader?'

'It's not the acront. He spends his time rushing hither and thither as if he's looking for something in the fortress,' Ilenis told him openly, as she arranged her silk cloak to flow attractively over her shoulders. 'There's a man with them, no one of consequence, it would seem. He's wrapped in stinking furs and is ordering the black armour wolves about. The beasts are fiendishly clever. Their eyes shine in the dark and they can smell fear in any living creature, it's said.'

'So maybe they are in charge of him, not the other way around,' Klaey joked. He could certainly find a use for animals of that nature.

'Who knows?' Ilenis took more bread out of the basket one of her servants was holding out to her, and gave it to the children who had come up to ask for a food handout. Loaves clutched tight, the children ran off again. The doulia slaves also carried supplies of dried meat and fruit to distribute in the temporary shelters.

'Why is—' Klaey broke off his question.

A freakish-looking individual, scrawny and unkempt, had appeared out of one of the side passages. Some malicious divinity must have caused him to come into the world with crooked limbs. His shoulders were unequal in height and his spine was disconcertingly malformed. As he walked, he dragged one leg behind him. His right hand had a constant tremor, such that he would never have been able to hold cutlery or a full glass. He had attempted to hide his disfigured physique under a wide robe made up of patches of odd pieces of material. He approached Kawutan.

'At long last, Omuthan!' His attractive clean-shaven face was in complete contrast to his general appearance. It was a countenance so bewitchingly beautiful that even an elf would have been envious. 'You've kept me waiting. That is something I do not appreciate.'

Two of the bodyguards blocked his advance, holding their lances crossed in his path.

'Nor this attitude, either,' was the cripple's comment. He threw back his capacious hood to rest it on his uneven shoulders.

'This is getting interesting.' Klaey took Ilenis along with him in order to have a good excuse for his continued presence in the tunnel. He was eager to listen in.

'Do you think *that* thing's their leader? That horror?' Ilenis asked sceptically. She sent her servants and the doulia slaves off to wait in the main corridor. 'Why would anyone follow him?'

Kawutan was keeping his distance from the strangely garbed newcomer, and he did not notice his wife and Klaey coming closer. 'It has not been possible before now, Hantu. You know we have been under siege. And that my brother was injured in the fighting. I have more important things to do than listen to your complaints.'

'Do not speak to me as if I were some lowly supplicant!' Hantu hissed. 'It was your brother who summoned *me* to come to you to help with the conquest. And what was I given in place of the promised reward?' With his shaking right hand he indicated the tunnel he had emerged from. 'Accommodation no orc would tolerate for a toilet!'

'I have checked your name on the list . . .'

'Speak to me in a proper manner!' Hantu shouted. 'Pay me the respect I am due. I am treating you courteously.'

'I found your name on my brother's list. That is the only reason why I have come. To show my goodwill.' Kawutan glanced past the man, looking into the tunnels behind. 'How many are you?'

'I am here on my own. My family is stuck on the other side of the blockage in the tunnel.' Hantu clasped his hands in front of his flat belly, the action seeming only to emphasise his odd proportions. 'Get me the sort of accommodation that reflects my status.'

'But as I do not know what you and my brother—'

'Ask him.'

'First, he has to recover. Then I shall ask him.'

Hantu took half a step forward, so that the tip of his nose came into contact with the guards' crossed spears. 'I am absolutely indifferent to the state of your brother's health, *Omuthan* Kawutan Berengart. The agreement with him and Brigantia is binding. I have in my possession a signed and sealed contract with your family's name and the official Omuthan endorsement on it. Do not make me pursue this with all the means at my disposal.'

'This is not a threat you are making here, I surmise, but a statement,' an angered Kawutan retorted.

'Exactly. One Omuthan is as good as another.' Hantu shot a quick glance at the guards. 'It may be some time, I presume, until I am granted the promised access through to Girdlegard, as detailed in our agreement. Your brother's annexation campaign seems not to have gone entirely to plan.'

'That is unfortunately the case.' Kawutan turned away. 'I shall keep you informed as to where you may go to find somewhere better to stay.'

'Not just better. You are to find me suitable accommodation appropriate for my standing, Omuthan-Replacement. That, too, is expressly detailed in the agreement with your family. I am acquainted with ways of keeping this matter to the forefront of your mind, from sun up to sun down.' Hantu placed his calmer hand on the spot, in front of his face, where the two lances crossed. 'Or, on the other hand, I could help you to win a victory over the army that is laying siege. Under certain conditions. That would also facilitate my entry to Girdlegard. Is Kràg Tahuum far from here?'

Klaey pricked up his ears. *What does he have in mind with the orc stronghold?*

Kawutan stopped short and gave Hantu a contemptuous glare. 'You? You would help me? Then you should get a move on. If you are a magus, all the magic power will be disappearing. The turn of the cycle is nigh.'

'What did your brother's list say about me?'

'It said you are . . . an Amrach. Or something like that.'

'It's *Rhamak*. You think that's another name for a magus, something to do with witchcraft, sorcery, magic powers?'

Kawutan felt uncertain now. 'Well, isn't it?'

Hantu laughed scornfully. 'Not in the slightest bit like that. But powers are involved that can match anything a wizard or a witch can conjure up.'

'What are you in need of, in order to exercise your power?' Kawutan had grown curious.

'I could do it without demanding anything more than is

agreed in the contract. That way I could get to Kràg Tahuum sooner. Otherwise I'll be stuck here in this pile of rocks for cycles.' Hantu reached into his shoulder bag and pulled out a stick of charcoal and a sheet of paper. Using his better-functioning hand, he wrote some words. 'This is for your eyes only, Replacement Omuthan. You would do well to keep it to yourself. If you don't . . . oh, read it yourself.' He handed the writing over to Kawutan.

Klaey watched his brother go chalk-white, as terror or shock hit home, draining the blood from his face. He immediately ripped the paper into tiny pieces and threw the shreds into Hantu's face. 'That will never happen.' He turned on his heel abruptly and saw his wife with Klaey. After a brief moment's hesitation he stormed past them both. 'Never.'

'Then I hope your brother will soon be restored sufficiently to make his own decisions,' Hantu called after him in a vicious tone. 'Otherwise this fortress will fall and you will have lost everything. Everything! And that is more than I was asking for!' He, too, disappeared.

Klaey and Ilenis looked at each other. 'Go after your husband. Find out what just happened,' he murmured to her, kissing her gently on the cheek. 'We can't let him put our rescue in jeopardy.'

'I know you would make a better Omuthan than him,' she whispered, leaving his embrace. 'I shall make that happen.' She quickly set off after Kawutan with her servants and the doulia in tow.

Klaey hurried over to where the shredded pieces of paper lay scattered on the floor. Hantu's script was clumsy and it was obviously not his own language he was writing. Some of the fragments were missing, so Klaey could not read what it was Hantu had been demanding.

Curses! Kawutan is such a fool. It was painful for Klaey to know that Brigantia could prevail. *But at what cost? Under what conditions?* Orweyn had recruited Hantu deliberately. *He knows the answer.* Klaey would have to depose his incompetent brother Kawutan, by ensuring that Orweyn recovered completely as soon as possible. *It's essential he be in charge of Brigantia and he must give Hantu a free hand.* Otherwise the besieging forces would soon be returning with a magus. Or perhaps with a number of them. *And that confounded dwarf that brought me down out of the sky.*

Klaey already knew how he would go about speeding up the healing process.

He did not want to have to rely only on Ilenis. She might be able to seduce her spouse into betraying some information, but she certainly would not be up for killing him. And Kawutan's death would not get them very far if Orweyn were not restored to power first.

That little ragana can help me. She can make Orweyn recover. Klaey hurried back. *And if she doesn't, then I'll have her arrested and executed.*

He soon reached the place where the puppet mistress and the moor-witch had been told to stay. The lock was quickly opened and he stepped into the rooms. 'Chòldunja!' Klaey slammed the door behind him. 'Come here!'

Both women appeared. Their hands and clothing were spotted with glue and wood shavings. They had begun making replacement puppets. They had covered their hair in headscarves.

'You have to use your powers to ensure my brother is restored to full health.' He went over swiftly to the young aprendisa and grabbed her by the upper arm. 'Right now! Today! Or your magic power will have vanished.'

'But . . . but I . . .' she stammered.

'I realise helping the sick and suffering is hardly the speciality of someone who likes to devour young children.' Klaey dragged her to the door and chucked a brown cloak over to her. 'Put that on, and mind you keep the hood up over your face.'

'I can't do it!' Chòldunja objected.

'You *will* do it!' He stopped and glared at her in fury. 'Otherwise the puppet woman will suffer, I promise you. Without me you are both done for here in Brigantia.'

Rodana stepped forward, wiping her dirty hands on her apron. Her dark fingertips and lips looked as if they had been painted; a fluke of nature had made them almost black. 'She really can't. Because Mostro stole her moor diamond.'

'So what?' Klaey stared at the puppeteer, who was fixing back behind her ear a stray strand of hair that had escaped from her headscarf. 'Then she'll have to do without it. The explosion worked without it.'

'Most of the energy the diamond held stemmed from the souls of young children.' Rodana cleared her throat. 'Without its power Chòldunja can't do any spells like a ragana might do. The explosion used up the last bit of power.'

Klaey uttered a hoarse cry of frustration. 'But you could heal someone if you had that energy?'

'Of course.'

'What if I get you a new stone? Has it got to be one of those clunky moor gems?'

'It would . . . work better,' Chòldunja stammered, looking to the puppeteer for help.

Klaey understood from this that a conventional diamond would do just as well. *Good! Then there's hope. Brigantia has a chance.*

Rodana came over. 'We are grateful to you, for having—'

'Be quiet! I'm talking to the ragana!' Klaey grabbed the younger girl by the shoulders. 'If you don't heal my brother in the next few orbits, Brigantia will fall. The besieging army will find you and execute you. If the fortress falls, you fall with it. Is that what you want?'

Sobbing, Chòldunja shook her head.

'Then heal my brother. He can make our new allies break the siege,' Klaey explained. 'Have you got it?'

Chòldunja nodded. 'Which . . . which new allies are these?'

'There's an acront who's turned up. And some black armour wolves and lots of other people that will only take commands from my eldest brother.' Klaey took a deep breath and did some thinking. 'Do you maybe know what a rhamak is?'

She shook her head.

'No matter. Good. In order to charge up your new magic gemstone with fresh energy, you'll need some young life to consume. Right, ragana?'

'Yes. But—'

'Understood.' Klaey let go of her arm and turned to leave. 'I hope you've got a big stomach. I'll bring you so many infants and toddlers you'll be kept busy eating them. And I'll get you the best, the rarest diamond I can find in Brigantia.' He yanked the door open, kissed his lucky amulet and hurried off.

The GARNET.

The stone has colours ranging from crimson to a deep dark red.

It dispels unchaste thoughts, protects against light-ning strikes and infections, with the unfortunate exception of the suihhi plague. Numerous people have paid with their lives for this misconception.

What makes the garnet even more valuable is its effect in repelling demonic influences.

Strangely, it seems that particularly the young dislike the stone and choose not to wear garnet jewellery. One might almost conclude that young people do not object to unchaste thoughts.

Excerpt from
*The Forgotten Power of Precious
and Semi-precious Stones*
by Sparklestone & Sons & Daughters

IV

Girdlegard

In the north of the United Great Kingdom of Gauragon
Foothills of the Grey Mountains
1023 P.Q. (7514th solar cycle in old reckoning), winter

I'm stuck fast here in the middle of my own nightmare. Sitting unhappily in the crate the orcs had constructed for him out of thick branches, Barbandor watched the last fire-eater settlement fall to Borkon and his fighting force, following the collapse of negotiations. *Nothing's getting any better.*

Not only had he been taken prisoner but his captors had robbed him of his last bit of dignity. The beasts had suspended him from the branches of lava beech tree at the edge of the village like some cute little songbird in its cage, so that he should have a good view of events as they occurred. *To Tion with the confounded pig-faces!*

The night-blue orc with the whole-body white tattoo markings had tried several times to engage Barbandor in civil conversation, in order to extract some useful facts out of him about the Children of Vraccas. Borkon seemed to be obsessed with finding out as much information as possible, and the orc's greyish-green subjects shared his keenness.

Barbandor was being treated well. They had let him keep his chainmail tunic and the sash of office. They gave him food and drink and allowed him washing facilities. In view of the increasingly cold weather, they had given him a fur coat that was far too big for him.

That was why it seemed doubly cruel of them to have feasted on the mortal remains of the unfortunate Gyndala. Her body had been roasted over the fire and the flesh finely sliced; bones and the tougher cuts of meat had been the basis for some soup. The monsters were ecstatic about the delicious meal she had provided. Barbandor had been unable to watch. He had kept his eyes firmly shut, and had stopped up his ears to try to keep out the sounds. This attempt had not been wholly successful.

He kept up a steady stream of prayers to Vraccas to let him survive his ordeal. To let him be able to avenge poor Gyndala and all the others who fell victim to the beasts. And got gobbled up.

The last settlement of the so-called fire eaters lay far off to the east, at the foot of the southern Grey Mountains. The orc village rose up proudly on an island in the middle of the lave fields, and was only accessible via a stone causeway through the broiling molten rock. At the end of the walkway there was a massive gate barring the entrance. The soles of one's feet could only withstand the searing heat if one ran across quickly. If your feet started to melt or catch fire this would make you an easy target for the village's defenders. All they had to do was slow would-be invaders down somewhat and they'd die on the natural bridge without ever reaching the orcs at all.

And yet Borkon had taken the settlement, quick as a flash.

Barbandor, confined to his cage, had not been able to see exactly how Borkon had effected this conquest. What he had been aware of was the usual general slaughter and mayhem he would have expected from a bunch of dumb orcs. He heard the screams and the clash of metal weaponry. And then the noise of battle subsided into near silence, followed by an outbreak of triumphant shouting and much excited drumming on shields. The fire-eater flag above the settlement was brought down and replaced with a white banner marked with dark blue runes and a star.

After a while a grey-skinned orc in full armour appeared and unhooked Barbandor's crate down from the branches of the lava beech tree in order to carry the prisoner in his cage over the causeway to the camp they had captured.

'Hey there, Flatnose. Tell me, am I supposed to be your victory feast?' Barbandor got to his feet and held fast to the wooden bars. 'Have the rest of the villages fallen to Borkon already?'

The orc ignored him, trotted swiftly off and hurried over the hot stone pathway to find the turning up to the huts.

The blood of the vanquished ran down the hill in streams. A severed head rolled down the stepped slope, earrings jangling and tongue hanging out and quivering each time the skull bumped on its way down.

As they made their way up the slope Barbandor saw the butchery tables set up for the preparation of the corpses. The orc females were cutting and roasting the cadavers of their own menfolk. Intestines unfit for consumption were chucked over the cliff straight into the boiling lava. 'By Vraccas! You've got plenty to eat, haven't you? You don't really need a dwarf for extra snacking.' He watched incredulously as the orcs worked away without a sign of mourning or anger. The children were helping with the task. 'So cruel!'

'No. They've volunteered to do it. They hadn't had any meat for a long time,' Borkon contradicted him, stepping over from the sidelines. 'We have released them from the oppression their menfolk held them under.' The grey-skinned orc placed the crate down and the orc leader sat down next to it. He was wearing heavy duty lamellar armour that was generously daubed with blood. His weapons belt had two different-sized clubs furnished with spikes and hooks. 'We did the same with the other fire eaters in the settlements we captured previously. The females had had more than enough of being subjugated to the males and they even helped our side in the fighting.'

Barbandor found this difficult to believe. He realised that he knew very little about the beasts who were their deadly enemies. 'And now you are the new oppressors.'

'No.' Borkon reached for a water-skin and drank from it. Then he poured a stream of water on to his black mane, cleansing the blood from the strands wrapped in gold wire. The filthy liquid running off formed droplets that dripped over the blue skin and white symbols. 'We are their liberators. That's the way it will stay. It's a beginning.'

Barbandor tried to fathom the meaning of these words. 'You mean, you want to do the same thing with the salt sea orcs and with Kràg Tahuum?' Laughing incredulously, he watched the slaughter party. 'How many were there? A hundred? If that?'

'It was easy.'

'The Salt Sea region has thousands of orcs. You'll be shot out of existence by the orcs on the fortress. You'll never even get across the moat.'

'In that case there'll be thousands of female orcs who are being treated by their menfolk the same as these ones had been. That's what I've been told.' Borkon indicated the orc womenfolk, who were busy chopping, sawing and scraping. 'They aren't merely scraping the meat off the bones, they're scraping away the indignities of the past. And then they will eat it.'

'Is that your spiel? Your chat-up line?' Barbandor looked at Borkon. 'Quite savvy, really. I have to hand it you. You spread the seeds of treason among your enemy.'

'It's not a spiel and it's not a plan with a hidden agenda to get them ready to accept the next lot of chains.'

'An orc who liberates them from the clutches of the orcs.' Barbandor tried to read the truth in the watery green eyes of his opposite number.

'It has taken many generations for the orc females to gather up sufficient courage to follow the leadership of one of their own, and start a revolution.' When he talked, the sharp fangs at the corner of his mouth became visible, conspicuous against the black gums. 'The males are very strong. You'll know that from experience.'

Barbandor hummed to himself. 'What are you planning?'

'I am going to unite my people. And we will multiply. We will produce a new generation. Prepared to take on any changes that may happen in Girdlegard.' Borkon gave off a noticeable pungent smell of blood and sweat. He waved his leather water bottle at the banner overhead. '*I* am the beginning of it all.'

Barbandor got the distinct impression that he was missing some vital information. It was not merely a question of liberating the female orcs from their aggressively proprietorial menfolk. And it was not clear at all that the situation for the Salt Sea and Kràg Tahuum orcs was similar. Perhaps the female orcs in those regions were treated better. Perhaps they were even especially favoured. *We know far too little about how the beasts live.* 'So you really see yourself as something akin to the Chosen One? Why is that? Is it your bewitching appearance with the stunning dark blue skin and the shiny silver toothypegs?'

'You are forgetting the small matter of my being immortal.' Borkon grinned and handed the water bottle in through the bars of the cage. The dwarf accepted it, after an initial hesitancy; he would have to drink, even if it meant his mouth touching where the monster's lips had been. 'You and your kind – for myself and my companions you were always creatures of myth and legend – bones and bits of armour found in the old abandoned tunnels. Pictures on the walls. Images in old books, friezes, statues from other ages. But then we saw that Girdlegard really exists. That the groundlings really exist.' His face took on a determined expression. 'This meant that so many other things were proved so much more true than what others had been dismissing as pure fantasy.'

'So there's a story about you?' Barbandor hazarded, trying to make sense of what he was being told. 'Is that the reason why the female orcs are on your side?'

'As I said: I am just the start. The Uniter. Who will bring victory over the groundlings who have the best and most delicious flesh I have ever tasted.' A smile played round Borkon's lips at the thought. 'But nutrition is not the reason I set off on my journey, putting myself in danger.'

I hope you choke and die on the first bite you take off my body. Barbandor kept his feelings under control. He had not yet found out what Borkon's main motivation was. *I'll try a different tack.* 'Why did you people attack Smallwater? What did they want that wooden box for? Was it really all about Goldhand's book?'

Borkon frowned, scrunching his black brows. 'What box? What book?'

Barbandor quickly filled him in on the story of how he had first come across those orcs down by the river, and how they had ended under catapult fire at the gates of Platinshine. 'Was that all part of your plan?'

'Ah, yes. That part of the project did not go exactly as intended. Not as I had commanded.' Borkon uttered a stifled curse in his own language. 'Divoc the Hustler did not want to wait and he set out to start the search. He nearly sabotaged the whole operation. He deserved the death that was meted out to him. After Platinshine burned to the ground no one ever mentioned him again. Thanks to you and your girlfriend we managed to lay a false trail to avoid discovery.'

Now it was becoming clear to Barbandor that he would not be leaving his cage alive if these orcs had any say in the matter. *Borkon knows I would run straight to warn my folk and Girdlegard.* And so he decided to find out more about the blue-skinned orc's mission before attempting his escape.

'How is it you are immortal? How does that come about? Is it something you were born with? Or is it magic?'

Borkon gave a quiet laugh, showing his shining fangs as he did so. 'If you're not going to enlighten me about the groundlings in the mountains, I'm hardly likely to want to volunteer my life-story, am I, Barbandor? Let me put it like this: I was never the only one. And soon there will be many more.' He got up with a sudden graceful energy and went over to where two female orcs and their children needed some help to heave the carcass of a particularly fat beast up on to the table for butchering. The insignia indicated the orc in question had been Grushuk Flameshout, the most feared fire eater of all.

And now he serves them as a snack. Barbandor shuddered. To drink from the leather flask he jetted the water directly into his mouth so that his lips would not come in contact with the spout. From the occasional glances coming his way from the other orcs he was quite clear in his mind that they would be very happy to dissect and consume him in just the same way. Up until now the dwarf had liked to think that it was the Brigantians who posed the greatest threat.

Or, of course, those älfar ships with the blood-red sails.

Or perhaps one of the remaining dragons.

Or any, in fact, of the rogues and monsters they already knew and who they and their allies were already at war with.

The appearance of Borkon and the hints he dropped, together with his undoubted capabilities, made the imprisoned dwarf reassess the situation. It had become more important than ever that Barbandor should survive. It was no help to anyone if he took his new-found knowledge with him to the grave. *Or rather, to the cooking pot.*

Girdlegard

Empire of Gautaya
1024 P.Q. (7515th solar cycle in old reckoning), winter

Using her spyglass on the eye that was black, Ascatoîa watched the älf that she had sent ahead as a scout. He was making his way across the snow-covered lower southern slopes of the Sword Tip mountain range. Despite the heavy sack he was carrying, he left as good as no footmarks at all.

The massive light-grey wall of rock had appeared little more than one thousand cycles ago, created during an earthquake. This mountain range was thus comparatively young. It had forced its way up in the north-western part of Girdlegard in the middle of the Empire of Gautaya and its cooled lava cone had given rise to shapes that reminded one of a row of swords held erect. Each sharp point had its own name and its own legend held dear by the humans who lived in the locality. The orcs in the adjoining Salt Sea region termed the formation simply Stickleback. And they had their own tales about how it had come into being.

For Ascatoîa these stories were all immaterial. *Stone is stone.*

She was in the area with a small group of the best warriors for a specific reason. The sunshine on the whiteness of the snow dazzled her, even though she had recourse to a coloured glass screen in front of the spyglass. 'The lad is doing very well,' she murmured to Ophîras, who was crouched down next to her as they sheltered under cover. 'It shouldn't be long now.'

'Who are we actually hiding from, Ascatoîa?' There were a

further thirty älfar with them here, behind the outcrop below the Nail Blade. They were all wearing thick furs and taking care not to be seen. In their greyish-white cloaks they were well camouflaged in the snowy landscape.

'We're hiding from eyes that shouldn't see us. You never know. There could be some huntsman out checking his traps, looking for snow leopards.' She kept her optical aid securely focused on the scout. 'Excellent work, by the way, getting us out of the mountains and across Girdlegard like that, unseen. Well done. There'll be more than just a good word from the Ganyeios in it for you. There should be a proper reward coming your way.'

To protect her parti-coloured face from the ravages of the cold air and the strong sunlight, Ascatoîa had donned a leather mask with narrow eye-slits. The unusual complexion, one half white and the other black, resulted presumably from the use her forebears had made of alchemical products when they had wanted to disguise themselves as elves in order to trick the inhabitants of Girdlegard. In this way they had managed to get through the border posts manned by the dwarves. The substances they had taken changed the make-up of their blood permanently and caused their eyes to react differently to light; these effects were passed down through the generations.

'It was quite simple. I was already familiar with the lesser-known paths,' Ophîras explained. 'Our spies used them. All the same, I thank you for your praise.'

'Not to speak too soon . . . We've still got to get back safely.' Ascatoîa gave a restrained smile. *But no one will succeed in stopping us. Not even Mòndarcai.*

'How do you know whether the scout has entered the Wonder Zone?' Ophîras could be heard taking out his own spyglass, and he used it to watch the älf making his way carefully across the open ground. 'And how did you know where the new source was?'

'Have you seen the ygota in the glass container I brought with me?' Ophîras put down his spyglass and looked at the jar in the snow next to the zhussa. 'These big flies the size of my finger, with the coloured chitin?'

'They're ygota?' Every single one of the insects had settled on one side of the glass container. On the westernmost side.

And it was to the west that the älf scout was walking.

'Ygota are fiendishly difficult to catch. In earlier times, when there were still permanent magic fields in Girdlegard, these flies were found in the houses where the magi and magae lived. They thrive on the invisible streams of the forces at work in the earth and in the general environment. The magic power affects the colour of their wings and makes them glow.' Ascatoîa saw the scout trip and stumble. On all fours now, he was coughing, choking and vomiting. Clots of dark red blood sloshed out of his mouth on to the otherwise spotless white snow. The älf struggled back up on to his feet and continued on his way. Ophîras had not noticed what had happened. 'Ygota are attracted to magic. Even the tiniest traces. They are very few and far between in these times. When I came across some of these insects in the Inàste temple in Dsôn Khamateion, I caught them. Cycles ago, it was. For my own experiments. As if I had known I should be needing them one day.'

'Cintalôr is walking to the right. But the ygotas' wings aren't glowing,' Ophîras observed after a while. 'And there's no change to their bodies. Are you sure about this?'

'Be patient.'

Ophîras set the eyepiece to his right eye. 'What is so dangerous about the Wonder Zone? Why did we have to send him on ahead?'

'The magic often changes everything. The land and the creatures living there. In particular immediately after the zone comes into being. I don't want to risk exposing us to dangers if this can be avoided.' Ascatoîa glanced sideways at Ophîras, using her white eye. 'There are terrible stories about people who set foot unawares in the Wonder Zone. Bodies bursting open. Spontaneous changes. Turning into beasts . . .' Ophîras nodded in agreement, hearing this. 'It's for our protection. Should Cintalôr suddenly turn into a monster we'll have plenty of time to know how best to react. He'll be far enough away. Quite apart from awful creatures ready to ambush unsuspecting visitors.'

'Why Cintalôr?'

Ascatoîa turned her gaze on the plain. 'Because he volunteered.' *And because I made him certain promises.*

A slight wind came up, wafting across the plateau, at the southern edge of which there was a sheer drop of hundreds of paces. In good weather there was a clear view from here all the way over to the Inland Sea and the coast of Gauragon. On the far side of the Sword Tip range of mountains lay the southern salt flats where the orcs had taken up residence. Ascatoîa was glad to be able to reassure herself of the fact that they rarely emerged out of its protective salty heat and certainly would never venture into the winter season's cold, thin air.

'How long will Girdlegard take to find out where the Wonder Zone is located?' Ophîras shifted the weight from his elbows to his forearms. There was no sound from the movement.

'It won't be found at all. Well, if it does get discovered, we'll be well prepared and will have recharged ourselves with magic energy by then, my good Ophîras.' Ascotoîa noticed a winged shadow on the dazzling white snow above where Cintalôr was. She raised her eyes in alarm to scan the sky, looking for something the same shape. *What for . . .?*

'It's the flight-mare!' Ophîras exclaimed. 'In the name of Inàste! He's seen our tracks somehow and wants to come back to us!'

And I know why. Ascatoîa looked over at Cintalôr. 'Its name is Phlavaros. And what he wants is our flesh. That ill-begotten Brigantian has trained him to go for älfar.'

The black stallion shot down out of the sun with a shrill whinnying call, aiming straight at the älfar scout. The beast's long neck was stretched forward and its muzzle wide open, teeth bared for a fatal attack.

Cintalôr saw the shadow on the snow grow ever larger; he tumbled to the ground just as the stallion's jaws closed on his neck with a deadly clack. The zhussa in her hiding place could clearly hear the sound. A large bite of flesh, together with the covering of fabric, was ripped out of Cintalôr's upper arm. Gliding along, Phlavaros took off again, having secured its mouthful of meat. Glinting crystals rose up in clouds under the mighty force of the two great wings. The injured scout was covered in a blanket of snow.

'We must kill the beast!' Ophîras shouted, about to get to his feet, his dark steel longbow at the ready. He had wrapped white fabric round the bow where he gripped it.

But Ascatoîa pulled him back down. 'Stay down, if you value your life!'

At that very moment there was a loud rushing noise in the air above them, and a thundering roar that went straight through you, overlaid with the terrified neighing from the black stallion.

'A dragon!' whispered Ophîras, rigid with fear, as he tried to make out the shape he had glimpsed through the blizzard-like snow.

'No. It's two of them.' Ascatoîa pointed towards the south, where a second outline was hurtling out of the bright-blue firmament straight into the whirling clouds of white. *Slibina and Szmajro! Just as I wanted.*

Phlavaros appearing had, however, not been part of her plan

and had nearly put paid to her scheme. *They can tear you to pieces and eat you up.* 'Don't anyone move,' she commanded her soldiers in an urgent whisper. 'Stay behind the rocky outcrop and under the overhang. Otherwise we're all lost.'

The snorting roars of the dragon siblings mixed with the fearful whinnying of the flight-mare, closely followed by the death scream of the scout. After that all that could be heard was an ugly tearing sound as Cintalôr's body was consumed by the scaled creatures who were fighting each other for the prize.

Gradually, the cloud of snow began to settle.

The ice crystals fell on to the rusty-brown bodies of the dragons as they lay on the plain moving only silently, blood dripping from their mouths. Their skulls were each adorned with three long horns and a coronet of thorny spikes.

Up in the blue sky, meanwhile, the injured flight-mare was trying to get away to safety, clumsily beating its bleeding, broken wings until all strength was lost and the animal dropped like a stone to disappear between the peaks of the mountain range below them.

Ascatoîa jumped up in some distress, picking up the jar of ygotas. 'Pull back, everyone!'

Ophîras called out, at her side, 'Retreat, as long as—'

'Silence! Nobody's going anywhere at all until I've got the dragons.' The zhussa vaulted over the rocks and ran over to where the anaesthetised creatures lay, each ten paces in length. Slibina and Szmajro were much smaller than either Ûra or Ardin, to whom these two had always been subordinate. The stronger ones controlled the weaker ones. *But they are more or less the last of the dragons that can ever be put to use.*

Ascatoîa approached the sibling dragons fearlessly. They had both been put out of action by the poison of the black-juice flower. Cintalôr's blood had contained the toxin and the meat in his rucksack, intended as bait, had been impregnated with the poison. The älf scout had been quite unaware of this. His task had never been one of reconnoitring or scouting. They were probably very far away from the new magic source, the Wonder Zone. The zhussa had only been interested in capturing the dragons, because she knew they overwintered here in the vicinity of the Nail Blade mountain, where there were hidden warm air currents.

The älfar bait was irresistible for them. Ascatoîa placed her left hand on Szmajro's snout. She could feel the warmth of his rust-brown scale-covered body through her thick gloves. *All just as I wanted it to happen. That rebellious flight-mare nearly ruined everything by turning up like that. Good thing we're rid of him now.*

Ophîras was the first to reach her. The other älfar spread out, swords drawn, surrounding the stunned beasts.

'By Inàste! Why are they asleep?'

'I think it's to do with the meat. Cintalôr's flesh didn't agree with them.'

The älf spat on Szmajro's belly. The scales, as big as roof tiles, shimmered like copper and rusty metal ore. 'Let's cut their throats. They killed one of us!'

'No. They are not to be hurt. I will use my magic powers to keep them in this harmless condition. You and your people, get some sledges built. Use the equipment we brought with us. We can take them down the mountain on sledges. Once we're down on the plain we'll get some horses and we can organise some proper transport sleighs.' Ascatoîa raised the glass jar with the ygotas, which were climbing over each other on its side. 'I must have been wrong. We'll have to go much further to the west.'

'But . . . what do we want with the scaled creatures?' Ophîras stared in confusion at the winged dragons, now snoozing and harmless. 'They'll never obey us. As soon as they wake up −'

'Let that be my concern.' She stroked the long black horn of the sleeping Szmajro, who was breathing deeply in and out. It had been the right thing not to go back to Klaey Berengart. The Brigantian could do nothing to help. Her new plan was much better. The Wonder Zone would provide a much bigger miracle than anything Girdlegard could ever imagine.

Goïmron was icy cold but he was extremely keen not to show any weakness to the other members of the group who were riding with him: humans, elves, meldriths and dwarves. Halfway up there on the Sword Tip mountain range the temperature fell sharply to well below freezing. The sunshine hardly helped at all.

'Are you sure this is the way the älfar went?' he called out through the thick scarf over his face. Sònuk was on his knees at the head of the column, investigating the state of the snow.

The srgāláh did not answer. He dug into the snow layer. The cold did not seem to be affecting him, although he only had a thin cloak over his leather armour.

'What would they have wanted on the mountain?' Brûgar rubbed the ice crystals off his blue-dyed beard. 'Do you think they came up here for the view?' The coat he was wearing over his armour was unfastened, as if it were a balmy spring day. He had a pipe in the corner of his mouth, but there was little smoke because the tobacco was not responding well. 'Maybe I should fill myself a little war pipe?'

'The Wonder Zone could be located anywhere. Even on the very top of a mountain.' Mostro gestured towards one of the volcano craters, which was smouldering. 'Or up there.'

'So how do the black-eyes know where to start looking? Do you think they've got a srgāláh of their own to help them?' Gata adjusted the heavy fabric across her face to make sure her nose was covered. Her breath had formed a crackling layer of ice on her scarf.

'It's a mystery to me.' Mostro was wearing several extravagantly tailored jackets and more expensive mantles over the top than any of his colleagues on the journey. If he had had to go any distance on foot it would have been impossible. His fur cap gave him the appearance of a bear in fancy dress. 'Maybe they're not looking for the magic source at all? Something else in their sights, perhaps?'

'Fine by me,' grumbled Brûgar, puffing determinedly at his pipe, but the tobacco was refusing to cooperate. 'Anyone got a couple of the alchemy matchsticks?'

'Sònuk said he could feel a slight trace of magic.'

Goïmron was glad they had in their number a skilled and reliable tracker with an excellent sense of smell. Sònuk was able to sense danger and could always help out when the tracks were hard to see.

A few orbits after they had set off from the camp with some armed soldiers, the srgäláh had picked up the trail of the älfar heading directly west. Their älfar foes were riding on ordinary horses, rather than night-mares, presumably to avoid the track being made obvious with the burn marks in the hoofprints.

But it would have been difficult indeed for them to fool Sònuk's nose.

Since Dsôn Khamateion had no allies in this neck of the woods, finding their tracks here could only indicate that they, too, were trying to locate the new magic zone. It was obvious to Goïmron: *They are eager to find it first, in order to prevent anyone else gaining access to its energy.* The Ganyeios knew full well that Vanéra and both her pupils would be in urgent need of this magic power source.

'They've been this way,' Sònuk came back to join them and swung himself back up into the saddle of his visok horse, which was a good one and a half times the size of a normal horse. This rendered the sight of the srgäláh even more impressive, as he held his spear in his right hand. 'Most of them were hiding under the stone overhang behind that outcrop on the Nail Blade, watching the plain in front of us. They sent one of the group down first.' He got his mount to speed up to a gallop. 'Come on! This is going to be good!'

'So it's not the Wonder Zone?' Goïmron wanted to know.

'No. But we're getting closer.'

The company followed Sònuk on to the plain just below the vegetation line.

Goïmron did not notice anything special. The snow had formed irregular drifts and piles around the rocks and boulders, as if the white stuff itself were seeking shelter from the biting cold wind.

Sònuk leaped out of the saddle and ran around excitedly, often going down on one knee, rubbing away the snow and picking up small particles. Then he raced off to the outer edge of the plain and gazed out towards the west, raising his long nose to the wind and taking deep in-breaths. On the out-breaths the air from his golden leathery nostrils made vapour clouds like those a dragon might produce.

'Anyone would think he's had a bit too much of that black tea that Brûgar makes,' Gata commented.

'Or has he been at my store and helped himself to the pepper tobacco?' Brûgar halted beside Goïmron for a better view of what was happening. 'What's he picking up?'

Mostro rode straight past them both, ignoring them as if they were servants he had nothing to do with. 'Hey! Sònuk! What have you got there?'

'Does anyone else reckon Mostro's behaving as if he's taken over from Ûra as supreme ruler?' Brûgar touched the war flail in its saddle holster, then tapped the cold tobacco out of his pipe. 'If I gave him a little tap with the flail it would bring him back down to earth.'

'Or it might kill him,' Telìnâs countered drily. Compared to all the extra outer garments the humans and dwarves were wearing, the elf's winter clothing looked both elegant and warming. 'Not a good plan, as we still need him.'

Brûgar nodded at the elf. 'Nice sense of humour, my pointy-eared friend.'

'Too kind.' Telìnâs had sculpted a little figure out of pressed snow. It was a dwarf with a twisted tuft of wool for pipe smoke. He grinned and placed it on a large rock as he rode by. Together with the others, Goïmron rode up to Mostro and the srgāláh.

'They've taken Slibina and Szmajro with them,' Sònuk announced, holding up two tiny pieces of dragon scales, one of them earth-coloured and the other rust-brown. 'The älfar have managed to knock them out, it seems, and they've carried them off on sledges they've made themselves.'

Mostro burst out laughing, and some of the soldiers from the besieging army joined in from sheer disbelief.

'At first I thought you were just a bit hyperactive, my good srgāláh, but now I see the black-eyes must have laid out some poisoned bait for you that's sent you mad.'

Goïmron was careful not to dismiss the words of their excellent scout. He knew that Sònuk could always be relied on. 'What makes you say that? Is it the fragments you found?'

Sònuk was unaffected by the jeers. The laughter ebbed away. 'I can smell the dragons. And I can feel the scratches their claws have made on the stone under the snow. The älfar have used a poisoned älf as bait to attract the dragon siblings. After the dragons had eaten him they fell into an enforced slumber. I would guess they used a distillation of black-juice flower essence.' He pointed to the west, where, at some distance, the vague shape of a fortified town could be glimpsed against the backdrop of the Red Mountains. 'They've gone over there. I can feel the traces of magic quite clearly.'

'With Slibina and Szmajro in tow, I presume?' Mostro chuckled. 'Captive dragons. Ridiculous.'

'Is it, though?' Gata looked over to the impressively large fortified settlement. 'That must be Fortgard. If the new Wonder Zone has emerged over there we're in trouble, I'm afraid.'

'Why would that be?' Telìnâs looked round at the others, wide-eyed. 'It's all part of Girdlegard. Are you saying they're not on our side?'

'They won't let either the black-eyes or us into the town.' Brûgar pushed his helmet more firmly on to his head, so the brim could protect his forehead and his eyes better from the strong rays of the sun. 'They're a bit eccentric over there.'

'Am I the only one of you to wonder why on earth the älfar might have taken the dragon siblings with them?' Mostro turned to the others, astonishment on his face. 'It's impossible! Utter stuff and nonsense. The beasts will never obey them. As soon as the anaesthetic poison wears off – and our clever srgäläh seems to know all about its effects – the dragons will fall on their älfar captors at once.'

'They won't have done it without good reason.' Sònuk was quite unflustered. 'The tracks made by those sledges they've built lead down the valley. Have a good look yourselves through your own spyglasses. You're bound to see the trail going towards Fortgard.'

Goïmron tried to remember the little he knew about one of the Free Towns. Like Malleniagard, Fortgard was not subject to the royal overlord and it sheltered some ten thousand souls, all of them armed to the teeth. The city was governed by a kind of council called a Consortio. *It'll be tricky trying to get heard.*

According to legend a rebellious general in the Gautayan army had escaped there immediately after the first earthquake, wanting to find a safe shelter for himself and his family. Most of the army, together with their own families, had followed suit. Protected by the Nail Blade range and the Red Mountains at their flanks, they had built a city and added successive rings of defence walls, surmounted by self-loading shooting machines. There was a sophisticated system of pulleys and lifts, which meant that a small number of defenders would be able to keep potential invaders at bay for several orbits at a time.

'With any luck the Wonder Zone won't lie entirely within their city limits,' said Gata, optimistically.

'Oh, I don't mind if our black-eyes run their heads against the Fortgard walls.' Brûgar sniffed into his scarf. 'Because we, of course, have the uniquely wonderful Mostro with his legendary sack full of useful artefacts to open the city gates for us.'

'I rather like this straightforward kind of thinking,' said Telìnâs. 'I do wish I had the knack of it myself.'

Brûgar winked. 'It was a joke,' he said under his breath. 'Don't tell it to the wand-fiddler.' He had his next smoke ready. 'Now for a combining pipe. I've got to do some working out.'

Goïmron sighed. 'I think we're in line for some long, drawn-out negotiations with the Consortio.' Seeing the inquisitive expression on the blond elf's face, he added quickly, 'That's what the city council is called.'

Telìnâs nodded, grateful for the explanation. 'How many are they? Can we maybe offer them some bribes?' He put his hand in his pocket and handed Brûgar a packet of matches.

'The Consortio consists of every adult resident who has been living in Fortgard for longer than five cycles.' Goïmron did some calculating, trying to imagine how long their discussions and voting procedures might take. Every single orbit's delay meant even longer without their getting to the Wonder Zone. This would all work to the Omuthan's advantage.

'Who knows what effect the magic fields may have had on the inhabitants.' Sònuk got back on his visok horse. 'Don't forget the kind of thing that can happen under the influence of unbridled magic energy. There's good. And there's bad.'

'Knowing our luck,' said Mostro, 'I'd wager that—'

'That we will be able to convince the Consortio to admit us,' Gata finished his sentence for him. 'We wouldn't, of course, need to be here at all if Goldhand had entered into the pact that Mòndarcai was offering.' She got her horse to walk on. 'Each loss we experience, each defeat, I put at the door of the ancient dwarf. We could have done with having the älf and his rune spear to help us against Slibina and Szmajro. He knows how to get rid of creatures like them.'

'Ha! Me too!' Brûgar waved his war flail and then rested it back against his shoulder. 'Just what I need for my trophy collection. Couple of splendid items for the chimney nook! I'd have Szmajro's horns on the windowsill. And Slibina's skull as a lamp base next to my reading armchair.' He quickly filled and lit his Thinking Pipe and tossed the matches back to the elf.

'One, you don't have an armchair, and two, I've never seen you open a book,' said Gata, laughing at the very thought. 'By Lorimbur! That would look odd, wouldn't it? You, and a book!'

'What kind of thing would you like to read, do you think?' Goïmron grinned behind his scarf. 'Poems? Sonnets? An ode to the power of love?'

All the dwarves joined in with the general mirth.

'I'd wrute my own.' This was Brûgar's retort.

'Wrute? What sort of a word is that?' Gata was holding her sides with laughter.

'Then I will wrote one, you uncultured idiots. It's the inner values that count in poetry. The actual form is negligetable,' Brûgar spluttered, having himself fallen victim to an attack of the hysterics.

Goïmron relished the enjoyment of the moment, particularly considering what awaited them. 'Come on, let's hear some poetry, Blue Beard,' he challenged his friend. 'Impress us, mighty bard.'

'Why not? Hear ye, hear ye! Gather round. I'll just have a couple of puffs before I start.' He stood up in the stirrups so everyone would have a good view. 'Listen to one of my many poetic works.' He cleared his throat and smoke puffed out of his mouth.

> *I killed an orc,*
> *Virtue in person.*
> *Just because I could.*
> *What do I know,*
> *Child of the Smith,*
> *Of orcish virtue?'*

His dwarf audience cheered and clapped and even the rest of the company looked amused.

'A masterpiece,' Mostro mocked. 'Verily, you have summed yourself up magnificently.'

'What do you mean by that, you would-be wand-waver?' Brûgar glared at him and the good mood vanished.

'You prefer to kill anything you don't understand, without trying to find out whether the creature might or might not be of further value,' Mostro explained.

Goïmron was surprised at how seriously the famulus had taken the silly rhyme.

'Oho, lightning strike of intellect here. Remind me, Gata, next time there's a pig-snout in my face, that I must stop and interrogate him and ask him whether he'd like to change sides. I could invite them in to tea and biscuits, for a little chat. So I can get to understand them better.' Brûgar howled with derision, delighted with his own wit. 'Perhaps I'll serve up a couple of baby goats to Slibina and Szmajro. That'll go down well.'

All the Children of the Smith joined in with his merriment.

Goïmron secretly had to admit that Mostro had hit the nail on the head. However, now was not the time, in the present circumstances, when it could never be possible for orcs and the other inhabitants of Girdlegard to sign a peace treaty. There was too deep-seated a hatred between them, too many old wounds, and most importantly: *No common enemy. Otherwise, it might have been a possibility.* He moved behind a little, coming fifth in the column that was moving slowly along the narrow winding pathway down the Sword Tip range below the Nail Blade peak. *But only a remote possibility.*

His horse followed the tracks of the one in front faithfully and so Goïmron could risk taking out his spyglass to look out for any fresh marks in the snow of the plain.

Fortgard lay near the steep slopes of the mountains where the Grey Range gave way to the Red. Thus it lay on the edge of the Firstlings' territory, further to the south. To the north the city had the protection of the Sword Blade foothills to keep out attackers, as Goïmron had once read, cycles ago, in an article about the Free Towns of Girdlegard. In addition, the city was surrounded by a number of small lakes and low-growing forests, whose trees tended to bend over to the west. The continuous strong wind formed them that way from the first seedlings.

As Sònuk had predicted, Goïmron's glass soon showed him the drag marks in the snow, leading from one clump of trees to the next. So the älfar were dodging from one safe shelter to the next bit of cover they could find – and they were definitely heading over to the unsuspecting settlement of Fortgard.

What do they want with the dragons? Goïmron lowered the spyglass and noticed a dark cloud of smoke issuing from one of the wooded areas where the last of the sledge marks had been leading. Slibina and Szmajro were young and small compared with Ardin and Ûra, but they were certainly used to combat and had made names for themselves as cattle-stealers. Goïmron was reminded of Brûgar's words: *trophies for my chimney nook. Szmarjro's horns*—He stopped. His train of thought changed track and he mused on the word *horns*. *Oh, Vraccas! Vraccas forbid! Don't let it happen! The thing I'm afraid of!*

You have no idea how I came to mutate into a being, how I was changed into a creature that was half älf and half dwarf.

How did this come to pass?

Potions and elixirs, distilled, brewed, and invented by älfar minds. Alchemical means rendered me a faithful and reliable servant who was completely unaware of his own transformation.

Excerpt from
The Adventures of Tungdil Goldhand,
as experienced in the Black Abyss
and written by himself.
First draft.

V

Girdlegard

Empire of Gautaya
1024 P.Q. (7515th solar cycle in old reckoning), winter

Goïmron and his companions were travelling through a region of the plain where there were several small lakes. Drawing nearer, they realised that one of the many wooded areas ahead of them was ablaze. A sheet of flame rose like a wall, impenetrable for any living creature that was not fire-proof. Clearly visible from far off, a column of dark grey smoke rose to the sky.

The sledge tracks, deeper now than before, seemed to lead straight into the sea of flames, as did also the strong magic radiation that Sònuk was detecting. Instead of engaging in combat the älfar had chosen the simplest of methods to keep pursuers and foes at bay: devastating fire.

Even if it will only work for a limited amount of time, sooner or later those trees will all be reduced to ashes. Goïmron reined in his nervous mount. The horse was anxious to get away from the smoke. *They have won some extra time to get themselves prepared. This is what I feared they would do!*

His company halted a good hundred paces away from the edge of the wood. Sònuk had warned them it would be dangerous to penetrate into the thicket to follow the sledge tracks.

There could be an älf hiding in the branches of one of the trees. Goïmron and the others would provide easy targets for the black arrows of their enemies.

'Lorimbur be praised.' Gata looked at Mostro. 'We have found the Wonder Zone. Now it's up to us to work out how we can get you in there safely. As soon as you've absorbed your new magic energy we'll be needing your wizardry. Otherwise those black-eyes will be causing us no end of trouble.'

'If Goïmron's assumption proves right, we've no time to lose.' Telìnâs looked over at the Fourthling dwarf. 'Thanks for your warning.'

'I disagree.' Mostro's adamant rebuttal was immediate. 'The älfar will be satisfied with defending the area against us.'

'Defending only makes sense if in the meantime there's an attack taking place on our camp in the Brown Mountains,' Brûgar argued. He was puffing away fiercely at his pipe, as if in competition with the smoke from the fire. 'The black-eyes know they won't be able to hold the area indefinitely and that the wood will all burn down. They'd have no protection left at all. Certainly not for a full cycle.'

'Then let's get a move on.' Gata watched the red and orange tongues of flame that could be glimpsed in the centre of the woodland and which occasionally shot upwards to envelop the crown of a tall tree. The smoke, growing denser now, swirled upwards in strange shapes and configurations that seemed almost alive. 'We've got reason enough.'

Watching the spectral shapes rising in the sky high over-head, Goïmron was reminded of the marvellous silhouette puppets Rodana employed to tell her stories. 'The magic is having its fun with us,' he murmured.

'Just as long as the fun and games stay harmless, that's fine with me.' Brûgar shouldered his war flail. 'Sònuk, how far away is this confounded magic zone?'

The srgāláh suddenly looked over to the right-hand side. 'We've got company. Mounted. Roughly fifty of them and their lances are sporting the Fortgard colours.'

'Reinforcements!' Gata cried out, cheerfully.

'Or perhaps more enemies,' Brûgar grumbled away into his blue beard. 'Right you are, wand-waver. Get ready. Pull one of your famous artefacts out of your sack. I'm not about to exhaust myself fighting the Fortgard long'uns. We've got to keep our strength up for tackling the black-eyes and killing a dragon or two.'

Mostro turned to Telìnâs. 'Would you please ride over to meet them and find out what they want?'

'Why send an elf when there are älfar all over the place? Not the cleverest thing to do. Could end badly.' Gata pulled her horse's head around, ready to gallop off. 'Come on, Goïmron. We'll be the ones to deal with this.'

Taken rather aback by her proposal, he followed the Thirdling queen. Then he looked at the smoke spewing upwards from the burning grove of trees, twisting, swirling, and forming the shapes of fabulous creatures locked in mortal combat until one or the other was victorious, then dispersing into the air, while the next figure emerged from the grey columns of dark cloud. *I have never seen anything like this.*

The band of warriors from Fortgard approached until they were only ten paces away. They were wearing light armour and dark red cloaks. 'Halt!' called the leader at the head of his entourage. He was around fifty years old. When he lifted his visor, he showed a scarred and clean-shaven countenance. 'What are dwarves doing here in Gautaya? Is the fire in our city forest anything to do with you?' Then he noticed the insignia on Gata's mantle and helmet. 'Ah, I see we have royal visitors. My greetings, Queen Regnorgata.'

'I am flattered that you know my name,' she answered in a friendly tone. 'But who are you?'

'A simple obrist from the city guard. My name is Emaro of Staine. News of your accession to the throne reached us even here in this far north-western corner of the land.' From his seat in the saddle, he bowed his head to show respect. 'But I must still ask you to explain your presence here. It wasn't the fire that brought you to us, I assume?'

Goïmron looked the riders over carefully, noting the hardened leather armour they wore under their red cloaks. They carried spears, short swords and light shields. *They won't stand a chance against the älfar, equipped like that.*

'Not the fire, no. But we came because of what has caused it. Or rather, *who*.' Indicating herself and Goïmron, Gata said, 'We and our companions, who you can see gathered round Famulus Mostro over there behind us, have been attempting to keep the new magic field safe from the älfar, who have, however, unfortunately reached it first. And now they are beyond our reach behind that wall of flames, together with two anaesthetised dragons. We need help from you and from Fortgard to win the Wonder Zone from them.'

'The Wonder Zone? On our territory?' Emaro smacked his open hand down on the saddlebow. 'Oh, Palandiell, I just *knew* it! I had a suspicion it could be that. Two or three orbits ago we found some odd-looking crows that weren't screeching as usual but singing beautifully. And their black plumage had turned all shiny peacock colours. Their birdsong was louder than a war drum. I knew it couldn't be an eccentricity of the natural world. Maybe a whim of the gods is what I thought.'

'Or magic.' Gata studied his companions' equipment. 'You are not heavily armoured.'

'We did not know we'd be meeting älfar in the field, did we? Or we'd have brought half the army with us.' Emaro's face showed he was somewhat in shock. 'Or dragons, for pity's sake! *Two* of them, you say? That can only mean . . .'

'Yes. Slibina and Szmajro, I'm afraid.'

'So you never noticed, up in your towers, how the älfar dragged their sledges with the dragons on, went straight past your town and then dodged from one little woodland to the next?' Goïmron found this difficult to believe.

'We did see the tracks, but we thought it must have been the loggers. We get them a lot here in winter, of course. Cutting trees down for lumber.' Emaro breathed steadily. 'Slibina, Szmajro. And älfar. Palendiell preserve us! What do they want the Wonder Zone for?'

Goïmron was about to impart his greatest fears to the Fortgard obrist. He worried that the city would have to turn out with their entire army and some portable catapults. 'I rather think they may—' he started, but Gata broke in.

'We think that they have only wickedness on their minds and that they want to prevent Famulus Mostro getting to the new magic source to replenish his powers. You see, we need him and his magic in the Brown Range of Mountains. The black-eyes are afraid that Brigantia will fall. They assume Dsôn Khamateion will be next on the list for a visit from the Children of the Smith.'

'I understand.' Emaro called his men over and gave the order for them to put Fortgard on an alarm footing, and then to come swiftly back with every available warrior and the mobile catapults. 'Perhaps they intend to tame the dragons with sorcery? Slibina and Szmajro would be well suited for breaking a siege, but I'd not fancy the idea of exposing two dragons to an unlimited amount of magic. Who knows what might happen?'

'Oh, just think back to those crows you saw. They were changed into something harmless and rather cute, really, weren't they?' Gata chipped in optimistically.

Goïmron guessed that she was trying to avoid the humans getting in a panic. But on the other hand he did not think it right to keep this man and his whole town in the dark about what the älfars' ultimate aim might be.

'What do we do about this blaze, obrist?' he asked.

Emaro looked at their random collection of dwarves, humans, meldriths and one elf. 'Didn't you say you had a famulus with you? Surely he will—'

'No use at all until he gets access to the new magic source,' said Goïmron. It sounded more spiteful than he had meant it to. *But it's true. Whereas I . . .* He still had Chòldunja's warning in the back of his mind, that he must never advertise the fact that he possessed any magic skills. *No. Not unless there was absolutely no other way.*

'If the fire doesn't burn itself out, I suppose it could go on smouldering for ten or eleven orbits before it reaches the perimeter of the wood. Until then there's no way we can go in. We had a dry summer and the undergrowth will burn like tinder. But the wood of the ironthorn trees isn't as vulnerable; it won't turn to ashes as quickly as the Red Spruce or the West Fir.' Emaro thought for a moment, then added, 'How many älfar did you reckon?'

'I'm afraid we don't know precisely,' said Gata, pretending to be contrite.

That was another untruth. Sònuk had told them exactly how many adversaries there were and how many horses they had. Goïmron could not work out what the dwarf queen was up to. *Any moment now she'll be offering the älfar in the wood some kind of pact to attack Mòndarcai.*

'We reckon it might be about thirty,' he added quickly.

'That may sound like quite a lot but as they don't have any magicians in their number, they won't be profiting from being in the Wonder Zone. Perhaps indirectly, by keeping the dragons on their side,' Gata said at once. 'You know about the innate powers the älfar possess, Obrist Staine? They bring fear with them. And darkness.'

Emaro nodded, hesitantly. 'We've heard of it but only anec-dotally. Old stories. We've never had anything to do with any black-eyes up till now. We've certainly never had to fight any. I'm glad to have you here with us, Queen Regnorgata.'

Gata smiled at him. 'Excellent, obrist. We'll make our plan together with the famulus about how to get through this ring of fire. As soon as your reinforcements arrive from Fortgard, we can set off.'

'I presume the soldiers won't be coming on their own. Some of the old-established families will not want to miss seeing what happens,' Emaro explained.

'Will they want to stop us?' Gata turned her horse round. 'We would not permit that. Please don't take this as any kind of threat, but you must understand there is more at stake here than simply winning back the Brown Mountains. We have only just had the luck to get rid of Ûra and Ardin. The last thing we want is to have two dragons controlled by the älfar, obeying the black-eyes like faithful hounds at their heels. It doesn't matter how small they may be.'

'I expect the families will have many questions to put to you. And that then they will stand side by side with us to enter the fray. They will want to make history, even though they will not be in the front line.' Emaro gave his troops the order to check their weapons and to hold themselves in readiness.

'I shall ensure your name will definitely be mentioned,' said Goïmron. 'You will be a hero.'

'Just as long as I'm alive to enjoy the fame.' The fifty-year-old veteran saluted.

Goïmron and Gata rode slowly back to the rest of their party, where it seemed arguments had broken out. Mostro was hand-ing out artefacts from his bag and was busy issuing instructions about them. Brûgar had refused point-blank to take any, but

Telìnâs had, with his fingertips, picked up something that looked like a vase.

'Why didn't you tell Emaro what the älfar are planning?' Goïmron looked at Gata from the side.

'I thought it better not to make them afraid. And it's not a case of knowing their actual *planning*. More a supposition on our part. I mean on *your* part.'

'That's right.' Goïmron glanced back at the fifty mounted Fortgarders. 'They seem to be taking it well, the fact that we'll be facing two dragons and three dozen älfar.'

'Drugged dragons. That's why we've got to be quick. If we'd had Mòndarcai with us it'd have taken us a matter of less than one sandglass to defeat these Dsôn Khamateion black-eyes and to chop up the dragon siblings into little pieces.' Gata's comment was delivered as if this were a foregone conclusion.

Goïmron was more confused than ever as to her intentions. 'How could anyone ever trust that älf?'

'Well. He's got every reason to hate the rest of his kind. Now he is standing to attention with thousands of his orc allies and he has plenty of time just to come up with ideas about what he'd like to do with them, instead of us having the pig-faces fight for us on our side.'

'I don't agree. The orcs will desert soon if they don't get offered a victory.'

'We could easily have got them to storm Brigantia, so we . . . oh, whatever – why do I bother discussing it with you?' Gata looked at him reproachfully. 'You and Goldhand, you always agree with each other, don't you?'

'Yes, I suppose so. Mostly. But not always.' Goïmron was remembering the dwarf hero's silence on hearing that Mòndarcai's offer of collaboration had been rejected. 'It doesn't matter. Today we're going to be fighting the älfar and the two dragons in a coma . . . What's the term? Night-dragons? The älfar will be wanting to alter the dragon siblings' nature to benefit their own plans.'

'That's your view. And I admit it's plausible.'

Gata's tone was more mollifying. 'Let's address this task first. And then we move on to the next one. Who knows? Perhaps in the end Goldhand will withdraw his decision about turning Mòndarcai down and he may yet send for the black-eyes and his orcs?'

I certainly hope not. Goïmron did not like the idea one little bit. 'And where would he be found?'

'In Kràg Tahuum, I expect. He's hardly likely to be in the salt flats. His flesh would dry out in the heat like meat being smoked for winter.' Gata whistled through her teeth to draw Mostro's attention. He threw her an artefact, which she handed straight to Goïmron. 'There you go, gem cutter. I'm sure you can do something or other clever with that. Why don't you leave all the fighting to me?'

'I shall.' He turned the object over. It was the size of his fist and looked like a miniature version of a surgeon's forceps. 'What is this thing supposed to do?' He looked up. 'Hey, there! Master Mostro! What can this thing do?'

'How am I supposed to know?' the famulus snapped back crossly. 'It was left over. Brûgar didn't want it.'

'That's because I'm a warrior, not an artefact waver,' the blue-bearded dwarf called, pipe in mouth as usual. He gestured with his war flail. 'I want to see this weapon smashing open a few black-eyes' heads. I'll have no truck with hocus-pocus nonsense that might do all the work for me. Where's the glory in that?'

The other dwarf warriors cheered, obviously agreeing with him.

'I'm not putting my trust in something if I haven't got a clue about how it functions. About what effect it might have on me.'

Telìnâs handed back the artefact he had been holding. It looked a bit like a quill pen. 'I'm sure you'll know better than me how to use this, Master Mostro.'

With a furious scowl the famulus handed it on to one of the Gauragon soldiers, who accepted it rather gingerly, asking, 'Any ideas about how we get through the wall of fire without turning in to ashes ourselves? Have the Fortgarders—'

Sònuk raised his hand. 'We are not alone. It's like what happened under the earth in the Grey Mountains.' He pointed at the clump of ironthorn trees a hundred paces further on, where the smoke belched out, swirling up to form contorted shapes in the air. 'The älfar have got scouts posted on this side of the flames. I can sense two of them. One of them is watching us from that thicket.'

This time no one was tempted to make fun of the srgäláh's keen nose. On their quest to find Goldhand in the mines, shafts and passageways he had proved often enough how reliable his sense of smell could be.

Goïmron was uneasy. They were well in range of the älfar steel war-bows. They would have to keep a good five hundred paces away to be sure of being out of range of their arrows. *They've thought of nearly everything.* With his left hand he grasped the sea sapphire in his pocket. *But they have no idea what I am capable of.*

I AM AT YOUR SERVICE, said the stone, speaking quietly inside his head. *BUT DO BEAR IN MIND THE DISTANCE. I CAN'T PERFORM AT INFINITE LENGTHS.*

The sapphire would not be asked to do that.

Goïmron turned to face the nearest little lake, which sported a layer of snow on its ice-bound surface. 'I have an idea,' he announced, speaking loud enough for all his companions to hear. 'Ice.'

'Ice?' Gata frowned. 'Tell us what you mean.'

Goïmron summarised his plan. 'We can saw off chunks of ice from the lake and send the blocks over to where the fire is. When they melt in the heat it'll extinguish the flames and keep the ground moist. The more ice we can bring over, the wider the path that'll get freed up for us to get at where the älfar are hiding.'

Telìnâs nodded encouragingly. 'Good idea!'

'Our gem cutter Chiselcut should know one end of a saw from the other, shouldn't he?' said Brûgar, grinning. 'But don't you go chipping away and making tiny ice sculptures, please. It'll only hold us up.'

'Don't anyone turn towards the lake,' warned Sònuk. 'Remember, they're watching us. Their spy will warn the rest of them as soon as they've worked out our intentions.'

'Let's chase him down from his lookout post and deal with him once and for all!' Brûgar shouted, spoiling for a fight. 'I'll just get my war pipe ready—'

'No. No pursuit. Nothing to attract attention at all. I can still see Hargorina and Goldhand in my mind's eye, stuck through with älfar arrows.' Gata addressed Telìnâs and Sònuk. 'Do you think you two could take their scout by surprise? As soon as he's out of action we can start sawing up the ice.'

'One moment! Why are you all so excited?' Mostro raised his hands to calm the others down. 'The notion may indeed be a good one in theory – but how are you going to get those ice blocks transported over to where the fire is? How do you know any of the artefacts will be up to doing that?'

RIGHT! TIME TO GET RID OF HIM! the sapphire offered eagerly.

'Because I know what the artefact you handed me can do.' Goïmron showed them all the tiny pair of tongs and began, from a distance of three paces, to grab Mostro with them by the collar of his extravagant mantle. As he closed the pincers in the air and lifted them up, all the time he was secretly gripping the dragon-set sapphire tight in his other hand.

AND OFF WITH THE BOASTER! A gentle laugh was faintly audible. YOU CAN STEER HIM WITH YOUR THOUGHTS AND WITH MY MAGIC POWER.

Goïmron moved the astonished Mostro, protesting wildly, up out of the saddle and made him float at approximately dwarf height in the air next to his horse, which rolled its eyes in amazement. 'This surgical instrument is supremely suited to move the blocks of ice, don't you think?' he said happily. 'You chose it well, Master Mostro!'

'Put me down this very instant!' the famulus ranted, going bright red in the face under his elaborate fur cap. This sight was greeted with howls of laughter. 'You are seriously undermining my authority. This is totally unacceptable! Undignified!'

'But I can send you back up on to your horse . . .'

'Let me down, Master Chiselcut,' Mostro called. He was furious at the humiliation that was moving him about in the air like a puppy being carried by its mother. His clothing slipped out of place and swirled around him, so that it looked as if the young man were being slowly swallowed by the luxurious textiles. 'Now!'

'As you wish.' Goïmron had been looking forward to this bit.

He opened the tongs and switched off his own floating-instruction thoughts, causing the famulus to be unceremoniously deposited in the snow from a height of one and a half paces. Mostro, struggling with his opulent garments, fell back into the pile of dazzling whiteness and disappeared from view in a shimmering cloud of snow, to the mirth of the general company.

Mostro sat up, cursing and trying to get the snow crystals off his face and to rearrange his attire. 'You'll pay for this,' he mouthed silently to Goïmron, narrowing his eyes. 'Give me those pincers back!' he demanded. 'I'll use them myself.'

'No,' said Gata. 'You gave them to me. I handed them to Goïmron and he knows what he's going to be doing with them.'

'And he's handling them extremely well,' added Sònuk, spurring his giant visok horse into action. 'Come on, Telìnâs, let's get that älfar spy so we can start flying in the ice blocks.'

The two of them raced off and worked their way all the way round the wood in order to draw the älfar scout's attention away.

'If you insist.' Mostro got to his feet and busied himself with organising his equipment and the items that had fallen out of his shoulder bag. The many layers of expensive fabric together with the fur mantle on top of his robes impeded his movements, making him appear clumsy. 'But then after that I want the pincers back. They are valuable.'

Among the things lying round about on the ground there was a small stick made of sigurdacia wood that he studied with a frown. Then he cast his eyes over to the Fourthling with a quizzical expression on his face.

This did not please Goïmron one bit.

Girdlegard

In the Brown Mountains
Brigantia
1024 P.Q. (7515th solar cycle in old reckoning), winter

'Mistress?'

Rodana woke with a start and saw the shape of Chòldunja's face floating above her own in the dim light. The candle had nearly burned itself out.

'What is it?' she mumbled.

'Escape. It's our only hope.'

Rodana sat up with her back against the wall, pulling the blanket up to cover her thin nightgown. Her aprendisa was already fully dressed and obviously ready to set off.

'Don't think I haven't been playing with the idea for ages,' she said, still half asleep. 'But the tunnel to the north-west through to the Outer Lands is completely blocked.'

'No. I mean *you* need to escape. Get out of here. Over the fortress walls. Go over to the besieging army,' Chòldunja said, with such determination that one might think there had never been any question of a different course of action.

Rodana was now fully awake. 'What are you going on about?'

'The most important thing, Mistress.' The ragana sat down next to her and took her hand. 'Because I know exactly what a rhamak is.'

'Rhamak,' Rodana repeated thoughtfully. She felt she had heard the word before but she had no recollection when or where or in what context.

'The new arrival that Klaey Berengart was talking about before he ran off to go and find me some infants,' Chòldunja said. 'And to get me a diamond. Because he's going to need my magic powers, as long as the new Wonder Zone hasn't been located.'

'Oh, yes, I remember.' Rodana rubbed the sleep out of her eyes. 'Tell me exactly why I've got to run away? To the besieging army? And on my own?' She was aware not only of the decisiveness of the young apprentice, but also of the young girl's fear. 'And what will you be doing in Brigantia in the meantime?'

'I'll be doing my best not to turn into a real ragana witch.' Chòldunja pressed her mistress's hand. 'My people in the swamps know all the arts that a rhamak has at their disposal. Once upon a time there were a small number of them in Girdlegard but their knowledge got lost over the ensuing cycles. Until now. Now the Omuthan has brought one of them back.' She sighed. 'I am sure that Berengart has no idea what he's let himself in for.'

Rodana picked up on the suppressed fear the young woman was feeling. Her heart started beating faster. 'You're making this quite scary.'

'I'm sorry. You taught me yourself how to tell a story so that the audience are on the edge of their seats.' Her smile was a little forced. The half-darkness accentuated the shadows on Chòldunja's countenance. 'My people had a different name for a rhamak. They called it a taikhom. Translated, that means *the summoner of hidden things* or *summoner of souls*. But the terms are both misleading, really.'

Rodana attempted to calm the girl by stroking her head. 'That surely won't matter as long as he doesn't get access to the new magic source. His power will have disappeared at the end of the cycle. He can't get over the walls to the besieging forces.'

'A taikhom does not need an external magic source. That's what makes him so dangerous.' Chòldunja pressed her temples. 'His power resides in his intellect. In his consciousness, which can be active in different spheres when he is in a trance. And he can summon up creatures from those other dimensions.'

Rodana looked puzzled. 'I'm finding this hard to understand.'

Chòldunja tried to explain. 'It's as if a human could make a thought connection to a fish in the water many miles away. He can send a thought message and make that fish jump out of the water on to the land,' she said. 'There are other dimensions here around us that cannot be seen with our eyes. We cannot grasp their existence. But they are there.'

'Like the world of the gods, you mean? A world a normal mortal would only enter after his death?'

'Yes, similar to that, Mistress. I know it's hard to grasp. The taikhom releases his astral body and lets it roam freely through various worlds that are closed to us. His spirit can then enter these worlds, encounter different beings and invite them to come into our own. Or he can force them to do so,' Chòldunja explained. 'Just imagine if we were ants. And a taikhom comes along and puts a creature in our ant-world that's as big as a bear. What could we ants hope to do against it?'

We would be totally at the creature's mercy. 'And you're saying that a taikhom can do all that without recourse to external magic?' Rodana asked with growing horror.

'Completely without magic.' Chòldunja pressed her mistress's hand once more before releasing it. 'Some of these beings only remain for a short time. Others stay for ever. Some will obey a taikhom. And then again others won't.'

Ye gods preserve us! 'So he can bring terrible danger into Girdlegard that is without precedent,' Rodana whispered.

'As soon as he has finished his preparations, yes, he can. Some of the creatures will need to be enticed here with specially prepared bait, if they are to undertake the arduous journey through the dimensions to this place.'

'And the bait's hardly likely just to be a pot of honey, like for a bear,' Rodana guessed.

'Indeed not, Mistress. Usually it will be the power of blood. Vital energy. Life. That's why taikhoms tend to collect a group of followers round them, fanatic enough to donate their own blood so that the taikhom can exercise his arts. Often this will be to the advantage of those who survive.' She stopped speaking for a moment, then went on. 'It can also happen that humans are forced to sacrifice themselves. And to donate all their blood.'

'It sounds as though the taikhom are no better than the ragana witches,' Rodana exclaimed. 'Oh, I'm sorry. I didn't mean you, of course.'

'You are right. The ragana do terrible things. But compared

to a taikhom – a rhamak, that is – what the ragana can do is nothing.' Chòldunja nodded to Rodana. 'You've got to go and warn Goldhand and the besieging army about what is happening here in the fortress. Without delay! Before some creature from another dimension turns up, with effects impossible to counteract. Not now and not in one thousand cycles.'

'But what will happen to you?' Rodana pushed to the back of her mind the fraught question of how she could possibly manage to escape unseen and cross Brigantia on foot. She thought she would be able to abseil down the walls without too much difficulty if she could make it over to them without being spotted. She was good at climbing.

'I'll stay here.' Chòldunja got to her feet and turned the lantern light towards the door. 'Get going now! I will try to keep the rhamak here by some means or other.'

'But how will you do that? Without your ragana powers? Does the rhamak have vulnerabilities?'

'He does.'

Rodana was well aware this was a lie. 'It would be better if I helped you to deal with the rhamak.'

Chòldunja's expression was miserable. 'I have a debt to repay. I shall never have a better opportunity to make up for what I did.' Before Rodana could enquire about this, the young woman went on, 'I'll have to have got away from this prison before Berengart turns up with babies and a ruby. Otherwise my charade will be seen through and one way or another I'll be executed.'

Rodana did not like the idea of leaving her aprendisa behind in the fortress. 'I did not save you from Mostro and the baying mob just to lose you to Berengart or someone else,' she announced, as she got up from her bed. 'You are my aprendisa! I want to keep teaching you about the art of puppetry and shadow-play. That's what *our* life is supposed to be like.'

'And it will be again, as soon as we have stopped this evil. An evil nobody can ever grasp the idea of, Mistress. Not even Berengart,' Chòldunja replied. 'I beg you, please, flee! Escape from the fortress and warn Goldhand and the others. You will be listened to. They have to launch their attack. Swiftly! Using all available means at their disposal!'

They may listen, but will they believe me? Rodana's only hope was the good sense of her friend Goïmron, who was with the army outside the walls. *I must find him. He will have a ready ear for my dire warning.* 'Right, I'll do it. You must promise to be careful and to look after yourself, my aprendisa?'

She nodded quickly. 'I shall! If only to be able to stop the rhamak. I'll do it stealthily, quiet as a little mouse. I will ruin his arts and then I shall run away and hide in a little hole somewhere and you can come and free me later.'

Chòldunja put her arms round her mistress. Rodana returned the embrace and held the young woman tenderly for a few moments.

'Now, get this lock broken so we can get out of here. Our mission brooks no further delay.' Chòldunja released her and shone the light on the lock plate just below the door handle. 'You're wonderful at lock-breaking, Mistress.'

Rodana bent down with a laugh and took the tools her apprentice held out to her. After a few breaths the lock cylinders yielded to Rodana's skilful fingers.

Rodana quickly threw on suitable clothing, grabbed a few possessions and stuffed them in a shoulder bag. The younger woman was already prepared for their escape. They stepped out into the corridor, one after the other, pulled the hoods of their cloaks up to conceal their faces, hugged for a final time, and parted.

Only when Rodana had gone round a few corners did she remember she had failed to ask a vital question. Namely, the matter of the secret debt that Chòldunja felt she must settle.

Girdlegard

United Great Kingdom of Gauragon
Province of Tschobad
1024 P.Q. (7515th solar cycle in old reckoning), winter

'Then you're not one of the Undead?' Barbandor was making use of every possible opportunity to find out more about this strange orc's miraculous immortality. As now, when the white-on-blue patterned Borkon was riding next to Barbandor's crate, which was being carried by a grey-skinned orc.

Borkon grunted a laugh. 'No, I'm not.'

'So is it a gift you were born with?' In his cage prison Barbandor was being rocked to and fro, as his muscular bearer-orc, for whom he seemed to weigh less than a large piece of cheese, galloped along. He had been given two stinking blankets to wrap himself in against the icy cold. At least he was not having to run along himself. These orcs were displaying great stamina and could put on quite a burst of sustained speed. Dark-bearded Barbandor was aware he would never have been able to keep up. *Unless they gave me a horse.*

'You really want to know all about it, don't you?' Borkon was moving swiftly through Girdlegard, heading north with his dwarf prisoner and his band of a score or so orc warriors. They had now left the one-time territory of the fire eaters behind them, had given the fortified dwarf settlements of Mountainshine and Goldenwall a wide berth, and their progress was steady and fast. Depending on the type of landscape they were traversing, the gang of orcs could cover between sixty and a hundred miles each orbit, running from dawn to sunset. And carrying, of course, all their equipment. They could move faster on foot than any humans, meldriths, dwarves, elves or even älfar could manage.

'It's just that I'm curious. At first I thought you were bringing back a demon. There was a demon rampaging here in Girdlegard thirteen hundred cycles ago, and anything or anyone that perished on his land he would bring back as one of the Undead.'

Thoroughly shaken up when his carrying orc had to jump over some obstacle in his path, Barbandor felt his teeth rattling in his head, and he had to take care while speaking to avoid the risk of biting his own tongue. Every bone in his body was sore from this uncomfortable form of transport. The continuous rolling motion of the crate he was subjected to made him feel slightly nauseous but he had got used to that. But the fact he had lost so much weight was a different matter. His clothing and his chainmail tunic hung on him much more loosely than usual and he had had to fasten his belt a few notches tighter.

'No, I am not in the control of a demon or any other magical being.' In his own orc language Borkon gave one or two concise commands, and the group's speed slowed. 'But there's one in particular I should like to encounter.'

'Which one is that?'

'Just be patient. You dwarves are long-lived, aren't you? Behave yourself and continue to serve as our lucky mascot and you'll maybe survive long enough to find out.' Borkon winked at him and burst out laughing, showing as he did so the silvery canine teeth set into black gums. 'Oh, you should see your face!'

'I don't need to look at my own face, I know what I look like.' Barbandor was at a loss to work out the enigmatic answers he was getting from Borkon. He was still completely in the dark about how this orc leader was apparently able to defy death. And he did not like the fact that he was obviously being regarded as some kind of amusing trinket, a comic keepsake. There was no way he wanted to contribute to the orcs' well-being and success by bringing them luck of any kind. 'Well, if you're so keen to keep the secret of your immortality to yourself, at least maybe tell me where the blazes you are taking me?'

'It seems you've never been far from Platinshine before now?'

'No. Born and bred there. And proud of it, by Vraccas!'

Borkon pointed over to the left, where a mountain range was visible. 'The slopes belong to the Landbolt. You'll see the western side of the mountain at dawn tomorrow. We're going to make camp tonight earlier than usual. I want my people to be well rested for tomorrow.'

Barbandor tried to calculate what kind of a distance they might all have covered in recent orbits. According to the constellations he could see at night, they were probably right in the centre of Girdlegard.

All of a sudden it all fell into place. 'You are heading for Kràg Tahuum.'

'Exactly.'

'And you want to suck up to the chief black-eyes there, who's said to be the arch-enemy of Dsôn Khamateion. It makes sense. He could use someone like you: you are immortal. You are different. He'll make you his second-in-command,' mused Barbandor. 'That's quite a wise move on your part.'

'Thank you.' Borkon bared his impressive painted teeth. 'But you are mistaken, angry little man.'

'Don't call me that!'

'But it's what you are. You've been angry ever since we first met.' Now that it was dusk, the blue-skinned orc ordered his troops to halt behind a rocky outcrop and set up camp in its shelter. 'Any idea why you are still alive and haven't yet been served up as stew like your lady friend?'

Barbandor grabbed the bars of his cage. 'Because Vraccas is protecting me and he will give me an opportunity to kill you.'

'Oh, that's a very good answer. But no, it's not the right one.'

Borkon gave orders for a lookout to be posted in a nearby sitalia oak on the hill, and for the campfire to be kept on the small side to avoid attracting attention. 'There have been prophecies, Barbandor. I want to follow them in order to achieve my aims.'

'And those would be?'

Borkon shrugged his broad shoulders. 'Like I said: dwarves can live a long time. You will live to see it. Try your best.' The orc who had been carrying Barbandor set the crate down near the fire for warmth, then groaned slightly as he stretched to relieve his muscles, and massaged his shoulders and back. 'I wish you good night, little angry man. Tomorrow will be an exciting orbit for us all.' Borkon stepped away from the firelight and climbed up the incline with such ease that it seemed the long journey had not affected him.

Nobody paid any more attention to Barbandor.

The orc band set up their camp and arranged a rota for the watch. Dried meat was distributed to the troops and after their simple meal the beasts lay down for their night's rest. Soon there was snoring and whistling from all quarters.

They're snoring loud enough to be heard miles off. Barbandor had once assumed that orcs always drank themselves into a stupor each evening after rampaging through the nearby villages, laying waste, and then indulging their unpleasant fancies. But he had come to realise that this was a highly disciplined group that Borkon had under him. Very well disciplined. This only added to Barbandor's sense of unease. *These are a different sort of monster altogether.* As far as circumstances permitted, he stretched his limbs and tried to find a comfortable position for the night.

He was about to close his eyes, ready for sleep, relieved not to be jiggled and rattled about for once, when he noticed a black orc with white markings putting a copper pot over the fire. He was wearing a clean grey embroidered tunic and had bracelets on his arms and amulets round his neck, which made him different in appearance from all the others. Next to the pot he set up some small scales such that healers might use to measure out ingredients. He weighed out some herbs and put them in the pot.

Herbs! Like the ones that Gyndala found left behind in the abandoned burnt-out shelters the pig-faces left in Platinshine? Barbandor was fully awake now but kept still, pretending to be in the world of dreams. *I must find out more.*

He observed how the black-and-white spotted orc added some powder that had been wrapped in waxed paper, and then stirred the mixture with a copper spoon. This produced an acrid smell that, with the steam from the pot, spread over the camp.

All of a sudden, Borkon stepped in out of the darkness and sat down next to the orc making the herbal brew. They chatted to each other, but Barbandor could not understand what they were saying. However, he was able to ascertain that the other one was called Torsuk.

Next, Borkon woke one of his people and had him taste a spoonful of the brew. The grey-skinned orc drank from the spoon without hesitation. The bright, watery liquid dripped out of the corner of his muzzle and ran down over his fur collar. The drops appeared bright red in the faint firelight.

Immediately the orc's eyes changed and took on a purple colour. The beast fell to its knees and held its throat.

I hope it dies. One less of the bastards.

Barbandor watched as the beverage taster, after coughing for a while, got to his feet, pulled out his dagger and dragged it along his own forearm. Black blood oozed out of the wound. The grey orc looked disappointed as he surveyed the injury, and clamped his lips firmly together.

Torsuk spoke some words and then bound up the cut. Borkon patted the victim on the shoulder approvingly.

After that the entire contents of the copper pot were poured out on to the fire. The flames shrank back as if in pain and for a few heartbeats the blaze turned bright red.

Dazzled, Barbandor shut his eyes. When he dared open them again to look at Torsuk, the black-and-white orc had vanished. Together with his equipment. *I assume he's researching into finding some method to give the orcs the same characteristic as their leader. I'll have to prevent that happening.*

As a dwarf, imprisoned and surrounded by enemies, he had quite a substantial list of important tasks. Each one more urgent than the last.

Vraccas preserve me. He closed his eyes once more. *I shall be able to do it soon. I feel it in my guts. I can avenge Gyndala's death.*

As he drifted into sleep Barbandor made one more decision. If Torsuk were to be successful in his brewing experiment, he would be one of the first to try it out. Because, as Borkon had stated, dwarves are long-lived. *If I had protection against sword blades and other weapons I'd be able to live even longer.*

These earthquakes and the distortion of the landscape brought fascinating changes to Girdlegard. I came across stone with such a high iron content that it turned rusty and fragile if it was stepped on or hit with a pick-axe. I saw basalt lava that flowed faster than water could. There was no escape from its path.

But the best things were the new minerals that were spewed up from the earth's core. They may prove useful for weaving magic. These unfamiliar minerals are so new that as yet they have no name and are so rare that they have only occurred once in a hundred cycles. Their value surpasses that of every other element. But the composition of their strange breath-like emanation, the vapour that attacks granite and makes it melt like butter, remains a mystery. A riddle I have not solved.

Excerpt from
The History of Girdlegard Followingthe Great Quake
(vol I, p.342)
as compiled by Master Ukentro Smallquill of Enaiko

VI

Girdlegard

Empire of Gautaya
1024 P.Q. (7515th solar cycle in old reckoning), winter

The next large glittering ice block, as thick as an arm and ten paces in length, was floating in the air, skilfully manipulated by Goïmron and directed with great precision to land in the flames next to the first recognisable gap in the trees. The frozen water melted in the heat and soaked the dampened ground; the tongues of flame were extinguished with a hiss of steam.

Then he raced out of the wood along the path that was being created. 'Excellent,' he called out to the workers sawing away at the lake's frozen surface. He ran to his horse. 'Carry on! We need plenty more blocks. You can make them smaller if that's easier and quicker. We're nearly through!'

He swiftly swung himself up into the saddle and quickly made his way, next to Brûgar, fifty paces further along where another entrance through the forest fire was being prepared. There was a third attempt happening on the opposite side. It was important that the älfar enemy be forced to defend their hideaway on several fronts simultaneously. Telìnâs and Sònuk had incapacitated the älfar lookouts before they could get a warning to their fellows in the centre of the ironthorn tree wood. The tripartite attack would thus come as a relative surprise.

In front of each of the openings there waited four hundred mounted human troops, armed to the teeth and supremely well trained for combat, as the town of Fortgard expected of each adult resident. The city's tradition as an army settlement demanded every healthy resident take part in regular military exercises.

Behind them were a range of catapults able to fire arrows, spears or bolts. These were mounted on light carts in case the anaesthetised dragons were suddenly to wake up. Slibina and Szmajro were young, hardly more than ten paces in length, and could in all probability be defeated with conventional projectiles. Their brownish and rust-coloured young scales would not have developed the same degree of hardness as those of a fully grown dragon.

Goïmron was reassured by this knowledge. *I do so hope that I'm wrong about what the älfar have in mind with these particular specimens.*

Fortgard was already organising reinforcements, but it might take till evening before those extra couple of thousand new troops could be suitably equipped. *I don't think we can wait that long.*

Goïmron and Brûgar reached the most westerly of the paths through the fire. The ice treatment had nearly broken through completely. 'Let's get everything ready,' Goïmron proposed, halting his horse. 'After that we use the other two openings.'

Brûgar nodded and jumped down out of the saddle as soon as his mount slowed its pace. Goïmron had never seen a better horseman among the dwarf folk. Being of squat stature seemed to be no disadvantage at all to this blue-bearded fighter, who was already chewing on the war pipe clenched between his teeth.

'I can't wait to snuff out a black-eyes' life-light!' he declared. 'My war flail is an excellent life-light swatter.'

Mostro and his artefacts were over on the eastern side. It was agreed that the famulus would give the signal to launch the attack. However diligently he had searched through his random collection of potentially magic objects, he had not yet located anything quite as practical as the surgical tongs for moving blocks of ice.

And how is he supposed to know that it was me doing that and not his silly artefact? Goïmron looked at the pile of ice blocks his helpers had cut out of the lake ice. With his mental powers of concentration at full stretch, he could have these hefty ice sections lifted up on command, then moved along by sea sapphire strength from the jewel he grasped tight in his fist, while he waved the pincers for show in his right hand.

The Fortgarders were no longer quite as surprised at these magic fire-fighting manoeuvres as they had been at the start, but they always made a point of keeping out of the way of the flying ice blocks as they made their way over to where the frozen chunks were slid into the fire to melt and put out the flames they touched.

'Another ten paces and we'll be through,' Brûgar announced, standing bravely close to the fire. 'The black-eyes might see us and realise what we're doing, if any of them are even keeping watch properly.'

'I know. I'll be careful.' Goïmron quickly collected the final few blocks of ice and got ready to shepherd them into place, issuing directions to those assisting him. They were to await the bugle call to action. 'At the signal you storm through,' he told obrist Emaro, who was in charge of the forces here.

'Understood, Master Chiselcut. We kill everything in our path.' The fifty-year-old was looking tense, his hand constantly on the hilt of his sword. His Fortgard men and women were in solid armour and bore spears and long shields. 'Neither älfar nor dragons will escape to lay claim to the Wonder Zone for themselves.'

'We are indebted to you. The whole of Girdlegard and my own folk are grateful to you for your service,' he said, although this seemed to embarrass Emaro somewhat. 'Nobody else could have stopped the älfar. Not as quickly.'

'You've said that eight times, Master Chiselcut.'

'Because it's the truth.'

'You don't have to thank us. Fortgard may not be subject to Gautaya but we are well aware of what the consequences might be for the fate of Girdlegard as a whole.' Emaro looked into the flames, which threw a glow on to his scarred and immobile face. 'What do you think we should be expecting? Did the famulus give you any idea?'

Goïmron did not know what was behind this question. Fear, perhaps, that the magic field might exert some strange influence on his troops and might change their natures. Mutations? Turning them into beasts or shredding them into a thousand pieces in a sudden explosion? 'To be honest, I must admit I don't know,' he said. 'Mostro thought the magic field would be harmless when we stepped inside. And that things would be different if the zone was still emerging to its full form.'

'Is he sure the zone has finished forming itself?'

Goïmron was sorry not to be able to give a better answer. He was apprehensive enough himself, despite having the magic sapphire in his pocket. Every so often it would speak to him and say calming words, namely that everything was going to be fine. 'I'd love to be able to tell you more but it wouldn't be fair or honest.'

Emaro took a few deep breaths. 'We have no other option if we are going to hold back the evil. We will take the risk for the sake of Girdlegard.'

Goïmron was full of admiration for the obrist, who would make the perfect model for the statue of a veteran soldier. 'Vraccas will be with us—'

A sudden loud blast on the bugle sounded out from over at the third pathway into the burning wood, where Mostro was positioned. The famulus was ordering the fighting forces to launch their assault on älfar and dragons alike.

Emaro looked at Goïmron in surprise. 'Is that a mistake, do you think?' He would have been pleased to think that it was, but the notes followed the agreed melody and the tune was repeated.

'The fire must have gone out quicker in other places,' Goïmron said, magically transporting the heavy ice blocks, which stood ready in a pile. He would have to act quickly now. 'Everyone get ready.'

'As if I had known this would happen, I've already packed the tobacco into my war pipe,' said Brûgar, before hastening off to jump into his saddle. He took the war flail out of its holder. 'I'll look out for you, gem cutter. The black-eyes shan't get you as long as I'm alive.' He nudged him playfully. 'But in the end it might turn out to be you saving my life and protecting me from all the magicking stuff.'

He puffed at his pipe and winked. There was a pleasant smell of cherry-flavoured tobacco.

With a stern look Goïmron warned the others not to speak. He went on shifting the ice blocks into place. On a track about three paces wide the fire was already extinguished.

Curses. I thought Brûgar might have forgotten by now. But the blue-bearded dwarf remembered very well that there had been a lot of wizardry going on during the battle of Two-Stream Hill. And that these strange events could not all be explained away by Mostro's powers or the use of artefacts. But in spite of that, Brûgar had not spoken to the others because he had not been totally sure of things. *I mustn't give him any excuse to start putting two and two together.*

Emaro's cavalry troops were readying for action even though they knew they no longer had the advantage of surprise.

Then the obrist gave the command to launch the attack. The warriors thundered along the narrow track to reach the burned-out centre of the wood and to enter the new Wonder Zone. With the fire raging on all sides, they rushed forward, lances lowered and shields held protectively before them. Ash and hot cinders flew up under their horses' hooves and the sparks rising from the ground seemed to be trying to escape from the enemy attack.

'Quite a spectacle!' Brûgar stayed close to Goïmron, though it was hard for him not to storm forward to be in the first row. 'These long'uns really have steel in their bones.' He gestured excitedly with the stem of his pipe towards the open track. 'What's happening now? Use the artefact pincers and grab yourself some älfar. Hurl them into the air. You can be a help without ever having to use your little axe.'

Mostro can use his magic spells and magic powers. He should be able to sort it. Goïmron was much more nervous than he had been in the Two-Stream Hill battle. This combat would be taking place in a more restricted terrain and there would be little or no chance to get out of the way of danger because of the surrounding inferno. *But there's nothing for it. I'll have to barge straight in, even if they don't really need me.*

'Let's see what we can do.'

Together they followed Emaro and his force of four hundred armoured cavalry, who were dragging their catapults on wagons behind them. To the right and to the left huge flames shot into the air. The fire was trying to recapture the ground it had been forced out of. The heat in the flame-ravine was unbearably powerful, and took one's breath away. Goïmron made sure his scarf was covering his nose and mouth. It was like going through an oven in which the baker's apprentice had put far too much wood.

At last he and Brûgar were through.

They found themselves standing in a big circular clearing covered in a layer of grey ash that was being swept around by the wind. The burnt ground had stored the warmth from the recent fire. They saw occasional black skeletons of dead trees holding up their branches as if in warning. They resembled the bones of strange creatures that had been killed in the fire.

'Over there!' Brûgar yelled, raising his war flail. His pipe hung from the corner of his mouth. 'Look!'

By Vraccas. We were all so wrong! Goïmron could not move; he was rooted to his saddle, with one hand on his sea sapphire, the other gripping the reins.

As he had assumed, Slibina and Szmajro were lying in the magic field, their big horns having been forcibly removed. Stuck on to each horn stump was the quivering body of a dying älf, blood cascading down, sacrificed to effect the change in the dragons, just the same way night-mares were formed out of unicorns. They must have wanted to turn the scaled beasts into something infinitely more terrible, permeated with evil and malice and equipped with greatly increased powers.

A female älf was standing between the two comatose dragon siblings. She raised her hands and described magic symbols in the air with her gestures. Her face was half white, half dark. The same with her eyes. The signs she used appeared in the air as coloured lights: a dusky red and a bright violet, overlapping and forming patterns on an otherwise invisible defensive wall around them and their accompanying fighters.

The Fortgarders could penetrate this wall neither on their horses nor with their missiles, whereas the adversaries were shooting out black arrows at them unimpeded, causing many deaths on the side of the attackers. The murderous force of the steel projectiles went through the Fortgard long shields to pierce the armour behind.

The älfar have a maga working for them! This was an idea that Goïmron had never even entertained and it was actually true. *And that was why they wanted to come to this place.* In the new Wonder Zone she could renew her magic powers in order to ensure the planned metamorphosis of the two dragons. *And to bring the dragon siblings under her control.*

Up until now Goïmron had been feeling fairly confident that things were going to get better and that the siege of the Brown Mountains fortress would soon be successful. But now there was a new terror facing them and it would be worse than anything Ûra and Ardin had ever confronted them with.

'What is the wand-waver up to? Why is he so useless?' Brûgar gestured towards Mostro, who was kneeling behind a protective row of shields next to the invisible barrier, a string of gemstones in his hand. He was presumably trying to break open the magic obstacle. 'Now!' Brûgar shouted furiously across the battlefield, holding his war pipe firmly in one hand. 'Come on, you useless piece of snot, do something for Vraccas' sake. Or I'll come over and make you work quicker!'

WE CAN ATTEMPT TO BREAK THE BARRIER, the sapphire told Goïmron. BUT YOU NEED TO GET CLOSER.

'How much closer?' he muttered under his breath.

NEAR ENOUGH FOR YOU TO PLACE YOUR HAND ON IT.

The envisaged combat with the superior numbers on their own side had turned into wholesale slaughter. All the black arrows were piercing shields and bodies, and swathes of brave Fortgard warriors were falling in droves without being able to fight back. Not only the Fortgarder soldiers but dwarves, meldriths, other humans and elves in the attacking forces were being hit, and casualties lay scattered everywhere on the ash-covered ground, often trampled by stampeding, panicking horses.

I SWEAR THE TWO OF US CAN DO THIS IF WE WORK TOGETHER. HURRY! BEFORE THE DRAGONS WAKE UP OR IT WILL BE TOO LATE.

Goïmron took a deep breath – and sat up straight in the saddle. 'Brûgar, get me to the front. You'll be better than me at spotting the best way through.'

'What have you got in mind?' Brûgar stared at him in amazement. 'Do you reckon those tongs can cope with the barrier?'

'No. It's enough if I can lay my hands on the älfar maga. I'll squeeze her with the pincers till she loses her concentration,' he answered.

'Good idea! Why not just pinch her head off with the tongs? Then we'll be all right.' Brûgar raced off, a cloud of cherry smoke streaming in his wake. 'Follow me! I'll lead the way but you must stick close behind.' He pulled a shield out of its fastening on the saddle of a riderless horse and raised it high. 'If I were to fall, then–'

'You won't fall.' Goïmron rode along in the wake of the blue-bearded dwarf.

At breakneck speed they raced over the scorched earth. From time to time they were swallowed up by clouds of ash. When it began to snow it was almost impossible to tell the difference between the snowflakes and the clumps of ash. The burned-out clearing was soon completely covered with a thick layer of both.

Brûgar swerved to the side and was now approaching the invisible barricade. He dismounted. He knocked the tobacco out and stowed his pipe away. Things were getting serious. 'Now we'll work our way through like busy little worms. Mind you don't get pecked at!'

Goïmron followed Brûgar's example and crawled after him.

His heart was hammering in his chest and the heavy clothing was making him sweat freely. From time to time an älf would hurry past with a loaded bow, not noticing them in all the flurry of snow and ash.

'Over there! Get over to that big tree stump,' said Brûgar as he squirmed his way forward, covered in snowflakes. 'They won't see us straight away.'

Panting with the effort, Goïmron arrived at the promised shelter of the ironthorn tree stump at the same time as his companion did. He could actually sense the vibrations from the magic fence when he put out his hand. He peeled off his glove. *Ready?*

READY.

'What are you doing?' Brûgar grasped him by the shoulder. 'Use the pincer artefact and pull the black-eye witch's head off!'

'I've . . . I've thought of something that might work better.' There was no time for long explanations. He placed the flat of his hand against the magic wall and focused his thoughts on breaking the spell.

'I knew it,' Brûgar muttered at his side. 'My Thinking Pipe set me on the right path with that riddle. I always knew it was you at the Two-Stream Hill—'

'Be quiet, please. And never say a word to anyone, whatever you do. Specially not to Mostro.' Goïmron was concentrating hard.

A hot sensation streamed out of the gemstone into his body, working its way out to the hand he was holding against the barrier. Shooting out from round where his fingers were placed, lines and cracks formed in all directions, such as you would see in a sheet of shattering ice.

But the wall did not give way.

YOU MAY BE FOCUSING TOO SHARPLY, said the sapphire. YOU ARE DOING NEEDLE STITCHES INSTEAD OF A BLOW

WITH A CLUB. RELEASE MORE ENERGY! USE MUCH MORE FORCE!

I'll have to risk it. Goïmron closed his eyes and set the constrained forces free.

'Hurry, Goïmron! That maga is looking this way. She knows we are here,' Brûgar warned him.

A low swishing sound indicated that arrows were being shot in their direction now. The thick ironthorn tree stump continued to protect them from the hail of missiles. For now.

Get rid of the wall! Goïmron yelled out as the energy suddenly sent a hot surge of pain through his whole body. It was as if he were being scourged with a thousand bolts of lightning. His body shook and it felt as though his insides were cooking in the terrible wave of heat. *I . . . I am dying from the inside.* The breath leaving his body in that scream was as hot as lava wind. He opened his eyes and was about to pull his hand away because of the tortuous spasms of pain. *I can't do this anymore!*

NO. DON'T STOP NOW. YOU'VE NEARLY DONE IT, MY FRIEND.

Goïmron was unable to reply – and suddenly, round his fingers, the whole invisible wall exploded. The älfar woman's spell collapsed into millions of sea-blue will-o'-the-wisps.

At that moment the signal horn sounded out, summoning the cavalry to carry out the annihilating assault that had been originally planned. The heavily armoured Fortgard divisions were at last able to use their superior numbers to overwhelm the älfar soldiers.

'I—' A black arrow whirred across, striking through the flesh and bone of Goïmron's hand before being stopped by the wood of the tree stump. He cried out with the pain and, still pale and exhausted from his exertions, collapsed behind the protective tree stump.

'You've done it,' Brûgar yelled enthusiastically, and, wild

with excitement, he thumped his friend on the back. 'By Lorimbur! A dwarf that can do magic as if he were the living embodiment of the maga Vanéra. Can I leave you here on your own? I've got to get into the battle and help Gata pound the black-eyes into porridge before those long'uns have all the fun and leave nothing for me to do.' He leaped to his feet and grabbed a length of linen from his first aid bag to wrap round Goïmron's injured hand to stem the bleeding. 'I'll bring you back the witch's head!'

Goïmron was struggling to get his breath. He pressed his injured hand against his chest. He was too exhausted to speak, so he just nodded. *I can't go another step. Not a single one. Never again.*

'Thank you, gem-cutter wizard!' In joyful exuberance, Brûgar plonked a kiss on his friend's forehead. Then he stuck his war pipe back in his mouth and raced off, the soles of his boots sending up clouds of ash.

Thank you, Vraccas! Goïmron twisted round to risk a glance past the edge of the tree trunk, which now had half a dozen arrows stuck in its bark. They had all been intended for him, of course. Without the ironthorn's help, both he and Brûgar would be lying face down in the ash and the snow, peppered with holes. Any other kind of wood might have let the arrows through.

The cavalry were setting up formations in waves of attack from different directions, making the enemy have to spread their efforts and fight on three fronts. And behind the mounted troops came the catapults, currently being put into place.

The älfar maga was pulling the cadavers of her people off the horn stumps of the dragon siblings and she knelt down between the two creatures as they slept. Placing a hand on each of their muzzles, she lowered her own head and her lips worked ceaselessly. All the jewellery round her neck, on her arms and wrists and fingers glowed brightly. A magic shimmer spread over the two dragons, disappearing in through their nostrils.

Almost at once, Goïmron saw the dragons jerk convulsively. Their tails twitched and their ribcages rose and fell faster now. *She is waking the beasts up!*

The älf woman knew that the dragons were her last chance of leaving the Wonder Zone alive. Thanks to Slibina and Szmajro, she might perhaps emerge victorious from this battle.

'What can we do?' Goïmron asked his sapphire jewel nervously.

I NEED TO RECUPERATE. THEY REALLY TOOK IT OUT OF ME, YOU KNOW. LET'S JUST HOPE THAT—

All of a sudden, three long tongues of lightning shot up out of the forest floor, sending the snow and ash drifts high into the air.

There was a crackling discharge that struck the jewellery on the älfar maga's neck and forehead. Other flashes hit the two rust-coloured scaled beasts, who reacted with deafening roars as they were forced awake.

The eyes of the sibling creatures flashed blood-red like those of night-mares, and when their claws scratched the ground they sent up white sparks. The dragons' bodies shuddered and shook and grew and grew in size until they were eighteen, twenty paces or more in length, from the original measurement of ten. The rusty brown of the scales acquired a black patterning like veins. The Wonder Zone was doing what many old stories had told of. It was changing the nature of these beasts.

The courageous Fortgard cavalry kept up their attack even though the dragons awoke and were rearing up threateningly and spreading their wings to appear yet more terrifying. They roared frighteningly, their muzzles agape and long teeth much in evidence. Before their transformations these dragons had been too young to breathe out fire. *But now?* Goïmron was struggling with overwhelming fatigue. *If Slíbina and Szmajro can spit out flames, we're done for. I must do something . . .*

THERE IS NOTHING ELSE WE CAN TACKLE AT THE MOMENT. I HAVE TO RECOVER MY STRENGTH AND I MUST RENEW MY MAGIC POWERS FROM THE SOURCE HERE IN THE EARTH.

Suddenly Szmajro gave a shriek of pain and pivoted round, slashing out with his tail and sweeping several älfar and Fortgard soldiers aside. The assault came to a halt and horses were bolting off in all directions. A large open wound appeared on the dragon's neck, without any obvious cause, and a second head on a slim neck sprang up out of the aperture. The second head grew rapidly larger. At the same time, the creature's wings increased in size and, flapping powerfully, created a veritable whirlwind. The gusts were strong enough to topple some of the armoured vehicles. Horses and warriors alike were sent head over heels into struggling heaps on the ground.

No! Szmajro has two heads! Goïmron pulled himself to his feet, using the tree stump to lean on. *And both heads are still growing!*

Slíbina and Szmajro had each attained a length of forty paces and were hollering out their anger and surprise at the changes they were undergoing. Where the älfar woman had cut off their longest three horns in order to facilitate the transformation, there were now bright white flames imitating in shape the structure of the previous growths.

Occasionally arrows were shot in the dragons' direction, but the metal tips were useless against the creatures' now fully hardened scales. A bolt was fired into one of the flame-horns but it vanished almost at once. Whatever the scaled monsters touched with these flames would be immediately incinerated without leaving a trace.

The älfar woman has created the worst of all possible monsters here. Much worse than Ûra and Ardin would have been.

Goïmron drew himself up to his full height. *It's her doing. The new Wonder Zone cannot be held responsible.*

All round about was mayhem and utter chaos. Riderless horses were running wild, trying to get away from Slibina and Szmajro. But the previously opened pathways through the fire had closed up again. No chance of the reinforcements getting through from the city to relieve the fighting force here. Goïmron alone was standing immobile, studying what was happening to the dragon siblings. Their heads shook as they roared. The incipient fiery breath from their throats promised destructive tongues of flame to follow. Their gullets glowed and smouldered.

Even Brûgar, Gata, Telìnâs and Sònuk had retreated from the fray. Nobody could approach the magic älfar woman, who had struggled up on to her feet, though she was still unsteadily swaying somewhat as she took her place between the two dragons. She was holding one hand to her head and there was blood dripping from her nose on to her jewellery and on to the armoured clothing and her open fur mantle. Surrounded by ash and snow, she stretched out the flat palm of her other hand to Slibina while calling out her name.

The rust-coloured dragon bent down slowly, lowering her mighty skull, so that the hardened snout could gently caress the outstretched fingers. The veins in the armour-plated scales turned darker and the creature's eyes glowed like live coals.

Slibina is acknowledging her as her mistress. Goïmron gripped the sapphire and pulled it out of his pocket. The time for keeping secrets was long gone. *I am going to do something about this.* He held the shimmering gemstone out towards the three adversaries, who stood no further away than thirty paces. 'Whoever you are, älf woman,' he called, 'I am going to destroy you!' All his thoughts were concentrated on imagining this maga vanishing, struck by bolts of lightning issuing from the jewel. But nothing of the kind occurred.

'Whoever I am?' She burst out laughing. 'But I am a zhussa! And you have no inkling of how close you are to death.' She raised her other arm and called to the double-headed Szmajro. 'I'm going to show you the extent of my powers. Your death will bear my name.'

Slowly and seemingly reluctantly, the larger of the dragon siblings bowed its two necks towards the älfar woman, as if unwilling to carry out her order. A dark, dangerous-sounding growl came from both throats. The voice pierced Goïmron's soul. The flame-horns flickered darkly and the dark veins in Szmajro's scales absorbed all the light.

COME. To his surprise Goïmron heard the word in his head. ACKNOWLEDGE ME!

Szmajro jerked round before the rusty brown snout touched the zhussa's hand. The two pairs of eyes flashed ruby red with anger. Making a mighty leap, he landed in front of the flabbergasted Goïmron, who had continued to hold out the sea sapphire towards the dragon. Under the dragon's claws there were flashes of white sparks that Goïmron could feel on his own body as a prickling sensation.

'This is nonsense! What are you doing?' he called out to the sapphire.

Szmajro's claw pitched forward and took careful hold of Goïmron, then he swivelled round to face the zhussa. His growling roar was sounding even more threatening by now.

She let out a yell and staggered back. 'Don't you dare!'

But before Goïmron could say a word, Szmajro took off and swung him up into the air.

Girdlegard

In the Brown Mountains
Brigantia
1024 P.Q. (7515th solar cycle in old reckoning), winter

Klaey opened the door to the accommodation where he had imprisoned the two women: the ragana and the puppeteer. On his way no one had asked him what the heavy enclosed handcart was for that he was dragging along behind him and which needed much complicated manoeuvring to turn the corner into the room. Seeing a junior officer in the supply corps delivering food and other goods was an everyday occurrence.

'I've brought you what you need, moor-witch.' Klaey closed the door behind him and opened the cover on the handcart. In the dim light six sleeping infants could be seen. They had been drugged with poppy milk. In his pocket he had a clear moon diamond that was not the most valuable but still comparatively rare outside of the Brown Mountains. If you had connections it was possible to get anything you wanted in a city under siege. 'Now get your cruel business done. I'm going to need both your healing powers and your destructive capabilities.'

He stepped slowly through the apartments. It was suspiciously quiet.

'I want you to know I don't approve of your sacrificing these innocent little lives, but I suppose you have to do it. Unless you've come up with a better idea in the meantime?' Klaey adjusted the wick of the lamp on the table to illuminate the rooms. 'Ragana? Puppet mistress? Where have you got to?'

There was no answer.

Damnation! Klaey opened all the cupboards and looked under the beds, but the two very different females had vanished. 'Come out, wherever you are! This is not a game! It's absolutely essential my brother's health be restored. Time's running out.'

Taking the lamp in his hand, he went over to examine the lock on the entrance door. The scratches he could see round the keyhole spoke volumes. His prisoners had made a run for it, in spite of the opprobrium and danger they risked incurring if they were seen outside the fortress.

Why on earth would they try to escape? It makes no sense. Klaey stood up straight again. The besieging army would capture the two women and condemn them, just as the posters and leaflets had announced. If they ever got out of Brigantia. Did they even intend trying to slip past the enemy at the gates? It would be utterly impossible. The adversaries outside the fortress walls had watchful sentries posted everywhere. *Where are they trying to get to?*

A possibility occurred to Klaey. He did not like the idea but thought it might help him to track the women down. The sleuth-hounds might overdo things in their eagerness to hunt them down. *But I have no choice—*

He suddenly felt a sharp knife being pressed against his neck.

'You're not very good at hide and seek, are you, Croaker?' It was Chòldunja's voice behind him. With her free hand she grabbed him between the legs and grasped his balls.

'*Whisperer* is a nicer name.' Klaey forced himself to keep still. The ragana had him literally in the palm of her hand. 'Where is your mistress?'

'That is not important.'

'And what do you intend to do?'

'You are going to take me to the rhamak.' She increased the pressure from the knife blade. 'You know, I can cut your throat quicker than you can jerk away from the blade.'

'Slow down. I've brought you the babies and the stone you need.' With exquisite caution Klaey extracted the moon diamond from his pocket to show her. *All is not yet lost!* The milky gemstone gave off a silvery sparkle in his fingers. 'For recharging your magic.'

'I would never harm the children.'

This confused Klaey. 'But I thought you were a ragana?'

'I only told you all that stuff to get you off my back and to give my mistress a head start to let her get away. I renounced the ragana cult and code that my sisters and my ancestors believed in.'

'By the mother of Cadengis! So she's really escaped?'

'Perhaps she has.' Chòldunja squeezed his scrotum tighter. It was particularly painful. 'Best not to bend forward like that. You might end up slitting your own throat.'

Klaey suppressed the reflex movement. 'What do you want with the rhamak?' he hissed between his teeth.

'I want to offer him my services and pledge him my loyalty. I'm not serving any of you Berengarts. Your time is over and done with.'

'How far do you think we'll get if we leave the room? Everybody knows your face.'

But she laughed at him. 'I doubt it.' Chòldunja moved round to his side without shifting the knife. 'We'll get to him quite easily. You know where he is to be found.'

Klaey sighed with relief as the painful pressure on his manhood was reduced. 'Right, if that's what you want. You can leave the knife at my throat. It's less noticeable,' he advised her sarcastically.

'I've already thought of that.' Chòldunja's smile was cool. 'The rhamak will be pleased to know he has a ragana on his side.'

Klaey did not believe a word of what she was saying. Because she was refusing to take advantage of the possibility of regaining her ragana powers, the rhamak would have no use for her at all. Unless, of course, she was planning to offer herself as a companion to help warm his bed. But that was not the impression he had of this feisty young woman. *What does she really want from the rhamak?* 'So you know what he is?'

'Yes.'

'And you know his power?'

'I do. And you lot don't,' she replied contemptuously. 'Your brother Orweyn has no idea what sort of monster he has invited into his fortress. The reward he will receive for that invitation will be the loss of half of his people. That much is certain.'

Klaey was listening intently. He had actually been planning to get the ragana to heal his injured brother so that Orweyn could grant Hantu a completely free hand in dealing with the besieging army. Kawutan, the Berengart brother, had, on the other hand, acting as interim Omuthan, decisively rejected the rhamak's conditions, tearing up the paper with his demands. For the time being.

'Come on, let's get going!' Chòldunja pressed herself against his body. The blade she wielded transferred itself neatly as she slipped her arm through, under Klaey's shirt and the sand-coloured uniform jacket. The tip of the knife blade was now placed at the base of his spine. 'A stab to the spinal column and your life is over before you've drawn breath. The knife tip is coated with poison,' she explained, using her free hand to drape a stole over her face and shoulders. 'Raganas don't need magic to use their knowledge of plants.'

Klaey opened the door so that they could step out into the corridor.

'If anyone should ask who I am, then you say—'

'I'll tell them you're my latest whore. People will all believe that.' Klaey was not planning to try to get rid of Chòldunja.

She was giving him the opportunity to learn something about Hantu. This seemed vitally important. 'It's quite a distance. My brother Kawutan has put the rhamak up at the back of the fortress.'

'I'm not in any great hurry.'

They set off, locked in a close embrace.

'What do you know about this fellow?' Klaey put the question anew.

'So why is it you don't know anything about him?'

'I . . . well, at the moment I'm not in charge of what happens here in the fortress. They keep a lot of things secret,' Klaey had to admit. *I think I know what you are after.* Chòldunja would be wanting to get to the rhamak to kill him, thus making victory for the army laying siege to the fortress much more likely. *I shall put a stop to that. When an opportunity presents itself.*

'If I read you aright, you do not care much about the lives of your own people.'

'That's not so. But why should I care less about them because of Hantu, than about the army at the gates of Brigantia who are keen to wipe us all out? You, too, of course, if I may remind you.'

'You should ask your brother Orweyn. He's the one who summoned him.'

'Orweyn is confined to his sickbed. And he refuses to see me. Or rather, his deputy refuses to let me into his presence.'

Chòldunja's laughter was bitter. 'I'd wager the Omuthan has absolutely no idea what it is he has brought in. He probably thinks the rhamak is some kind of magus or a wizard.'

'Why don't you tell me more?'

'Why should I bother? As if you'd want to try to stop Hantu! You want your victory and you want to stay alive.'

By this point the ragana had shown him her true intentions in the matter. *She really wants to kill him. But she must realise she won't escape with her life if she kills him. If she's prepared to sacrifice herself to ensure the rhamak's death, it's clear that Hantu is a force for evil.* 'Convince me, go on.'

People were walking down the corridor towards them, not paying the couple any attention. Only one person called out a greeting to Klaey.

'I shan't be able to do that.' Chòldunja made a big show of fluttering her eyelashes at him, giving a splendid impression of being a street-walker. 'But it's true what I said about losing half the garrison. The rhamak is demanding something of that order if he is going to destroy a thousand of your enemy and all their siege engines for you.'

'How can he destroy them without magic?'

'He won't need any. His mind can summon up vicious beings from another sphere. Our magicians have no access to those other dimensions. The creatures are fed for the most part on blood. Or life-spirit, pure and simple.'

She lowered her head and her youthful face vanished from sight beneath the scarf she wore. 'Once these beings arrive there is nothing that can be done. There are no means of getting rid of them again.'

Now Klaey could understand why Kawutan had angrily torn up the paper with the demands. *It had been a list of the number of souls. The number of sacrifices.* Whereas Orweyn would probably have been ready to pay that price. Without the slightest compunction.

'I knew you didn't care. You brought me innocent infants to kill so I would help you.' Chòldunja spat out her contempt for him. 'You Berengarts have got to be eradicated. You have done nothing good for Girdlegard ever.'

'And it's a ragana who feels she can accuse me here?' Klaey had not enjoyed the task of providing infants to be eaten, but he was even less inclined to serve up hundreds of his own Brigantian people for slaughter.

'And I'm not a ragana anymore. Don't forget that. *Because* I refuse to take innocent lives.'

'I've long ago worked out your real intention in wanting to get to Hantu,' Klaey said thoughtfully. 'And it'll mean certain death for you.'

'My life is forfeit. Because I lost the moor diamond and because I let myself do something I should never ever have done. Why don't you think about those babies you dragged along, from wherever you got them?' Chòldunja pressed the knife tip harder. 'But put a happy face on, Berengart. You're supposed to be my lover and you're expecting a wonderful time in the sack soon.' She gave a high false laugh as another group of people came towards them, looking inquisitively at the pair.

'Oh, I shall make you so happy,' she said out loud, and surprised him by planting a kiss on his lips.

Even though Klaey was taken unawares by her play-acting, he did find he was quite enjoying it – and was also able to make use of it: moving his body forward meant his spine was further away from the tip of the knife.

He swiftly thrust his right elbow backwards and pushed Chòldunja's arm, holding the poisoned blade, away from his backbone; he made a half turn towards her and shoved her away from himself with the flat of his hand. There was a tearing sound as the knife blade slit through his shirt and his jacket. The Brigantians who had been strolling past were already round the corner.

The ragana cursed and pointed the knife at him. 'Get away from me, Berengart!'

Klaey chose not to draw his rapier. Instead he touched his lucky charm and kissed it. 'Do you want to get to Hantu without my help?'

'No other way.'

'I'd only have to call out and the guards will come running.'

Chòldunja held the knife hilt tight. 'So why haven't you shouted?'

'Your story about the rhamak has made me think. A victory involving the loss of half of our people would only help the älfar. It will be a breeze for them to take Brigantia once Hantu has moved on.'

'Good thinking. What are you going to do with the thought?' The ragana looked nervously to see if anyone was approaching.

She can still be useful. Klaey started to improvise.

'I'll help you—'

Growling fiercely, a black shadow with glowing eyes leaped out from a side corridor at Chòldunja and pushed her to the floor with its long snout. Her swift stabbing motion with the knife struck the hardened skin of the narshân beast and her blade shattered.

The creature's jaws snapped shut and its long fangs sank into the ragana's throat and tore it out. The scream the young woman gave turned into a wet, gurgling noise.

'No! No!' Klaey shouted, not daring to seize the wild creature, which was bigger than a wolf. 'Get off!'

But the narshân was not going to relinquish its prey. The brutal beast shook its head frantically, growling and grunting. It hurled the bleeding body of the girl gripped between its teeth to and fro. Then it moved backwards, dragging the girl as if she were a rag doll.

Klaey spread out his arms and waved them, shouting, trying to frighten the narshân beast. It was as long as he was tall and it was probably the same weight as he was. 'Get out of here!' he croaked.

The beast growled a warning, its large glowing eyes fixed on Klaey, its fangs still sunk in the girl's neck. The jaws opened and shut. Chòldunja's head was severed from her body as if sliced off with shears.

The armour-skinned black animal grabbed the girl's torso and was about to make its escape with it. Alarmed by the uproar, a detachment of guards turned up. The beast let go of the corpse and trotted off with an offended air.

Klaey dived down a side corridor and watched.

'Is that the . . . the ragana? It looks like the face off those posters we passed when we were retreating,' said one of the guards, coming closer and turning the severed head over with his foot so her features were visible.

'Yes, that's her. There's been a price on her head in Girdle-gard for some time. That devil of a narshân beast has done for her!'

The guards were busily exchanging theories and wild ideas about what could have happened here. How could the moor-witch have got into the fortress unnoticed? And who was going to collect on the reward that the other army had offered? And how could one claim the prize without risking capture oneself? And probably ending up being hanged?

Idiots. Klaey made use of the opportunity to disappear before he was noticed. *May the mother of Cadengis swallow them all up.* He had a good deal to reproach himself for. It was definitely his fault that Chòldunja had been killed by the narshân. It had been he who trained the narshân pack to her scent with old bits of her clothing. He had done the same for Rodana. The inten-tion had been to get the narshâns to track the women down in case they did ever escape. He had completely underestimated the strength of the beasts' hunting instinct, in spite of the kennel master's repeated warnings. However much of an incen-tive Klaey had offered him, the man had refused to guarantee the women's safety if tracked by a narshân.

He knew what he was talking about, obviously. The beast totally ignored my commands. Klaey was more upset by the ragana's death than he had expected. Her decision to eschew the use of her magical potential had brought her to a swift and ugly end. *No. It was me. It was me that killed her.*

He turned his steps back to the women's rooms, where the infants were still peacefully slumbering, unaware of the carnage. Klaey still had the taste of the young woman's kiss on his mouth. He felt it would stay on his skin for ever, as a reminder. As a warning. As a punishment. He would restore the babies safely to their mothers, as Chòldunja had insisted he do.

Klay was aware of an inner transformation brought about by the young girl's words to him, and he was also inspired by her readiness to sacrifice herself. Perhaps the gods were sending him a new sign, since the älfar woman had not come to meet him as arranged to hear his decision.

The siege must be lifted without Hantu's help. Kawutan would be able to rely on his assistance with this. Deep in thought, he rubbed his mouth, feeling for burn marks from Chòldunja's kiss. *She gave her life. Without—'*

'Hey, Banner Officer!' He heard the call behind him.

He stopped and turned around to face the guard, who was hurrying after him. 'What is it?'

'You're to come to the conference chamber. Your Omuthan wants to see you.'

'Tell Kawutan that I—'

'I mean the proper Omuthan. Not his deputy,' the guard interrupted, urging him to attend. 'Orweyn Berengart is out of his coma. Hurry. Get going!'

He indicated the badge on his shoulder showing his superior rank. 'At once.'

By Cadengis! Why now? That's all I need. Deeply uneasy, Klaey obeyed.

Girdlegard

In the Red Mountains
Realm of the Firstlings
Seahold (Eastern harbour)
1024 P.Q. (7515th solar cycle in old reckoning), winter

Xanomir Waveheart took a deep breath of the sea air that was blowing in over the land and wafting through his long curly hair and grey beard. The breeze carried the taste of departing winter and a sharp salty tang. It also brought the quayside sounds of work that was going on at the improvised wharf, which had once been the fortified town of Seahold. Xanomir could also hear the creaking of ropes from the many vessels tied up at the harbour wall. *Things are moving on. The black-eyes won't know what has hit them.*

People had rowed or sailed over to help from the surrounding villages and towns, bringing carpenters, craftsmen and materials to the stricken port as soon as news spread of the devastation and of the älfar defeat. Xanomir was struck by how the local communities were collaborating to assist the Firstlings with the reconstruction work.

'Are you coming? There are some questions only you can deal with.' Buvendil Shellgrip climbed up the scaffold built round his project so that he could check the exterior. Like his friend he was wearing a light tunic that did not get in the way when he was working. He had woven in some small black spiked shells to adorn his blond beard.

'Yes, of course.'

Xanomir had managed to attract a good half of the available workforce to help him on his special project, which had nothing to do with the reconstruction of the fortress. He had been delighted to find there were three ship builders: two male and one female. They had immediately understood what he was trying to do.

While he applied the beaten metal sheets to the outside of his submersible, his team of skilled workers were transforming a swift merchant ship that could carry his finished craft.

His invention could be quickly transported to wherever it was most needed for a diving task. His diving bell, which as yet still had no name, was too slow underwater and when it was up on the surface it tended just to bob around like a cork. The advantages of the invention were obvious once it was in place under the waves.

Few breaks in the work were allowed. They worked in shifts. Day and night were filled with the sounds of hammering, sawing, planning and generally improvising. The teams of craftspeople had nearly completed their work on both vessels. A test dive for the submersible was scheduled before they could wrap the project up.

'You're doing great.' Buvendil tapped the layer of thin metal. 'How deep can we go with this? We have to mind the under-water pressure.'

'I'm almost done here. Just got to check the welding seams. We ought to make it down to thirty paces without any trouble.'

'Thirty?' Buvendil's eyes were big with surprise. 'But this one's not like the *Elria Bonnet* with its thick walls. This is just . . . sheets of rolled tin. On wooden struts. Ten paces long, four paces high and two paces wide. It'll be a tight fit in there. And stuffy.'

Xanomir smiled at his friend, understanding his concern. 'Is that fear I can hear?'

'Respect for the sea, for the goddess Elria and for the under-sea currents,' Buvendil listed his worries and grinned back at Xanomir. 'Fear? Not really. No.'

Xanomir put an arm round his friend's shoulder and gave him a playful shake. 'Great! I want to have you at my side when we go diving with the fish.'

'I'm up for that.' Buvendil climbed up a couple of steps, curious to have a look through the upper access shaft. 'Did you manage to solve our drive problem?'

'Yes. I've put in a double-wheel wind-up clockwork mechanism. Cogwheels driving the propellors at the rear. If need be we can switch to manual if the springs or small cogs break. We've got the ballast tank that we can pump to empty it, we've got the adjustable weights for the dive and the external air containers,' Xanomir said, rattling off his new wheezes proudly. 'So we can stay down for four full sand-glasses without needing to surface.'

Buvendil looked at him admiringly. 'And you've sorted all that out in these last few orbits?' He fiddled with the black shell decorations in his beard.

'No, of course not. I had my plans ready to go all along in my head.'

'What? With all those details?' His friend shook his head in wonder. 'You've made an undersea boat quicker than anyone else could make a conventional one.'

'I've got the best blacksmiths and carpenters anyone could want. And with this model I've got the opportunity to sort out the faults that made my father's first one fail.' *Taking his life with it.*

'Elria will hate you. And love you.' Buvendil jumped down from the scaffolding. 'Have you got some kind of shooting device there at the back, or do my eyes deceive me?'

'I'll explain it all when we're at sea. Not here in the dry dock. You'll be stunned at what I've thought up.' Xanomir drummed on the thin but resistant tin wall of the craft. 'We'll be transforming the concept of marine warfare, dear fellow-engineer. We dwarves know what we are doing when it comes to moving about under the surface. Whether that's underground or underwater.'

The two of them hurried over to the completed transport vessel, which had been adapted using components from the damaged älfar ships. The wrecks had served as a source of spare parts and material for repairs.

Every time Xanomir looked at the improvements, he was filled with pride. Two additional lightweight masts had been installed and a couple of capstans at the bow, intended for sail-kites to be sent up to add speed if the wind was favourable. On either side of the narrow craft's stern there were outriggers for extra stability.

Alreth, the foreman for the team, came over, looking enthusiastic. 'It's going to be really great,' he said excitedly. This sturdily built giant had a layer of sawdust on his clothing and his leather apron and in his long black hair. 'Even with two diving boats on board she'd sail quicker than anything else on the water.'

'That's thanks to your good ideas.' Xanomir shook his hand. 'You've come up with some questions?'

Alreth grinned broadly. 'Only one.'

'Namely?'

'When?'

Xanomir was surprised. 'Could you—'

'*When* are we off?' He stepped aside so that the dwarves could admire the glorious-looking vessel. 'The *Sea Blade* is ready for her launch.'

The men and women on board the transporter craft raised a cheer, throwing their caps in the air, and breaking into applause for the dwarves and in recognition of their own skilled work.

'Let's bring invisible death over to the älfar, shall we? You two do the rest with your diving boat.' Alreth was stepping up the gangway on to the vessel.

'Come on board. I'll show you the latest improvements.'

'Amazing!' Xanomir called out, running up the plank to shake everyone's hands to thank and congratulate them for their work. 'May Elria and Vraccas bless you, one and all!'

The dwarves went along with the foreman to explore the whole ship and have everything explained. The Seablade's crew were already on board in their quarters or at their stations, waiting to hoist the red and white sails. The silk had been salvaged from the älfar wrecks and had been cleverly combined with the more conventional canvas rigging. In the hold where the undersea boat would be kept, Xanomir had requested the installation of a workshop so that running repairs could be carried out at sea.

'We haven't done a test run yet, but the Seablade under full sail can do at least twenty knots. The faster she is, the further she lifts up out of the water and the less resistance her keel and the outriggers offer to the waves,' said Alreth, concluding his guided tour on the main deck. 'It would be an honour to serve as her captain.'

'Who else, indeed? No one knows the ship better than yourself.' With the greatest of pleasure Xanomir stretched out his right hand. 'Unbelievable work.' He turned to the craftspeople, who all had tankards in their hands. 'From this orbit on the Seablade will be dedicated to the good of Girdlegard! Wherever injustice reigns we will be at hand!'

There was new applause from the ship's company and from the crowd on the quayside who had come along to admire the finished Seablade.

'When will your diving boat be ready?' Alreth enquired. 'We can lift it up with the hook and pulley mechanism and lower it straight down into the hold.'

'I want to try it out at least once in the harbour first. There's a lot to check: the drive, the seals, the steering,' Xanomir listed, earning an approving nod from Buvendil. 'If we find any snags we can get out easily and bring it to the surface.'

'That would be hard in open sea, of course. Getting it lifted up, I mean,' his friend chipped in.

'Watch out!' the lookout in the crow's nest called. 'The crane! It's about to fall on the diving boat!'

All eyes turned to the open wharf and there was a collective shriek of horror. The crane had broken free of its anchor points and the long arm was no longer horizontal but hanging diagonally, its point heading straight for the access shaft of the undersea boat.

If it falls now, it'll go straight through my craft like a nail hammered into an apple. 'Quick, Buvendil!' Xanomir raced down the creaking wooden gangplank to the quayside and shoved his way through the crowd.

'What's your plan?' His friend followed close on his heels.

He had no idea as yet. *One thing for sure: the crane must not be allowed to collapse in this direction.* 'Fetch rope and pulleys,' he shouted to the bystanders. 'Get a loop over the crane jib and pull as soon as it starts to fall. We have to adjust the line of descent. Over to the left!'

The people jumped into action to do what he had told them. Swift as the wind, weighted ropes were being cast up high to wrap themselves around the damaged jib of the crane. When the wooden arm gave way with a crack, Xanomir directed the workers to pull – and dozens of hands worked in unison. The movable jib arm plunged downwards and was jerked over to one side, so that it missed the diving boat by the decisive few paces, crashing to the ground and splintering into pieces.

Thanks be to the goddess Elria! Catastrophe averted! Xanomir was just drawing a breath to give a sigh of relief and join in the general rejoicing when all of a sudden they saw some of the scaffolding give way. The cascade of destruction continued at speed, with clanging and crashing. Any moment it would reach the wooden supports for the undersea craft. *We won't be able to stop it.*

Xanomir looked at Buvendil and Alreth. 'Quick!' he yelled through the excited noise of the crowd. 'Get the boat up on to the lifting hook!'

At this point Xanomir noticed the dark figure making its way out of the forest of wooden scaffolding. *No accidents, then! Sabotage!* 'Over there!' he shouted, pointing. 'Stop that man! He's a saboteur! Guards, arrest him!'

While Alreth and the crew of the *Sea Blade* immediately, having understood what to do, started deploying the ship's loading crane to get the submersible on to its hook, the dwarf's shout regarding the miscreant went unheard in the general uproar. Not until more and more of the wooden supports, scaffolding walkways and ladders crashed to the ground did the people move apart in horror. Xanomir set off after the saboteur but soon lost sight of him. The confusion on the quayside gave the evil-doer exactly what he needed to cover his escape. *Curses! Who was that?*

A shout was heard and one of the guards at the first fortification wall collapsed. It seemed that the saboteur had attempted to hide in the bastion's defence wall but had been found by the sentry. The watchmen up on the top walls answering the alarm call fired bolts and arrows at the figure in the long mantle.

At first the figure was able to avoid the rain of missiles, but the sixth crossbow bolt struck him in the chest and he went staggering. Thereafter he presented an easy target and collapsed in a veritable pool of blood, stuck with arrows.

Xanomir was first to arrive on the scene and saw the fine-featured face under the hood that had slipped. Even in death the eyes were clear and bright blue. The blood streaming out of the many wounds was fresh and red.

'It's an elf!' he exclaimed in astonishment. 'What on earth was it doing that for?'

'Stand aside! Let me through.' An officer approached and examined the dead body and casually pulled out the arrows and crossbow bolts so he could check the clothing. He was unaffected by all the blood. 'The pointy-ears doesn't have anything on him. Oh, except for this here.' He held up the remains of a broken glass tube. 'This is not good news,' he murmured, sniffing it. 'No smell at all. A few drops left. We'll have to get an alchemist to check them out.'

I think I know what the results will show. The älfar were known to have found a way, not only to affect a permanent colour change to their eyes, but also to give their blood a harmless appearance, feigning innocence.

'This one certainly won't have been acting in isolation,' Xanomir said to Buvendil, who had run up to him, gasping for breath from the exertion. 'We'll load up the diving craft on to the *Sea Blade* and make for open sea.'

'Good idea. We can do the trials, checking the seams and the workings in shallow water somewhere.'

'No. We sail for Undarimar. The älfar know all about our submersible now and they know they can't defend themselves against it. Not yet, that is. Before they've worked out how to deal with it I want to have sunk their entire fleet.'

'But ... what if there's some fault in the—' Buvendil countered.

'Well, we'll find out soon enough, won't we?' Xanomir interrupted and turned back to the quay. Chances were, the next act of sabotage the älfar and their allies attempted would be successful. He had to avoid this at all costs.

You know the elf realm Tî Silândur.

It is ruled by a child empress called Kisâri, whose appearance never alters. She is said to be a virgin. And has been, apparently, for four hundred cycles. Because as long as she refuses the advances of any elf or mortal suitor, she stays looking the same and she keeps her hold on power.

The Kisâri is said to have special capabilities. She is thought to be intrinsically linked to the natural world and able to influence nature anywhere in Tî Silândur. But she is also closely linked to death, which makes many fear that the Kisâri may have älfar blood.

Ucerius, priest of Palandiell

VII

Girdlegard

Empire of Gautaya
1024 P.Q. (7515th *solar cycle in old reckoning), winter*

'By the axe of Lorimbur! It's grabbed Goïmron and taken him off!' Gata cried out, distraught, gesturing at the two-headed dragon far away in the sky, after the whirling cloud of ash and snow had descended on the clearing. 'It will eat him alive!'

The battle was still raging between the remaining älfar and Slibina on the one side, and Fortgard troops together with the besieging army with Telìnâs and Sònuk on the other.

'No. Szmajro doesn't want to eat him or he'd have gobbled him up straight away, right here, wouldn't he?' Brûgar ducked to avoid an arrow whirring towards him. He battered an unsuspecting älf, striking him in the face with his vicious war flail, dislodging the metal visor. His adversary was floored and lay there, gasping for breath. 'Let's deal with this lot of black-eyes first and this dragon of theirs. They are our immediate concern.' To make certain of his opponent he struck him again, shattering the älf's skull. 'Telìnâs is manning the catapult. He'll keep the scaled monster off us.'

Gata watched Szmajro fly off. She cried out in frustration and swept her axe sword through the air. 'How can you be so sure?'

'Believe me, Queen. Our gem cutter will be all right. He's got magic on his side.' Brûgar dodged some more arrows and looked around to identify his next victim.

'Did I hear you say he's got access to *magic*?' Surprised, Gata turned to face him.

'That's right. I suspected it at the time of the Two-Stream Hill battle.' Brûgar took the queen by the arm and pulled her to safety. 'He's got this sapphire thing – it's in a dragon-shaped setting. Must be from the maga's artefact hoard. Don't worry about him. He probably wanted Szmajro to carry him away like that.' He attempted an encouraging smile. 'I'll wager he'll be flying off with the dragon to the Fourthling stronghold and he'll be annihilating the Brigantians by now.'

May Lorimbur be at his side! If that were the case, Gata thought, she would not expend further effort worrying about Goïmron, however difficult this was. After all, she could do absolutely nothing about the situation herself. 'You're quite right. Let's deal with these enemies here.'

Brûgar pointed ahead to the figures of Slibina and the älfar sorceress. 'These two are ours. Let's show the black-eyes we're not afraid of any dragon. No matter how big she is. And despite her three magic horns.' He got to his feet and raced along the path that was clogged with dead bodies, horse cadavers and fallen tree trunks. 'Follow me, my queen!'

'You'd enjoy that, wouldn't you? No. *You* follow *me*, if you please, not the other way round!' She pushed her fears for Goïmron's safety to the back of her mind and sprinted past Brûgar, heavy axe sword in her hand.

Under covering fire from Telìnâs and Sònuk, who had set up and manned the two heavy-duty bolt-firing catapults, Gata and Brûgar set off together with a handful of dwarves and some soldiers from Fortgard, to get closer to the dragon.

Seen from up close, the monster was impressive: the height of a house and thirty paces in length. Conventional blades would, in the dragon's present incarnation, be utterly useless against her hardened rust-brown scales. That option was over and done with. Gata gave the command to target the älf woman first. If the dragon's controller were killed, Slibina would surely either flee or be easier to fight with. *At least, I hope so.*

The Fortgard troop numbers were by now worryingly small. Obrist Emaro Staine led them bravely to attack the devious älf woman, who was using her innate magic powers against the human soldiers. The attacking forces were overcome by paralysing moments of darkness and fear. The enemies were merciless in taking advantage of this, slaughtering to the right and to the left with swords and daggers.

There came the abrupt sound of a horn signal, summoning two thousand Fortgard reinforcements to come galloping in along the pathway through the fire to join the fray. The last of the ice blocks had been manoeuvred into place and the meltwater had extinguished the flames.

The continuous hail of heavy metal bolts and spiked balls was starting to affect Slibina. Gata could see the wounds inflicted on the dragon's brownish-black scales, and she caught sight of the boiling bright-red blood coursing down in streams. Whenever the mighty beast attempted to destroy the trebuchets, Telìnâs and Sònuk increased their fire, targeting the creature's sensitive snout and eyes.

She may have changed shape but she's still a young, inexperienced dragon. Ûra or Ardin would certainly have wiped out their opponents by now.

The soldiers righted the catapult transporters that had been overturned and they got the devices ready for action. The steel rain attacking the dragon swelled to a torrent and there were several holes in the creature's wings.

Gata and Brûgar reached the älf, who had discarded her heavy fur mantle to fight in a leather armour covering. In her left hand she wielded an elegantly curved sword blade against four soldiers. The way she moved made the interplay look less like deadly combat and more like a dance, at the end of which, however, all four brave Fortgard souls lay dead in the ashes at her feet. The one white and one black eye in the parti-coloured face gave her the appearance of a vengeful demon of death, dispatched by Tion and Inàste personally.

An arrow whirred across, unseen by the älf. The metal adornment on her forehead glowed brightly and the arrow was deflected from her person a good arm's length away without her having had to use a spoken spell.

She is protecting herself using only artefact magic. Gata signalled to the impetuous Brûgar coming up in her wake not to attack. *We need Mostro and his special formulae. Urgently!*

All of a sudden the battlefield fell oddly quiet. The catapult fire stopped.

When Gata looked round, she saw every one of their älfar adversaries stretched out dead on the ground, pierced with missiles, or upright, stuck through with pikes. All, that is, except for the sorceress herself. Troops from Fortgard had encircled the maga. Slibina was up on all four legs, hissing threateningly and sending fearsome roars in all directions, but apparently not daring to launch an actual attack.

Working together with the soldiers, Telìnâs and Sònuk were exchanging the catapult magazines and re-tightening the springs. The machines were aimed towards the dragon and the maga.

'Don't anyone move,' Mostro commanded in a decisive tone. His input was completely superfluous in the circumstances, since no one was moving.

'He's as much of a fool now as he was in his speech at the hill,' commented Brûgar quietly, speaking to his sovereign. He made use of the pause in the action to take out his war pipe and stick it firmly between his teeth. 'I hope the silly wand-fiddler has got all the right spells off by heart.'

'Be ready,' Gata replied. 'As soon as the protective glow of her jewellery fades, we attack. Tell the others.' She grasped her axe sword, her light-coloured eyes fixed on this, the final opponent.

'A female älf who can do magic.' Mostro was obviously enjoying his big moment. The troops made way for him, closing the gap behind him again as he walked through to the edge of the circle. He was dressed in a sable mantle of a grandeur that would not have disgraced an emperor. For the purposes of appearing on the battlefield he had replaced the fur cap with a sparkling metal helmet shaped like a crown. 'What a miracle Inàste has sent us with you. Although it is not one that pleases me at all.'

The älf woman's uncanny eyes looked him up and down. 'So you are the famulus who bestowed that resounding defeat on your own Omuthan.' She stood very erect and waved nonchalantly behind her to indicate the presence of Slibina. 'It won't be so easy this time. A forty-pace-long dragon you will find more difficult to fight.'

'Best not to avoid the obvious conclusion here. You have as good as lost. Surrender and I will spare your life,' Mostro announced pompously. (And without having consulted Gata, which made the queen furious.) 'Slibina is to obey me from now on,' Mostro declared. 'I offer you, in return, the chance to leave Girdlegard without a hair of your head being harmed.'

Astonished murmurs were heard among the allied troops, for whom Mostro's promises were not to everyone's liking.

'To Tion with the idiot! Any moment now I'm going to finish him off myself!' Brûgar spluttered into his blue-dyed beard. The bowl of his pipe glowed brightly because he was drawing in his breath so hard. 'What on earth is going on in his little brain?'

'Only stupid thoughts.' Gata felt unable to continue watching this scene without stepping in. She strode forward to Mostro's side. 'I am Regnorgata Mortalblow of the clan of the Orc Slayers, queen of the Thirdlings,' she said, by way of introduction. 'What's your name? And what are you?'

'What are you doing?' Mostro hissed at her out of the corner of his mouth.

'Me? Gaining us some time,' she responded quietly. 'It will give you every opportunity to get your spells sorted so you can break through her magic barrier. This black-eyes will not be leaving the Wonder Zone alive. Focus on her ornaments. She's got a protective artefact.' Aloud she said, 'We had no idea that the älfar were able to employ magic arts.'

'And I did not expect it of a groundling either,' the unusual figure responded. 'And a dwarf, above all, who has managed to abscond with one of my dragons. It seems that Girdlegard is witnessing the dawn of a new age. Don't you agree, of the Thirdling queen?'

'What?' laughed Mostro. 'That ... Goïmron ... does ... magic, you say? By Palandiell!'

'Indeed he does,' the älfar maga confirmed. 'I saw a sea sapphire in his hand. He used it to destroy my magic wall.'

'No! Never! It was thanks to *me*! I destroyed your barrier.' Mostro was getting agitated. Too excited to be credible. The allied troops were starting to protest more loudly. 'Apart from Famula Adelia and the Esteemed Maga Vanéra and myself, nobody knows how to break a protective spell. Nobody else, do you hear?'

'Indeed. I hear you. But you seem to have overlooked my own arts, Famulus.' The älf wiped her bloodied sword on the carcass of a fallen Fortgarder. 'You were asking, Queen, who or what I am. My name is Ascatoîa, and I am a zhussa. If you really believe that you and your friends can defeat me in battle, let me tell you now that you are wrong. You will die.'

'Absolutely not!' Mostro opened his fists and spread his hands, palm up, displaying a white nephrite and a dark green jasper stone, both emitting sparks. 'We are in the new Wonder Zone here. Magic energy is bubbling up within me, Zhussa! I know lots of spells, with which I can—'

'So do you actually know what a zhussa is?' Ascatoîa interrupted Mostro's self-important flow. 'Do you know what I am capable of? Or what Slibina can do, now she has been transformed? I changed her nature by infusing älfar blood into her circulation with a bolt of magic lightning.'

Gata saw Mostro's arms begin to shake. *He has absolutely no idea.*

'You are to be killed, if need be. And your dragon, too,' Gata responded.

'I am aware that the famulus was speaking out of turn just now. I see he did not have your permission to make his generous offer,' said Ascatoîa. 'So let *me* make you one. I am speaking with the authority from the Ganyeios, who told me to say this.' She slowly replaced her sword in its scabbard. 'Dsôn Khamateion offers you a free hand in Brigantia. Take over the fortress, kill the Brigantians and whatever else is roaming around in the tunnels and corridors. The Fourthlings are to be allowed to return to the Brown Mountains. We will leave them in peace as long as Girdlegard is prepared to leave us älfar similarly unhindered. Remember that in the Two-Stream Hill battle we did not attack. We left you to savour that victory.' She placed one hand on her breast and the ornaments on her torso glowed brightly, as if to emphasise her words. 'I can promise you this in the name of the Ganyeios. He suggests you send a representative delegation to negotiate further treaty details.'

Mostro shot Gata a worried glance. He closed his hands round the jasper and the nephrite. 'We will discuss it as soon as we reach the siege. Is that correct, Queen Regnorgata?'

The älfar would never countenance an agreement of that nature. *They want the whole of Girdlegard under their yoke. They plan to enslave the entire population and exterminate the elves.* Gata considered this offer to have been a bold deception on the part of the zhussa. A trick. But at the same time the queen was attracted to part of the suggestion. 'Tell me, what has prompted this change of attitude?'

'Do not confuse us with those other älfar who lived in your homeland in the past,' Ascatoîa said. 'The ones that called themselves the Originals were certainly not keen to achieve peace. But we are.'

Brûgar exploded. 'You've changed, have you? That's a good one, Black-and-White-Eyes. Because you're from the Outer Lands? Is that it?'

'We were *always* different, but you misunderstood us.'

'Oh, I see. *Misunderstood*,' the dwarf exclaimed, outraged. 'How comes it that a black-eyes with a rune spear offers us his services and those of his pig-face underlings—'

'Brûgar!' warned the queen, reprimanding him.

For two heartbeats Ascatoîa's eyes narrowed and black anger lines flashed across her visage as if her inner fury were trying to break out of her and burst into a thousand pieces. 'We need the dragons to protect us. To protect us from *you*. If you are bent on destroying Dsôn Khamateion's very existence, then we will annihilate you. We already sent you a warning to that effect. Think what happened to the delegations. Our assassins.' She spoke calmly, while stepping slowly backwards. With each step she floated up further from the ground until she was on Slibina's back. Her magic adornments flared up once more. The young dragon's injuries healed over and the bleeding stopped.

'Take Brigantia and be content with that. We are not the enemies of Girdlegard. But beware of Mòndarcai. He is a liar and a cheat.'

'Mostro,' Gata murmured. 'Are you ready? She'll be flying off any moment if we don't stop her.'

Slibina raised her head with its three magic horns and blew hot fire-breath out of her nostrils. She stretched out her wings, about to take off.

'If you attack me or my dragon, Ascatoîa shall be the name your death bears,' the zhussa said calmly, as she stroked the rust-brown scales of the dragon's skull with her right hand. 'Let me leave and we have a deal.'

The powerful muscles of the dragon's hindquarters tensed as the creature readied itself for a vertical leap into the air.

'Mostro!' Gata's head shot round to challenge him. 'Aren't you going to do anything?'

The dragon's wings beat down once and Slibina took off. The wind of their passage sent up clouds of grey and white flakes, whirling them over into the faces of the Fortgard troops and their allies. Gata waited in vain for the famulus to cast some kind of spell that would stop the dragon escaping. Or for some wizardry that would bring Slibina and the zhussa crashing down. 'You are a useless coward!' she whispered into this artificial storm, which fell away instantly. The noise of the dragon's wings grew fainter and there was an irritating whistling sound the air made as it passed through the holes. 'A coward and an incompetent. To Tion with you! In my eyes you will always be a failure of a famulus, too scared to enter a fight.' Gata turned away. 'To horse, everyone! We have to get back to Brigantia. Our powerful would-be magus is overwhelmed with his own strength. We need to take advantage of it.'

After several steps she heard Mostro's pathetic voice behind her. 'I shall never forget or forgive your insulting words, Thirdling Queen!'

I don't want you to. Gata spat in his direction and went to get her horse. Part of her was glad that Ascatoîa had got away unharmed. This meant that, according to what the zhussa had said, there were grounds for a treaty with Dsòn Khamateion.

Girdlegard

In the Brown Mountains
Brigantia
1024 P.Q. (7575th solar cycle in old reckoning), winter

Rodana could be seen from afar, hurrying along the first fortified walkway, a leather roll in her hand. She was breathing heavily under the weight of the helmet she was wearing. *How on earth can anyone fight in one of these?*

She had garnered this headgear, together with a Brigantian tunic and a stamped leather pouch, in an opportunistic visit to the supplies chamber. The helmet covered her face, hiding her otherwise conspicuously dark lips, and it would also protect her from enemy fire. The leather roll made her look like a messenger on a legitimate errand to deliver orders to the next command post on the ramparts. Nobody challenged her or tried to stop her. Her mission was too important.

Rodana was actually just running to and fro in search of a convenient place from which she could get over the fortress walls. She had not been able, given the lack of time, to locate any of the secret gateways at the foot of the stone structure, so she was steeling herself for the long climb down. She had got herself two rolls of rope, each of them fifteen paces in length, and had secured them ready to hand.

She would have to wait for an opportune moment when she would not be seen by either Brigantians or the besieging army.

The former would think her a spy trying to escape from the fortress, and the others would think she was a saboteur tasked with immobilising the giant war-wolf catapults or maybe intending to poison the water supply. In either eventuality, she would be shot on sight.

Rodana looked up at the evening sky, now gradually growing dark. With the present amount of cloud cover there was a good chance it would soon snow again. *Perfect conditions for my escape.*

The leather padding on the inside of the metal helmet stank of stale sweat. Rodana found it impossible to imagine how anyone could stand wearing the thing for longer than a single sandglass. And it must be utterly unbearable in summer.

She had picked out a location on the northern side of the first ring of ramparts where she thought she could get down, using one of the ropes, to where there was a large wooden bolt sticking out of the masonry. This was where she tied the second rope. The bolt must have been fired by the army attacking Brigantia. They had probably been intending to anchor a siege ladder to it.

All in all, there was a drop of about eighty paces to overcome before she could reach the snow-covered ground. A little further down, wedged into the stonework, there was a broken spiked metal ball. It reminded her of a horse chestnut case. However much she disliked the idea, from then on she would have to improvise and find something to help her climb down the rest of the way.

As soon as the snowstorm hits I can make a start. She moved out of the wind to shelter beside one of the corner towers. She would not be seen by the sentries here. The Brigantians were supposed to think she was collecting new orders from the section commander's office. *Palandiell and Samusin, I beseech you, be gracious.*

The warning about the sudden appearance of the rhamak

called Hantu must reach the besieging army or the victory at Two-Stream Hill would have been in vain. No one would know anything yet about the Omuthan's unexpected new ally, because Goldhand and his companions thought the way through from the Outer Lands had been sealed shut. That was true, of course. But evil enough had been able to slip through before the closure had been affected.

The wind got up. Snowflakes from the heavy clouds started to swirl through the air, reducing the visibility. *Good!* Rodana blew on her hands to warm them, and tightened the tunic belt to keep out the cold draught. *I should have stolen an extra uniform.* She would definitely need to organise some gloves before starting the descent. Fingers stiff with cold would make climbing down dangerous. And naked skin would stick painfully to any metal items she used. What she would do once she reached the foot of the wall she would decide in situ. *First the dangerous descent. Once that's done, then I'll see about the rest.*

From the far side of the corner tower she heard the sound of snuffling. A long black snout, like a wolf's muzzle, appeared – but it was the size of one belonging to an isegrim. Instead of fur the creature had tiny dark scales like snakeskin.

Rodana realised what the creature was that was approaching her, catching her scent. *It was one of the narshân beasts.* Without knowing how the idea occurred, she realised it was her that the predator was seeking. *Curses!*

She quickly climbed up three or four paces over the top of the tower's oriel window and looked down. The beast had its nose to the ground on the walkway below. Its ears were pricked up – and suddenly it wheeled round and stared at the puppet mistress with glowing white eyes. The whirling snow reflected the light.

'Be off with you! Find something else to hunt!' she called out, climbing higher still. If she went over the roof she could access a side arch that would take her back over to the wall. *But what good is that if this horrid animal wants to eat me? It'll certainly run quicker than I can.*

'What are you doing up there?' came a man's surprised shout. The guardsman, in helmet and mantle, had some kind of silver badge on his shoulder that she did not recognise. 'Aren't you supposed to be delivering messages?' He stroked the growling narshân beast's black head.

'That's what I was trying to do. But that thing of yours was not letting me. It probably hasn't been fed,' Rodana answered. 'It seems to think I'm its dinner.'

'That's odd. It *has* just been fed, the kennel master told me.' The soldier was about to pull the beast back into the guard-room by the scruff of its neck. But the growling got louder and more threatening. 'There you are! It seems to have taken a real dislike to you for some reason.'

'It's mutual.' Rodana lifted the leather pouch. 'I've got to get on. These orders have got to go back to the north wall. The idiot scribe gave me the wrong ones for you. I've just checked the seal. Can you keep that animal off me?'

The armoured guardsman closed the wrought iron door to the tower, cutting off the part of the walkway behind the beast. 'Climb over the roof and go quick. I'll try and calm the animal down and explain that messengers are not food. Or playthings.'

'How come the beast obeys you?' With fingers numb with cold, Rodana started to climb. She hoped the sentry would not notice the black tips to her fingers and get curious.

The sentry showed a pendant he had round his neck. 'This has the special smell they like. All the zabitay commanders wear these. I'm surprised you don't know that.'

'Oh yes, that's it. I was concentrating on not getting eaten. I think messengers should have those as well.' Rodana made no further enquiries about where the pendant was from. She did not want to risk arousing suspicion. 'I'll be back soon. Then I'll have the proper message for you, zabitay.' She went quickly over the little roof and used the side archway to take her to the part of the walkway the guard had made safe for her.

Rodana ran off while gusts sent snowflakes in through her visor. The crystals felt ice cold as they met her skin and melted.

And of course she was having second thoughts.

The fact that the narshân beast had seemed to be tracking her probably had a different cause. Not hunger. Like a bloodhound it had been specifically hunting her down. The beast had not threatened any of the other soldiers on the walkway. Rodana supposed this was due to Klaey Berengart's having wanted to be sure his valuable prisoner did not escape. *It doesn't look as though it was going to deliver me nicely to Berengart. It would have savaged me.* Rodana was glad to note that the visibility was even worse now. She could hardly see further than the length of her outstretched arm. No more time to look for suitable gloves. She wanted to be away from the wall before that zabitay let go of the narshân.

Her two prepared climbing ropes, knotted at regular intervals for hand-holds, were in place. She coiled one over her shoulder and fastened one end of the other to the battlements and let the rope down on the outside of the wall. Reassuring herself that no one was watching, she swung herself over the coping stones and let herself down on the thick rope. The knots made hand-over-hand progress relatively easy.

Reaching the end of the rope in the midst of a blizzard, she was relieved to locate the large wooden bolt stuck in a crack between the stones of the wall. *Exactly where I expected I'd find it.* She fashioned a loop with a quick-release knot and fastened the second rope firmly. Down again she climbed, starting from the bolt, step by step, knot by knot. She was losing all feeling in her fingers. The whirling snow made it impossible to judge distances – and for all she knew, the ground might be a mile away or perhaps just a little jump. There was no difference. *Except if I fall.*

Her toes encountered the broken spiked metal ball. It gave a little under her weight. Anchored in the stonework by only two of the spikes, it was unlikely to be stable for long. *I'll have to be very quick.* Rodana stepped on to the projectile and released the rope, tying it again to one of the spikes, then abseiled further down. The muscles in her arms were threatening to cramp and her hands were so cold she found it difficult to grip.

She had worked her way past several of the rope-knots when something snakelike rushed down past her. *That's my first rope! They must have found it.* It would not be long before they would be chucking stones and the gods knew what else over the wall on the off chance of hitting whoever had used the rope.

Speeding up her descent, she soon reached the end of the rope, but could find nothing suitable to reattach it to. According to her calculations there must be about thirty-five paces still to cover. With the ground iced over, the impact of the fall would certainly kill her. *I need to swing on the rope like a pendulum to see if I can find an anchor point.* She sent a prayer up to Samusin. *Please let it hold!* She placed her feet on the wall and began to walk one way and the other in search of something suitable, maybe a snapped-off spear or a missile lodged in the masonry.

The arcs she described on the end of her rope got wider and wider. The combination of half-light and blizzard meant Rodana could hardly see anything at all. She felt with her free hand and found – nothing.

Without any warning a huge stone whizzed past, only just missing her. The fortress's defenders were obviously able to aim at her because they could hear the rope creaking and the sound her feet made on the wall.

Can't do this for much longer! Her strength was ebbing away. *I—*Another stone hit the anchorage point supporting her rope and the projection broke off. Then the loop slipped and she was on the point of falling.

No! I'll never make it alive! Grabbing the hefty rope with both hands, she could only pray that it would snag on something.

With a sudden jerk the rope caught on the shaft of a bolt that had recently been fired at the walls. She let out a cry of joy – until a small boulder struck her. Her cry of joy changed swiftly to a shout of pain as a hot stabbing spasm from her shoulder numbed her arm, opening her grip, and she fell again.

After a short drop she landed in a drift of powdery snow at the foot of the wall. She felt herself sinking down as if she were on soft ice-cold blankets. The snow crystals closed over her as if they wanted to protect her from any more missiles thrown down from the ramparts.

I've done it! Gasping for breath, she struggled out of the mound of snow, spluttering. There was snow inside her clothes. *I've made it! I'm down!*

Missiles were hurtling her way, some stones as big as a fist. Then came two leather bags of flaming pitch. They burst on impact with the ground, illuminating the area, the contents splashing out far and wide but not touching her. She staggered forward to get out of range. The blizzard meant it was impossible to know which direction she was going in. Nothing but whirling whiteness all around.

Suddenly a round shield shot up in front of her, hitting her in the chest and face. Stunned, Rodana fell backwards on to the snow. She glimpsed an angry pair of dark eyes glaring at her from inside an ice-encrusted scarf.

'A saboteur!' the man shouted. 'I've got him.' Her helmet was yanked off, revealing her chin-length blonde hair. 'Don't move or I'll slit your throat.'

More armoured soldiers emerged from the snowstorm, wearing heavy-duty mantles. They all had their spears pointing at her.

'She's not a saboteur! That's the puppet woman!' one of the female warriors declared in surprise. 'You know – she's friends with the child-eater witch. There's a price on her head.'

'She could still be planning sabotage, though,' insisted the man who had caught her. 'The reward is mine!'

'Then why not knock her head off and let's get out of here,' the female soldier suggested. 'The Brigantians have seen us and they're chucking down stones and firebombs and being very unfriendly. I have no intention of turning into a flaming torch for their amusement, even if I am freezing my whatnots off in this weather.'

This was greeted with coarse laughter from her companions.

Rodana tried hard to explain why she had escaped, but her mind was less than clear since being hit on the head with that shield. She was not producing much more than stammers and groans. *Don't let this be happening! I escaped from that narshân beast safely but now I'll be ending up dead all for the sake of the price on my head.*

'I have to speak to Goldhand,' she finally managed to stutter.

'I'll take you,' the man replied, pressing the tip of his spear to her throat. 'Well, I'll take your head. That'll do. You'll have a nice quick death. Heads don't always come off easy.'

Rodana felt the spear tip poke in under her skin and then it was suddenly pulled back out. There was a loud clang and a muffled shout from the warrior, who fell to one side.

A black-bearded dwarf appeared and stood in front of her, protecting her. His long-handled battleaxe was still raised. He must have hit the soldier with the flat side. She recognised the traditional kilted black armour often adopted by Thirdlings that he wore under his heavy mantle. The insignia were also familiar to her. *Thanks be to Samusin!*

'Belîngor,' she groaned. 'I absolutely have to see Goldhand. The Brigantians have got a terrible ... There's such danger for you all! I must tell him.'

'Oy! *I'm* having that reward money. Get off her!' the furious soldier yelled, staggering back up to his feet. The three-man group united against the dwarf, drawing their weapons and circling him like a pack of wolves closing in on their prey.

Rodana wanted to get up but the silent dwarf pushed her back down into the snow with his foot, all without taking his eyes off the guards. He swapped his grip on the axe handle from hand to hand and then whirled the heavy blade over his head as a sign he was not prepared to back down and yield to the superior numbers.

'We don't want to hurt you,' said the female warrior, obviously wanting a sensible outcome. 'Come on, we're all allies, aren't we? It's surely not worth fighting over among ourselves.'

'For *that* reward? Oh, yes, it certainly is!' came the challenge from her fellow soldier. 'Watch it, dwarf! We'll just knock you about a bit. But if you were to die while we were doing that, then–'

'Hang on! Just wait!' the third soldier broke in. 'This bloke is one of Goldhand's friends. I recognise the axe and the runes on his face. We can't do away with him.'

'But now he knows that we'd have done away with any other groundling,' the man objected. Belîngor motioned to the group to go away.

The three warriors looked at each other and hesitated. Now it had become more than a question of losing the reward, more a matter of punishment they could expect from their superiors for an egregious action. And that penalty was unlikely to be insignificant.

From the fortress walls there came a clink and a scraping sound and suddenly, out of the snow flurries, a black shadow

MARKUS HEITZ | 193

the size of a wolf sprang at them into the circle of burning pitch lights. It struck at one of the soldiers with one paw, its claws slicing through mantle, leather armour and flesh beneath. Blood spurted out in an arc, freezing into solid drops in mid-air and raining down on to Rodana. The creature's long black muzzle opened wide and shining white fangs buried themselves in the screaming warrior's back, making the man fall to the ground. The creature was intent on biting through the man's spine despite the layers of cloth and metal.

It's that narshân beast! Rodana was utterly petrified. *Did it follow me over the wall?*

The two remaining soldiers beat at the predatory animal. One of their swords broke in half on impact with the armoured hide. The other's blade was as damaged as if it had been used against a granite boulder.

Barking furiously, the narshân beast pounced at the female soldier, who was only just able to protect herself with her shield before she was hurled to the snowy ground by the beast leaping at her. The creature planted its front legs on her chest, its jaws snapping at her face. She fell silent at once. Her helmet buckled and her bones were crunched.

Rodana sat up and looked round for some weapon she could use in order to come to the dwarf's defence. If Belîngor were to succumb to this predator she herself would stand no chance.

Belîngor raised his weapon for a mighty blow. The sharp end of the axe blade smashed straight into the open maw of the monstrous creature, just as it was snapping at the third soldier. The axe head slid along the line of teeth but its progress was halted when the jaws slammed shut.

Belîngor abruptly released his hold on the axe shaft and delivered a kick to the blunt end so that the axe blade dug deeper into the beast's mouth where the hardened scales were less in evidence. Glowing white blood dripped out of the gaping wound and the narshân beast sprang back, howling with fury and pain, and trying desperately to shake the axe out. But the polished steel blade was buried in the jawbone.

Furiously snarling, the narshân beast attacked the fleeing survivor with its claws, slicing open the man's belly. Then it turned for Belîngor. Growling, it crouched down, ready to spring, the axe still in its jaw.

Rodana had in the meantime struggled to her feet, picking up the dead female soldier's sword. Adrenalin surged through her. 'What do we do?'

The dwarf without a word picked up the two round shields and held them in front of himself before stomping forward towards the narshân. When the creature leaped, Belîngor rushed forward with a shout. The two of them clashed together in mid-air and fell to the ground in a furious knot. The snow covered them and their struggle was hidden from sight by the blizzard. Then there came the sound as if of a heavy tree branch breaking.

Rodana staggered past the corpses of the three soldiers. 'Belîngor?' She screwed up her eyes against the snow to see better.

She saw the dwarf standing, panting with exertion, next to the wild monster. He had both hands on the handle of his axe. The vicious creature's eyes were wide open and had lost their previous glow. Belîngor was obviously using the axe shaft as a lever, twisting the animal's head round to break its neck. As no blade could pierce the creature's armoured coat, this dangerous method of attack was the only approach Belîngor could take.

'Praise be to Vraccas,' she exclaimed, dropping her sword before sinking into the dwarf's arms. 'Take me to Goldhand,' she mouthed, all her energy now vanished. 'As quick as you can!'

What walks on four feet in the morning, two at noon, and three in the evening?

A drunken orc, a sobering orc, and three one-legged orcs running away from the battlefield.

Traditional dwarf riddle

VIII

Girdlegard

United Great Kingdom of Gauragon
Province of Fire
1024 P.Q. (7515th solar cycle in old reckoning), winter

Barbandor came to with a start when his cage was plonked down unceremoniously. The noise and the jolt were a stimulus to his thinking but painful for his body. 'Oy. Gently! Mind how you're doing that! You won't want your dinner covered in bruises, now, will you?' he muttered, poking his nose out of the mass of blankets and furs he had wrapped himself in. Ice crystals and snowflakes fell out of the plaits in his dark beard. The sun was high in the winter sky but the air was freezing cold.

Borkon stood in front of the dwarf's portable prison cell and pointed forward. 'Now you will witness the start of something bigger than we can ever have imagined,' he announced sententiously. 'Or it might all end in less than half a sandglass. For me, my companions, and possibly also for you.' He took a step to one side.

Barbandor gazed at the fortress standing proud in the flat landscape. It was surrounded by a deep ditch. *Kràg Tahuum!*

So often he had heard merchants and other travellers speak of this orc stronghold. The reports had always seemed exaggerated. But now he could see this hundred-pace, deep-cut defensive ditch with his own eyes. The moat was spanned by broad bridges, one from each point of the compass. Above, one saw the stepped curtain walls with corner defence towers, enclosing an area at least one thousand by one thousand paces. *In the name of the Eternal Smith! So it's true, what folk always said!*

In the centre there was an unadorned building several storeys high. It sported towers that were either round or seven-sided, reaching way above the height of the defence walls. How it might look behind those walls, Barbandor could not imagine.

Orcs were not generally known for their sense of order or aesthetics, so the perfection of these edifices in Kràg Tahuum surprised him. The architectural style was unfamiliar. To assess the quality of the stonework he would have had to get much nearer.

There'll be room for thousands in there. Hundreds of thousands perhaps. Barbandor started to laugh. 'You want to capture Kràg Tahuum with a handful of warriors? Twenty against a whole army? Is *that* your plan?'

'That's why I said: either it starts now or it ends here pretty soon – something really great.' Borkon tapped on the roof of the wooden cage, whose bars were fastened together with rope and wire. 'Your eyes will be witnessing events on behalf of all the residents of Girdlegard. I think you know the honour you bear.'

Barbandor would rather have had the honour of a good tankard of beer. A dead orc would have pleased him, too. *But this?* 'Are you going to get them to join forces with you by winning the womenfolk over like you did with the fire eaters?'

Borkon nodded so earnestly that Barbandor was inclined to laugh again, but he controlled the urge. 'I'd rather rely on different measures here.'

'Meaning? Gold?' the dwarf teased, stretching his limbs and brushing off the snow that had settled on his clothing. 'Am I the bait? I don't think there's enough meat on me to feed the whole stronghold.'

'I like your sense of humour.' Borkon grasped the horn at his belt. It had an unusual patterning in red and silver and seemed to have come from some animal that was not native to Girdlegard. *Where did he get that? He must have stored it away with the rest of the equipment during the journey. I've not seen it before.*

'Pay attention.' Borkon placed the mouthpiece to his lips. Barbandor had never heard tones like this. He did not like the sound. His innards objected both to the timbre and to the melody the orc was playing.

The tune echoed round on all sides, rising up to the top of the walls, and was certainly heard not only by the sentries on watch on the walkways.

While Borkon blasted the tune, a companion hoisted the white banner with dark blue runes and a star on an improvised flagpole made of three spears tied together. The fabric fluttered bravely in the breeze, announcing clearly that these were not salt sea orcs demanding entry at the gates. *Negotiation, capitulation, whatever.*

Barbandor held his hands over his ears but the vibrations went straight through his skull. There was no escape.

Borkon played the tune a second time and then placed the horn on his thigh before standing up and hurling his mantle aside. Underneath, his upper body was naked, and the decorative scar patterns and tattooed blue designs on the skin clearly visible. The rippling muscles could not be ignored. This was a physically powerful being.

Barbandor expected a shower of arrows and spears would meet this bold challenge. He thought the arrows would be followed up by the launch of a huge boulder flying their way to crush them all. *Mashed orc pudding, maybe. With a subtle hint of unwashed dwarf. The fortress orcs will be licking their lips.*

But instead, a short while later there was a loud rumbling as the great entrance gate was rolled open. A smartly armoured unit, fifty strong, marched out. At the front of the squad were four figures, two and a half paces in height, with long shields ready to protect those coming in their wake. There would be no getting past those shield-bearers.

'What did I tell you?' Displaying his silver canine teeth, Borkon smiled rather smugly at the dwarf.

'Don't count your chickens before they've hatched. They'll have archers in the rear,' Barbandor retorted. 'They think you're a rare type of bluebird and they're coming to catch you and put you in chains. They've never seen the like. You'll be their lucky mascot.'

'Is that what you think?'

'By Vraccas, do *they* look peaceful?' Barbandor took a closer look, and now saw that behind the shields there were twenty human slaves carrying dishes of food and amphorae of drink. *Never! How can that be?*

'Do you think they are threatening me with their gifts?' Borkon was enjoying his moment of triumph. 'Could it all be poisoned, perhaps?'

'I hope so,' muttered Barbandor.

The slaves were flanked by guards. Behind them came orcs, male and female, in opulent fur mantles and imposing bejewelled headwear. They clearly belonged to the highest-ranking society of Kràg Tahuum. *Or could they be from the priestly class?*

'To Tion with you,' he cursed. 'You did all that with the tune you blasted on that wretched horn?'

'Let's find out.' Borkon winked at him and burst out laughing. 'You're making such a face. I'd like to have a picture of you like that.' He strode slowly forward. 'As you do not speak our language you will have to try and work out what is happening. But I think you'll be able to understand.'

Watching through the bars of his cage, Barbandor saw the blue-skinned orc walk to the edge of the nearest bridge to receive the delegation while his troops followed him to stand in a triangular formation, at attention, but not drawing their weapons. The huge orcs carrying long shields moved aside and guards and slaves alike knelt down to form a gangway. The orcs in costly raiments stepped forward. Borkon sketched a bow in their direction and displayed the signal horn to them as if it were a kind of regalia. The orc at the head of the procession accepted it after making it a respectful bow. This was acknowledged approvingly by both parties in a series of ritual gestures. The leader's high-ranking companions kept up a chant of certain repeated syllables, sounding like a prayer mill. Subsequently Borkon spread his powerful arms out, right and left, turning his palms upwards like a dancer might, and he pivoted round.

They are inspecting him and that calling-horn of his. Why? Is this a ritual? . . . or a mating dance? Barbandor could make no sense of it. *And Borkon? Who exactly is he?* It was a pity his own people had never bothered with finding out about orc culture. *Why would they have? You have to exterminate them because orcs are nothing but trouble. Always have been.* What he was witnessing here, however, did not contribute anything to affect the long-standing prejudice that had held sway for thousands of cycles. *The whole thing reeks of nothing but strife and tribulation for Girdlegard.*

Borkon had completed his boastful rotation. The delegation made appreciative declarations and two of their number came forward and encircled the blue orc. They traced the white lines on his skin with their fingers and consulted several sheets of parchment that they took out of their shoulder bags. From time to time they laid the parchment illustrations close to Borkon's body to make comparisons. *There would seem to be records. About him? About the designs?* Barbandor kept wishing he understood the monsters' language.

'Out of my way!' came the charismatic tone using the common vernacular, coloured with an arrogant bleak-sounding accent. 'What in Inaste's name is happening here?'

It's a black-eyes! Barbandor saw a dark-haired älf hurrying across the bridge. In his left hand he brandished a rune-encrusted spear fashioned of tionium, while the right hand was encased in a gauntlet made of the same metal. Clothing his slim figure was a dark, close-fitting, tailored garment that flared out to billow around his leather-booted lower limbs as he strode forward. *This must be the one that defeated Ûra! What was his name again? ... Mòndarcai!* Either the älf did not speak the orc language or he was refusing to employ it, which, knowing the normal älfar arrogance and general attitude, would be the likelier explanation. *That's helpful for me.*

'This is Borkon Gràc Hâl, overturner of worlds,' said one of the high-ranking official delegates, who was holding the calling-horn reverently in his hands. 'He has restored to us the horn of Corschnok and he bears the symbols of the Twisted Strands on his body.' He gestured to the orcs who had inspected the patterns to approach. 'Each detail is perfect and so fashioned that—'

'I did not ask what kind of a specimen it is and what sort of gifts it came bearing, but I demanded to know what is happening here!' Mòndarcai had so far not directed the gaze of his black-dyed eyes to look at Borkon. Dark lines of fury had spread over the älf's pale face. 'Why did you open the gates?'

'Because he played Heshbaar's tune,' one of the female orcs explained, staring, fascinated, at Borkon. 'Exactly as the prophecy of Nushrok the Ripper foretold.'

Barbandor saw the expression of stunned surprise on the älf's features. He was obviously not able to work out what had just happened to his allies. *Oh, this is going to be fun!*

Mòndarcai hit the ground with the end of his rune spear.

'It appears I must ask that this joke be explained.' He held the sharp tip of this unique magic weapon pointing towards the base of the blue-skinned orc's broad throat, and the älfar symbols on the spear glowed a dangerous toxic green. With his other hand he opened his mantle and revealed dark red leather armour that left free those parts of his torso that had tionium plates sewn directly into the flesh. 'What does a world-overthrower want at my fortress gates?'

Horrified murmurs and gruntings went through the delegation. Warning shouts and threatening noises even rang out from up on the ramparts of Kràg Tahuum. This caused Mòndarcai to turn his head slowly in order to glare up at them until the orcs fell silent. *So now the little black-eyes is in trouble!* Barbandor was at a loss as to why the orcs would want to defend Borkon against Mòndarcai. Against this lethally dangerous älf who had recourse to such sensational powers and who had vanquished the dragon Ûra.

'The stronghold is now mine,' Borkon replied, with no trace of false pride or of being intimidated, but with the air, on the contrary, of the rightful overlord returning to his realm after a victorious military campaign, ready to oust an unsuitable deputy.

The filigree work of anger lines now covered most of Mòndarcai's face, appearing like an artist's sketch in black ink. 'Either you are the court jester or—'

'The very incarnation of Nushrok the Ripper's prophecy,' the female orc quickly broke in. 'We have been familiar with Nushrok's words since earliest childhood. He foretells that on an orbit in winter an orc with the skin of night and stars will appear and will play the melody of Heshbaar as no one else could. With blood and with silver.' She indicated the strange ornamentation on the instrument. 'Behold! It has all come to pass!'

'And does the prophecy also state that there already exists an agreement, Shashka, between us, on the fulfilment of which I intend to insist?' Mòndarcai had not lowered the spear. Its point remained at Borkon's throat.

'If the orc with skin of night and stars appears then the whole situation is altered. And Great Things will soon come,' Shashka continued. 'Great things that will give us a position of power.'

'I am glad to hear it.'

'No. Give *us*, the orcs, I mean. There is no mention of any älfar in the prophecy.' Shashka sounded excited and overcome with happiness, without being aware what consequences her words might involve.

Barbandor would have wished for a warming mug of spiced beer, some toasted cheese and a crispy bacon snack, in order to enjoy watching this dramatic spectacle properly. *By Vraccas, what we have here is a serious rift: the breaching of a treaty.* All it takes is for Mòndarcai to say something unwise and orcs will all attack him, no matter what powers he possesses. *He may have killed that dragon but thousands of angry pig-faces are a different matter entirely. He would soon be exhausted, worn out with all the slaughter and butchery.* He studied the älf carefully and noticed a hole, a small gap in the tionium armour plating attached to the light skin between the items of red leather protection. *I spot a weak point – he is vulnerable there. A skilled archer might target that spot successfully.*

'So Borkon has appeared. The long-awaited orc from wherever,' Mòndarcai summed up sarcastically. 'And apparently he lays claim to the fortress of Kràg Tahuum, which you then cede to him, just like that, after the stronghold has been so fiercely defended against the humans for so many hundreds of cycles? And you abandon your agreement with myself?'

Borkon seemed to be following the exchange from a position

of moral superiority and remained silent and aloof. He did not attempt to cover himself with his mantle. He was the very essence of strength and self-confidence.

'The prophecy is older than Kràg Tahuum and many other parts of Girdlegard. We yield to its import with humility and joy because a new era awaits us,' Shashka explained.

'But what,' Mòndarcai looked at the blue-skinned orc contemptuously, 'what if I kill him? What happens to your precious prophecy then?'

'We would cancel the pact that we entered into with you and would consider you our enemy and we would pursue you to the death. At any price,' Shashka declared, her facial expression one of lethal animosity.

'I destroyed Ûra. Do you think I am afraid of you?' Mòndarcai did not let his gaze waver from the Chosen Orc. 'But I choose to demonstrate my goodwill. I suggest we –'

Borkon took one step forward. The tip of the älf's spear pierced the flesh of his throat as if slicing through butter. The symbols on the spear shaft glowed – but the orc did not die. Mòndarcai immediately pulled his weapon back and the wound closed up of its own accord. The only reminder of that potentially fatal injury was the stream of blue-black blood dripping down over the white pattern lines. Loud shouts and joyful whoops resounded from those orcs on the ramparts and bridge of Kràg Tahuum. This was the proof they had longed for. Evidence that he was indeed the Bringer of the New Era.

'That is merely some trickery,' the älf said quietly. 'The skin patterns are painted on, so are the symbols, and he's used a bit of healing magic. And you race to follow him?'

'It is better you do not ever come back to Kràg Tahuum,' Shashka responded coldly. 'Our pact is no longer valid. If you want a new alliance' – she indicated Borkon – 'you will have to negotiate with the Overturner of Worlds.'

Barbandor was laughing to himself, but on the inside. He allowed only a quiet giggle to escape. *That's how quickly you can lose a whole army. And an impregnable fortress.*

Mòndarcai's face was completely covered with the tracery of anger lines and his dark eye sockets shone like polished shadows. But he was clever enough not to lose his temper or to risk making an attack. 'I have understood that I am at present not welcome.' He ignored Shashka and her entourage completely and turned to Borkon. 'I assume you will also be heading north to pay your respects to the Salt Sea?'

'Indeed.'

Mòndarcai laughed mirthlessly. 'And so I have one ally less, I see. Inàste is testing me harshly.' He nodded slowly. 'Right, I shall collect my things and leave Kràg Tahuum. When one cycle has passed I shall return and I shall then ask you, Borkon, Overturner of Worlds, whether you wish to enter into an alliance with me. Together with all that follow you.'

'You are welcome to do that, älf. You will receive hospitality, but nothing more than that.' The blue-skinned orc raised his voice and thrust his broad fist high into the air. 'The time of servitude is over!'

All the orc residents up on the fortress walls were vying with each other in exuberant welcoming of their Chosen One, as Mòndarcai turned away. He checked his movement when he noticed the dwarf in the cage. 'Why have you got a groundling with you? Is he to serve as your provisions for the journey?'

'Oh no. I'm their lucky charm,' Barbandor piped up, removing the scarf from his face so he could grin at the älf. 'They are fonder of me than of you. Look – they carry me around as if I were their king.' He tapped the wooden bars. 'And they keep me safe. Aren't they sweet?'

Borkon burst out laughing.

Mòndarcai turned back to the fortress again. The blue-skinned orc requested the special horn with the silver and red patterns, and placed it to his lips again in order to play Heshbaar's melody for the third time.

Barbandor placed his fingers in his ears. *Not again!* If he ever managed to escape from his prison, he vowed the first thing he would do would be to destroy the instrument of torture.

Girdlegard

In the Brown Mountains
Brigantia
1024 P.Q. (7515th solar cycle in old reckoning), winter

On entering the building Gata embraced Hargorina, who was dressed for combat. They met in the largest of the eight longhouses that had been erected for strategy meetings or to house the delegations and the commanding officers. The accommodation was anything but luxurious, with unadorned wooden panelling, but it was warm, heated by stoves burning coal and peat. There were lamps overhead to provide illumination.

'It's so good to see you, my mentor,' said Gata.

'I hear you bring special news.' Red-haired Hargorina looked at the group who had followed the Thirdling queen. 'There's someone missing. Where is our gem cutter?'

Gata pulled a face. Mostro, Telìnâs, Sònuk and Brûgar – the latter puffing away at his pipe – were all showing signs of the journey's hardships. They had travelled at speed. But the meeting was urgent and could not be delayed. 'Well, *that* is one of the bits of news.'

Hargorina raised the copper-coloured eyebrows that emphasised the dark blue tattoo patterns on her face. 'By Lorimbur! Don't tell me he's dead . . .?'

Gata's response was to sigh deeply. 'You will soon hear more.' She patted the warrior queen on her armoured shoulder. As she did so she noticed the numerous representatives from various territories already seated in a horseshoe formation round the table, with Goldhand at the head. And sitting next to him ... 'But that's the puppet mistress!' Gata exclaimed, incredulous. 'How did she get here?'

'We have news, too.' Hargorina led Gata to her chair. 'But I don't know whether it's good news.'

'The same as our own, then.' As she passed him, she stretched out a hand to Belîngor, who was standing at the side. 'Good to see you again.'

Grinning broadly, he bowed.

Brûgar thumped his friend on the back, discarding his pipe for a moment in order to give the dwarf a vigorous hug.

'I've missed you! Travelling with Mostro, I've certainly learned to appreciate the way you always stay nice and quiet.'

They both laughed.

'It was Belîngor who saved Rodana,' Hargorina explained.

Gata chose a seat near Tungdil Goldhand. 'You mean, he *captured* her.'

'No. He rescued her. He saved her from a wild narshân and three over-enthusiastic Gauragon soldiers who were super keen to bring Goldhand the prize of her head. Without the rest of her, that is.' Like Belîngor and Brûgar, Hargorina remained standing behind Gata.

'Vanéra's turned up as well, I see.' Gata watched the brown-haired maga, who was wearing a lustrous robe of white and gold, in conversation with a well-dressed elf. 'When did she arrive?'

'Soon after you left. She brought a selection of artefacts with her that are thought to be useful in warfare,' Hargorina answered. 'The troops seemed relieved to see her. They had been worried about Mostro not being there. There are a whole lot of rumours going round in the camp about the Brigantians having magic powers at their disposal.'

Telînâs went to sit with the elf delegates. Sònuk took a seat at the open fireside, spreading his hands out to the warmth.

Mostro could not resist shifting his own chair nearer to where the opulently attired Vanéra was sitting, as if to make it clear that he considered that the two of them were of similar standing when it came to wisdom and knowledge. He did not respond to the maga's reproving glance.

Ever since the victory at Two-Stream Hill he seems very full of himself – but in reality he achieved spectacularly little, Gata thought. She helped herself to some hot tea and relished being in the warm for once. She would have to be careful not to nod off, particularly given the effect of the clouds of Brûgar's cinnamon and mint pipe smoke. She was tired enough to be in danger of falling asleep, and her eyelids felt heavy as lead.

White-haired Goldhand turned his ancient face towards her. He had eschewed his elaborate armour and was wearing a comfortable garment of dark brown cloth. 'Before we open the session with discussion of the state of the siege and the worrying new information we have been brought by the guest here at my side, tell me, please. Where is Goïmron?'

Gata was aware that the aged dwarf particularly wanted his trusted confidant at his side. Goïmron acted as Goldhand's voice whenever the waves of älfar poison in his bones overwhelmed him and left him unable to speak. She stood up and made her way through the clouds of smoke. Being on the move would help her not to fall asleep. 'At present he is in Szmajro's clutches. Or maybe Szmajro is in his. I do not know which.'

The others in the meeting started murmuring.

'Explain, please, if you will.' Goldhand reached for his beaker, his hand trembling. The mark on his hand glowed gold in the lamplight, as if the inlaid metal were wanting to remind everyone of the legend.

'It all started when we reached the Wonder Zone near Fortgard,' Gata began. She related their adventures, telling how they had encountered the zhussa and the älfar, how they and the Fortgarders had been triumphant, how Goïmron had used magic and how the dragon Szmajro had seized the dwarf and flown off with him. She stated that Mostro had not interceded. He had done nothing. At all. *Everyone here in the longhouse shall hear that the famulus did not move a muscle to help.* 'After that we came back to rejoin the siege as quickly as we could.' She pointed to the famulus. 'His power is fully recharged. With the appropriate spells he will now, I hope, forge a break in the walls or break open the gates so we can march in and restore to the Fourthlings what is rightfully theirs.' Slightly hoarse from speaking, Gata sat down again and drank some more tea. Adrenalin had done its work and she no longer felt sleepy.

'And you've seen no trace of Goïmron since?' Vanéra asked, touching the red bead necklace at her throat. 'Anyone might think a forty-pace-long dragon with two heads would be quite conspicuous.'

When Gata shook her head, her long blonde plait swung from side to side. 'On the way back we kept making enquiries to see if anyone had seen anything. No one had.'

'But that means there's still hope that Goïmron's alive,' said Goldhand. 'Let us pray to Vraccas to use his shield to protect him. And use his hammer to smash the dragon to pieces.' The news about Goïmron was obviously affecting the white-bearded old dwarf. The furrows on his lined face had deepened perceptibly. 'But we have a significant task to address. For the welfare of Girdlegard and of all who live there. Not merely for the sake of the Fourthling dwarves.' He nodded at the famulus. 'Master Mostro, you are now adequately charged with sufficient new magic energy to be able to force an opening for us into the fortress using your knowledge of spells, in a way that our war-wolf catapults have not managed to do.'

'Indeed.' Mostro got to his feet slowly, enjoying his moment. The ceremonial attire made him appear yet more arrogant. 'But what do we do if the thief returns to us?'

Gata was at a loss to understand his words and noticed that others in the room were similarly confused. 'What do you mean? What thief?'

'Goïmron Chiselcut is a common criminal,' Mostro began. 'I know you want to tell me that it was his magic power that helped me to chase away the zhussa—'

'Oh, come on! Don't twist things like that,' Gata interrupted angrily. 'You allowed her to make her escape!'

'And, anyway, the sea sapphire that he used at Fortgard was stolen. He took it clandestinely, when he went into the Chamber of Wonders many orbits ago. I caught him at the door to the Chamber.' Mostro held up his piece of sigurdacia wood. The wand was engraved with numerous runes and had inlaid gems. 'This is my magic-indicator. I employed it when Chòldunja took flight from the army encampment because I thought it would show me where she was. The artefact led me to the sea sapphire and the thief so that I could confront him.'

'Are these old stories of any relevance to us this evening?' Telìnâs asked, hoping to stem the flow of Mostro's narrative. The elf was busily folding and tearing a sheet of paper into the shape of a tree in blossom. 'The situation is different now.'

'But what if Goïmron Chiselcut turns up tomorrow? I want us to decide what punishment he will receive for defrauding the Esteemed Maga Vanéra,' Mostro insisted. 'Theft is theft.'

'But it was him found the carnelian knife that healed Hargorina and Goldhand,' Gata countered. 'I knew he wanted to get into the Chamber. No, I . . . it was me who asked him to go there. He told me that he'd be better able to locate the knife than the maga would. Because, as a Fourthling, he had a feeling for gemstones generally.'

'And he had light fingers and a big bag to hide stuff in,' Mostro snapped. 'So it was him who made such a mess of the archive and brought the drinx to life! A dwarf who could not resist laying his hands on the valuable items in that storeroom. Do we want to place our trust in him? That's if he hasn't already been eaten by Szmajro. Do we let him do magic? And why did he not tell us what a unique gift he has? This makes me very concerned. I know that he was in cahoots with this person' – he pointed at Rodana – 'and the child-eater. What arts has the moor-witch taught him? Is Goïmron's soul pure or does it harbour the seeds of darkness, implanted by the ragana?'

There was a loud rumble of disagreement among the dwarves in the meeting, objecting strongly to these allegations.

Goldhand slammed his fist down on the table. 'Quiet here! This is a serious accusation Master Mostro is making. We must discuss the issue, however unpleasant it is for us all.' He turned to Vanéra. 'Esteemed Maga, do you know what kind of stone Goïmron is said to have purloined?'

Vanéra got to her feet, a frown on her face. 'I'm afraid I know exactly what it is. It is a sea sapphire in a carved setting in the form of a dragon. I did not realise at the time what else had been on the same shelf as the drinx and the carnelian knife. And then I remembered.'

'You ae absolutely sure?'

Vanéra nodded, a regretful expression on her face. 'Unfortunately I do not know where the artefact was originally from, but I do remember my predecessor's mother mentioning it once. She spoke of it with a mixture of fear and awe.'

'I can tell you why, Esteemed Maga.' Bendoïn Feinunz got to his feet and inclined his head respectfully. Gata remembered having met him on a previous occasion. He had played an important role, and not only during the siege. He had been present in Rhuta when her father had drunk himself to death with the bewitched beer tankard. The stocky Fourthling and the bushy moustache looked at Vanéra directly. 'We spoke about it. It was on the list you gave me of the gemstones your famulus wanted. I did some research. And I am certain: it is the Stone of Trouble.'

There was more lively discussion in the room.

'Then . . . then it had been in my store chamber for hundreds of cycles?' Vanéra clearly found this as hard to believe as did Mostro, whose face was suffused with an angry red. 'So close at hand.' She looked at her famulus. 'So close, indeed, to your hand.'

'And it was stolen,' he whispered, but not quietly enough not to be overheard, 'by a presumptuous dwarf.'

'The old stories are true,' Bendoïn explained. 'The sea sapphire will allow a magus or a maga to accomplish any magic, no matter how dangerous or complicated the spell might be. But with every incantation put into effect it brings the holder of the stone, and the land he is in, nearer to disaster.'

'How many times can spells be used?' Gata interrupted.

'Well, it keeps going. Until the disaster happens.' Bendoïn took his seat again. 'I cannot say exactly what form the curse would take. You all know that our records are incomplete. It might be possible to find out more details in the Brown Mountains. Or in the fortress.'

Mostro covered his face with his hands. 'We'd have broken into the fortress long ago if the thief had left the stone for me to find and use,' he said, speaking with restraint. He jerked suddenly to attention. 'Because of Chiselcut we've lost the sapphire for ever. Good people have lost their lives in this prolonged siege. And now this stone forms the foundation of a dragon's hoard!'

'Calm yourself, Master Mostro,' Goldhand said, his voice brittle. 'All of you, calm down. Vraccas will restore Goïmron to us and we will challenge him on how he happens to be in possession of this sea sapphire. I am sure he will have had his reasons for taking it.' Goldhand drank from his beaker and then held it out, pointing at Vanéra with it. 'After that it will be up to the Esteemed Maga, and only her, to decide what happens. She is the one whose property was stolen, after all. Not yourself, Master Mostro.'

Gata could see the famulus grinding his teeth. If he had been in receipt of the gemstone's magic power, and had used it to break down the fortress gates, then his reaction would have been understandable. Very understandable. But the way this young man was making his case, always demanding and insisting, did not make a favourable impression on the people in the room. *He really considers himself to be a genuine master of his arts. Looks like he wants to supplant the maga.*

'We will decide the matter, should Goïmron ever manage to return,' Vanéra agreed. 'And when I make my decision I shall not be overlooking his heroic deeds.'

'His misdeeds, you mean, Esteemed Maga,' Mostro muttered to her.

'Let us leave the issue for now. Now, to our guest.' By now Goldhand was deliberately speaking more slowly and having to concentrate hard. It was clear he was having to contend with a wave of the toxic effects from the älfar poison that was in his bones and his blood, and thus could attack his mind. 'You all know Doria Rodana de Psalí. Our good Belîngor saved her from a narshân beast that had pursued her out of the fortress. Rodana risked her life to flee from Brigantia to bring us a warning. She warns us of a danger that calls for immediate action.' He leaned forward. For a moment it appeared he might topple over and crash down on to the table. He put out a hand just in time. 'She swears that the allegations made against her person have no foundation. Neither those against herself nor those accusations faced by her aprendisa. Please listen. She will relate what happened following the battle at Two-Stream Hill.'

Mostro opened his mouth ready to object, but he was silenced by a stern look from Vanéra.

Rodana got to her feet and bowed to all those present. She had been given a light-brown winter dress from the Fourthling supplies; it fitted reasonably well. She also had a multi-layered shawl over her shoulders to keep her warm. As she stood there in the midst of the humans, dwarves and meldriths she looked as fragile as if she were made of glass. She looked like an elf, except that she was too short.

'I swear on my life and before the gods that I will speak the truth and will not try to mislead you on anything at all,' she began. Her voice projected strongly and, surprisingly, was able to fill the room. 'I am deeply concerned for the safety of my homeland. That is why I have risked imprisonment. My information must be heard.'

How small and delicate she is for a human. Her flight from the fortress and the time she had spent inside had left her even thinner than before. *Whatever is it that Goïmron finds so attractive?* thought Gata, fighting with her feelings of jealousy. *Probably those darkened lips. And her fingertips. Looks like she's been digging around in someone's grave!*

Rodana told them how she and Chòldunja had fled after Mostro had made his accusations; she explained how the two of them had encountered Klaey Berengart, whose life they had saved. They had then ridden with him to Brigantia; she told them how, before the connecting tunnels had been destroyed, Hantu and the weird collection of monsters had been summoned through from the Outer Lands by the Omuthan, wanting to increase his troop capabilities. Finally she told them of the powers the rhamak possessed and that there was as good as nothing at all that could be used to combat or defeat him as soon as he summoned up beings from another dimension. 'My apprentice sent me away to bring you this warning. She chose to stay behind to try to kill Hantu. Only the gods know how she would manage to do that,' Rodana concluded her speech.

Once again the furious Mostro had to be restrained by the brown-haired maga. He glared at the puppet mistress, rolling his eyes and drumming with his fists on his knees. Gata could not recall ever having heard tell of a magus who could successfully use invocations without recourse to actual magic. *So in fact it isn't magic at all but something more dangerous still.* Anyone with access to such arts could deploy them at any time, providing only that sufficient sacrifices and blood were made available. 'Have you ever heard of a person with powers of that nature, Esteemed Maga?'

Vanéra said no. 'Never. Not under the concept of a rhamak or taikhom or even a Summoner of Hidden Things. It's possible that the archives in the City of Knowledge may have records that mention it, but I am afraid we seem to be dealing with an art that was rightly forgotten once the magic fields started to occur.'

'If you will permit: I do not believe a word of anything this infamous woman has told us.' Mostro found it impossible to remain silent. 'She is purely intent on getting the price removed from her head. So she tells us some made-up nonsense while that child-eater girl is doubtless hiding near the wall just waiting for us to ask her back in. Then she'll pretend to have tried absolutely everything to stop this Summoner—'

Goldhand slammed his fist down on the table again, this time with such force that beakers, goblets and tankards jumped. His old strength flared up. 'I believe her! And I know honesty when I hear it and see it.'

These authoritative words did not prevent a lively dispute breaking out. In a few blinks of an eye it was apparent that the majority of those present were unwilling to go with Rodana's evidence. They thought it was a trick.

Gata said nothing, preferring to listen and to think through what she heard. *She is certainly courageous.* On the other hand, her words might well be a proficiently delivered set of lies with aspects of the truth woven in for effect.

Rodana was still on her feet, watching the session's participants. 'What can I do to convince you all?' she called out above the hubbub of voices. 'Every grain that falls in the sandglass brings the danger one step nearer of his summoning beings from another dimension, and events occurring in Brigantia we have no means of combatting.'

'Pah!' said Mostro contemptuously, as he pulled at his pointed beard. 'We shan't believe you even if you cut your own throat in front of us to try to convince us.'

Quick as lightning Rodana grabbed a dagger from the guard standing next to her and placed it at her throat. 'Believe me. Believe my words. And if you find my aprendisa alive, let her live. She is innocent.'

Before Rodana could draw the blade through skin, flesh and arteries to reinforce her message, Gata picked up a beaker and hurled it accurately at the girl's forehead. The cup shattered on impact and the young woman was knocked senseless. The dagger fell harmlessly to the floor.

'I believe her,' Gata declared, wiping away the tea she had spilled. 'There is no need for her to sacrifice her life to convince us. We'll deal with the case against her once we have captured the fortress. Agreed?' she asked. This was greeted with applause. 'Until then she is not to be harmed.'

The guards picked up the unconscious figure and carried her out of the longhouse.

Goldhand raised his beaker of tea in a salute to the queen of the Thirdlings. 'By Vraccas. Well done indeed.' He took a sip. 'Let us start the proceedings to discuss how the fortress is to be stormed. Using both earthly and magic means.' He looked at Vanéra. 'You and your famulus will give us important support in this.'

'May I say something first?' Gata broke in.

'Of course. Feel free.' Goldhand invited her to speak.

'You have all heard about the offer the zhussa made. If we stay away from Dsôn Khamateion the älfar will leave us in peace,' she summarised. 'We have already rejected one pact with a very powerful älf who has an army of orcs under him able to inflict a disastrous defeat on us. In my opinion it was a serious error to turn down Mòndarcai's proposal of an alliance.' Gata gently touched the badge of office on the collar of her inner robe. It seemed to give her confidence. 'I suggest most strongly that, after securing the fortress, we should send a delegation to the Ganyeios to speak to the ruler to negotiate terms for collaboration.' She was unfazed by the cries of dissent coming particularly from the corner where the elves and meldriths were sitting. 'Make no mistake. Ascatoîa is a zhussa equally as powerful as the famulus. If not more so. And on top of that she is in possession of a fully grown dragon who follows her orders. Also, do not forget the fleet of eight mighty älfar ships at anchor in the Inland Sea, ready to spread death and destruction on the coastal regions.' Gata was aware of the effect her words would have. It was worth reminding the assembly that the expected fall of Brigantia would not represent the end of the problems to be faced by the peoples of Girdlegard. 'The black-eyes are dangerous enough adversaries even without the zhussa and her scale-covered helpmeet. We all know this to be true. But now they are more lethal a threat than ever before.'

'Silence!' thundered Goldhand, suppressing the tumult of voices in the room. 'Please. Quiet, all of you. Let us hear her out.'

'Goïmron was the only one who could have used his powers to counteract those of the zhussa. Only he, and no one else, was able to break through the magic barrier. But we don't have him here,' Gata continued, ignoring the interruptions.

'Victory in the Brown Mountains and the defeat of the Omuthan's army will not be secured without great losses on our part. The battles will leave us weakened, and thus vulnerable to attack by other enemies. I think we need the non-aggression treaty with Dsôn,' she urged. 'Do not ignore this option, my honoured comrades in arms.'

Elves and meldriths were loudly and emphatically against her proposal. Some of the dwarves showed they could not understand Gata's reasoning. Memories of the recent assassination campaigns were still fresh.

Gata let the noisy discussion die down. She had said what she had wanted to say – what had needed, in her mind, to be said. Girdlegard would have to decide to deal with terrible threat. After much thought, she considered an enormous orc army constituted the greater evil. Sooner or later Mòndarcai might forfeit his hold over the unstable beasts, and the orcs from Kràg Tahuum and the Salt Desert could devastate entire regions and then head south-west with a view to re-establishing an empire in their original territory of Toboribor.

We will have to be ready for that. They could not win a war on three fronts. Impossible. *They will see it makes sense.* Gata asked for more tea to be brought. She waited for calm.

But in the meantime Goldhand was beginning to flag. The meeting was ended and it was agreed to reconvene on the following orbit.

I shall get my way. Gata stood up and strolled to the door, holding her cup of tea. She was looking forward to taking a hot bath – after a short visit she planned on making first.

Sitting on her bunk, Rodana was holding a cloth containing some ice to her painful head wound. A piece of waxed paper prevented the melting ice dripping into the open gash on her forehead.

She had not seen the object flying towards her. Luckily she had not been unconscious for very long. When she was brought to a simple cell in one of the longhouses, she was told by one of the guards that it had been the Thirdling queen who had stymied her suicide attempt.

The light in the longhouse was low, with Rodana being granted only a couple of petroleum lamps. Apart from herself there were no other prisoners. This meant it was quiet, at least, which helped with the pounding headache. A small brazier afforded a source of heat, and she also had thick clothes and a shawl.

At least I got the assembly to consider bringing forward their attack on Brigantia. Rodana inspected the compress and saw the bleeding must have stopped. *At least I won't need stitches. A scar, though, probably.*

She heard footsteps approaching on the other side of the bars.

'I am sorry, but I could not risk you killing yourself just to be taken seriously.' In the half dark she could recognise the figure of Gata in full armour, a mug of tea in her hand. Steam wafted up, curling round the blue tattoos on the skin of her face. 'Don't worry, I'm not going to throw this one at you.'

Rodana smiled painfully. 'Thank you. My head is still buzzing.' She tried a gentle nod. 'And thanks, too, for saving my life.'

'Any idea why?'

Rodana had been asking herself the same thing. 'Maybe you appreciate my theatrical skills,' she said, attempting a joke.

'True. But that's not the reason.' Gata assessed her. 'You are my rival, you know.'

Rodana could not believe her ears. 'Forgive me, what . . .'

'Goïmron. His heart beats for your sake. I know this because he turned down the offer of my own. And then I saw how he was looking at you. Secretly.'

Rodana tried to recall the meetings and conversations she had had with Goïmron. With her good friend. She would never in a million cycles have guessed he held a candle for her. *Oh heavens! I have been so blind.* 'I knew you had an eye on him and I even told him that. Because I thought you would make a splendid couple.' She pressed the iced cloth to her head.

'Too kind.'

'Don't mock. It was meant honestly. I was happy for Goïmron. It would be a good match. A queen.' Rodana laughed. 'But that wasn't the thing. I considered you a dwarf that one could trust, that one could rely on.'

Gata leaned against the bars of the cell. 'But yet he did not listen to you, did he? He was utterly distraught when we heard that you and child-eater girl—'

'Don't call her that. She had forsworn the ways of the ragana people.'

'. . . that you and the apprentice girl were thought to be spies for Brigantia, as that slimy little famulus never tires of claiming.' Gata looked at Rodana again. 'In truth I'd say Mostro wanted to get you and your aprendisa beneath him. And because he was never going to get his wicked way with you, he wants you destroyed.'

Rodana's brain was not working at full strength because of the blow to her head. 'Then . . . you saved my life . . . because Goïmron is . . . secretly in love with me?' she stammered, perplexed.

Gata nodded. 'Yes. I want him to be happy. The fact he's

disappeared doesn't mean he's dead. And when he comes back he ought to see that you are well and happy. That will ensure that *he* is well and happy. And that will make *me* happy.'

Rodana could not think of anything to say to that. Her thoughts were whirling around her head. And some of them were sticking fast.

'A heart cannot be coerced into loving. If one is not the chosen one, life still has to go on. Even if I am envious of you,' the queen said solemnly, 'Goïmron will always be very important to me. He means a lot to me. And that is why I would always try to spare him pain and sadness where I can. Your death would have been awful for him.' She looked at Rodana. 'Nothing can force your heart to love where it does not. But perhaps circumstances may change once you are aware of his feelings for you?' She tapped her beaker against the bars. 'You will be well treated here. Mostro can't get at you.' Pulling a tiny knife out of her belt, she handed it to Rodana. 'If I can't always be at your side to protect you, here, take this. It should help you to sleep easy.'

'Thank you.' Rodana concealed the weapon under her shawl.

'If Goïmron returns and tells you of his feelings, please be kind to him,' said Gata, turning to go. 'I don't want to see him unhappy.'

Rodana watched the dwarf queen leave. It must have cost her dear to speak those words.

And as if from nowhere Goïmron's face arrived unprompted in her thoughts.

The Magic Realm of Rhuta is the least sensible of all the territorial formats in Girdlegard. This silly diamond shape stems from the calculations made in ancient times by the Magus Cnus Kolknat, who claimed he could justify the mathematics for the perfect magic shape. His calculations were adopted by half a dozen magae and magi. Absolute nonsense! Magus Kolknat also came up with what he considered the ideal shape for a loaf of bread, a perfect cloud, the exemplary format for a brick and all kinds of ridiculous things. Completely disregarding mathematical principles. No further comment needed.

Dar Whjenn, academic expert
in the fields of flora,
fauna and the laws of nature

IX

Girdlegard

United Great Kingdom of Gauragon
Province of Grasslands
1024 P.Q. (7515th solar cycle in old reckoning), winter

Stémna moved the soaped brush forwards and backwards over the wooden boards with both hands to remove the stains and layers of dirt from the floor. Her fingers were swollen from the effect of the water and her nasal passages stung from the fumes of the cleaning fluid. She was sure she would hear the constantly repeated *shh shh shh* sounds of the bristles even in her sleep. The whole orbit so far she had been on her knees, scrubbing away, dressed in the grey robe of a candidate doulia, a headscarf covering her hair. The more she scrubbed, the more often filthy boots seemed to arrive, ruining her work. As soon as she had cleaned the last bit, a stable lad would come through, or a maid, or some dogs. Boots, shoes, paws . . .

Stémna went on with the cleaning without complaint and without a break. She could hardly feel her back, knees or legs anymore. She was thirsty and her stomach was grumbling, particularly now the smell of a tasty stew was wafting through the rooms.

Having arrived at the end of the corridor, she looked up and stretched her neck. *I've done it!* She listened out in case someone turned up to spoil all her hard work. Through the narrow window she caught sight of the stars. All sense of time passing had been lost and already it was night.

All quiet.

Done it! Getting to her feet, she felt like the old woman she actually was. For two hundred cycles now she had been wandering throughout Girdlegard, to all intents and purposes in the form of a forty-year-old, but she had never before had to carry out physical work of this nature.

Or doing laundry. Doing the cooking. Polishing the silver. Slopping out the latrines. Cleaning shoes. Fetching water. And much else besides.

Cup of tea in her hand, Gubnara, a graceful woman of about sixty, came strolling past from the kitchens. She stopped and looked at Stémna. 'You took your time.' Like all the other doulia, she wore her hair very short and with a green lock of horsehair woven in, to indicate her status. So far Stémna had avoided having her head shorn in that way.

Gubnara was her instructor, her breaker-in, the person who decided who was ready for higher service in Girdlegard and who was to remain behind at headquarters. Simple doulia were offered out locally. But if service with noble families, in the household of celebrities, or even in the homes of elves were aspired to, a further course of training was essential. This was what Stémna was presently undergoing. She was being taught about specific customs, how to handle special requests and understand particular forms of speech.

'There was a lot of coming and going. I had to keep starting over, Mistress,' she explained, speaking meekly and humbly, as she had been taught. It had been hard for her at first. The pride she carried from her long history and from her career as the messenger of the white dragon persisted still. With every humiliating task she was given she became more compliant, suppressing feelings of anger or resentment. 'May I have permission to take food and drink now, Mistress?'

'As soon as you have finished your work.' Gubnara smoothed down the folds in her ankle-length dark grey dress, which sported a wide black belt embroidered in white as a striking focal point.

'I have finished, Mistress.' Stémna glanced back at the shining floors drying off in the warmth from the stoves.

'This is good work, Stémna. I am pleased.' Gubnara took a sip of the tea, fragrant with apple and spices. 'You realise you are the only outsider ever to train as a doulia, the only one not of our own folk?'

'Yes, Mistress.'

'This is because we see in you the oldest slave in Girdlegard, always doing loyal service. Until her death you obeyed your mistress faithfully. No one could have done more.'

'Thank you, Mistress.' Stémna was familiar with praise such as this, intended to flatter her and remind her of her station. Her present and future place in life.

'In a few orbits' time we could be accepting you into the ranks of the doulia. You will receive the shearing and the lock of hair. And your new name. You will swear allegiance to the great doulia mission and soon you will be given your reward. Your gifts are a blessing for us.' Gubnara watched the steam rising from her cup. 'Then you will be sent to a household as a slave. As a doulia. You will soon learn what that entails.'

'Thank you, Mistress.'

'There are certain tests that await you. If you fail any of them, you lose everything you have gained so far.' Gubnara tipped up her cup slowly, letting the contents spill on to the floorboards. 'I see you have missed a bit.'

'I shall clean it up at once, Mistress.' Stémna was familiar with these little games, designed to try her patience.

'Take off your robe and rub it dry with that. I shall want to see you in a laundered garment tomorrow at roll-call,' Gubnara declared. Then she hurled the empty cup at the wall, sending sharp fragments everywhere. 'That was my favourite cup. Mend it. And hand it to me in the morning.'

'Yes, Mistress.'

'Very good, Stémna.' Gubnara turned to go back to the kitchen. 'The stable lad is waiting for you in your room. Satisfy him. You are still attractive for your age. This will please your owners. Mature but not worn out, thus you will not represent any threat to the woman of the house where you are sent.' The doulia instructor disappeared over the threshold. 'Enjoy yourself with the stable lad and see you don't fall asleep.'

'No, Mistress. He will have no cause to complain.' Stémna took off her dress as instructed, dried the floor and then picked up the pieces of broken crockery before collecting a pot of glue from the workshop. She was not bothered by her nakedness. This would be yet one more orbit on which she would get no sleep. But there might well be some pleasure in it. Or so she hoped.

Stémna had been playing along, pretending to Gubnara that she wanted to become the perfect doulia slave. She would not let herself be broken by the treatment. She had goals of her own to achieve and in order to reach them she must accept this temporary existence of a slave. The role would protect her until Girdlegard had forgotten who she had once been.

Until Mòndarcai had forgotten who she was.

And then I will get him. When he least expects it. She had sworn to avenge her dragon mistress's death, if need be with the very last breath in her body. Mòndarcai, the extraordinary, all-powerful älf, would be paying for what he had done. For that she would need to collect new orange feathers so she could mete out the deadly demon fire that dissolved all and every type of material. Not even Mòndarcai's peculiar armour would be able to withstand those scorching hot flames. She had, in the course of the many cycles of her life, deposited hidden stores of these feathers in secret locations so that she would never be without. Ûra had given them to her in the past without divulging where they came from. Stémna had had her suspicions about their provenance but had never had the chance to follow up on her ideas. And certainly not after the death of the dragon.

As she was about to climb the stairs to prepare for pleasing the stable boy, before dealing with the broken cup and the dirty dress, she noticed a light shining on the first step. It came from underneath the wooden floorboards.

What's that?

This had been the dirtiest, sandiest spot of all, Stémna remembered, when she was scrubbing the floor. There was encrusted soil wedged between the boards. It had taken her two full sandglasses to clean that section, which she had found odd, given that there did not seem to really be any reason for that part to be much trodden.

Placing the broken cup down on the stair and putting her soiled robe back on, Stémna knelt and peered through the gap. *That's definitely candlelight.* Taking a quick look round in the dark corridor, she verified that she was alone. *Is it some kind of secret cellar?* She got up, feeling along the walls, the friezes and the borders in search of any irregularity in the panelling.

At long last in one of the slave frescoes she found a whip that could be rotated. *I should have guessed. A cat o'nine tails.* With a soft click the floor lowered slightly and then swung to one side, revealing a steep staircase. The light had been shining up through a hole. *Secrets. Well, well. What do you know?* Stémna listened out for steps. Hearing nothing, she felt it safe to go down.

She found herself in a low, dry, vaulted cellar. On the walls were maps of Girdlegard displaying tiny flags with numbers and script. Two petroleum lamps and a candle were still alight, having obviously been forgotten. It was difficult to see in the dim light how far back the cellar went. There were sets of shelves up to the ceiling, with drawers full of cards covered in closely written text. Stémna caught sight of the names of the male and female slaves together with the details of their current placements – and all the secrets of those households.

Raising her gaze, she looked around. *So the doulia are spying in Girdlegard. They've noted down everything they think is important.* Stémna shrugged off the last of her tiredness. *So that's what Gubnara meant when she said I could be one of them.* And it explained why they had not ever taken on any outsiders. *Until now. Until me. I am an outsider for them.*

Her attention fell on one drawer in particular labelled *Newcomers*, where she found her own name on a list. And there was an abbreviation next to it. *Does that mean I'm already assigned to a situation?* She looked for her own flag on the map and located it in a town in the Sinterich region. *That's no good. I've got no feathers stored in the vicinity.*

She swapped her flag with another. Now her little symbol was in the north of Gautaya, next to a heraldic emblem she did not recognise. From there it would only be ten miles to the nearest cache of feathers. She could do that on foot at night, surely, without her absence being noted. In great excitement she left the archive and closed the door, after removing all traces of her presence.

I just wanted to stay safe. I'm obviously part now of some grand plan. A conspiracy. She would have to wait to learn exactly what the doulias' intentions were. *And I need to find out what they want me to do.*

After that Stémna collected the broken pottery and the glue and went up to the dormitory, taking off her dress again as she went, ready to attend to the needs of the stable lad.

It would have to be quick. She still had to wash her robe and mend that cup.

Girdlegard

In the Brown Mountains
Brigantia
1024 P.Q. (7515th solar cycle in old reckoning), winter

Klaey was too late.

He realised this when he saw the male and female zabitay commanders coming away from his eldest brother's suite of rooms. The orders had obviously already been given and the session was over.

So Klaey was not being given any significant role to play in whatever the Omuthan was planning. Or maybe not any role at all. Or, worse still, *Am I about to have an audience with the Omuthan to hear my own death sentence?*

Shortly before reaching the large chamber, heart in mouth, he encountered Kawutan, who had had to relinquish his temporary control of Brigantia when Orweyn regained his senses. His regency was over and his resentment was clear. Others had taken over the highest offices in the land, but for Kawutan personally the Omuthan's recovery had meant a downgrading of his status.

Wearing a tantalisingly attractive shimmering gold silk robe, Ilenis was accompanying Kawutan. She darted a passionate look at Klaey without her husband's noticing.

'Brother dear! What have I missed?' Klaey called, greeting the pair effusively. Suddenly, even in his own sand-coloured military dress bearing the insignia of a junior banner officer candidate in the supplies department he felt superior to this brother in the green uniform. *The braggart deserved his downfall.* He would never forget how Kawutan had nearly sent him to the cells. 'Has our Omuthan chucked everyone out in a fit of pique or did I just get the time wrong?'

'You did not get the time wrong.' Ilenis smiled and linked arms with her spouse so that her loyalty could not be doubted. 'But I'm afraid we can't reveal anything about the meeting.' She looked at Kawutan.

'What? You're keeping secrets?' Klaey looked round at the departing zabitays, who were already halfway down the corridor. 'Nearly everyone in the Brown Mountains seems to know what's going to happen and they've all got their orders, but—'

'You know very well why you're not exactly in his good books,' Kawutan interrupted. He looked distracted, and freed his arm from his wife's. He was seething with anger. 'Orweyn has imposed our silence on the matter. Under threat of dire punishment, Klaey. So don't even ask.'

'Right. Then I'll listen to whatever he wants me for.'

Unexpectedly Kawutan stepped in close and grabbed him by the shoulders. 'You know about Hantu. The rhamak. The one from the Outer Lands.'

'Know about him? I've only seen him that one time, talking to you. There are the wildest rumours going round about the recent influx of guests,' Klaey responded. 'Narshân beasts. The Tower That Walks. And then this strange mystical being, of course. What name did you give him just now?'

'I presume our brother will give you his orders . . . it would be a good idea to consider them carefully.' Kawutan chose his words with precision in order to steer clear of actually committing treason. 'Whatever you may have heard about the rhamak, it's worse than that.'

'Much worse,' Ilenis added, her expression now one of deep concern.

'His task for me can hardly be of great significance,' Klaey returned, although he was feeling increasingly unsettled. 'Otherwise he would surely have invited me to be part of the meeting just now.'

'I think it's the other way about. You will have to weigh up the likely consequences for yourself.' Kawutan slowly released his hold on his younger brother's shoulder. 'A decisive battle is about to be fought, but victory at just any price ought not to be sought.' The message in his eyes was a determined warning.

Klaey did not understand. He had never known his brother as serious as this. 'Now I'm really curious as to what to expect.'

'Don't say anything about having met us. Just act naïve and contrite. This will only be the second time you have seen him since he came round. It would be appropriate to show remorse.' Ilenis went past him and took Kawutan's hand. 'If you want to talk later, you know where to find me.'

'Right.' Klaey gave her a meaningful look and strode quickly along the corridor until he reached the Omuthan's apartments.

On coming round from his coma the Omuthan had summoned him, but had not spoken a word to him. All Klaey had been able to glimpse of the patient had been the eyes, the rest of him having been wrapped in bandages. But the message in the disappointed and resentful expression in those eyes had told Klaey what his eldest brother thought of him. He was soon told to leave.

Try not to let on. The guards on the door let him pass through to the enormous salon, where he found the Omuthan seated in an upholstered chair. 'You called for me?'

Servants were busily removing the used crockery and glassware from the side tables where the commanding officers had been seated. Fresh confectionery and four different types of tea were brought in. A delightful smell from the herbal tea and the cakes spread throughout the room. There was a plan of the fortress on a large table, also showing the enemy siege engines and encampment. Their own and the enemy units were marked with wooden figures.

Orweyn gestured to the chair opposite him and waited until the servants had left. He had a wide mantle of a soft fabric round his shoulders, resting loosely so as not to aggravate the discomfort from the burns he had received. He was still bandaged up to the chin but his face was free, with new skin showing bright pink. 'You have heard that the enemy is about to launch a final assault on Brigantia?'

'I have heard rumours. As a banner officer cadet in the supply unit I don't get to be on the ramparts,' Klaey responded, his voice a mere croak. He poured himself some white tea.

'Can you think what has caused this change in the enemy's approach?'

'How would I know what is going on in Goldhand's head? Or the other idiots he has round him? They will get themselves bloody noses if they try to storm the fortress.' Klaey watched the Omuthan expectantly to see what he would request as refreshment. Orweyn selected red tea. 'And anyway, your zabitays will know more about the art of warfare than I do.'

'The fact that the besieging army is preparing to attack means they must have recourse to magic strong enough to broach our gates. Their war-wolf catapults are still hurling missiles but this is just to distract us and to make us think they don't have any more powerful means to attack us with.' He pointed to the diagram of the beleaguered fortress. 'I had been thinking we should take the long view in planning our defence tactics. I was wrong.'

Klaey pursed his lips. 'What have we got to offer against magic?'

'It could also be the case that they might have heard about our new guests and the rhamak,' Orweyn went on, as if he had not heard the question. 'The corpse of the little ragana has been found in one of the corridors, I hear?'

'Yes. Savaged to death by a narshân. Some madmen have gone to some lengths to preserve her head in a jar of honey in order to be able to claim the Girdlegard reward once the siege is over.' Klaey was doing well in hiding his nervousness. He helped himself to biscuits. 'So, as you commanded, the moor-witch has been killed.'

Orweyn kept his eyes fixed on his youngest brother. 'That corridor. The one where they found the body. It leads to where the rhamak is. It would seem she was trying to get to see him.'

'Possible.' Klaey chewed a biscuit, but was not able to enjoy the buttery taste. He was feeling increasingly tense. *It's probably a good thing my voice always sounds this way.* 'Why are you concerned?'

'I'm wondering where the puppet woman has got to.' Orweyn accepted the cup of tea and breathed in the fragrant steam.

So he knows. Any moment now the guards will storm in and arrest me! Cadengis, I place my life in your hands. 'Somewhere in Girdle-gard, I expect, carving new marionettes for her theatre. She won't have been stupid enough to have come to Brigantia along with her aprendisa.' Klaey quickly drank some tea. His mouth felt very dry.

'There was a great deal of upheaval in the enemy encampment a few orbits ago. The same night that our sentries found a rope hanging over the fortress walls. And one of the narshân beasts has disappeared.' Orweyn put down his cup. 'I think Goldhand was playing a trick on us when he placed rewards on the women's heads. He wanted them to come here and pretend they were on our side. All pretence. They were to spy on us.'

'Aha?' Klaey started to relax somewhat. *So he doesn't suspect me.* 'You think Rodana was here and has made her escape over the ramparts to tell Goldhand about the rhamak?'

'Exactly. And the ragana was trying to confront him to kill

him, I assume. Think about where she was found.' Orweyn seemed utterly convinced. 'On the retreat from the Two-Stream Hill there was so much confusion. Who knows how many spies Goldhand has smuggled in?'

'I understand. It's certainly worth thinking about. Thank you.' Klaey leaned back. 'What are your immediate plans, Omuthan? And what is my part in them?'

Orweyn put his burn-scarred hands together. 'If the puppeteer has managed to collect information about Hantu and things happen as I fear, then we lose the element of surprise about the rhamak's special gifts. So it is vital that Hantu uses his powers immediately.'

'Immediately means . . .?'

'At once.' Orweyn cleared his throat. 'I have given the order for a sortie. In two sandglasses the main gate will open, as well as the two secondary gates to let our troops storm out to attack the enemy.'

Not such a good move, I fear. 'You know that our numbers —' Klaey began.

'Hantu will summon beings from another dimension, invulnerable to sword blades and magic,' Orweyn interrupted triumphantly. 'Side by side with our warriors and the Tower That Walks and the narshân beasts. With our combined resources we shall sweep away their siege and destroy them all.'

Klaey did not dare offer any estimation of the probable consequences of such an attack. He was more immediately concerned with a different issue. 'And what about me?'

'Have you got your flying horse back?'

'No. Deathwing has vanished.'

'Good! I was afraid you might set fire to me again from up in the air.' The Omuthan laughed. 'Your task is to ensure that all the non-combatants gather in the big shelter room. It is near the collapsed section of the right-hand tunnel. This should include, of course, all the families.'

It seemed to Klaey that very little time was being allotted to this exercise. 'Inside of two sandglasses?'

'As a junior stores-and-supplies officer you will be accustomed to dispositions of the kind being carried out at speed. They will need provisions and water, in case they have to remain there for a long time. It may be that our troops will be away after the attack hunting down the surviving enemies, to make sure that the last of the siege forces have been eliminated.' Orweyn sounded as if he were concerned about the safety of those left behind. 'To protect the weak and the families you will remain with them. You will have a unit with you. I don't want Goldhand's spies and assassins wreaking havoc and seeking revenge for the defeat he will have suffered.'

In principle Klaey approved of the task he had been allotted. It was very good. This way he would not be at the front fighting for his life. He could sit it out and wait and see how things developed. But he was well aware that there was something else implicit in this order. 'I have only twenty swords at my disposal. Do you think that will be sufficient?'

'Access to the shelter was deliberately kept narrow and so it can be easily defended by a small number of soldiers.' Orweyn smiled and, as he did so, a small crack appeared in the delicate new skin under the cheekbone. Blood started to ooze out. He dabbed it away with his sleeve. 'I had to promise the zabitays I wouldn't give you anything important to do because it might affect our success. Quite a few of them wanted me to punish you. In fact, they wanted me to have you executed, because you lost us the battle at Two-Stream Hill.'

'To the Mother of Cadengis with the lot of them!' Klaey sat up, angrily. 'I've explained time and again that it was that dwarf, Goïmron Chiselcut, that sent me off course with his magic and then the firepots—'

'Calm down.' Orweyn held up his hand, revealing blood-stains on the bandages on his wrist. 'I know that, little brother. And we shall ensure it will be this groundling that is thoroughly punished for it. Not you.'

'Thank you.'

'Now be off with you.' The Omuthan pointed to the door. 'The sortie will be going ahead inside of two sandglasses. Get all the non-combatants taken to safety.'

Klaey stood up and bowed, but then stretched out a hand to the plate of cakes and biscuits. 'I'll take these for on the way. I didn't get any dinner.'

'Help yourself.' Orweyn gave a friendly smile. 'We shall celebrate our victory together, little brother. And then I shall promote you, even if the commanders all disapprove. What can they do? I am their Omuthan, after all!' He laughed.

In his croaking voice Klaey joined in the mirth, and waved as he left the room.

As soon as he was out of sight and hearing of his brother, his fake light mood disappeared. *You absolute bastard! You swine, son of all swine!* Incensed, he stuffed cake into his mouth and hurried through the corridors to reach the tiny cupboard that served as the quartermaster's office, where the tedious lists of provisions and equipment for the fortress were kept. *Did you think I wouldn't work out what you are up to?*

The people he was to shepherd into the shelter were intended to be bait and fodder for the beings from other spheres that Hantu would be summoning. Crowded into the cave and without any prospect of ever getting out alive. Orweyn's hoped-for victory would be paid for in a double reckoning of blood: the lives that would be lost on the battlefield and the lives of the unsuspecting victims who would be butchered in the shelter.

Women and children. The old and the sick. Klaey nearly choked on the cake. He shoved the plate into the hands of an astonished guard and raced off. The Omuthan would surely be already thinking up how to blame someone else entirely for the terrible death toll. *Probably Goldhand's assassins. And I'm supposed to die in the cave alongside the others. That much is clear.* Without expressly saying so, his brother had condemned him to death. *Duplicitous wretched hole of a scumbag!* He played through various scenarios in his head, working out what might be feasible. But one fact remained indisputable: his brother planned for him to die. Irrespective of whether or not he saved the lives of the pitiful victims in the shelter. And irrespective of whether the fortress defenders' sortie was successful or not.

I absolutely have to get out of Brigantia. This realm is going to go down. Or else it will be upheld by means I am not prepared to have anything to do with. As far as Klaey was concerned Hantu could gather his own sacrificial lambs and slit their throats himself. *I'm certainly not going to help do it.*

However, it was clear that an unthinking reckless flight was out of the question. *I need a plan for getting through the army lines.*

And the basis for this very plan occurred to him before he had drawn his next breath.

'The water cannon – now!' Hargorina commanded. She was supervising procedures for the artillery crews. It was essential to iron out any miscalculations and the constant rhythm of attack had to be maintained.

Gata, nearby, was impressed by the simplicity of this idea. The huge water-filled skins, sewn together from animal hides, burst on impact when hurled at the ramparts, flooding the walkways and coursing down the walls. Given the current air temperature, it did not take long for the water to freeze over. The Brigantian soldiers were struggling to keep their footing.

In other places the icy water expanding between the stones weakened the masonry, so that the siege engines and catapults were finally being effective.

Five of these giant hide sacks shot through the air, accurately striking the stronghold defences and bursting open. Floods of water streamed everywhere, adding to the sheet-ice already on the walls.

'Excellent,' said Gata, approaching Hargorina, the woman who had originally trained her in the military arts. 'That will have taken the Omuthan by surprise.'

'And how! They're sending out all their reinforcements to tackle the ice with hot coal.' Hargorina was checking targeting success rates and studying enemy activity with her glass seeing-scope. Her copper-red hair was concealed for now under a cap, making it easier to wear a helmet. 'It won't be any use, though.'

Gata glanced at the war-wolf catapults, which had recently been adjusted for this new procedure. *The new strategy is working well.* The payload was being flung in a higher trajectory. Instead of bombarding the lower walls the catapults were aiming at the iced-over ramparts on the east side of the fortress.

And with notable success. The masonry built up on top of the walls over the course of many hundreds of cycles by the Brigantians was being taken down, bit by bit, with the debris crashing below to form great piles in the depths of the moat-ditch.

Gata lifted her eyes up to the lookout post. Semaphore messages were being relayed down to themselves and the other battlefield commanders. 'The signal says Brigantia is expecting an onslaught soon. They have seen our troops assembling.'

'Just what we wanted them to think.' On Hargorina's orders, larger twelve-sided blocks were now being loaded into the slings of the gigantic war-wolf siege engines. The shape of the missiles brought the advantage on impact of a greater destructive force. If they made it over the walls they would continue down into the heart of the fortress, crushing anything in their path: soldiers, vehicles, equipment, supplies and even whole buildings. 'How long now?'

'One run of the sandglass,' Gata replied, observing the empty area outside the main fortress entrance. Positions and trenches were abandoned and empty. Dwarves, elves, humans and meldriths were assembling on the eastern side. They were carrying siege ladders and storm hooks with chain pulleys; mobile catapults would shoot the anchor-sized hooks up to the walls. Counterweights and guide rollers would take the boldest of the first wave of attackers up in support slings. 'Then everything will be decided once and for all.'

'Brigantia will fall.'

'I can only hope that the rhamak hasn't already sent out his summons to the other dimensions. Or our plan is for naught.' Gata pulled a leather strap tighter. There would be no time to correct anything in the heat of battle. 'See you again soon.'

'Where are you off to?' Hargorina asked.

'A final prayer to Lorimbur. We are in urgent need of his aid.' Gata hurried past the catapult operators and masons chipping away at the stone blocks, until she reached the far end of the longhouse where her own quarters were. She knelt before the statue of Lorimbur, the tribal father of all the Thirdlings, and lit the brazier, scattering incense and fragrant herbs on the coals. She added bonemeal and iron filings.

'I shall win this victory for you, Lorimbur,' Gata whispered to the sculpted figure. She placed her axe sword on the ground in front of it. 'It will be in your name, Lorimbur, that I shall destroy Brigantia, even if the army shouts out the name of my own dead father. The Thirdlings will forget him soon enough. I shall ensure this.'

Gata had no proof that Vanéra was behind her father's

sudden demise. It was evident that he had drunk himself to death with the goblet the maga had expressly warned him about. The magic goblet that had been a gift was capable of changing its nature, the maga had said, if misused.

The Thirdling queen had no axe to grind with Vanéra, who had in effect made Gata's secret wish come true, but she was angry with Goldhand for refusing Mòndarcai's offer of a pact. *Of course, no älf can be trusted. Mostly.* But something told her this rule did not always hold true. In an unconscious reflex she touched the brooch inherited from her ancestors and which had once been her father's. *Lorimbur, you will be victorious over Vraccas. All the dwarf tribes will realise this. This is how it will be in the coming battle.* Gata had ordered her troops to wear Lorimbur's rune marked on their armour when they went into battle, honouring their tribal founder. The name of Vraccas would not be issuing from Gata's throat.

She ended her prayer with a deep sigh, but she remained in place. Her thoughts were with Goïmron, the dwarf who had managed to win her heart. Every conversation with him had intensified her emotions. And although she was aware he admired Rodana, this did not change her feelings for him. *Lorimbur, do not allow darkness and malice to enter my heart.* It had certainly occurred to Gata that she might encourage Mostro in his demands for severe punishment for Rodana. A death sentence would remove her as a rival in love. For ever.

But this was something she could never do to Goïmron. Gata was putting her money on the possibility that his love for the human would fade when he realised that his affections were not being returned. *He will recognise that I have so much more to offer than she does.*

Following the battle and the victory she would set off to find Goïmron. She refused to believe that Szmajro had spirited him off purely in order to devour him in peace somewhere safe.

Whatever the dragon intends, I'm bringing back my future spouse. Gata grasped the handle of her axe sword and studied the weapon. *No scaled dragon creature is going to stop me.*

Bugle calls sounded outside.

That's the first signal! Gata got quickly to her feet and bowed her head to the Lorimbur statuette. Then she hurried out of the room and out of the longhouse, running in a slight curve to reach the entrance to the trench that would bring her to the front line.

'Ah, there you are.' Brûgar moved to her side to join her. His shiny blue beard was freshly dyed, oiled and groomed. He had his war flail over his shoulder and the inevitable war pipe in the corner of his mouth. This tobacco smelled of sweetwood and orange. 'We were starting to think you weren't going to turn up till we'd done all the fighting.'

Belîngor was at her other side, his battleaxe in his left hand. *'This is going to be fun,'* he told them in sign language. *'For us. Not for the Brigantians.'*

To her surprise Gata saw a human female in a suit of armour of an unfamiliar kind: a combination of lamellar and scale armour, but with the torso covered in rigid plate metal. 'Is that Vanéra?' Glancing back at the maga, Gata saw that a maid was helping her to fit a helmet over the pinned-up coiffure, while a squire was buckling the straps on her leg protectors. Another man held out a two-handed sword, one and a half paces long, and surely so heavy that it would only have been suitable for a fully grown orc. 'What's she going to do with that? She'll never be able to carry it.'

'It's all stuff from the Chamber of Wonders, apparently,' Brûgar explained. Like the others, this fast jogging was having no adverse effects on his breathing. 'It's said the armour is as easy to wear as a silken dress and the sword is as light as a feather . . .'

'We'll find out soon enough.' This from Belîngor. 'She wouldn't do it if she knew it wasn't safe.'

'True enough.' Gata could not imagine how the maga would cope in a swordfight with an aggressor. *She's no warrior.* 'Has she had any kind of training? Do either of you know?'

'She will probably spin round like a top. Best not to get too close,' Brûgar advised, laughing through clenched teeth, so as not to drop his pipe. 'A wand-wielder thrashing about with a giant's sword blade. Could be quite a spectacle, by Lorimbur!' He puffed noisily.

'What else has she got?' Gata stepped into the trench corridor, the two warrior dwarves close on her heels. 'Hope her artefacts are better than Mostro's.'

'Supposed to be. She's equipped the long'uns in the front line with special weapons – magic blades from the Chamber of Wonders.' Brûgar's tone of voice made it clear he did not approve. 'As long as she takes the heat off us in the battle, that's fine by me.'

Belîngor laughed.

Gata and her companions made their way quickly along the deep trench without coming across anyone else. The thumps coming from the war-wolves and the noise of the boulders thudding into the walls of the fortress were softened by the high sides of the trench. The rattling and clanging of the advancing troops was quieter down there. It smelled of damp earth and mud.

A second horn signal was sounded from the crow's nest.

Soon the smell will be of blood. A lot of blood. Gata had reached the first cross trench, and she placed her foot on the step that had been cut into the walls to make it easier to surge up and attack. 'So here we are.'

The main gate, undamaged and impenetrable, loomed up not a hundred paces away in front of the trio. No one else was around far and wide. All the other Girdlegard forces were massing on the eastern side, ready to storm the fortress.

Then the third signal sounded out and a wild shout was uttered in unison from thousands of throats. The attack began. Gata found the whole atmosphere unreal. She looked at the empty area in front of the double-winged gate. 'We are the only ones.'

'We are indeed. But our hearts are strong enough for a thousand.' Brûgar gave a wolfish grin, smoke pouring out of mouth and nose. He raised his war flail. 'I am ready.'

'*Me too*,' Belîngor signed, gesticulating with his long-handled axe. '*After you, my queen. The honour is yours.*'

Gata took a deep breath, grabbed hold of the icy soil and pulled herself up out of the trench. She swung her axe sword. 'For Lorimbur!' was her battle cry as she charged forward.

Brûgar and Belîngor followed without a second's hesitation.

Humans do not stumble over mountains, they trip over molehills.

Dwarves on the other hand are never on top of the mountains in the first place. No stumbling at all. Much more important.

Old dwarf saying

X

Girdlegard

In the Brown Mountains
Brigantia
1024 P.Q. (7515th solar cycle in old reckoning), winter

'Off with you. Everybody to the East Wall,' Klaey shouted, hurrying through the beginnings of a light snowfall towards the westernmost tower. He approached the foot of the edifice, where a fifty-strong troop of armed guards was on duty. Four men and one woman were standing round a brazier. There was light up in the tower and the rest of the company were inside, keeping warm. 'The Omuthan needs you over on the east side.'

One of the commanders detached herself from the group and came over to meet him. 'Since when does a junior banner officer candidate get to give me orders?' She had a scarf over her mouth and nose and the padded helmet left only her piercing green eyes visible. Klaey had ten of his own supply corps soldiers in his wake – they were trusted colleagues who were also keen to make their escape.

'We're taking over sentry duty here,' Klaey lied. 'Combat units are needed at the front. Did you not see the size of the Girdlegard army?'

'Our orders are normally delivered by official messenger, banner officer candidate.'

'There was no time for that, zabitaya.' Klaey took off his hood to display the symbolic family brand on his forehead. 'I bring you this command in the name of the Berengart family. Get a move on! Or the fortress will fall and we shall all die!'

Still hesitating, the zabitaya looked at the soldiers behind Klaey. 'Are you telling me those random fellows are going to be on watch here? They're just supply corps, aren't they?'

'All we've been asked to do is sound the alarm if we see anything happening at the west gate,' he replied. 'There's ten of us, and we're all messengers, if you like.' He pointed up at the tower. 'Tell the others. They need every sword and every shield over on the east. If we can repel the enemy attack there's a sortie planned with our own troops.'

'A sortie?' The zabitaya stared in surprise. 'That's the first I've heard about it.'

'That would be because I'm a Berengart and you're not. My eldest brother is dead set on eradicating the enemy so he can take over Girdlegard himself.' Klaey made shooing gestures with his arms. 'Come on, be off with you. Can't you hear the alarm horns? The eastern wall is under heavy fire.'

The zabitaya gave him another searching look and then, to Klaey's immense relief, she gave the order to get ready to depart. Her colleagues climbed the tower's spiral stairs to inform the rest of the company they were to leave.

'May Cadengis be with you,' the commander said.

'And with yourselves.' Klaey gave a friendly nod in acknowledgement. 'We'll keep guard here. You go and save the realm. We will always be in your debt.'

The zabitaya rolled her eyes a little at that and disappeared up the stairs.

Klaey slowly turned round with a cheeky grin on his face. 'What did I tell you?'

His companions laughed and stepped forward, ready to

remove the bolts and bars on the low iron door that led to the outside. From the exterior it looked like part of the stone cladding in the wall beneath the tower. The dwarves of old had devised this secret entrance for spies to come and go. It gave access to a narrow pathway that wound through Girdlegard. Since the earthquakes this path was no longer functional, but the portal for spies and scouts was still in existence.

The besieging armies had of course been aware of this, but the extremely small opening was totally unsuitable for any attempt at storming the fortress: too low, very narrow, securely barricaded and too well defended. That was why the battle was being fought on the eastern side, where the besieging army had been belabouring the walls with a combination of freezing water and the twelve-cornered stones.

This all suited Klaey's plan. This little doorway would provide their escape route from Brigantia's impending defeat. 'Kiil and Irmon, go and fetch our provisions and equipment. Then we set off while the main attack is still under way.'

The men saluted and raced off to collect the rucksacks they had prepared earlier.

Even if he tried his best to hide it, Klaey was extremely apprehensive, remembering the last time he had set out with a gang of soldiers on a secret mission to make his fortune, and how it had ended in catastrophe, and very nearly in his own death.

Today will be different. Klaey kept a weather eye open in case a messenger or one of the zabitays turned up. That would certainly put paid to their chances. He kept one hand on the long dagger that he was absolutely ready to use. *I am not heading for destruction along with my idiot shit of a brother. May the demons get him!*

Their preparations over, Kiil and Irmon were soon back and the bolts and bars had been removed from the door.

'Right you are. Stick to our agreed plan.' Klaey watched his group of ten. Two of them were holding Gauragon uniform tunics ready to don once they were safely a couple of hundred paces away from the fortress. Then they would transform themselves into Gauragonians who had captured nine spies from Brigantia and were taking them off to be interrogated. They would surely be allowed through the battle lines. That is, if anyone even noticed them at all.

Klaey opened up the spy-door, crawled along the narrow tunnel under the ramparts and removed the rusty fittings on the door at the far side. It was some time before he was able to venture a cautious glance outside. At the other end of the stronghold the war-wolves were bombarding the ramparts with rock after rock. The besieging forces were getting into position to storm the walls.

'There's nobody here,' he called back over his shoulder to the others. 'Let's go!' He was the first to set off, bending double to avoid being seen. His heavy rucksack was making him lean forward at a precarious angle and the muscles of leg and buttocks were protesting at the length of this mode of travel. His people followed him, their footsteps crunching in new-fallen snow over the coating of ice.

'Will you look at that!' exclaimed one of them. 'Over there at the main gate!'

Klaey turned – and saw three dwarves launching themselves out of the trench, weapons drawn, and heading for the main entrance, to all intents and purposes as if they thought the gate was about to swing open to receive them and Brigantia was going to surrender.

'That's not how you do a surprise attack,' he said. His companions laughed quietly.

Behind them a woman's furious voice was heard. 'Banner Officer Candidate Berengart! Halt in the name of the Omuthan!'

To Cadengis with her! It was that confounded female zabitaya. She had come back! 'Keep going!' he ordered his group. He crouched down, making himself smaller. 'There should be a side trench we can jump into.'

There was a soft whirring sound and he felt a jolt in his back. The projectile had lodged in his rucksack and gone nearly all the way through, but had not pierced his armour.

'The next arrow will get you!' the zabitaya called. 'Come back here and give yourself up. Or you and your soldiers will all be shot like the cowards you are!'

Klaey stopped and looked at his group. 'Carry on,' he ordered softly. 'Keep it slow. Don't run.' He looked back at the zabitaya standing at the open door of the spies' entrance with a handful of her soldiers. He waved to her. 'No! You go back!' he responded in his croaky voice, affecting impatience. 'You are endangering our mission!'

'No one knows anything about any mission. Or that you are supposed to be guarding the gate.' She made a sign and the archers placed arrows to their bowstrings. 'On the contrary. We've been told you have disobeyed orders. This is your last warning.'

'Listen! I am Klaey Brengart—'

'Exactly. Turn back or die.' The zabitaya stretched her bowstring back, ready to fire. 'Well?'

Why would we turn back, just to get executed anyway? However dire his predicament, he could not help laughing at the thought. 'Neither option is attractive, zabitaya.' When selecting the type of death awaiting him the choice was only one of the relative speediness of dispatch. And the rucksack could absorb quite a few hits. He would risk it. 'I bid you farewell. Tell the Omuthan that I prefer not to be sacrificed. He will know what I mean.'

'I shall tell him.' The zabitaya lowered her hand slowly – and, without completing the command to fire, released a smothered sound. An arrow had pierced her side, penetrating the leather armour. She took half a step back before collapsing in front of the small open door into the fortress.

Klaey was astonished to see a srgāláh racing over, zigzagging and whirling his sword-staff. He deflected two arrows with the broad blade of his weapon. All the other shots missed him. *A scout on reconnaissance!*

Close on the heels of the srgāláh came a blond elf who was taking out the fortress defenders one by one with his short bow. Three or four slashes of the srgāláh's spear-like weapon and all the Brigantians lay dead at the feet of this unequal pair.

Klaey did not for a moment think of stopping to confront them. They had dealt with the zabitaya for him, thus preventing or delaying his execution. *And it's not my fault the spy-door has been breached*, he thought, well pleased. *Oh, this is turning out very well.* He even dared to give the elf and the srgāláh a cheerful wave. 'Good luck!' he called to them. 'Kill the Omuthan for me, won't you? You have my blessing, you really do.'

As Klaey turned round to follow his troops he caught sight of events at the main gates where, but a few heartbeats earlier, three barmy dwarves had been the only ones far and wide.

By the mother of Cadengis! He was so surprised that he almost staggered and nearly fell, brought down by the weight of his rucksack. He had to stand and stare. *What is happening?*

Gata felt the prickling that meant Mostro's spell was fading. He had been concealing the true location of the attack.

The war-wolves were hurling their multi-cornered stone projectiles and the water-filled leather bags ceaselessly against the eastern side of the fortress. But the troops massed at the foot of those walls suddenly blurred into nothingness and the whole illusion dissolved away. At the same time the apparently empty space in front of the gate revealed the presence of the whole army, furnished with siege ladders and storming hooks, ready to take the undefended main ramparts of the fortress.

Gata, Brûgar and Belîngor had taken up their agreed positions in order to get through the broad open path in the mass of troops so as to head off the onslaught.

'Master Mostro, open up the gate for us,' Hargorina shouted as she joined the trio, with her sharp chin jutting belligerently. 'Children of the Smith and Heirs of Lorimbur: stand ready! Let us liberate the Brown Mountains. Let's get the scum kicked out!'

A battle cry arose from thousands of throats to echo against the walls. Siege ladders and catapulted grappling hooks were deployed. The advance party rushed fearlessly up the rungs of the sky-high ladders to hurl themselves on to the pitiful numbers of defenders. Some of the Brigantian slingshot devices were quickly operated but without enough time to adjust their aim, so that many of the bolts and spears and arrows they shot went wide of the targets.

'Behold, ye of little faith!' Mostro stood at the gates, legs planted wide and arms outstretched. He waved a watery-coloured noble topaz on the palm of one hand, directing it towards the barred entrance. 'You, all of you who mocked me as a useless famulus.' With his free left hand he pointed at the double gates. 'I shall tear down what is in my way! Get ready and remember for ever who it is making this miracle possible!'

He's got up like the emperor of Girdlegard, the self-important little famulus! Gata was getting impatient. She glanced over to the eastern side of the fortress. The Brigantians had worked out they had been duped by some magic trick or other and they were dispatching their forces over at full speed. 'He's so full of himself. All talk!'

Mostro closed his eyes and lowered his head, stretching

the fingers of his left hand out towards the portal. The noble topaz sent out glowing rays. 'Brigantia! Surrender! Give in to my power!'

Brûgar took the war pipe out of his mouth and spat on the ground. 'Can't he get this damned door open?' He quickly replaced the pipe and drew on it. As he puffed away he produced great clouds of smoke. 'The fool is totally besotted with himself.'

Belîngor's face darkened. *'Mostro is throwing away our advantage of a surprise attack.'* He kept his eye on the battlements, where the first of the Girdlegard attackers were doing well and were endeavouring to get over to the catapults before they could be reloaded.

'The Brigantians will be here soon.'

Vanéra arrived to stand next to her famulus in her magic armour. 'Come on, hurry up. Get going and cut out your ridiculous prattle,' she said, taking him to task brusquely, her two-hander sword raised in just the one hand. 'You'll have plenty of time for your heroic speeches later on.'

Mostro went red. He was obviously mortified at the rebuke. This made the topaz lose its glow. The maga's harsh words had ruined his concentration and his prepared spell began to falter.

'Oh, for pity's sake!' Gata saw catastrophe in the offing. If they did not get inside the stronghold within the next sixty heartbeats the whole attack on the ramparts would fail. As soon as the Omuthan moved his troops round, the army at the gates would be an easy target for them.

All of a sudden Telìnâs turned up. 'Queen, call up your best people,' he said, speaking quickly. There was perspiration coating his brow. 'And follow me.'

'What is it?'

'Sònuk and I have secured the spy-gate access into the fortress.'

'What?'

'Sònuk picked up the scent of a Brigantian outside the walls. One of the Berengart family. The one who used to have that flight-mare. He was making his escape.' The young elf ran off.

Gata gave the commands and the company of Thirdlings moved over to the west, following Telìnâs at speed. 'That is fantastic news.'

'That cursed wretch of a famulus!' Brûgar was running along beside her. 'Lorimbur's benevolence has given us the opportunity to overwhelm the Brigantians from behind their back.'

'I'm sure Mostro will want to take the credit for that, too,' Belîngor joked.

'Let's make sure this victory doesn't slip through our fingers. Then all the tribes will be grateful to us for ever.' Gata and her unit had now reached the expertly camouflaged secret entrance into the fortress.

Sònuk was at the threshold, saluting her, his ears pricked and alert. Blood was dripping from the blade of his spear. Many dead Brigantians lay strewn on the ground by the low doorway, which was only waist-high. 'The Berengart coward and his mates are over there, running off to the horizon.' He pointed to the silhouettes in the distance. 'I'll get them,' he growled, 'when we've finished here. I shan't forget his scent.'

'Don't be too hard on him. It's thanks to him we've found this little doorway.' Telìnâs slapped his friend on the shoulder and then crawled in. 'Let's make the entrance a bit bigger.'

Gata grasped her axe sword firmly. 'Right. What the famulus was not able to get done, we will do ourselves. Let's get the main gate open!' She made her way carefully through, followed by her unit, all ready for combat.

Mostro's confidence had taken a knock. It had gone the same way as his failed spell.

The words of the maga had downgraded him to a simple famulus in the first year of training, neither quick enough nor skilled enough to be of any use. Vanéra seemed unwilling to acknowledge that he was the only one in a position to weave spells and cast them effectively. *But all she can do is apply artefacts. Nothing more than that. Who does she think she is, treating me like that?*

'What's the matter? What are you waiting for?' He heard her cutting tones. 'The Brigantians will soon be outnumbering our people up there on the walkway. The whole army has got to get through into the fortress.'

Mostro felt heavy as lead and was unsure of what to do. Thousands of encouraging glances were focused on him but this did not help. And more and more alarm horns were being sounded inside the fortress. He saw a multitude of shadows rushing about behind the battlement walls, heard the clashing of weapons on armour and the screams of the bold soldiers who had already swung themselves up over the ramparts. The dying had started.

The famulus started to tremble violently. The noble topaz in his hand had lost its effectiveness. It no longer held any energy. Mostro would have to begin all over again using his own magic. He was not able to pronounce the incantation for broaching the doors and walls. The syllables were getting mixed up and making no sense at all. He could not force the enchantment to work, however desperately it was needed.

'By Palandiell, Sitalia and Elria! Just say the wretched formula like I sent you off to Enaiko to learn!' Vanéra raged. 'What else are you good for if you can't use your talents and your knowledge when it's needed? Shall I send to Rhuta for Adelia to come? She can replace you, maybe. I'm sure she'll be quicker on the uptake than you seem to be, Mostro. Come on! Or we'll end up with our people dying in their droves because of you!'

By now the advancing army had realised that Mostro's magic

had faltered and ceased. They started drumming on their shields to encourage the famulus.

This meant even greater performance pressure for Mostro. Thousands of expectations for him to fulfil.

Individual syllables were slipping through his mind like silvery fish, but he was unable to grab hold of any of them. Another part of his brain could see the terrible consequences of failure: a field of butchered troops in front of the solid portal still resolutely shut. And Brigantians crowding the ramparts and laughing themselves silly.

I can't! Mostro was overcome with fear. His throat closed up and his hands were shaking. The topaz quivered in his open palm. At the thought of Vanéra also lying dead in the field of corpses his feelings altered. Relief at first, then satisfaction. Followed by delight.

'Send a signal to the catapults,' one of the commanders near him yelled. 'They must adjust the range. Our confounded famulus is as good as useless. We've got to save what we can. Quick! Up the walls. It's too late to retreat.'

So, I'll always be the confounded useless famulus, as long as Vanéra is still around. Mostro's thoughts were still thrilling to the idea of the maga lying dead. He would only be free once she was dead. Free of the maga who had trained him. Free of her criticism. Free of all the petty humiliations of the past. *She has got to die in order for me to become a true magus.*

With a dull thud the bolts on the inside of the fifty-pace-high double doors were drawn back. A loud rumbling sound accompanied the mighty steel gates' opening, allowing the attacking forces free access to the fortress. At this success the whole army cheered the famulus, calling Mostro's name. They started to take up position in a wedge-shaped formation so they could force their way through the ranks of the defending army, like an arrow penetrating unprotected flesh.

'I know it wasn't you doing that,' Vanéra said, as the flood of warriors swept past them to the right and to the left. 'Just stay back, famulus.' She raised her two-handed sword and joined the storming troops. 'Leave this to those who know what they're doing.'

Stunned, Mostro stood motionless in the stream of weaponry, shields and armoured soldiers. He was thrust aside, and nearly pushed over several times, but he could not move from the spot. *She must die.* The words went round and round in his head.

The storm-charge of the besieging army lessened in intensity when the gates were fully opened, revealing piles of dead Brigantians in the courtyard, spears still in their hands. Others were clutching wounds in bellies or throats. Something else completely had killed them – not the besieging army.

Narshân beasts were investigating the piled bodies, freshly slaughtered, some still convulsing. The beasts kept their white eyes fixed on the rows of attackers, who had come to a shocked standstill at this gruesome sight.

At the other end of the yard stood a huge acront in silver armour. Dazzling yellow light streamed out of the ugly eye pieces of the helmet's demonic visor. The imposing figure, three paces tall, was swinging a double-bladed axe and a war club in its gauntleted hands. The glowing eyes were directed towards the superior numbers of the attackers, as if offering an individual challenge to each and every warrior.

Finally, a misshapen lump of a man in a ragged, patched garment came limping along to stand at the acront's side. Slowly he raised his arms as if conducting an invisible orchestra, but his right hand showed the continuous tremor of a chronic disability. One shoulder was noticeably higher than the other and the man's back was twisted and bent like a reed in the wind.

That is the rhamak. Mostro was fascinated. *Did he kill all those soldiers?*

At this point a golden shimmer appeared above each of the corpses, streaming upwards and coalescing to form a cone-shaped flickering cloud, from which there suddenly emerged red claws at the end of a muscular forearm. The leathery skin was ablaze, with the flames burning a threatening yellowish green.

'Forward!' Vanéra yelled. 'Let's attack before it has a chance to finish materialising. I'll hold it back, you capture the fortress.' She started running, her two-handed sword lifted high, ready to strike. Arrows aimed at her by the archers on the high walkway were deflected by her magic armour. Nothing could halt the maga's progress. The river of steel stopped momentarily and then restarted. The attacking soldiers shouted in unison to give themselves encouragement.

It must have been poison, Mostro presumed. *The Brigantians have been sacrificed in order to tempt this being down out of his other sphere.* He stayed motionless while the rear-guard of the army streamed past him. The famulus followed the course of the action from a safe distance, watching the narshân beasts and the acront confronting the attackers and gouging great gaps out of their ranks. He saw a creature with six arms lunge forward out of the glittering gold cloud. It was covered in burning metal armour and equipped with four long swords and two huge clubs. The earth shook when this creature attacked. Each time it struck home, ten or twenty lives were lost.

But as Vanéra had commanded, the Girdlegard troops surged through into the passages and alleyways of the fortress, quelling the resistance of the Brigantians and winning ground step by step.

It started snowing. The chilly flakes landed on Mostro as he stood by himself out on the plain in front of the ramparts. He did not move. He watched his maga in combat with the unknown creature. Her enchanted armour sent out sparks each time she was hit but it continued to protect her. On the other hand, however, she was having no success with her two-handed sword as it failed to make any impression on the extraordinary adversary she was facing. Vanéra cleverly managed to prevent the creature attacking any of the Girdlegard soldiers.

Up on the battlements the castle defenders had been beaten back and defeated. The clashing sound of steel on steel ebbed away and the heart of the armed struggle was now inside the fortress. From what Mostro could gather it looked as if the acront had fallen at the hands of a band of dwarves led by Gata. Brûgar and Belîngor, helped by Telìnâs and Sònuk, were locked in combat with the pack of narshân beasts. There was no sign of the rhamak.

When the dwarves joined in the fighting against the monster from the far-off dimension, more and more magic artefacts were being deployed, distracting the creature, and Vanéra landed a blow on its underbelly. With a bloodcurdling, ear-piercingly loud scream, the likes of which had never been heard in Girdlegard before, the strange being fell on its side in its death throes. Mostro had to hold his hands to his ears, and all the soldiers in the immediate vicinity of the convulsing creature collapsed to the ground. The overwhelming sound of the scream of agony knocked them all unconscious – humans, dwarves, elves and meldriths alike. Silence fell in the fortress.

Now Mostro stepped forward.

Having arrived in the courtyard, he lifted a broken-off section of the creature's claw. He stopped where Vanéra had fainted and looked down with utter disdain as she lay there.

I have finished. I have completed my training. He bent swiftly and pressed the sharp fragment into her throat, severing the jugular. *And I have finished with you.*

Coming to, the maga opened her eyes and pressed her right hand on to the wound in her throat, trying to pull the sharp object out. But Mostro stamped on her wrist. He stared wordlessly into her eyes to watch her life force die away.

A slight noise made him swing round, drawing his short sword and pointing it at the misshapen human behind him in the patched robe. The figure held a dagger in one trembling hand.

'Are you Hantu?' Mostro placed the tip of his sword at the man's throat.

The man, wearing a white hood, nodded carefully. He was obviously well versed in the exigencies of close combat. His smooth-shaven and regular facial features were surprisingly attractive. It was as if his head had been placed on the wrong body.

'You know what will happen when they get you?' Mostro threatened.

Eyes wide, Hantu nodded.

'Do you want to die with the Omuthan and the Brigantians?'

'No! Really not! Please —'

'Very well. I shall make you an offer.' Mostro checked that nobody could overhear. All the soldiers were still unconscious. 'I am prepared to hide you in Rhuta. I can protect you. But you have to teach me your craft. I want to be the mightiest magus in the whole of Girdlegard. With or without having to rely on magic energy.'

Hantu sank to his knees and dropped his dagger. 'Let me instruct you. And serve you. I will accept any conditions, Master, if you let me live.'

'Quiet.' Mostro gave the man a small cut through the fabric and into the flesh near the crooked collarbone. Then he took a thumbnail-sized slice of black onyx out of his bag of gems and inserted it under the man's skin, murmuring a simple formula. The enchantment immediately permeated the rhamak's form and features and transformed the twisted human into a youth of healthy stature and strong bones.

'If you remove the onyx-disc, you will die. If you attempt to flee from me and more than one orbit passes before I hear from you, I shall detonate the stone,' Mostro announced. 'Do not abuse my kindness. We have an agreement. Your life for your knowledge.'

'I shall never deceive you.' Hantu kissed Mostro's boots.

'Take some clothing and armour off some of the Gauragon dead. Rub their blood and guts on yourself. You need to get past the srgāláh's nose. Get yourself out of the fortress and come to my tent after dark. You are now my servant and bodyguard.' He gave the transformed man a kick to send him on his way. 'Get out before the others turn up, or before any of these soldiers wake up again.'

Hantu hurried to the pile of the dead and selected a corpse to drag over to a niche at the side of the courtyard.

Mostro noticed some of the unconscious soldiers were starting to come round. *It's time to begin composing the legend that suits my purposes best.*

He quickly grasped the maga's two-handed magic sword and, rushing over to where the strange creature lay dead, plunged the weapon into the cadaver. Vanéra would not be praised as the heroine of the orbit for long. He would find a suitable story to accompany the action. *Who's going to gainsay it?* Mostro closed his eyes with an expression of satisfaction and waited for all the troops to wake up.

Gata sat up, gasping for air. Her ears were still ringing and her hearing was affected. The creature's death-cry had over-whelmed her senses and made her pass out. *Is it still dead?*

Brûgar was soon at her side to help her up. 'Is everything all right, queen?' He picked up the war pipe that she had dropped. The tobacco was no longer alight.

'I think so. But I can't hear properly.' To Gata's surprise, she saw the famulus lying next to the dead six-armed creature that would easily have killed them all had they not had recourse to the artefacts and the magic sword. Mostro was holding the two-hander, and had pierced the monster's body. *He did that?*

Horrified, Belîngor knelt down at Vanéra's side. '*She's dead!*' he signed.

'What?' As Gata went over with Brûgar, she stumbled a little. She saw the fragment of claw in the maga's throat and took in the image of the empty eyes. Snowflakes were covering the maga's immobile upturned face. 'By Lorimbur! What . . . what happened after we all passed out?'

Mostro stood up, groaning, and let go of the hilt of the sword. 'Is she . . . is the maga unharmed?' he stammered, apparently full of concern for her welfare. He almost slipped on the blood-ied snow in his rush to get to her. 'No! Palandiell! No!' Sobbing violently, he threw himself on to her dead body. 'I thought I had been able to prevent that!'

'Whatever happened?' Gata pushed him off Vanéra's body. 'But we'd already killed the creature!'

'No. It wasn't completely dead.' Mostro sniffed and wiped away some tears and some blood with his sleeve. 'After the crea-ture gave that scream and fell, you all fainted. I was standing by the gate like Vanéra told me to. Because I was further away the noise did not affect me the same way. It just made me dizzy. But then it got up again. So I ran over and used the strongest magic spell I had – the same one I'd used to open the fortress gates – I wanted to make the creature explode,' he said, speaking all in a rush. 'But in my excitement the spell did not work, so I grabbed the sword when the monster started to attack my Esteemed Maga. My sword blow felled the creature.' He moved the bloodied brown strands of hair from her face, revealing thin red lines on her skin. 'And then I passed out when it screamed the second time.' Mostro sobbed again. 'My only thought was to save her! And I thought I had!' He buried his face in his hands. 'O ye gods!'

'You did what you could. It was courageous of you,' said Brûgar. Surprised, he grasped his blue beard. 'We owe you our lives, in that case.'

'Don't thank me. I only did what anyone would have done,' the famulus said through his fingers.

Belîngor looked down at the creature and the dead maga lying in the snow. After a long glance at Gata, he shook his head. He did not believe the young man's words.

Gata was also doubtful about the truth of the story. 'You have indeed done something amazing. You opened the gates, you killed the beast,' she said, her tone full of praise, but the gesture she made towards the two dwarves indicated the opposite.

What really happened? Gata could not remember seeing the maga near the creature at all. Her magic armour would surely have protected her if she had been struck. She studied the famulus, so distraught, keening and mourning the loss of the maga. *Would he really kill her? And why? Just to inherit her legacy?* There was not enough evidence for an accusation to be made. And there had been no witnesses. Only the wind and the clouds and the stone walls had been there on the courtyard. *I'll loosen his tongue with strong dwarf beer at the victory celebrations. Let's see what he lets slip when he's boasting about everything.*

'We've got him!' Telìnâs ran up with Sònuk.

'You mean the rhamak? Excellent!' Brûgar delivered a kick to the dead, many-armed creature. 'I don't ever want to see another one of these.'

'No. It's the Omuthan. We've got him, some of his family and the last of his followers.' Sònuk looked downcast. 'But I can't pick up a track for Hantu. Maybe he knows I'm on their trail and he's disguising his scent.'

'Don't worry. We can rely on your nose. You'll find him.'

Telìnâs came upon the body of the maga. 'May Sitalia have mercy on her! Whatever happened?'

Brûgar summed up what Mostro had told them. Gata realised that the srgãlâh and the young elf were giving exactly the same amount of credence to this version as her two warriors and she herself had done.

When Telìnâs opened his mouth, probably to voice his doubts, she gave him a hidden sign not to say anything for now. It was not the right time. If the famulus started to feel under attack he might use his magic against them, and they would be vulnerable in the extreme.

How we miss Goïmron. Gata was sure that things would never have come so far if he had been there to help them. *Where can he have got to?*

The orc stronghold in the centre of Girdlegard has many a myth connected to it.

Its name, Kràg Tahuum, was not made up by the orcs.

Did you not know that?

The orcs adopted the name because they thought it sounded suitably dark.

Very few of them realised that the letters of the words could be rearranged to say Hutu'rag Ka'm. In an ancient Gauragon dialect that more or less means bottomless evil.

That should give us pause for thought.

Ucerius, priest of Palandiell

XI

Girdlegard

Empire of Gautaya
1024 P.Q. (7515th solar cycle in old reckoning), winter

Goïmron was trying to understand what had happened.

The fact that he was on the easternmost peak of the Sword Tip range, in a cave warmed by hot lava winds from the mountain's core, and that Szmajro was sitting next to him, did nothing to make things easier to comprehend. The thin atmosphere was making it difficult to breathe.

The two-headed dragon had grabbed him outside Fortgard and carried him off him to the Sword Tip mountain range. Szmajro had then retreated with him into the concealed cave under the Three Prong Head Peak. This was where he and his sibling dragon Slibina would habitually take shelter, it would seem, judging by the piles of bones and objects stolen from farmsteads and villages. The newly acquired dimensions of the dragon no longer made this a suitable home. Szmajro had been augmented in size by magic. He now had to roll up as small as possible and tuck his wings in carefully.

After depositing Goïmron he had positioned himself at the cave mouth, blocking the entrance to ensure the dwarf could not escape. He had then closed his eyes and gone to sleep. Occasionally a shimmer would cross his rusty-brown, black-veined scales. The beast was still increasing in size, even if this was happening slowly.

How long have I got to wait? The glowing moss on the walls gave off enough light for Goïmron to get his bearings. No matter how hard he tried to find an escape route from the cave, there was no other way out. He did not dare to wake the dragon for fear he would be attacked.

HE WON'T HURT YOU, said the sea sapphire calmingly, inside his mind.

'Yes, but what if I starve to death?' Goïmron had investigated and found some lichen and a few edible fungi. He collected meltwater from what was dripping from the roof of the cave. It tasted of salt and of stone. 'I suppose I should be happy to have found something, at least.'

He had lost all sense of time passing. He would sleep and wake in his own rhythm. He reckoned it might be about six or seven orbits since he had been carried off to the dragon's lair. Even the wound in his hand where the arrow had gone through was healing without his having to use the magic gemstone.

'I wonder if the battle is over? And what if it's in full swing and Brigantia wins the upper hand?' Goïmron was impatient. 'By Vraccas, I can't hang around here! They're depending on me. They need me!' Distractedly he ran his fingers through his curly black hair.

And each time he woke his fear for Rodana's safety grew. What would happen to her if she fell into Mostro's hands? Or the Omuthan's? *Or what if she is injured in the fighting? Or even killed?* Goïmron uttered a loud curse.

THEN WAKE UP SZMAJRO.

'Right – just so's he can attack me?'

HE WON'T ATTACK YOU. HE ACKNOWLEDGED YOU AS HIS MASTER. AS I COMMANDED HE SHOULD. OTHERWISE HE WOULD HAVE DEVOURED YOU BACK IN FORTGARD.

'I suppose you are right.' Goïmron summoned up enough courage to approach the sleeping dragon, taking with him one of the long bones he had found among the remains of the dragon's meals. He used it to poke the dragon's second head gently. 'Sorry to bother you.' He tried it cautiously at first and then prodded more forcefully. Finally, to attract attention, he used it to knock loudly as if demanding admittance at a castle gate. 'Can you hear me?'

Grudgingly Szmajro lifted one eyelid to reveal an oval black pupil that looked as if it were swimming on a bed of cold liquid fire. A loud hiss shot out of both nostrils. The dragon was angry at being disturbed.

'I am Goïmron Chiselcut from the clan of the Silver Beards of the tribe of the Fourthlings,' he said by way of introduction. He held the sea sapphire tight, without having the slightest idea what kind of magic could be deployed against a dragon that had been magically transformed through contact with the Wonder Zone. The beast outclassed him a hundredfold in size, speed and magic.

YOU NEED TO BE MORE ASSERTIVE.

'You have agreed to submit to me. In Fortgard, Szmajro.' Goïmron made every effort to speak decisively but his voice came out a little too high. 'So I am ordering you to take me to the Brown Mountains.'

'I did not say I would submit. I said I would acknowledge you.' Szmajro was specific. He spoke inside Goïmron's head, just as the jewel did. But the sheer presence of the monster made it impossible for the dwarf to dismiss the words as fabrication. The glowing red eye remained fixed on him. 'What has happened to me, groundling?'

'I want you to—'

'We shall not be leaving the Sword Tip range and this nice safe cave before I know more.' The head with the three magic flame-horns moved sideways and the other eye opened. 'I remember that Slibina and I caught an älf and we shared him. He tasted a bit odd. And then after that, I woke up in great pain. And without my proper horns. Only these fire things in their place. And it was all in a burning forest and everything was shouting and screaming and running about, and then that black-eyes that wanted to possess me. Ascatoîa! That was her name. It is her name.'

'Possess you?' Goïmron slowly sat down on a boulder.

Szmajro had the advantage. All Goïmron could do was wait.

'She changed me and she claimed it would make me stronger. And she said my sister and I were both to be her servants from that moment on.' The dragon gave a snort. This time with both heads. 'But something in me refused, I protested and defended myself against the älf woman who caused me all that pain and distress.'

Goïmron was acutely aware of the hatred the dragon had for Ascatoîa. 'She transformed you the same way the älfar change unicorns into night-mares. To bind you to herself and to give you certain powers,' he explained. 'That was why she took you and your sister to the Wonder Zone.' He remembered the magic forcefield had appeared around the dragons and the zhussa.

'So my transformation is due to forces in the earth? My whole body has grown. I am like a dragon that is two hundred cycles old.'

'I expect it was a concerted effort.' Goïmron was gradually losing his fear of this scale-covered creature, which was now getting on for fifty paces long and had claws it could easily dissect him with.

'We swallowed her bait like stupid beginners.'

'The bait?'

'That älf. In the mountains. The zhussa sacrificed one of her people in order to catch us.' Szmajro shut his eyes. 'Ûra and

Ardin are dead. That makes us two the oldest and the largest dragons in Girdlegard. There's only Grasstooth apart from me and Slibina, and he's no competition.'

'I don't suppose anything much could compete with you both, now that you've been transformed.' Goïmron's impatience and concern about his friends returned. 'After I've answered your questions, can we—?'

'We just stole cattle. We were harmless cattle thieves. We sometimes robbed a village for something to eat,' Szmajro went on. 'We only devoured humans in an emergency. When there was nothing else. Or if they attacked us. We had no ambitions about taking over territories or kingdoms. We were content. Our life was good.' The eyelids sprang open again. 'And now? I have power and size I never asked for. Girdlegard will be hunting me and my sister down to kill us!'

Goïmron found the dragon's argument well-founded. Apparently the creature's intelligence had matured along with the growth in its physical dimensions. 'I have to get to Brigantia,' he insisted.

'What's with my sister?'

'I don't know what's happened to her.'

Both dragon-heads were now raised. 'Seeing as she's not here, she's probably under the älfar woman's influence.' The dragon moved its wings slightly. 'I hate black-eyes and will bring them death! To each and every one of them! And death to all who follow them!'

'I am with you on that score.' Goïmron glimpsed an opportunity to prod Szmajro into action. 'Please listen. There is a battle raging in the Brown Mountains. It's quite likely that Ascatoîa is there. And your sister.' He pointed to the mouth of the cave. 'All we'd have to do would be fly there and take a look.'

'No,' came the immediate response.

'No?' Goïmron could not understand. 'Who would . . .'

Szmajro's look made Goïmron fall silent. 'I don't want to fight my sister. Since she has been made submissive to the zhussa she will have to obey her, I fear. This is why I am aiming to get at the black-eyes without involving Slibina.'

Goïmron attempted a new tactic. 'Let's fly to Brigantia first. Then we can consider our next course of action.'

'Why do you say *we*?'

'You have agreed to . . . no, I mean, you have acknowledged me. I shall therefore remain with you and you will stay with me. Until I tell you different,' said Goïmron in a sudden onrush of courageous cunning born of impatience.

The piercing stare of Szmajro's four eyes did not waver from Goïmron's face. 'Are you sure that you are a dwarf? You look more like a misshapen shrunken human. Sometimes the villages used to sacrifice their handicapped or deformed specimens to us. That's why I recognise the look.'

The long'uns are cruel. The dwarf opened his eyes wide and stood up. 'I am a dwarf! A true Fourthling and a Child of the Smith!'

'Ah, of course. You had mentioned what tribe you were from. So the Fourthlings really are a puny stock. Don't take offence. Since getting to this size everything looks tiny to me.' Szmajro's two heads both roared with laughter. The cave resounded with the deafening noise. 'And you've had nothing proper to eat for ages, have you?' One of the heads turned to look at the cave wall. 'There's no strength to be had from moss and lichen. I'll just fly off and get us both some meat. There's nothing to beat meat.' The dragon made itself smaller and crawled, turning with difficulty in the cave entrance. White flashes sparked round its claws and left burn marks on the rocks. 'Don't try to escape, groundling. The temperature outside will kill you in a couple of breaths.' And off it flew.

Ice-cold air swept through the opening.

Goïmron found himself a sheltered niche and cursed under his breath. 'That is not what I had planned.'

OH, DON'T WORRY. IT'LL BE ALL RIGHT, said the sea sapphire. THE TWO OF YOU HAVE MUTUAL ENEMIES.

'But how can I trust him? A dragon is never a good thing. And on top of that, Szmajro has received an infusion of älfar blood. That's the height of corruption!' Goïmron set about lighting a little fire for warmth, using a spark from his flint, some old moss and a few dried bones.

WHO SAID ALL DRAGONS ARE EVIL?

'History?' Goïmron answered mockingly. 'Or did we all get it wrong for hundreds of cycles about Ardin and Ûra? And have we been wrong about these two cattle stealers?'

WELL, YOU ARE RIGHT ABOUT ÛRA, I ADMIT. BUT TAKE ADVANTAGE OF THE SITUATION. SZMAJRO WILL FOLLOW YOU. HE ACKNOWLEDGED YOU.

'*I wish to Vraccas you wouldn't keep saying that! However many times you repeat it I still shan't understand what that actually entails.*' Goïmron's impatience was threatening to turn into utter despair. He picked up an old rib bone and poked the fire. 'How will I ever . . .?'

A cloud of snowflakes suddenly erupted and through the blizzard Szmajro's silhouette came up to the entrance. 'I've found something.' With its right claw it chucked a black-skinned animal into the cave. 'No need for a long hunting expedition.'

When he saw what the dragon had brought back Goïmron was so surprised that he dropped the bone he had been using as a poker. 'But that's the flight-mare!'

'Yes, I know. It had tried some of that älfar bait just before Slibina and I did. I just wish we had both waited.' Szmajro laughed. 'But the flight-mare will be useful after all. I thought the warm flesh could feed us. And it will mean we're getting rid of a bit of älfishness for Girdlegard.' The dragon crouched down and pushed the black stallion with one of his snouts. 'Look, it's still alive. We won't have to wait for it to thaw before we can eat it. Do you want to roast your share of the meat over the flames?'

'It is injured.' As Goïmron cautiously approached the trembling animal, he saw its coat had lumps of ice in the black fur of its hide.

'Of course! Slibina broke one of its wings. As a punishment.'

Szmajro licked the flight-mare's frozen hind leg. 'I've eaten cows and sheep and horses and whatnot in the past – anything I could garner from a farm. But I've never tried night-mare.' The dragon was drooling with anticipation. 'What a delicious snack awaits my bite!'

WHAT ARE YOU PLANNING TO DO? asked the sea sapphire.

Goïmron placed his hand on the flight-mare's white blaze and studied the place where the horn had been removed. 'Such a beautiful animal.'

'Corrupted innocence. Contaminated with the blood of an älf.' Szmajro opened the mouth of one of his heads. 'Let us relieve it of its suffering.'

'I think it is an ally.' Goïmron stood between the dragon and the flight-mare, holding the sea sapphire tight in one hand. 'I am convinced it hates the älfar just as much as you do because of what they did to it. Deep within its once pure soul.'

'Oh, sure. You know, I used to have a pure soul once.' Szmajro giggled. 'We've had enough fun. Let me bite first, I'll leave some for you.'

Goïmron placed a hand on the stallion's side and concentrated on healing the broken wing and the frostbitten parts of its body.

'Are you serious?' Szmajro snorted impatiently. 'You want to deprive me of my meal? I can't believe it!'

THE FLIGHT-MARE WON'T BE THANKING YOU, the stone prophesied. IT WILL BE WASTED EFFORT AND WASTED MEAT.

'I don't need to eat. And the flight-mare could take me to the Brown Mountains. I don't want to wait until hoity-toity Lord Dragon decides to help out,' he answered quietly. He felt the power of the sapphire going through his own body and into the stallion. The place by his fingers grew warmer, the ice crusts melted and fell away. At the same time the broken wing started to move. The bones mended with a crack and the feathers regrew. The stallion opened its blood-red eyes and whinnied, its fiery gaze focused on the dwarf.

'Quiet now. I'm only trying to help.' Goïmron was impressed by the size of the dagger-like fangs of the creature, but he remembered that, of course, the dragon had far more teeth. 'You will soon be able to fly again.' If back home in Mallenia-gard someone had told him half a cycle ago that he would be sitting here in a cave with a winged night-mare and a two-headed dragon, he would have said they were mad. He slowly removed his hand from the stallion's coat, which was now, after his treatment, giving off heat. 'Feeling better?'

The animal snorted and sprang to its feet. Lightning flashes shot from its hooves. It neighed loudly as soon as it saw the dragon. Unfolding its wings, it leaped into the air, flying upwards to the cave roof.

'Calm down. Szmajro won't hurt you. We have an enemy in common,' Goïmron reassured him. 'Why else would I have healed you? We want to find and kill älfar.'

'Ah! Flying food! Practical idea,' said the dragon, licking its lips.

'No! You are to leave it alone!' Goïmron felt like an animal trainer at the circus. *I'd ask high ticket prices and be the richest dwarf in Girdlegard.* 'And you, flight-mare, come down from up there. We are allies.'

The stallion actually came in to land but then flew a sharp-angled curve and took a bite of Szmajro's tail. The dragon whirled round, snarling and hissing, and snapped at the horse with both sets of jaws. But the flight-mare escaped in a death-defying manoeuvre through the gap that had opened at the mouth of the cave. And disappeared out into the open air.

'I'll get that ungrateful piece of shit!' Szmajro crouched to crawl out of the cave.

'No. Let it go.'

'It will be my dinner if it's not going to be your ally.'

Goïmron was struck with a mixture of disappointment and relief. Turning up riding up on a night-mare and accompanied by a dragon might have been a bit too much for his friends. 'Perhaps I gave the creature a little hope that for him, too, something might change.' He was pleased to see that the healing effect had also dealt satisfactorily with the injury on his own hand. There remained no trace of his wound.

'Oh ye dragon gods! What are you going on about?' Szmajro uttered a tortured sound. 'It's a night-mare. Created with the terrible arts of the black-eyes. Corrupt through and through!'

'Like yourself, then,' Goïmron let slip.

'No. I came about because of the Wonder Zone. And I hate the älfar.' Szmajro's stomach rumbled like faraway thunder. The sight of that fresh meat, now whisked away from under his nose, had triggered his appetite. 'Enough time has been lost. You wanted to get to the Brown Mountains.' The dragon lowered one wing to let the dwarf climb up. 'I'll take you there.'

'What? You'll suddenly do it now?' Goïmron mounted the huge creature's back, starting to feel rather apprehensive.

'I'm hungry. I can't be bothered to search up here for some

skinny little goat or a stinky ibex. We'll find a farm with some nice cows.'

'Don't drop me. Did you hear, Szmajro?' Before Goïmron could say anything else they were out of the cave shelter and plunging down over the edge.

Goïmron yelled out. The ride had begun.

Girdlegard

In the Brown Mountains
Brigantia
1024 P.Q. (7515th solar cycle in old reckoning), winter

Gata was standing at the far end of the Fourthlings' largest hall. It had previously served the Omuthan as his conference chamber. She watched the crowd dancing merrily to the music of the players on the platform.

Visibly moved, Bendoïn Feinunz had taken the stand to address his thanks to the other dwarves, elves, humans and meldriths at the beginning of his tribe's victory celebrations. In great relief, the highborn and the nobility had embraced each other, and had given due thanks to Palandiell, Elria, Sitalia and Vraccas. Even Samusin had been awarded a word of praise.

But not Lorimbur. Gata took a sip of beer and touched the brooch on the collar of her tunic. *Even though it was us that took the spy-hole entrance and made the victory possible.* Now she emptied the tankard at one draught. *What else have I got to do to demote Vraccas from first position?*

Apart from Gata everyone else was in the best of humours. After two protracted and exhausting battles, entertainment was welcome. The Fourthlings had moved out all of the furniture and anything else that still spoke of Brigantia. With great speed they had repaired the decor and removed the damage to the stonework in order to celebrate the victory with the highest status allies. The ordinary soldiers were being fêted in the outlying halls.

'It will be nice when the Gem Cutters have got round to polishing up their realm and chucking out all the Brigantian rubbish.' Brûgar came up to Gata and handed her a full tankard. The bowl of the pipe he had gripped between his teeth was as big as a teacup. It smoked like an incense burner and smelled like one. He had added some kind of resin to the tobacco. 'I can see you are thirsty.'

Gata accepted the tankard and put the empty one to one side. She and Brûgar clinked their mugs together in a toast. Neither of them was wearing heavy armour. He sported a padded greyish-blue tunic that bore the arms of Lorimbur. The war flail had been safely stowed away safely in his accommodation, but there were a pair of daggers hanging from his belt.

'Indeed, it will look great,' she agreed. 'And I shall always remind the Fourthlings that for the most part it is us they have to thank for the return of their homeland.'

'I'll drink to that!' Brûgar tasted the beer and made a face that said the drink was not to his liking. 'It's grim, having to make do with this thin Gauragon piss-water, isn't it? I wonder what Fourthling brewers can come up with.' He puffed at his pipe again, the tattoos on his face disappearing behind a cloud of smoke. 'I would never have thought I'd have to smoke to make the beer drinkable.'

'Goïmron always went on about how good theirs was.'

'Any news of him?'

Gata shook her head. 'No one's seen either him or the two-headed dragon.' It made her sad. *I so wish I knew how he was. Whether he's still alive.*

'And how do we deal with Szmajro?' Brûgar swilled the beer

MARKUS HEITZ | 283

round and looked disappointedly at the foam on top. He drew on his pipe again and filled their corner of the room with fresh clouds.

'We do nothing at first. The army is exhausted. They can't take arms against a scale-skinned creature of that size. And we need to acquire some more efficient weaponry that is easily portable.' Gata felt the resin smell going to her head. 'Who knows how the Wonder Zone may have altered the beast. Perhaps it's got a third head by now?'

'We do still have the famulus, of course.' Brûgar was either puffing at his pipe or making slurping sounds as he drank. 'With any luck he'll have a go at the dragon. And die in the attempt.'

'The magus, you mean. That's how he's officially known.' She laughed. 'I see you're no friend of his.'

'In my eyes he'll always be a shitty little famulus and a rotten stinking liar.' Brûgar cast a wary eye up at the podium, where Mostro, extravagantly attired, was chatting to one of the musicians. 'It wasn't him at all that vanquished that weird thing from the other dimensions. Telìnâs and Sònuk both say so.' He took another mouthful of beer and then offered Gata the pipe; she declined politely. 'That filthy piece of shit murdered his own maga!'

'We've no witnesses. Signs in the snow won't work as evidence,' Gata said in warning, and grabbed his arm to get him to lower his voice. The effect of the resin was making him forget all caution. 'Yes. He is our best defence against the dragon apart from the catapults that the dwarves have. Or those älfar ships in Undarimar. They did manage to shoot Ardin down, you know.'

'Well, let's get hold of those ships. We should capture them. Or at least steal the blueprints. That might be easier to do. Or we could sink them and then salvage the weaponry.' Brûgar sounded keen.

Gata drew her fair eyebrows together in a thoughtful frown, not sure whether to be amused or surprised. 'What makes you so jolly, in Lorimbur's name? Is it just the resin in your pipe tobacco?'

'The incense may have something to do with it, but it's actually the prospect of another battle. A real battle.' He relaxed the muscles in arms and shoulders, being careful not to spill his drink. 'We've had enough of killing escaped trolls. We'll at last be able to show what Thirdlings can do on the battlefield.'

'But you must still grant our allies time to rest and recuperate.' Gata gestured with her tankard over to the assembled company. 'Just take a look. They're all exhausted and they long for peace.'

'There won't be any of that. Not with the pig-faces on the loose. And the black-eyes. We've had it up to here with both. In every corner of our world.' He raised his tankard again in a toast. 'I'll be getting myself a nice collection of new war flails to be on the safe side. They wear out so quickly nowadays.' He waved his pipe. 'And so do these things. I've thought of making a nice one out of stone. Nice and warm in the hand.'

Gata bestowed a tired smile on him. 'Where is Belîngor?'

'He's found a deaf and dumb servant-maid he can talk to. I hope they'll keep each other warm at night.' Brûgar winked. 'But your words make me concerned, queen.'

There goes another who's found solace, then. It seems I'm the only one who hasn't. 'Why?'

'Well, I was hoping for a fight. Against Dsôn, for example.'

'Nothing doing.' Gata's answer came swiftly.

Brûgar had been about to draw on his pipe, but stopped abruptly. 'Why is that? Has Goldhand ordered us to leave them in peace?' His visage cleared. 'Oh, I understand! We go for the pig-faces first.'

'I shall be travelling to Dsôn Khamateion to speak to the

Ganyeios, as the zhussa suggested.' Gata was enjoying the dwarf warrior's look of horror as he puffed frantically on his pipe. 'Remember?'

'A treaty?'

Yes, a pact.'

'Without telling Goldhand?'

'In principle it was already decided in the moment when Ascatoîa flew off.' Gata had thought it through thoroughly. 'A campaign against Dsôn Khamateion is too dangerous an undertaking, Brûgar. The combined powers of the zhussa and the dragon would be way too much. They would wipe us out completely, even if the Fourthlings say they know their way around those mountains. They haven't been back here for hundreds of cycles.' This time she touched the warrior's tankard with her own. 'Let's take care of the threats in Girdlegard first.'

'Such as the älfar in the Inland Sea?' Brûgar prompted.

'No. As far as I know, they are allies of Dsôn. We won't do anything until I have negotiated a position with the Ganyeios. And anyway, those eight ships are moored in the harbour at Arimar and not causing any trouble. Well, not much. As far as I know.'

'Time I started a Thinking-Things-Through pipe.' Brûgar stared at her and stroked his blue beard. 'Tell me: how long have you been taking the side of the black-eyes?'

'Don't be ridiculous. But as you said, we have to set our priorities. We can't afford to spread ourselves too thinly between the various projects. Otherwise we risk losing in just one cycle everything we have just secured for Girdlegard. Particularly given the situation with the two dragon siblings.'

'I see. You'll be wanting to speak to Mòndarcai, too? He's in charge of all the pig-faces. And he'd be perfect when it comes to getting rid of dragons.'

'First I want to hear from the Ganyeios what's behind that

rune-staff älf's doings. Whoever controls the salt desert beasts and the ones from Kràg Tahuum and manages to unite them is to be handled with caution.' Gata leaned against the wall and watched the celebrations.

'What if we were to play him against the zhussa? Let the magic black-eyes kill each other.' Brûgar smacked his lips and emptied the cold tobacco out of his pipe on to the floor. 'Lorimbur will be at our side and will help you start something of the kind. Praise for our forefathers.'

'That would be it, yes.' She looked at him. 'While I'm away, Brûgar, make sure at the strategy meetings that no one suggests opening negotiations with Mòndarcai.'

'Sure thing. I don't think Goldhand will try. No one has forgotten the black-eyes' recent assassinations. You are the only one to even consider siding with him, if you don't mind my saying so.'

'I don't mind.' Gata called a servant over with a silver tray of delicacies. The beer they had found lacking in taste had made them both hungry. 'I wonder if Sònak likes this sort of stuff?'

'He's not here,' said the warrior, speaking with his mouth full.

'Sentry duty?'

'No. He is trying to track down Klaey Berengart. He's furious, Telìnâs says, that the last member of the murderous family has escaped. And he thinks Hantu is to be found among Berengart's retinue.' He grinned, revealing bits of spiced food stuck between his front teeth. 'Berengart will soon know what it's like to have a srgāláh on his tail. He won't be able to shake him off.'

'Oh, that's good. Then we don't have to worry about the rhamak anymore.'

The Omuthan had had his own people poisoned to provide energy to the summoner of souls from other spheres. The amount had, however, scarcely been sufficient to summon one of the smaller beings, as they had heard from one member of the Berengart household. It had originally been planned to sacrifice hundreds of the sick, the old, the injured and young families.

We'd have been lost if they'd actually done that. Just as Rodana had feared. The puppeteer woman was in prison along with Orweyn Berengart and his immediate family and would remain there until the trial. Nobody was in a rush to start proceedings.

Gata drank more slowly, and let her thoughts stray. She would prevent Rodana being hanged, that was clear. The woman had risked her own life and what she had achieved more than made up for the actions she was being accused of. Whether Chòldunja had really been a ragana could not now be proved one way or the other. Mostro was still insisting she was a moor-witch. *But he has no evidence, either.*

Orweyn Berengart, on the other hand, could expect no mercy. Not even from his own subjects. They all hated him, since he had poisoned his own troops. Maybe thirty or forty blinkered followers were still loyal. No more than that. The rest had deserted his cause and were hoping for lasting peace with Girdlegard.

I wonder! Gata selected a chicken portion and stuffed it in her mouth, chewing vigorously. That beer had an effect on stomach and mood. One good, one not so good.

Suddenly the music died away.

Everyone's eyes turned to the podium, where Mostro had approached the guardrail, arms widespread in a grandiose gesture. Coiffure and beard were groomed and his robes had probably cost more than any fine farmstead would pay in taxes in a whole cycle. 'My dear friends,' he intoned, obviously having had quite a lot to drink. 'Let us raise a glass to the friends we have lost, the fallen of the two recent battles. They gave their lives to drive injustice from Girdlegard!'

Glasses and tankards were raised.

'First and foremost, to the memory of my Esteemed Maga, Vanéra, without whom we would hardly have been able to vanquish the terrible being that the Omuthan sent after us! But for that crime Orweyn Berengart will be receiving his due punishment.'

'Hear, hear,' Brûgar called out.

'It is due to the maga that I received my training and, from being a famulus, I became the magus who opened the gates for you all. I opened the double portal and the spy's entrance! I delivered the deadliest of blows to the awful beast and made my mistress proud of me,' he declared, visibly touched by what he was saying. 'I avenged her death!'

The throng, who had been indulging in drink, did not notice that what Mostro was really doing was praising himself and laying claim to the main portion of glory for the victory. Oblivious to that, they cheered him.

'If he announced that he is now the emperor they'd swallow it,' Brûgar commented sarcastically. He called for more beer. 'Any more of this and I'll chuck my tankard at him. And my aim is good. Want a bet, anyone?'

'One gold piece,' said Gata, taking up the challenge. 'But you've got to get him on the forehead.'

'Let me tell you, dear friends, that it is a great honour for me to be able to step into the maga's shoes. Our good Adelia will now become my famula and I shall run Rhuta in the way my Esteemed Maga Vanéra did,' he announced, wiping tears from the corners of his eyes.

Brûgar looked alarmed. 'Isn't Adelia older than him? Isn't she his senior in the hierarchy?'

'In principle, yes.' Gata shook her blonde locks. 'It will be quite the snub for her. Our talkative fellow here is going for a fait accompli. Adelia wanted to come to the mountains to collect Vanéra's body to take it home to Rhuta for burial.'

'But?'

'Mostro will send her back as soon as she arrives.' Gata sipped her beer. 'He buried his mistress with the rest of the bodies from the battle. Buried her like a warrior, to rest among other warriors. At the place of her greatest and most heroic acts.'

Brûgar gave an angry laugh. 'He got rid of her, that's what. So he wouldn't have to trouble about it. And so when he goes back to Rhuta he will go in triumph. He doesn't want people remembering Vanéra and he doesn't want there to be a memorial in Rhuta to remind them. I hope Adelia takes the time to box his ears.'

'Long live the Esteemed Magus Mostro!' someone in the crowd shouted. 'Three cheers! Hip, hip, hooray!'

The rest of the company joined in.

Brûgar hurled the full tankard, but he missed the young man by an arm's length. One of the musicians was covered in beer and the glass mug shattered on the wall. 'Awfully sorry. It slipped out of my hand, I was cheering so much,' he said. 'Carry on playing, do! We've had quite enough talk.'

Mostro shot him a furious glance and opened his mouth to respond, but the music had started up afresh and drowned out his words. The celebrations were soon in full swing again.

Gata tapped Brûgar on the shoulder and handed him a gold coin. 'It was worth it, even if you missed his head. I'm off to bed. I'll set off for Dsôn tomorrow. Don't tell anyone, though.'

'I shan't.' Brûgar had got himself a new mug of beer, and he raised it in a toast to her. 'Here's a health and long life to Lorimbur's people!'

They shall live long. Gata had to steady herself with one hand on the wall on her way out of the celebrations. *Longer than all the others.*

It is a well-kept secret that some Children of the Smith founded new settlements on the recently emerged mountain ranges because the young mountains are the work of Vraccas and thus it must be the will of Vraccas that dwarves should reside there. And not in the circle of mountains surrounding Girdlegard.

This caused trouble with the princes and rulers of the various realms. It led to the question of whether the Children of the Smith should really be living there? Is this to be their new homeland? This is a controversial topic among the tribes themselves, but the matter is never discussed when outsiders are present. It is rumoured that dwarf settlers on the slopes of volcanoes had even entered into agreements with the local dragon, in order to be able to live in peace.

Dar Whienn, academic expert in the fields
of flora, fauna and the laws of nature

XII

Girdlegard

Empire of Gautaya
1024 P.Q. (7515th solar cycle in old reckoning), winter

'Who would have thought it? It's just as bad as I'd imagined.' Barbandor had never before set foot in the salt desert that made up a considerable part of the Gautayan empire. It had not been the salt itself that constituted a problem for successive rulers, but rather the orcs that lived there. The beasts would plague the outlying areas with raiding parties, thereafter immediately retreating deep into the salt plain that protected them. Even in winter the landscape remained inhospitable, as the snow melt-water formed huge lakes, the high salt content preventing freezing. Instead a thin layer of salt crystals would often form. 'I'd hoped it would be warm.'

'Because it's called a desert?' Borkon ran alongside the dwarf's carrying cage. He took a drink from his waterskin flask. 'Bad luck, groundling. In summer, yes, it is. But now it's icy cold like everywhere else. Skin dries out quickly in these conditions. Because of the salt in the air we need to rub grease into our hides.'

During the whole of their long journey from Kràg Tahuum to Gautaya's north-west, Barbandor, wrapped in furs and blankets, had been travelling in the wooden contraption carried by an uncomplaining orc. Because he was conveyed on the huge orc's back, he seldom saw what was in front of them, only what they had already passed. 'How much further?'

'I can make out the village.' Borkon stretched and touched the long red and silver signal horn at his side. 'You'll see, the next time I sound my horn, I'll get even more followers. They've been supporting Mòndarcai, but they'll soon swarm over to join me.'

'You're getting a bit over-confident, aren't you?' Barbandor did not bother to mind his tongue. Any orbit now they would be slicing him up for their dinner, and he did not want to have to reproach himself with having held back when addressing the blue-skinned orc. He had to remember he was a dwarf by nature. 'It's going to your head, all this success. Or maybe the salt is drying out your brain. That's if you've even got one.'

'You groundlings are an extraordinary folk, aren't you? Quite different from what I'd imagined.' Borkon watched him in amusement. 'But there it is. If you only have written records to go on . . .'

'Better or worse than you thought?'

'More entertaining, at any rate. It was a good idea to bring you along as our lucky mascot.' The white patterns on his tattooed blue skin were visible under his mantle. He would be displaying them on reaching the gates of the village as proof of his unique status.

A loud bugle call sounded from the distance and low, threatening, rhythmical drum rolls accompanied the tones.

'Ha! It doesn't sound like they're looking forward to joining you.' Barbandor got up as well as he could, given the restrictions of the cage. He tried to peek out over the shoulder of the orc carrying him. 'They're going to send you a greeting. With arrows. Aimed directly at you.' He patted the grey orc on the back, reaching through the bars to do so. 'Good thing you're so big. You'll catch all their fire.'

'Your orc can swivel round any time he wants, of course.

Then you'll be the one providing the target, you Big Mouth.'
Borkon's expression was no longer so relaxed.

'You weren't expecting war drums, though, were you? I can
tell. Shall I show you what your face looks like?' Barbandor was
feeling apprehensive. A fortified village would not be easy to
capture with only a handful of grey-skins, however immortal.
After a while even the risen dead would be hacked to pieces.
The dwarf assumed that Borkon's special horn signal would not
be affecting a welcome opening of the gates as had happened
back in Kràg Tahuum. They knew it was Borkon coming. *And
they're not keen on meeting him.*

It seemed the salt sea orcs' leader was not eager to surrender
his position to some jumped-up come-lately random figure
citing a half-forgotten prophecy. 'How many arrows can you
take before you die?'

'I cannot die.'

'What if your head comes off? Or if your heart is taken out?'

'You won't see either of those eventualities occurring.'
Borkon roared out a command and the company came to a halt.
Without his having to say any more, his grey-skinned soldiers
took up a circular formation, with the archers behind a defensive ring of shields and pikes.

*I hope I do, though. Perhaps I'll have a chance to do the beheading
myself.* Barbandor's prison-crate was placed on the ground.
Through the forest of legs, shields and armour he glimpsed an
army approaching: more than a thousand orcs riding bastard-
horses. This was a larger reception party than the one in
Kràg Tahuum had been. And they did not look welcoming in
the slightest.

We'll never survive this encounter. Barbandor gave a whistle to
alert one of the orcs. 'Hey! Let me out and give me an axe! I
don't want to wait like a chicken in a hencoop for the salt sea
orcs to wring my neck!'

They ignored his demand.

By Vraccas. To end like this! Barbandor rattled the bars of his cage but could not break them. The rope and wire fastenings held.

Borkon insisted on attempting a signal with the silver and red horn, playing the tune that had secured him the loyalty of the fortress orcs. The village cavalry swiftly surrounded them. Clouds of snow and salt mist wafted around under the hooves of their mounts. The melody could not be heard above the thundering sounds of galloping hooves. The blue-skinned orc then stopped blowing the horn. And waited.

Barbandor watched as a stockily built female orc from the village left the ring of animals and beasts and rode slowly over to them. Her light-green skin was decorated with a whitish layer of salt paste. She wore armour protecting her upper torso and her long platinum-grey hair blew freely in the wind. She had mysterious ornaments on her brow and in her left hand she carried a martial slaughtering axe with a jagged blade.

At a signal from her, the advancing party halted. 'I am Akrosha the Beheader, ruler of the Salt Sea,' she declared in dreadful tones. To Barbandor's delight, she used the common vernacular; she must have assumed the foreign visitor would otherwise not understand. There were golden rings attached to her pointed, sharpened tusks. 'And you, apparently, are the orc the prophecies tell of.'

Borkon turned to address her. The wall of shields opened for him and he cast off his mantle once again to display his tattooed markings and the lines on his body. 'I am he.'

Akroshsa regarded him closely. 'You come to make demands?'

'I make no demands. Kràg Tahuum joined me voluntarily because they recognised that I am the one our people have long awaited. Have awaited for thousands of cycles.' Borkon raised his arms and was about to execute his customary authoritative pivot to show himself from all aspects. 'And now—'

'Spare us the speech.' Akrosha leaped from the saddle without stowing her axe. The blade was the size of a ten-year-old child. 'We heard you were coming. Some of my people believe the prophecies of Nushrok the Ripper. Others don't.' In a well-practised motion she twirled the weapon. It had a widened tip designed to cause maximum damage. 'So we need a solution.' She gave a challenging nod. 'One of us two will now die. That will provide the decision.'

Barbandor grinned to himself. *She may be a pig-face, but I like her style.* This female orc was not succumbing to Borkon's charm. And since there was already a female here in charge of the Salt Sea realm there would not be any prospective revolt of the females against the males to be incited.

'Will the unbelievers not continue to doubt?'

'If I fall, all doubts will be removed. The salt sea orcs will then follow you like our enemy brothers and sisters from Kràg Tahuum.' Akrosha gave her killing-axe an experimental swing. It swished as if the blade were slicing the air in half. Ice and salt whirled up from the tips of her boots. 'If I win, we shall remain with Mòndarcai. I am not one to give up a pact as quickly as the colourfully dressed weaklings from the fortress.'

Her mounted escort laughed out loud – a malicious and vulgar sound.

'It is your decision.' From his belt Borkon drew out his two differently sized, spike-studded clubs, and stepped up to meet her without stopping to don any armour. 'You will soon see how wrong—'

Without any warning Akrosha struck diagonally down with her axe, her muscles bulging under the clothing and the armour. Borkon parried the blow, but his club shuddered under its impact. He had to dodge to one side to avoid being hit.

That blow would have sliced me in half! Barbandor followed the fight intently.

Akrosha struck the blue-skinned orc with an elbow to his face, driving him back. She followed up with a kick to his chest and then stabbed at him with the blade of her axe.

Again, Borkon could do nothing but leap to one side. This elemental force could not be blocked.

Now I can understand why she is the ruler here. Barbandor was careful not to actively cheer her on although he wanted to. He had no wish to be executed by his keepers if he made them angry.

Once more Akrosha hit her opponent with an elbow blow to the middle of his face that sent him staggering. Blood shot out of Borkon's nose and from a cut on his forehead, running down into his eyes. With a yell of triumph Akrosha drove her axe deep into her adversary's side, set her boot against his chest to give purchase, and thrust the blade through flesh and bone. Barbandor knew he would never forget the bestial noise that the jagged edges of the sharp axe made as they severed the rib-cage. The steel blade emerged from Borkon's body in a torrent of blood.

'It is decided!' shouted Akrosha with a laugh of triumph, holding her axe above her head with both hands.

It isn't. No, it isn't. 'Aren't you called the Beheader? Cut his head off!' Barbandor yelled. This piece of advice was drowned out by the roar of victory shouts from Akrosha's cavalry. 'Cut his heart out!'

Akrosha had turned full circle – and then stared as Borkon got to his feet in front of her very eyes. The wound had closed up and he was not even unsteady on his feet. 'To the demons with you!' she roared at him. 'How can you not be dead?'

'I am the One Foretold.' Borkon took one step forward and thrust a club-spike through the leader-female's body, ramming it home and then lifting her up on the weapon as her dark blood sprayed out from her mouth. Horror-struck, her throng of mounted fighters fell instantly silent. 'And I have defeated you because I am immortal.' He lifted the groaning orc's body up, higher still, as she clutched and dragged at the chain round his neck, wanting to strangle him even as she was dying. 'And you were wrong.'

She should have paid attention to what I was telling her. Barbandor would have been glad to see Borkon dead. *Now the salt sea orcs will be joining him, too. To Tion with him!*

Borkon lowered Akrosha, stuck as on a spit, back to the ground, feet first. He took a small flask from his belt and removed the cork, placing the phial to her lips.

'Prepare to witness the miracle that is available to those who choose to follow me.'

Akrosha tried hard not to swallow any of the potion she was offered, but in her death throes she was unable to resist. She had hardly taken it in before Borkon removed the spike from her belly and then stepped back away. Akrosha fell to her knees, gasping and pressing her hands on the wound. Then she went stiff as a board. Only her eyes moved. She focused on her conqueror.

'How did you do that?' she whispered.

'Behold! Your leader lives. Because of my gift to her,' he called out. Borkon reached out a hand to help her up.

Akrosha got to her feet, cast off her armour and pushed her clothing aside, staring at the place where she had been injured. Barbandor was able to see the light-green skin and the bruise made by the head of the war club.

'You are indeed the One who was Foretold in the prophecy,' she announced, deeply moved. Attempting to prostrate herself in the salty snow at his feet, she was prevented by his actions. 'You really are the Foretold One! You have power over life and death.' Her wide hand gesture of acknowledgement was visible from afar.

Her soldiers all dismounted and knelt, bowing their heads and murmuring prayers.

Vraccas, why on earth? Why does this guy have to win at everything? Barbandor watched the monsters near him, all of them reverential now. *They will all be following him. This will be an army capable of tremendous impact.* He looked at the flask that hung at the blue-skinned orc's belt. *The contents of that bottle can restore an orc to life. And they are more or less totally invulnerable.*

'Hear my words.' Borkon raised his voice and the army's murmuring died away. 'The prophecies of Nushrok the Ripper are true! You have all been witnesses to the miracle that just occurred.' He indicated his own wound, completely healed now, then the site of Akrosha's recent major injury. 'Thus all the orc tribes are united under my banner. I vow to lead you all to victory as soon as the preordained orbit arrives. This, too, is foretold in Nushrok's promise.'

The monsters erupted in cheers once more.

Right. Now black-eyes can give up. Borkon has wiped the board clean of any opposition. That would be it, now, with his plan for an allied force. Barbandor sat down in his travelling prison.

Borkon looked at Akrosha. 'You are undoubtedly the strongest female I have ever seen. Up to this point no one has ever defeated me.' With his fingers he wiped some of her blood off the spike of his weapon. He tasted it. 'Will you join me as my companion, ready to turn the whole of Girdlegard upside down?'

In response, Akrosha rubbed some of his blood from the blade of her axe on her lips, to lick. 'You shall be my companion, Borkon. Now and forever more.'

The throng of orcs broke out in roars of delighted cheering.

Oh, Vraccas. I get the feeling I know why Borkon dragged me along. Barbandor's cage was being lifted up anew, and they were off at a run towards the orc village. *I bet I'm to furnish their wedding feast. I'm going to be served up in a huge celebration pie.*

Girdlegard

In the Brown Mountains
Dsôn Khamateion
1024 P.Q. (7515th solar cycle in old reckoning), winter

Gata was in the circular chamber, keenly awaiting what was to come. The room resembled a huge egg with gold and silver ornamentation on the interior walls, in which an expert sculptor had chiselled out filigree patterns and shapes. The axe sword lay before her, because she had had neither armour nor weapons taken away. The älfar were not afraid of her.

The warm light entering the chamber from outside was distributed evenly off reflective surfaces. There were no lamps. There was tea in a porcelain dish on the bone and black ravenwood table. She did not drink any of it, not wanting to have to visit the lavatory. It would not be the proper impression she wanted to make as the queen of the Thirdlings when meeting the Ganyeios: Regnorata Smallbladder was not a nickname she wanted to acquire.

Gata had reached Dsôn Khamateion relatively easily, particularly because, after two full orbits of swift marching, she had been intercepted by an älfar reconnaissance party. The zhussa had been expecting a visit from her and had told her scouts to escort the dwarf. During some parts of the journey Gata had been made to wear a blindfold in order that she should not be able to see the landmarks and note her exact path. She was not allowed to see traps the älfar had laid or their secret stations in the rocks.

She was finally brought to Dsôn along confusingly meandering paths and through underground passages. They had wanted to prevent her having sight of the city known throughout

Girdlegard only from strange stories and obscure descriptions of the cruel nature of the art to be found there.

I should really have liked to see Dsôn Khamateion. Gata leaned back against the comfortable upholstery. She appreciated the scent of fresh flowers combined with the fragrance from the incense sticks. Her present accommodation was far less morbidly grim than she had thought it might be. The älfar sense of the aesthetic she found somehow strangely appealing. She was rather drawn to their ideas of beauty, although it seemed inappropriate to admit it. There was a sudden clicking sound. Part of the ceiling was slowly lowered, revealing a set of stairs and a ramp, apparently an invitation to approach for her interview with the ruler of Dsôn Khamateion. *Climb the stairs. As if approaching a divine being.* Gata smiled at the symbolism, which was so obviously intended to impress her before her audience with the Ganyeios. She stood up, picked up her axe sword and walked up the gold and marble staircase.

A circular hall with a radius of thirty paces came into view. The domed ceiling, having no visible support columns, had the appearance of a second sky. Rays of sunlight, filtering in through decorative stained-glass inserts in the walls, were focused to draw the onlooker's attention to various artworks either displayed on plinths or seeming to float in mid-air.

As she walked up, Gata's gaze fell on abstract objects made of bone and finest gold, perfectly executed life-size statues of unfamiliar or imaginary beings; she saw paintings on canvas that was artistically formed and convoluted to bestow an additional dimension on the aesthetic creations.

'I bid you welcome, Regnorgata Mortalblow of the clan of the Orc Slayers, queen of the Thirdlings and heiress to the legacy of Lorimbur.' Gata heard the velvet smooth tones coming from somewhere within the dome-ceilinged room. She was unsure whether they were spoken by a male or a female voice. The ceremonious words were enhanced by echoing vibrations. 'It is an honour for us to make your acquaintance. We have heard much of your reputation.'

It must be the Ganyeios. It was impossible for her to discern where in the room the älf might be standing.

Before she could make a response, some of the artworks moved aside to form a broad path, at the end of which she saw a low platform with a throne seemingly composed only of light. On it sat an upright figure in wide black robes, the countenance covered by a transparent veil.

Gata walked slowly towards the podium. 'I also deem it a great pleasure to speak to, and, of course, to see, the ruler of Dsôn Khamateion. The view is widespread that you are a legend.'

'We are pleased to be thought a legend. But We are, however, not a figment of the imagination.' The smoothly modulated tones were still not assignable to one gender or another. The common vernacular was being used, with no noticeable accent, and the diction was crystal clear. The veil hardly moved with the breath. 'Approach. And please dispense with long titles when addressing Us. Say Ganyeios.'

'Likewise let me be simply a queen.' Gata went closer, stopping ten paces from the throne. Serving personnel in dark attire stepped from behind the sculptures, bringing an upholstered chair, a table, something to eat, a pitcher and a goblet, all of which they set up halfway between Gata and the podium.

'Then we are equal.' A gesture from the Ganyeios invited her to sit. 'Come, queen. Please help yourself to the refreshments We have selected for you. And let us talk.'

Gata sat down, laying the axe sword at her side. She attempted to make out the älf's features through the thin gauze. The ruler's throne, made of bone that had been skilfully turned and carved, glowed from within, emphasising the beauty of the inlaid patterns of precious metal. 'I am curious to hear your words.'

'Have you come here without either the knowledge or the express agreement of Girdlegard?'

'Yes,' she replied, speaking freely. 'No one would have understood why I wanted to meet with enemies. They say you are not to be trusted. Particularly following the attacks on the delegations and on Girdlegard's royal houses.'

'Politely phrased. We are aware of the prejudices that are levelled against us älfar,' the Ganyeios said. 'However, we have never been guilty of any serious atrocities. For we have nothing to do with those älfar that Girdlegard was familiar with from earlier times and who present, under the leadership of Mòndarcai, a significant threat.'

'So the assassinations were not atrocities?'

'Well. We admit that the actions were over-hasty. It was intended that a warning be delivered. It appears to have got slightly out of hand. We therefore understand why Girdlegard is angry with us at present. But We guarantee to offer recompense for the lives that were lost. In addition to what We have already undertaken: namely, no active involvement on Brigantia's side in the current hostilities.'

'I doubt whether your not having actively joined Brigantia will serve as compensation for all the deaths.' Gata looked at the delicacies displayed and smelled the fragrance of the drink on offer. She was able to resist. 'We are aware that Mòndarcai is set on destroying you and Dsòn Khamateion.'

'He told you so?'

'Yes.'

'Did he give his reasons?'

'Not convincingly, in my opinion.' Gata did not mention that she had been ready to enter a pact with Mòndarcai, but that this move had been stymied by Goldhand's veto. 'This is why I have come to see you. To understand your own position.'

'A praiseworthy and sensible decision, Queen Regnorgata.'

'Praiseworthy? None of my acquaintance would agree with you on that count.' Gata smiled and looked round the hall. 'The architecture is impressive.'

'How kind. This is nothing in comparison with the beauties of the city. Or compared with the magnificence of Our art galleries. Or the skills of the other artists among Our people. I hope you will consider making another visit in the future?'

'Shall we see how these negotiations pan out?' Gata turned her attention back to the Ganyeios. 'Tell me what the situation is with you and Mòndarcai?'

'As Our zhussa has already warned you, We hereby give you, as the representative of Girdlegard, the well-meant advice not to put your trust in him. For a long time We held him to be only a myth, a tale thought up to put fear into the hearts of children.' The älf's long pale hands gripped the arms of the throne. 'But then he appeared. He stole sacred relics from us and used them to increase his power. Fortunately for all concerned, he, together with Ardin, fell foul of our fleet in Undarimar.'

'So he is not intent on destroying Dsòn?'

'He certainly does want to destroy me,' the Ganyeios declared. 'And Girdlegard. He is eager to see its downfall, even if he insists he is exclusively against Dsòn Khamateon.'

'What have we done to him?'

'He primarily sees the humans and the elves as the guilty parties responsible for the death of his father. An appalling death,' the ruler explained. 'He may lull you into a false state of security with his promises, but he will turn against you as soon as Dsòn falls.' As the Ganyeios leaned forward a ray of light fell through the fabric, making the outline of the graceful features visible. 'Mòndarcai is the enemy that must be confronted first. Him and the army of orcs he has gathered around himself. The mere fact that he has allied himself with that scum shows his true nature.'

Gata was glad to finally have an explanation for the mystery. 'So who was his father?'

'According to the stories and the old poems, his father was Carmondai.' The Ganyeios sat back again. 'You will have heard of him, I expect? It will have been more than one thousand cycles ago that he played a role in Girdlegard.'

Gata was unsure. She had heard of an älf that had once helped to defeat Aiphatòn, who had been made mad by a love spell. *Wasn't he the one who liked to draw and write?* 'I shall have to read up about that.'

'You should, queen. We think Mòndarcai is spreading a lie about his heritage to make himself more important. Using the famous name for more effect. To all intents and purposes, he remains nothing but an arrogant thief at the head of a horde of low-life monsters he has collected around him.' The ruler of Dsòn Khamateion sat bolt upright on the throne as if tethered to a pole. 'We want to stress that Our warriors did not intercede in either battle: neither at Two-Stream Hill nor at the siege of Brigantia. We would have been able to sweep your army from the field, particularly since Ascatoîa secured the services of a dragon. This was Our signal to Girdlegard, an indication of Our intention of co-existing with you undisturbed and in peace. An initial gesture of restitution to compensate for the tragic occurrences involving the delegations. Who knows? On some future orbit trading relationships may be established between our countries.'

'What country do you mean?'

'Well, Dsòn Khamateion is an independent realm.'

'But it is located within the Brown Mountains, a territory that the Fourthlings claim for themselves.'

'It has not belonged to them for over a thousand cycles. They therefore have no claim to it. And We have also found no indication that there had ever been any Fourthlings around in this area. And certainly none were ever resident here.' The ruler's tone remained courteous but determined. 'We want to receive your assurances, Queen Regnorgata, that you will prevent Girdlegard attacking Us. Until we have been able to prove that Our aim is for peaceful co-existence. We are not the same as the traditional *black-eyes* of old. We have come to see many things quite differently.'

Gata was keen to believe these fine words because, if true, Girdlegard would be spared the burden of potential future distress. 'The älfar fleet that came through the Firstlings' sea gate and destroyed the dwarf strongholds gives a contrary picture, I believe.' She touched the insignia brooch on the collar. 'How do you explain that? This was not a trading party, was it?'

'Oh, on that issue We were taken completely by surprise, I assure you! We have no idea who sent the fleet. We did not summon those ships. We swear it on Our immortal life, queen.'

'Then it was perhaps someone powerful in your entourage who sees Dsòn Khamateion as the prospective overall ruler of Girdlegard? Is there a council or a politically motivated group?'

The Ganyeios smiled slightly. 'No. No one acts without Our agreement. Dsòn does in fact possess a Secret Chamber that makes decisions. It is Ourself who signs them off. For the truth of this We also are prepared to swear an oath.'

Gata believed the strength of the oath. *No älf would gamble with their immortal life.*

'We do not want war, Queen Regnorgata. And do you know why this is?'

'Tell me.'

'It would bring us no advantage. What would We want with such a huge area? Thousands of miles in all directions, a large number of nations, many different mentalities and a long history of various instances of inter-racial enmity. It all has to be governed and supervised, the subjects have to be kept content, uprisings have to be suppressed, whole territories have to be looked after and defended. This all takes time and effort. No wealth can make up for wasted time.' The älf listed the problems in a bored voice. 'Even for those who have eternal life. Instead we dedicate our orbits and cycles to the cause of art. In the fine arts.'

Gata touched her brooch as she considered these words. 'You can convince me. But there are so many others who would never trust an älf. Not after everything that has happened recently.'

'They don't have to. All they have to do is to leave us in peace. We deliberately chose this place, isolated as it is from everything. But if Girdlegard wants war, incited by and led by Fourthling dwarves or by some heroic figure intent on glory, We shall defend ourselves.' The Ganyeios gave this declaration in relaxed tones but the voice took on a dark note. 'Defend ourselves to the point of utter destruction of any enemy. With the dragon. With the zhussa's magic. With all the martial skills of the älfar warrior class. Compared to this, the battles at Two-Stream Hill and in Brigantia were nothing.'

Gata believed every word of this, too. 'If I agree to our secret treaty, what would I get for risking my reputation if I prevent anyone marching on Dsòn? You know that people have been alleging that the Thirdlings and I – purely because of something that happened in the past – might secretly be in sympathy with the älfar.'

'Over one thousand cycles ago and still not forgotten?' The ruler laughed. 'Remind them that the Thirdlings only gave the impression of being on the side of the black-eyes. Today and in the past, Queen Regnorgata, hasn't it always been, as it is now, first and foremost the Thirdlings' priority to protect Girdle-gard? Are We not correct?'

Indeed, the Ganyeios is right. Gata nodded. 'But I shall have to give the elves, dwarves, humans and meldriths something to fight against,' she said. 'Some deadly threat that they can over-come. To distract their attention away from Dsòn Khamateion.'

'Why not Mòndarcai, his Originals and his orcs?'

'That won't be enough,' Gata argued. 'I shall need your per-mission to attack and destroy the älfar fleet in Undarimar, without Dsòn retaliating. That would serve as evidence of Dsòn's peaceful intentions. And anyway, I believe you told me the ships had not come in answer to a summons from yourself?'

There was a sharp intake of breath from the Ganyeios.

'This fight will occupy Girdlegard for many cycles to come. Until the älfar fleet and their island kingdom allies are defeated, I can, behind the scenes, introduce a non-aggression pact with Dsòn Khamateion,' Gata suggested. 'And we'll add lots of extra gifts and concessions as compensation payments to be made for the assassinations. You will have to be ready to make that sacri-fice if you want your city state kept safe. Give up the fleet. And Undarimar, too.'

For quite some time the Ganyeios remained motionless. The veil over their face did not move. It was almost as if the ruler had omitted to continue drawing breath, and had expired, stone-cold dead on the throne from sheer fury at the outra-geous demand.

I wonder if I've made a mistake. Not daring to speak, Gata kept her eyes firmly fixed on the Ganyeios.

'Queen Regnorgata, We agree to your terms,' the älf announced, so suddenly that Gata jumped. 'We shall sacrifice the ships to Girdlegard and we shall put together a list of valu-able items to offer as compensation. May no further älfar lives be wasted and may from this time forward an age of peaceful cooperation begin.' The ruler raised their left hand, took up a bone dagger in their right and made a cut in the palm. The cut was not so deep that it might endanger tendons and muscles, but deep enough to cause bleeding. 'Let us seal our secret treaty, which will bring prosperity and happiness to our lands, as We hope.' The open hand, dripping with red-black blood, was illuminated by a multi-coloured ray of light from the window.

It seemed entirely right to Gata that an important agreement such as this should be ceremoniously sealed in blood. Standing up and making her way over to the podium, she took out her own dagger and gave herself a similar wound on the palm of her hand. 'For prosperity and happiness,' she said, repeating the words as she shook hands with the älf ruler.

The handshake the Ganyeios gave was firmer than she had expected, those slim älfar fingers exerting a surprising degree of pressure.

Gata felt light-headed and she thought the brooch on her collar was glowing especially brightly in the light. 'Then it is agreed, Ganyeios.'

'It is, indeed, queen.' The ruler released her fingers. 'Return now to Girdlegard and arrange what has to be done. Always think of this: we are not your enemy. Mòndarcai is the double traitor: he betrayed us älfar and he betrayed all the inhabitants of Girdlegard. Let us call him to account before he can carry out his appalling plans.'

'Let it be held even so.'

'If you need our help against the orcs, let us know. We can then send you appropriate measures.' The Ganyeios gestured towards the staircase. 'Travel safe and well, Queen Regnorgata. Our scouts will see you safely to the border. From there you will be able to make your own way to the Fourthling realm.' They rose and inclined their head respectfully. 'It has been an honour for Us. And a pleasure.'

Gata mirrored the bow they had made in her direction.

She started to feel somewhat euphoric as she turned, picking up her axe sword as she went over to the steps to descend. Although this treaty was a dangerous one for herself, she had achieved more for Girdlegard than all the other four dwarf tribes had managed in the last thousand cycles. *The orbit will soon come when I can reveal what I have achieved. And then the rejoicing will be greater than the misgivings.*

She strode swiftly down the stairs and was surprised to find herself in a completely different chamber. Instead of the egg-shaped hall she saw a floor-to-ceiling window ten paces square, through which she had a panoramic view of Dsòn in the evening light.

Proof that I have won the trust of the Ganyeios! Gata walked up to the glass and surveyed the sea of lights, and the illuminated facades of all the buildings whose shapes and colours she could hardly take in.

All of a sudden a rust-coloured dragon, forty paces long, shot up in front of the window, blocking her view with the outspread wings that kept the creature suspended in the air. On Slibina's scale-covered back rode the zhussa dressed in her black armoured robe with a black cloak over it. She greeted Gata with an expansive wave towards the right, a movement that could well have been intended as a mocking gesture.

What? Why? Gata turned in the direction indicated.

She saw a second dragon approaching out of the darkening evening, significantly smaller than Slibina and with a white and grey patterning on the chitin plates. It screeched and a long tongue of green fire emerged from its gorge and shot out through the twilight sky.

Gata realised the mistake she had made.

The Ganyeios had indeed wished to show her something:

their zhussa had made use of the time to overcome Girdlegard's last dragon and to effect its transformation.

This meant that Dsòn Khamateion possessed at least two winged beasts and one of them could spit burning flames. If this was a male dragon, the älfar could soon breed more of these lethal creatures.

Lorimbur, I praise you. Gata moved slowly back from the glass pane, watching the zhussa take her leave, leading Slibina to a headlong dive. *It has never been more important to have a treaty.*

An axe does not mind what it strikes. Always use it with care, with a swing and with a steady hand.

Dwarf axiom

XIII

Girdlegard

The Inland Sea
1024 P.Q. (7515th solar cycle in old reckoning), winter

'Curses on this storm!' Xanomir, down in the ship's hold, struggled to keep his balance, hardly able to place his equipment correctly where it was needed for the test. The *Sea Blade* was going wildly up and down and lurching from one side to the other as if waves were coming at them from all directions simultaneously. Without its stabilising outriggers, the narrow craft would have capsized and sunk long ago.

'Captain Alreth says he's never seen it like this before – the waves are coming from alternate sides. It's a complete anomaly.' Buvendil was extremely pale. He vomited into the bucket for what felt to him like the hundredth time, holding his blond hair back out of the way with his free hand.

'It's impossible.' Xanomir had more or less completed the repairs to the diving bell. The scaffolding that had collapsed on top of it had left scratches and dents on the thin outer metal skin and he was patching up the damage. A number of adjustments were still necessary to the sensitive clockwork mechanisms, which had suffered from the over-hasty loading procedure. It was quite a challenge, regulating some of the tiny cogwheels and having to replace others, and all while the boat was attempting to keep to its course through these raging seas. 'I'm going to have to wait till the wind drops.'

'Is there still much to do?'

He fixed his rubber-faced hammer into its wall-clip to ensure the heavy item did not go flying through the air with the next wave. 'I noticed one of the lateral rudders needs attention. I'll have to adjust the trim or we'll be taking pot luck when we try to send the craft down. Or up.' Xanomir was not enjoying the constant movement, either, although he would normally have classed both of them as being strong-stomached seafarers. These adverse weather conditions were extremely unusual. 'Shall we go up and get some fresh air? We can have a look at the waves,' he joked.

'What? Go up top and get washed overboard like rats?' Buvendil belched, his face a shade of green. 'No, thanks.'

The voyage had started so well. The *Sea Blade* was moved even more swiftly than Alreth had predicted, and, true to her name, she had cut through the sea like a knife. With the towing kite sails set, the vessel shot along at such a speed that the crew had initially been concerned about her stability.

But the *Sea Blade* had come through the test with flying colours, bringing them closer to Undarimar.

Then the first clouds had appeared and there was no escape from the wind. The storm had the mother ship held fast as in a cauldron and the sailors were starting to wonder whether magic could be involved. Whereas Buvendil thought it was Elria and Samusin working in tandem to destroy the dwarves, the crew were convinced the älfar and their zhussa were behind the terrible weather.

Xanomir did not go with either explanation. There were always storms at this time of the cycle. And he had heard of heavy seas like this occurring. *I'll put my trust in Vraccas.* He was starting to feel hungry. 'Let's see what the galley has to offer.'

'You're actually able to think of food?'

'I'm not only thinking about food. I'm actually going to go and get some.' Xanomir put on his waxed coat, climbed up the companionway ladder that led up to the deck. 'Shall I bring you a snack?' he asked before lifting the hatch cover.

Buvendil's reply was the sound of him retching.

The violent storm gusts tore at Xanomir as soon as he put his grey-haired head outside. The wind hoicked him up, made his waxcloth crumple, flapped his woollen scarf up over his face and hurled him against the railings before he had had a chance to grab hold of a support.

Most of the crew had gone below to find shelter. There was nothing they could do apart from pray to the gods and trust to the skill of the boat-builders. Two smaller sails were still set to guarantee forward propulsion, so the vessel was not totally at the mercy of the waves.

By grasping one of the shroud ropes Xanomir just managed to avoid being swept overboard, but he was immediately soaked through by a wall of icy sea water breaking over him. The sheer weight of water had him off his feet. Sliding across the deck, he slammed into one of the masts, and was able to grab hold of it.

Vraccas, what kind of a storm-beast have we got here? Xanomir peered through the curtain of rain over to the wheelhouse, where the captain and three other sailors were trying with their combined strengths to control the helm, battling to keep the *Sea Blade* on course and on an even keel. *I ought to give them a hand instead of going to the galley to find some dinner.*

On the other hand, he would need some food if he were going to be able to help out against the forces of nature. *A couple of slices of bread would do it for now, then I'll join them on the bridge.* He staggered from obstacle to obstacle, clinging to whatever he could find as he made his way aft, where he opened the sliding door to enter the galley.

Inside, the roar of the storm lessened but the noises the ship herself was making were even more frightening: a clattering and a creaking on all sides. Most of the crew were standing about in the gangway dressed in oilskins, ready to rush out and respond to any orders Captain Alreth might shout. Ready to do their utmost, anything to get safely away from these threatening conditions. The sailors, male and female, nodded to Xanomir and made room for him to pass. Their faces were pale, but it was not their upset stomachs – it was fear, pure and simple.

He disappeared into the galley, where Ólstrum, the ship's cook, was trying to prevent the pots and pans flying around. However stained it was, his cook's jacket was something he wore with pride, as if it were made of gold cloth. 'Aha, the engineer! Hot food's off the menu. Or have you got an invention that will let me do a fry-up in the middle of a storm? I wouldn't mind preparing something for you, as long as it took my mind off the weather.'

'Sorry. All I've got for you is my hunger.'

'Hunger? I've heard everything now.' Ólstrum laughed, adjusting the patterned headscarf covering his light-coloured hair. Or most of it. 'You dwarves must have strong stomachs.'

'No, not all of us. But I have.' Xanomir collected bread, cheese and a slab of ham, plus a fragrant uti fruit the size of an apple. 'Thank you. That'll be enough.' He sat in a swaying chair that was fastened to the ceiling by four ropes, which made it easier to cope with the movement of the ship. 'Are the crew afraid?'

'A storm like this is very rare. And it's rarer still to survive one,' Ólstrum admitted. 'We've all heard stories about weather like this. But nobody wants to experience it.' He deftly caught a saucepan lid that was sailing through the air. 'Except for little Fridgatt. He was in the jolliest of moods when this weather started up.'

'Oh, that's strange.'

'That's what I said. But he told me a good storm brought him properly to life. He liked it when it was really rough. He must be from one of the coastal regions. Crazy little fellow.' Ólstrum watched the dwarf happily. 'I'm amazed at your appetite, given the circumstances.'

Xanomir winked at him. 'You should be pleased you've got Fridgatt and me to help you use up the stores. We'll be making the ship a bit lighter and she can get through the storm easier.'

Ólstrum laughed. 'Good thinking.'

Xanomir shoved the last morsels into his mouth, his hunger satisfied. 'I'm off to the wheelhouse to see if Alreth needs any help. It looked as if it was tough going for him and the crew just now. They were struggling to keep hold of the wheel.'

'They'll appreciate the strong hand of a dwarf.' The ship's cook pressed a small box into his hand. 'Something sweet. For the crew. Their nerves will be needing food, not just their muscles.'

Xanomir pocketed it and went back outside.

Again he was assaulted by wind and water, which nearly swept him off the steps of the companionway up to the wheelhouse at the stern. The *Sea Blade* shuddered, shook and shifted from her course as each successive wave struck home from a new direction, battering her timbers.

Xanomir found it more difficult than he had envisaged to clamber up and then pull the door aside and step in. 'Permission to enter the wheelhouse, captain?' he asked, wiping the salt water from his face.

What he then saw took the next words out of his mouth.

Alreth and the three mariners all lay dead on the floor, their throats cut. There was blood coursing this way and that on the floorboards. The wheel had been smashed and the driving chain taken off the cogs. It was rattling free like a toothed-saw blade.

'No!' Xanomir could not believe his eyes. But the implication finally filtered through to his brain. *We are in the middle of a storm with no means of steering the ship. We are lost. We will capsize and sink.*

'I'm glad you've come. I shan't have to go down to the hold to find you,' said a voice behind him.

Instinct told Xanomir to duck. The sword swirled past his head. He turned and drew his knife; his axe was back in his quarters. In front of him he saw Fridgatt looking delighted, with the blade in his hand dripping with blood. The sailor was smaller and slimmer than the dwarf. 'Surprised? You thought it'd be an älf, didn't you?'

'Why would you do this?'

'Why do you think? I'm from Undarimar, that's why. You'll never take the *Sea Blade* to my land. You can take all your clever knowledge about evil diving boats to your watery grave,' Fridgatt declared. 'Your invention is the work of a demon. An insult to the sea!' And with those words he wielded his sword again.

Vraccas and Elria! From down on the floor, Xanomir parried the vicious blow using his knife. The clashing of the blades jarred his shoulder painfully. It was too late to try negotiating his way out of this confrontation. Fridgatt's bloody acts spoke for themselves. His only hope was to kill him and warn the crew. They would surely know how the ship could best be managed without its steering apparatus. *That's why Fridgatt was in such a good mood. The storm was just what he wanted.*

'A vessel like that should never have been built!' Fridgatt waved his sword, gripping the hilt with both hands. 'And it will never be done again!'

Xanomir adroitly managed to avoid the swiping blade. The sword sliced through the captain's body and lodged in the boards of the deck. Without hesitating, Xanomir seized the opportunity to plunge his dagger into the inside of his adversary's upper thigh, causing Fridgatt to utter a long scream of pain. Groaning, the young Undarimarian tried to kick at the dwarf, but his leg muscles had been partially severed, and he fell to the floor.

Like Xanomir and the bodies of his victims, Fridgatt, too, was rolling to and fro with the movement of the ship. Blood sprayed from his wound. 'I'll get you,' he threatened, but his voice sounded faint. He tried to get hold of a rapier that had belonged to one of the dead sailors. 'Then I'll go down in the hold and kill your friend.' But before he could pick the weapon up, he collapsed over the sailor's body. And lay still.

Xanomir struggled to his feet. The door was being opened from the outside.

Drenched through, Ólstrum stood on the threshold, staring in astonishment at the interior of the wheelhouse. 'By all the demons of the deep,' he exclaimed in horror. 'What . . .?'

'Fridgatt. Saboteur and murderer. He's from Undarimar,' Xanomir summarised breathlessly. 'Alert the crew! We've got to work out how to get the *Sea Blade* under control.'

But Ólstrum shook his head. 'I came to tell Alreth we've sprung a leak. The hold is filling up with water. Your mate Buvendil discovered several holes that have been made in the hull.'

'Fridgatt again! The swine! He's done this for Undarimar!' Xanomir put his knife away. 'What do we do?'

Ólstrum looked at the corpses. 'I presume the captain would have ordered you and your friend to launch your diving bell,' he said calmly. 'The two of you have to reach Arimar and sink the älfar fleet. Now more than ever. The whole island should burn for this treachery.'

'What about you?'

The cook gave a twisted smile. 'A sailor's grave for us. Straight down into Elria's arms.'

'No!'

'The lifeboats are no better than nutshells in seas like these. We'll drown, one way or the other. But we'll be going down in a unique sailing vessel and with the best captain anyone could ever wish for.' Ólstrum grabbed Xanomir by the collar. 'Now be off with you. You and your friend must get diving! Untie the submersible and we'll get you launched!'

'But—'

'There's no time to delay! Otherwise our deaths will be for naught.'

Ólstrum pushed him roughly down on to the deck and manhandled him into the hold. 'As soon as you're both ready, get in. Then we'll heave your craft up and over the side,' he said. 'May Elria and Vraccas protect you.'

The cook hurried off. The first mate's whistle sounded clearly through the raging wind. Without a word Buvendil and Xanomir worked hand in hand, loading the diving craft with the tools they would be needing to complete the repair job, which they would now, of course, have to complete under water.

'If it doesn't work, we'll sink to the bottom.' Buvendil spoke out loud what both of them were afraid of. 'Like our mother ship, the Sea Blade.'

'But before that we are going to destroy those älfar ships. And we'll avenge the deaths of Alreth and his crew.' He swung himself over into the entry hatch and checked the fixtures. 'Looks like it's watertight. Get in!'

'This porthole will hold. Let's hope all the others will, too.'

Buvendil pushed his way past and got into the steel belly of the diving bell and moved to its stern. 'Ready!' His voice sounded hollow as it echoed.

Xanomir looked up. The hatchway above them opened up and three ropes with hooks at the ends were lowered. Ólstrum peered down over the edge of the opening and chucked in another box of sweets, then he saluted.

'It has been an honour to sail with you,' said Xanomir, saluting too; then he went down the rungs of the ladder, closed and bolted the hatch-lid behind himself. A small oil lamp gave light enough for dwarf eyes to see by.

Almost immediately there was a clanging and a banging and the craft was hoisted up and swung from side to side before it suddenly jerked downwards and splashed into the sea. Buvendil and Xanomir realised the winch must have broken.

The deeper they sank, the less their vessel swayed.

It became quieter until the ticking of the clockwork mechanism and the friends' breathing were the only sounds to be heard.

We shall avenge your deaths. Xanomir consulted the on-board compass and set his course for Undarimar.

Girdlegard

Empire of Gautaya
1024 P.Q. (7515th solar cycle in old reckoning), winter

Stémna hurried back through the forest along the track she had made to the place where one of her stores of orange feathers had been concealed. Using a broken-off pine branch, she swept away the footprints behind herself. By daybreak the snow that had started to fall would have covered the last of the fresh marks.

It was the middle of the night. The moon stood high in the sky, giving Stémna the light she needed for her illicit outing, so she had not needed to bring a lantern. The moonlight reflecting off the white snow was sufficient even in the woods.

She had taken a couple of dozen feathers from her secret supply. There were still about forty left for another time. She felt secure in knowing she had protection against complaints or in fights she might encounter. *I'm making good time. It's gone even quicker than I'd thought.*

For warmth she was wrapped in a thick woollen mantle with a sheep fleece draped over her shoulders. Underneath she had on the simple beige tunic her mistress had given her to wear. In less than one and a half sandglasses' time she would be back in her bed in the narrow chamber. She slept there alone, being the slave of highest standing in Tithmar of Widestone's household. Here she was known as Elora.

Her workplace was a country estate that included the village of Wideholm with its five hundred souls, all bonded serfs belonging to the Widestone family.

Stémna had initially assumed she would be acting as a nurse for young children, or as a companion for Tithmar's bored lady wife, but on the orbit following her arrival she had realised that she would be responsible for handing out punishments. Being whipped or beaten with a rod or even merely being supervised in their daily work by a doulia would be an additional humiliation for the village serfs.

The cruelty characteristic of the vulgar figure who owned the estate did not let his many children off the hook. They loved him, and idolised him, he thought. So it was Stémna who was expected to exact harsh discipline for the slightest misdemeanour. The father thus was spared any resentment the children might feel. Their mother Helka, however, would run from the room, sobbing and trembling at the sight of the pain inflicted on them.

In her previous capacity as the envoy of the white dragon, Stémna had been accustomed to seeing distress. But the scourged backs of the children, the bruises and cuts, the fractured toes and fingers of the three boys and the seven girls, aged between six and fourteen, showed that Tithmar had always been cruel in the extreme. He remained in the room when the punishments were meted out, whether it was in the village or within the family, and he enjoyed watching. He liked to hear them whimper and beg. He liked to see the blood and the tears.

How does his wife stand it? Stémna hurried to the edge of the wood. *And how does the perverted swine manage to avoid being murdered? Why don't the villagers down tools and leave? Being outlawed must be better than living under this yoke.*

She did not intend to remain long in the service of this family. Even though she wished to be a good doulia, she felt she was within her rights to tell Gubnara that she had not undergone her onerous course of training in order to be nothing more than a torturer. If that was what was required, then surely a less well-qualified doulia could carry out the duties satisfactorily.

Stémna discarded the pine-tree branch and left the thicket to step out on to the snowy open field.

Less than five paces from where she emerged from the wood, she heard the sound of a horse snorting, accompanied by whining from a brace of hounds. *Curses!* Turning her head, she tried to make herself as small as possible. *A huntsman?*

'Don't try and hide.' It was Tithmar himself, wrapped in warm clothing, with a high fur collar and a cap. He was mounted on a dapple grey. The two hounds, Snaig and Snog, lay by the horse's feet and glared at her watchfully. 'I was about to let them off the leash to track you. What are you doing here in the middle of the night, out without my permission, Elora?'

'My Lord, forgive me.' Striking a humble attitude that was not natural to her, Stémna went on, 'I am troubled by the moon. At full moon I have these problems and I sleepwalk. Often I don't realise at all until I wake up somewhere strange.'

'Is that so?' Tithmar pointed down at her. 'But you're perfectly dressed for a cold country walk. I expect you've even taken provisions?'

'No, not provisions, Lord.' Stémna lowered her shaven head. It still felt strange to her to have no hair under her cap. There was one last strand of her own light hair, with a black extension plaited in, made of horsehair and running from the brow to the nape. 'My thanks that you were concerned for my safety and came to find me.'

'Concerned for your safety? No. I assumed you had run away.'

She hoped that her acting was convincing. 'But my Lord, I am a doulia! I live only to serve. To serve with all my devotion, as you know and as you have witnessed. No doulia would ever deceive their master.' She pointed up again at the night-star's globe. 'The moon bears the guilt. Pardon me. I should have informed you about my weakness but I did not guess that the pull would be as strong as it has been tonight. I woke from my sleepwalking and found I was already on the way back home to you.'

Tithmar did not budge. 'Your explanation seems credible.'

'Yes, Master.' Stémna moved past the growling pair of dogs and approached to kiss the toe of Tithmar's boot. 'The next time the moon is full I'll tie my feet together, so I don't cause you any trouble.'

'An excellent idea.' Tithmar observed her closely. 'You don't wonder about it?'

'About the lunar feelings? Well, my mother—'

'You don't wonder why I noticed you had gone?' He pushed her away with his foot.

'Yes, indeed, now you mention it, Master. I thought maybe you had heard me leave. Or Snaig and Snog had barked perhaps.'

'That's not the reason. I wanted to fuck you. Quite simple. Your orange eyes drive me wild.' Tithmar laughed quietly. 'I wanted my wife to watch while I did it, so she can learn what I like.'

Stémna was glad her face was covered with the scarf. She bowed her head so the look in her eyes would not betray her. 'And I have deprived you of your pleasure. I am very sorry, Master.'

'So am I.' He slowly unwound a length of rope from his saddle. 'And that is why I am going to punish you. In order for us to reach home quicker I will pull you along behind my horse. It will be like sledging. But without a sledge.' Tithmar watched her. 'I don't want you to enjoy it. Take your clothes off.'

Stémna nodded obediently. 'Of course, Master.' She slowly undid the fastenings on her mantle. 'I have deserved this.'

'I agree. It's only six miles that you'll be dragged. If you are lucky there won't be much ice on top of the snow. Because that would shred your skin, wouldn't it?' Tithmar sat upright in the saddle and looked over towards the west. 'Oh, you know what? I think I'll make a little detour. Through the Tay stream. That will be nice and refreshing for you.'

Stémna placed her sheepskin and then the folded mantle down on the snow. She opened the beige tunic she wore underneath. 'As you see fit, Master.'

'As soon as we are at home you will come straight back here on foot to collect your clothing. It is expensive. I don't want some woodsman to take it for his ugly thing of a woman,' he said, making a loop in the rope to attach to her wrists. 'Maybe this will help alleviate your moon sickness, Elora. And if it doesn't, then at least it will serve as compensation to me for my frustrated desires.'

'How right you are, Master.' Stémna bent over as if to unlace her boots. But she actually released the saddle belt under the horse's belly, grabbed the end and heaved it up, thus making the saddle tip over, taking Tithmar with it.

The stocky estate owner landed in the snow, shouting curses. Stémna took hold of the reins of the dappled grey as it reared up; she pulled it round to face the front and she slapped its rump as hard as she could.

The frightened mare whinnied with shock and kicked out with its hind legs. The metal horseshoes struck Tithmar repeatedly in the chest and on his face. Blood sprayed out over the snow. Not knowing what to do, the two hounds leaped around, barking furiously and excitedly circling their master, whose death rattle was audible by now. His deformed features were totally unrecognisable. After a final spasm Tithmar lay still.

'Well done, girl,' Stémna said soothingly to the horse, stroking its soft muzzle. 'You have done well.' No way had she been going to let that piece of scum drag her to her death through the snow. 'Snaig! Snog! Sit!'

The bloodhounds obeyed her command.

Stémna swiftly re-donned her clothes and placed the prepared loop of rope over the man's wrists to give the impression that he had previously been tied up. Then she used his blood to write slogans in the snow in large letters, and again on the saddle in smaller script, such as: *This is how a merciless oppressor dies. This is just the start! Freedom for the North!* To make sure, she opened his clothing and cut a spontaneously invented symbol into the skin of his chest, and then she rammed his own dagger through his heart.

Perfect! Stémna straightened up. The city fathers and the guards could try to work out which band of rebels had wrought this vengeance on their local estate-master. She chased Snaig, Snog and the horse off. Sooner or later they would make their way back to the farm.

Striding quickly along the horses' hoofprint track, she made her way through the snow back to the farmyard. She reached her attic bedroom by clambering over the roof and in through the window. She stripped off her thick outer garments and slipped beneath the covers. The warmth, combined with her exhaustion, soon sent her to sleep. No one would suspect she had anything to do with the occurrence. First and foremost, she was a doulia, loyal, submissive, born to serve. Moreover, her privileged status ensured she had no reason to feel any resentment and so would not have sought to join the roving squads of rebel murderers. *This was not what I had planned.* About to doze off, Stémna glanced out of the window and saw the snow was stopping. *But well executed. And the message written in blood*—

'Is he dead?' It was a quiet voice, sounding anxious and yet hopeful.

Under her blankets Stémna went stiff with apprehension. *Helka!* The lady of the house was sitting in the dark and had apparently been waiting for Tithmar to return. She was supposed to watch her spouse having his way with the doulia. *He even told me that it was planned.* Stémna was furious with herself for slipping up.

'Yes, he is,' she answered truthfully, sitting up, her right hand on the hilt of the knife she had concealed at the edge of her bed. If the estate owner's wife had to die, too, one more corpse would surely make no difference. She deserved to die, perhaps, for failing to speak out against her husband's cruelty and for not preventing his vicious actions.

'Good.' The door opened and a ray of light entered the chamber as Helka went to leave. 'I shan't say anything. And I'll be eternally grateful to you.' She left the chamber.

Stémna laughed and fell back on to her pillow.

Girdlegard

In the Brown Mountains
Brigantia
1024 P.Q. (7515th solar cycle in old reckoning), winter

Rodana slipped through the encampment at the foot of the besieged city. The camp was decreasing in size daily, with many of the coastal region troops heading back home to defend their homelands against the Undarimarians and their älfar allies, and others were preferring to shelter more comfortably from the winter weather by moving inside the Fourthlings' stronghold. There were many reminders still of the Brigantian occupancy but the dwarves, on returning to their own territory, had burned wagonloads of furniture and furnishings on great bonfires out on the field and in the fireplaces of the forges.

There was much coming and going in the camp and so Rodana was able to escape notice, wearing, as she did, a long, hooded cloak. Her target was clear: she was heading for the quarters of the recently promoted magus, who appeared to prefer to be accommodated outside the walls of the Brown Mountains area. He had arranged to have six large conference tents erected for himself, where he resided away from the rest in opulent splendour. Until all the negotiations were complete Mostro was keen to remain here, rather than return to Rhuta.

He thinks he is incredibly important. Rodana ducked down behind a canvas shelter to avoid being seen by a gang of laughing guards. If she were discovered, she would be sent straight back to the cells she had so recently escaped from. She had cleverly used Gata's knife to aid her escape, having shattered it on the icy ground to make a tool that would serve as a lock-pick. The guards stomped straight past her in the snow, all looking forward to their evening glass of beer, brought in from Sinterich. *Go on, go and get drunk. I'm going to exact my revenge.* Rodana waited until the soldiers had left.

While in her cell she had heard the sentries talking about how Mostro had come up with further allegations about her. He was utterly obsessed with dragging her to trial, furious as he was that, some time ago, she had beaten him in her theatre caravan; but this might not suffice to have her hanged, so more accusations had needed to be thought up. *I shall never let myself be punished for crimes I did not commit.* Rodana kept the broken dagger concealed under her mantle. At the end of four orbits the current talks would all be over and Mostro would be leaving, it was rumoured. She was intent on preventing his departure – by killing him.

He was responsible for Chòldunja's death. *And the Omuthan was culpable, too, for having summoned the rhamak that the girl had stayed behind to confront.* The guilty ones would have to die. They would be allowed no chance of avoiding their punishment. She doubted she would be able to get near the Omuthan. He was under armed guard in a cell and was surrounded by the other members of his family. *But I shall try. After I've killed the famulus for his terrible lies.* She was not worried about his magic powers. A sleeping magus would be an easy target. *He won't even notice what's happening before his soul leaves his body.*

She hurried on. After the murder she would slip back into her prison cell and innocently relish hearing the news of the death of the magus.

She reached the first of Mostro's six brightly lit yurts. Listening out, she walked carefully round its perimeter. Inside, the servants seemed to be complaining about the unfair demands their master had been making of them. His people were washing up kitchen utensils and dishes and preparing the next meal, to judge by the clattering noises, the smoke from the tin chimney and the smell of food.

Rodana counted half a dozen staff who were in Mostro's service. *I'll have to be careful none of them sees me.*

In the largest of his three private tents Mostro's voice could be heard, muffled by the expanses of thick canvas fabric walls. From the shadows on the tent's side it would appear he was talking energetically with another man, and walking up and down while he spoke. He had a goblet in his right hand, and drank from it every so often.

I've got you! Rodana sliced a gap through the dense textile behind one of the cupboards, wide enough for her to slip into the warm, but staying hidden behind the furniture. *Now all I have to do is wait till he's on his own.*

'. . . me an initial skill, honoured Hantu?' Rodana furrowed her brow. *I must have misheard.* She risked a cautious glance out past the cupboard.

A young Gauragon soldier was lolling in an upholstered chair, his uniform jacket unbuttoned and opened for comfort. He had laid aside his helmet, mantle and weapons belt. He did not seem to be deferring respectfully to a person of a higher rank than himself. 'You've done all the practice I told you to do? To relax and empty the mind?'

'How can one empty a spirit?' Mostro gestured dramatically. He was wearing an embroidered housecoat; his wavy hair was perfectly groomed and his pointed beard glossy and trim. 'It is impossible not to be thinking of something!'

'You will learn. Then you will be ready for the next stage: focusing on extraction. Perhaps you need more aquamarines and mountain crystals? They will help you. It's a good thing we have the Fourthlings near at hand.' The soldier, who could not be much older than seventeen or eighteen, gave a satisfied sigh and drank from a steaming cup.

'I'll give you till the end of the cycle to teach me how to reach the other hidden spheres in order to summon the beings from there like you can. Otherwise –'

'Oh come now! No need to threaten me, magus!' The juvenile soldier laughed and raised his drink in a salute. 'I'll do my best if you do the same.'

'I am doing my best, Hantu. I really am doing my best.' Mostro emptied his goblet and put it down on a table already covered in parchment rolls and piles of books. 'I should be happier once I've mastered a form of defence that does not depend on either an artefact or the vicinity of a magic energy source.'

So that's your game! Rodana could hardly believe it. That was why she had not been able to locate the rhamak. The magus had helped him to change his appearance. *And in return he's teaching the magus his own egregious arts!*

She altered her plan.

'I understand. Always better to have three legs to stand on,' the soldier said. 'Most of those artefacts turned out to be nothing but playthings, if you don't mind my saying so. Apart from the magic blade and that special armour. Your mistress—'

'Vanéra is no proper maga. She lacked magic arts and I overwhelmed her with my superior skill. But she was good at deception. She acted the part and put on a good show.' Mostro threw himself down in an empty chair and reached for a dish of candied fruit. 'How long did you need, Hantu? How many cycles does it take to be able to summon the hidden souls?'

'One never arrives at perfection,' the other admitted. 'You'll see, each time you achieve one level there's another one waiting. And then another one. And yet another. Each more beguiling and more dangerous than the last. A rapturous intoxication, without resorting to alcohol or herbal concoctions,' he enthused. 'These journeys are addictive, Mostro. I'm warning you.'

'Yes, you already told me that. But I am eager to submit to this rapturous state.' He chewed on a handful of fruit and belched. 'Excuse me. The human side of things needs a moment of quiet.' Mostro got to his feet. 'Help yourself. I'll be back soon.' He left the tent.

'Take as long as you like with your shit,' the newly youthful form of Hantu murmured. 'The orbit will arrive, you utter fool, on which I will use your magician's blood to let me reach a far-off sphere.'

Samusin, god of retribution and justice. Thank you for the opportunity you have presented me with! Rodana crept out through the rip in the fabric and hastened along the sides of the tent to get to the latrines. Mostro had arranged to have his own personal amenities. *Stabbed to death while at stool. A fitting end.*

Now Rodana understood why the magus had not wanted to move his quarters into the fortress; here outside the walls there were fewer curious pairs of eyes and ears. He could see the transformed rhamak as often as he wanted for lessons without anyone noticing.

Rodana reached the little shack before the magus did. He had stopped to don a sable mantle before striding over through the wind and snowy weather. She crouched down silently. But then a hand was placed over her mouth and an arm hard as steel grabbed her upper body, preventing her from using her hands.

There was a sudden smell of vanilla and roast nuts. 'You can thank your lucky stars it was Belîngor and me that found you,' Brûgar whispered in her ear. 'Or there'd have been a summary execution for you for escaping from custody. Don't give them the excuse they want.'

Rodana gave a cursory nod.

Mostro disappeared into his private latrine shack. There was a noise from the inside.

'So you want to kill our little wand-fiddler. But that is not a good idea,' he murmured. 'He will be protected by his magic. For sure.'

She stayed very still. There was no point struggling against the strength of this warrior dwarf.

Blue-bearded Brûgar was at her side, so it must be Belîngor holding her.

'Don't make a sound!' he warned, pipe in the corner of his mouth as usual. 'I have no wish to be turned into something else by that conceited famulus.' Rodana was lifted off her feet and carried off. 'We will talk. Soon. Very soon.'

Despair flooded through her. Revenge and justice had been close enough to grasp but the moment was gone, all because of these two dwarves, who had had their wits about them. *I will never get a chance like that again.* And then, there was Hantu, sitting in the magus's tent, unsuspecting – an easy target.

Once Belîngor had got her a good twenty paces away from the latrines, and safely behind one of the carts, he removed his hand from her mouth. The steely grip on her body remained, stopping her from running off.

'Right. Now tell us about your earth-shatteringly intelligent plan.' Brûgar faced her, hands on hips, as if he were a mother remonstrating with a naughty child. 'No. Let me guess: stab the wand-fiddler and run away? After Gata's done so much on your behalf, risking her own reputation? Is that what you call gratitude?' He drew on his pipe. 'And don't you lie to me! This here is my special Thinking-Things-Through Pipe. It lets me see right through falsehoods.'

'Hantu is with Mostro,' Rodana blurted out, although she had intended to say something quite different. 'In that tent. He's changed his shape!'

Belîngor let her go and made a sign asking for her pardon for having held her so firmly. The dwarves looked at each other and at Rodana, eyebrows raised in question.

'You're telling me the wand-fiddler and the rhamak are in cahoots?' Brûgar found this hard to believe. 'How do you know?'

At the speed of the wind Rodana summarised how she had got into the tent and what she had overheard. 'The three of us together could attack and kill them. Take them by surprise,' she finished off. 'Otherwise Mostro will be able to defend himself with a banning spell. And maybe Hantu will summon one of the sphere beings quicker than we think he can.' She ran a few steps towards the extravagantly adorned tent and the private latrine. 'Come with me! We can't waste a moment!'

But Belîngor held her fast again and pulled her back behind the wagon.

'Wait, wait!' Brûgar narrowed his eyes, watching the latrine shack. He drew on his pipe. 'He's heading back. I think we should try to listen in. That would mean you wouldn't be the sole witness – and a witness, at that, who's actually supposed to be in her prison cell. Your word, I'm sorry to say, won't be taken seriously.'

Belîngor made a dismissive gesture. *It is too dangerous,* his signing implied. Brûgar interpreted. *'Magus, rhamak, artefacts. We'd be dead before we could raise our weapons.'*

'Nonsense! We'd have surprise on our side!' Rodana's eyes filled with angry tears. 'Please listen! We've got to stop them.'

'Belîngor's right, though. We need to set a trap for them so they will expose their own treachery in everyone's eyes.' Smoking his pipe thoughtfully, Brûgar watched Mostro depart, adjusting his clothing and humming to himself, loudly, but out of tune. 'What we need is Goîmron, of course. He's the only one able to confront the wand-fiddler with magic of his own.'

'But Goîmron's not here, is he? And nobody knows if he's even still alive.' Rodana considered sprinting off in Mostro's direction. Dwarf legs were not renowned for speed. Maybe she could risk it.

'He's sure to be alive.' Belîngor's face bore an expression intended to calm her concerns. 'Please, Rodana. Be sensible. We gain nothing if Mostro kills you and claims you attacked him first.'

Rodana sighed. *So near and yet so far. And now they talk about being sensible and reasonable.* 'How did you find me?'

'When Gata came back—' Brûgar began and then broke off, horrified.

'She's been away? Where was she then?' Rodana wanted to know.

'I mean . . . she came back after some strategy meeting. She told us to come and get you from the cells. You are still under her supervision. Until the court case is settled.' Brûgar went red, which made the blue of his beard and his tattoos stand out more than ever. He was puffing so fast at his pipe that his face was covered in a cloud of smoke. 'Gata does not want the case to come to court, she told us. She did not want you imprisoned any longer.'

Belîngor indicated two small items in the palm of his hand that had come from Gata's knife.

'It wasn't hard to guess what your plan was. And I was correct.' Brûgar pointed to the group of six illuminated yurts. 'It would have been madness!'

Rodana had given up. This orbit would not see the deaths of either Mostro or Hantu at her instigation. *Samusin, my trust is in you.* 'Let's at least slip over to the tents and listen to the two of them, like Brûgar just suggested. So you can testify to the truth of my words.'

Belîngor reluctantly agreed and they made their way cautiously over to the magus's accommodation. To be on the safe side, the blue-bearded dwarf extinguished his pipe, so the scent would not betray their presence. But when they reached the tent, the two they sought were no longer there. They had moved to a different part of Mostro's quarters to continue their talk.

'Let's look for them,' Brûgar said quietly. 'I'm curious to see what the rhamak looks like now.'

The trio was about to set off when the whole camp erupted in cries of jubilation. Mostro's servants joined in the celebration, applauding wildly. Figures seen in silhouette were hugging and embracing. There was no hope of being able to overhear any conversations.

'It's about Goïmron!' Rodana called out, delirious with happiness. 'He's back! Let's go and find him. He has to be told what's happened.'

'Yes! Off to find our wizard of a gem cutter! Let's go!' Rodana took the lead, with Brûgar following and Belîngor bringing up the rear.

They had hardly reached the army encampment before they realised that Rodana had jumped to the wrong conclusion. It was not Goïmron's return that was being celebrated but the death of the Omuthan. He and his retinue had been found dead in their cell, poisoned. The same poison he had used to sacrifice his own soldiers to serve the rhamak's needs. The troops were speculating about whether this was an act of revenge by some of the Brigantians who had defected.

They won't forgive Orweyn Berengart for his treachery. Rodana could not suppress a grim laugh. *The life of one of those who are to blame for Chòldunja's death has now been ended.* Just a matter of time before the other two got their comeuppance.

Her mood was still high until she realised that it did not have to have been Brigantians who had served the poisoned water to the Omuthan and his followers. It could just as well have been Gauragon guards.

To be specific: *one* of the very young Gauragon guards, in need of the life-strength of the Omuthan and his people in order to call spirits from another sphere. *And who now sits side by side with Mostro.*

In the conference chamber Gata allowed her thoughts to wander during Mostro's speech. She looked at the agenda to see which discussion points had been ticked off. There was still no hint of where Goïmron and Szmajro, the double-headed dragon, had got to, so the participants had decided to omit that item. Gata was still desperate to hear of a sign of life from the Fourthling.

There were enough other places 'where order had to be imposed,' as Mostro had put it, now that Brigantia had been defeated. Mostro was letting the victories go to his head, because he saw himself as Vanéra's successor, and thus equal in status to Girdlegard's monarchs.

In this estimation, however, he was alone.

Thanks to what she had been told by Brûgar, Belîngor and Rodana, Gata knew about the secret doings of the magus. She shared the view that he should not be confronted publicly until they had some kind of effective remedy. This could be provided, they thought, by either Goïmron or Ascatoîa. Or perhaps a suitable artefact. All three similarly difficult to come by. This was why she stayed silent, however hard it was and how dangerous it might turn out to be. *Provoking this awful little man might bring a catastrophe down on us all.*

Gata had at least been able to insist that Rodana should be cleared of all allegations of wrongdoing. There was no proof to back up the accusations against her, but there was, conversely, evidence of false witness statements. Mostro had objected furiously, but the puppet mistress had been released from custody. The aprendisa, since deceased, had been exonerated posthumously of the crime of killing infants.

Rodana had announced that she wished to stay. Officially in order to collect stories to use in her puppet shows. Her real reason was that she did not want to let the magus and Hantu, now in the shape of a young Gauragon soldier, out of her sight. *I hope*, thought Gata, *she doesn't do anything stupid.*

'And what do you say, Queen Regnorgata?'

'Mmm?' Gata raised her head to see everyone was looking

her way. Mostro was seated now. It had been Randûlas speaking, leader of the elf delegation from the realm of Tîlandur. Telînas sat next to him, folding the figure of a unicorn out of two pieces of coloured paper. 'I apologise. I was deep in thought.'

The dark-blond elf smiled and pointed to the map of Girdlegard with the tip of his slim rapier, indicating the location of Dsôn Khamateion. 'I proposed that we should pay a visit first to the älfar here, to free the Brown Mountains from their pernicious darkness. My Kisâri is of the opinion that they present our greatest threat. And as our combined forces are more or less at the very doors of the enemy it seems the ideal opportunity.'

Gata cleared her throat and stood up to speak. 'That's exactly what I was thinking about.' She took up a pointer and placed its tip on Arimar, Undarimar's main island. 'There are black-eyes here too. Eight ships, easy to attack. No zhussa. No dragons,' she said, inviting them to change their minds. 'They are causing concern to many of the nations based round the edge of the Inland Sea.' Her gaze went to the representatives from those very lands. 'There was good reason for the coastal regions to recall their troops many orbits ago. I propose we should start there and go for a swift and achievable victory.'

Randûlas blinked in irritation. 'But Dsôn Khamateion is much closer. To get to the Inland Sea we'd have to move a vast army column right across the whole of Girdlegard.'

'And *that* is just what is needed for an ambitious programme of action to succeed. It is reported that there is a new banner flying over Kràg Tahuum, indicating that they have a new ruler, who has chosen to disassociate the place from Mòndarcai. Thus he won't have the same support to call on.' Gata moved her pointing stick further up the map to the symbol for the fortress. 'We have five war-wolf catapults that can be taken apart for transport. Why not eradicate the orc strongholds on our way south? They have presented a threat for many cycles, standing for wholesale pillaging and murder. With a magus at our side we can do away with this danger once and for all. And we can show Girdlegard's peoples a further resounding victory.'

The conference attendees started to discuss the issue among themselves.

'Why are you assuming we would lose against Dsôn Khamateion? Our numbers are superior. And as you said, Queen Regnorgata, we have the services of the esteemed magus Mostro,' Randûlas argued, his brow furrowed.

'You are forgetting Slibina. The monster is controlled by the zhussa. And we have no idea where Szmajro has got to. If the two-headed dragon has returned to its mistress we'll have two flying enemies to contend with.' Gata, reading the faces of those present, realised there was a readiness in the room to follow her proposal. So she added: 'I have heard rumours that with Slibina's help the älfar witch has also subjugated the only remaining dragon – Grasstooth.'

The discussions round the table grew louder.

Randûlas left his sword on the map. 'Where did you hear that?'

'Some farmers bringing supplies to the camp told us about a dragon fight. A little one against a large beast. As we didn't find a cadaver I put two and two together.'

'Three dragons in Dsôn Khamateion,' somebody groaned. 'By Palandiell! It'd be suicide to attack now!'

'Indeed it would,' said Telìnâs, speaking up. 'I support Queen Regnorgata's suggestion. Let's take out Kràg Tahuum and the älfar fleet in Undarimar.' He deposited the winged paper unicorn in front of him. 'The dwarves of the Firstling tribe can help us enormously, given their knowledge of seafaring.'

Randûlas shot him an angry glance. 'If we do that we'd have Dsôn Khamateion constantly at our backs. If the Ganyeios were to decide to attack the Fourthlings, then—'

'He won't,' Gata interrupted. 'Think about it. He held back in the recent armed confrontations. His troops took part neither in the Battle of Two-Stream Hill nor in the Brigantia siege, even though they already had the dragons. They could have wiped us out long ago.'

The arguments round the table turned into hefty disputes.

'And what do you deduce from that, Queen Regnorgata?' Mostro chipped in, inquisitively. His attire for this occasion was as sumptuous as any king or emperor might wear. 'That the älfar in the north wanted peace after shedding too much of Girdlegard's noble blood in their recent attacks?'

His comment was met with loud laughter.

'Hardly. But it could be an indication that they did not wish to appear a threat,' Gata returned.

'In the end Inàste's fiendish monstrosities will be asking for a peace treaty and a trade agreement?' Randûlas was indignant. 'Never! Not with Tî Silândur. The älfar are all duplicitous. They will deceive us in order to attack when we least expect it. Remember the fate of so many of the delegations!'

'With respect, they did not do it when it would have been strategically crucial.' Telìnâs continued to take Gata's side, contradicting his superior officer. 'So why would they do it later on?'

'How should I know what they may be planning? It'll be evil enough, at all events.' Randûlas sat down, leaving the tip of his sword still pointing unmistakably at the älfar realm. 'Who's going to tell us they won't send in their dragons as soon as we attack the ships at Arimar?'

'Only a fool would rule out that eventuality. I am not a fool.' Gata also sat down. 'But judging by how they have acted so far I think it unlikely.'

'We know where Dsôn Khamateion is,' said Bendoïn Fein-unz, raising his voice unexpectedly. He had been chosen by his tribe as King of the Fourthlings. 'We've known it for a long time. There are very few locations suitable for settlements in the north-western parts of the Brown Mountains. It's difficult terrain. There are relatively few roads and the black-eyes will have laid traps and prepared ambushes all along the routes.' He turned to Mostro and smoothed his bushy moustache. 'I don't want to offend you, but you would not be able to prevent our losses. I reckon we might lose four or five thousand on the way. And then that's when the fighting would start in earnest. Given the circumstances, I'm afraid to say I doubt we could win.'

'I like Queen Regnorgata's suggestions,' declared the representative from Gauragon. 'It makes sense. If we destroy Kràg Tahuum we'd be sending the orcs in the salt flats a stark warning. They'd shape up and behave because they'd know there was a new unity among the various kingdoms, resulting in an effective army.'

The participants hammered on the table with mugs and tankards to show their approval. Only Randûlas and the elf delegates remained aloof.

'Good. It is resolved we march south,' Bendoïn announced. 'The orc stronghold will fall in the winter, meaning we can use the spring storms to get at the älfar ships and sink them, finishing off all the black-eyes in Arimar.' He glanced round the room. 'All those in favour, raise your hands.'

To Gata's intense relief all the delegations voted to support her proposal.

Except for Randûlas. 'Tî Silândur is against it,' he stated, speaking slowly to give his words more weight. 'Of course, the Kisâri will support the enterprise. We stand beside all the humans, dwarves and meldriths. But in our opinion our deadliest enemy is to be found in Dsôn Khamateion. And we are not willing to overlook the treacherous murders they have committed.'

'Noble Randûlas, rest assured: we shall be taking on that depraved brood in two or three cycles' time,' Mostro promised grandiosely, while gesturing for more wine. 'By that time I shall have many new powers at my disposal that a zhussa would never be able to match, even with the greatest dragons in the known world. You have my oath on it!'

This was greeted with loud applause and a friendly nod from the elf spokesman.

Gata had an idea where Mostro's self-confidence came from. He had not mentioned magic spells. He had spoken only of 'powers'. *He will have meant the beings he hopes to have summoned from other spheres. And the arts that Hantu was teaching him.*

All at once she was uneasy. Randûlas might have been mistaken when he claimed their most dangerous enemy was to be found in Dsôn.

From the stones that are put in our path we can build a fortress, from the top of whose battlements we can spit on our foes and those who mock us.

Dwarf saying

XIV

Girdlegard

United Great Kingdom of Gauragon
Province of Fire
1024 P.Q. (7515th solar cycle in old reckoning), late winter

Gata, Brûgar and Belîngor were riding with the vanguard of the army in order to get any scouts' reports as soon as possible. Hargorina was in command of the Thirdling dwarves; they had grown to appreciate her leadership during the recent siege and they trusted her implicitly. The long column of soldiers, vehicles, animals, equipment and weaponry wound in a procession many miles in length as they all journeyed across Girdlegard, eager to confront the forces of Kràg Tahuum.

Dawn approached, bringing them within twenty miles of the fortress, meaning they would be in danger of being observed if the orcs had any concealed outposts. That was why they had sent out reconnaissance teams and advance parties to examine the snow for tracks, locate any hidden stations and take them out if found, wanting to avoid news of their arrival getting back to Kràg Tahuum. The stronghold's defenders should not be given any opportunity to prepare the ground for the coming siege, for example by flooding the area or setting traps.

'I'm willing to wager four gold coins we can take the fortress within seven orbits,' said Brûgar, on his favourite topic. As he rode along he stuffed the bowl of his pipe with a special blend of Boredom tobacco. You had to smoke your way through several layers of it. The resulting build-up of aromas formed an interesting interplay of flavours. 'I've checked our ammunition and equipment. And we mustn't forget our wand-fiddler.'

'*Never!*' Belîngor said in sign language. He turned to Gata. '*Nobody knows exactly how the walls are constructed – what the foundations are like and how the support arches are arranged. We might have got it completely wrong.*'

'Surely it doesn't matter how they're built if our arrogant little magus sends in one of his fireballs?' Brûgar sang out as he tamped down his tobacco. 'The fireballs will go straight through the thickest of stone blocks and can knock out their strongest pillars.'

Gata found it strange how the two friends always found a new subject for speculation. She assumed it was out of boredom, just to pass the time. The war-wolf catapults had been taken apart for easier transport, with the heavy components carried on numerous wagons; the carthorses and oxen were pulling steadily, but necessarily only at a snail's pace.

'Don't forget the moat,' she reminded them. 'A ditch one hundred paces deep. Crossed by four bridges, which they'll find it easy to defend.'

'Correct. We've got to get across them.' Brûgar rubbed his blue-dyed beard thoughtfully.

'*Then let the magus magic us a fifth drawbridge conjured up of rays of pure light,*' Belîngor suggested. '*It can be like a rainbow. That should confuse the orcs.*'

'No. That's a stupid idea. Something tells me we would be annoying some unknown divinities if we did that,' said Gata. She had noticed a lone rider galloping towards them. 'Look! We're going to get some news!'

'*Good? Or bad?*' Belîngor put his flask to his lips.

'The way that long'un is riding, I'd say it's going to be good news.' Brûgar finished preparing his pipe. 'Oh, maybe the pig-faces have seen us coming and they're sending out an advance party to annoy us?' He pulled his war flail out of its holster. 'A bit of exercise would suit me fine. Or I'll be getting rusty.'

The rider, wearing the dark green attire of a messenger-scout, flourished a document. 'Look! He's got a bit of paper. Could be Kràg Tahuum asking if they can please surrender to us.' Brûgar chuckled. He carefully stowed away the pipe he had been preparing. 'Somebody's told them a bad joke and they've lost the will to live.'

'Perhaps it was that one about the orc asking a dwarf the way,' Gata interjected, before turning to greet the messenger, who had halted his horse near them. 'May Lorimbur be with you. Show me that note.' She was handed the paper covered in drawings. 'What am I seeing here?'

'It is a sketch of the new banner, Queen Regnorgata,' the man reported. 'We saw it from the last place we stopped.'

Gata glanced at it. A white flag with some dark blue runes that she was at a loss to interpret, and then a star emblem. 'This isn't a symbol normally used by the pig-faces, or the black-eyes either. Or have I got this wrong? What do you both think?' She handed the drawing over to the warriors for verification.

'This device is shown on all the flags on the battlements.' The scout used his sleeve to wipe away the hoarfrost and the snowflakes from his face.

'I wonder if they've hoisted the flags in honour of some eminent visitor from the Salt Sea area. He might have already arrived. Or perhaps they're about to welcome him?' This was Brûgar's suggestion. 'Maybe the beasts have developed a taste for collaboration with others, even without that weird black-eyes with the luminous spear?'

Why go to all that bother? Unless, of course, it were to welcome a king.' Belîngor studied the sketch and traced over the runes with his forefinger. '*I think this is the standard of Kràg Tahuum's new ruler. Obviously got an artistic bent.*'

Gata was trying to remember whether she had ever come across these symbols before. 'Wasn't there a beast once at the Eastern Gate in the Black Mountains with a similar banner?'

'Hang on – you were the commander there,' Brûgar answered, retrieving his pipe again. He clamped it between his teeth and sucked on it, but without lighting the tobacco. 'How do you expect me to know?'

'*Yes! Have a proper think about it!*' Belîngor encouraged.

Gata was unable to say with certainty. It would have been noted in the guard records, she knew, but their archives were stored in the homeland, a long way away. And since the tunnel collapses, anyway, they would have been lost. 'Oh well. I expect we'll find out soon enough.'

'In seven orbits' time, I think you'll find. I'm happy to ride over a rainbow bridge if necessary,' Brûgar said firmly. 'How about it? Bet you four gold pieces.' He turned to the scout. 'What do you say?'

'I . . . I don't understand,' said the soldier, confused. 'What do you mean about the four gold coins? Is it a wager? I'd rather not. It might be bad luck for the battle.'

Gata raised her head. Her clear eyes had spotted a thin column of smoke in the distance. 'That was stupid,' she reprimanded the scout.

The scout was as confused as ever. 'What do you mean, queen? Are you saying I should take the wager on?'

'No, I mean it was stupid of you to set fire to the abandoned outpost. The pig-faces will–'

'What? No. We didn't set fire to it!' He swivelled round in the saddle. 'And anyway, that's not where we were. It's the wrong direction.'

The thin grey thread of smoke soon became a swollen black cloud spreading out and up as if trying to colour the whole sky. Then the earth shook, making the horses fret and whinny with fear; they were pawing the ground ready to bolt. *What, in the name of Lorimbur, is happening?* Gata gave her horse its head. 'Come on, everyone! Let's take a look.'

Brûgar and Belîngor raced after her, riding round the chain of hills that had been obstructing their view of Kràg Tahuum. Before the scout and the three dwarves had their first sighting of the fortress there came a double roar, followed by more black clouds billowing up and the crash of masonry collapsing. The gusts of air coming from that direction were not seasonally cold, but warm. And they carried the smell of fire and hot rock, burnt leather and charred flesh.

Surely not? Gata rounded a wooded hillock and raced across a dry riverbed and up the slope on the other side where giant ferns flourished. As the long-leaved foliage parted, she gasped at what she saw.

Kràg Tahuum was no longer an indestructible citadel enclosed by moats, protective walls and defence towers. Instead it resembled nothing more than a burning, blackened, single tooth crumbling away before her eyes, much like a sugar loaf doused in brandy and set alight. Towers and walls had collapsed into the deep ditch.

The cause of this destruction was now flying a low pass over the plains, spitting out vivid scarlet tongues of flame from both muzzles, aimed at the orcs massing together in their efforts to escape over the bridges.

It's Szmajro! Gata felt ice-cold shivers down her spine. This dragon was displaying his strength and had reduced the hither-to impregnable fortress to rubble in a few overflights. *It's grown even bigger! Lorimbur! Behold! And intervene!* She estimated the dragon's body to be now about forty paces in length, plus the tail, the two necks and the heads with their flame-horns. The giant wings sent ice crystals and snowflakes whirling up from the ground in sweeping flurries. As Szmajro looked about to crash into the damaged fortress walls he suddenly pulled up short and, after filling the inner courtyards with blazing fire, slid in over the battlements. Tongues of flame shot out of the gates and arrow-slits together with clouds of ash and the remains of the fallen beasts. Gusts of wind from the dragon's passage sent whole groups of armoured orc warriors flying through the air. Up to that point they had courageously and stubbornly remained at their posts on the walkways, firing their crossbows in vain. All the largest of their catapults had been flattened or were on fire, like the rest of Kràg Tahuum.

Gata put her spyglass to her eye and observed how useless it was proving to shoot at the rust-brown dragon with its black-veined scales. Everything glanced off the hardened chitin plates. The fêted weapons the älfar fleet was said to be equipped with were of growing interest. They would be decisive in any future combat with dragons. *And then there's the damned magus, too.*

Szmajro landed, claws outstretched, on the wall of one of the towers, from which black clouds of smoke were billowing. He moved his wings frantically to and fro and the top third of the tower broke off, to fall into the main courtyard below. The scaled creature hovered in the air, roaring, and shooting out more fire into the ruins.

Is that . . .? Gata adjusted the focus at the front of the spyglass. 'Brûgar, Belîngor. Quickly!' she commanded. 'Look what's on its back!'

'What is it?'

'Just look!' She could hardly believe what she thought her eyes were telling her. *Don't let me be wrong.* 'What do you see?'

'Oh! By the axe of Lorimbur! It's our gemstone magician!'

Brûgar laughed out loud, his pipe falling out of his mouth and landing in a fold of his mantle. 'So he didn't get eaten up, after all!'

'No. It's him directing the dragon's movements.' As Szmajro sailed past, Gata kept her eyes on Goïmron, who was gripping a dorsal spike on the dragon's spine behind one of the creature's two necks. The dwarf's lips seemed to be moving.

'Unmistakeable. He's definitely telling it what to do,' Brûgar agreed. He was impressed. He told Belîngor, 'My praises to Lorimbur for sending us this Fourthling!'

'It would be better still if he was one of us Thirdlings. Like Goldhand,' was the sign-language response.

'That old hero Goldhand has been no help at all,' Gata said, pointing ahead. 'That's our future there, flying off. He's everything we need.'

'What *we* need? What do you mean?' Brûgar raised his eyebrows questioningly. 'What is it we're trying to do?'

Gata laughed. 'I mean it. We. Us. Girdlegard. With Szmajro we can root out and destroy all the evil in the land. The älfar in Undarimar, for example. The salt sea orcs. All the other monsters that have been making our lives a misery for so long. And we can fend off any threats from outside if they were ever to get through our defences.'

'You seem to have forgotten Dsôn Khamateion.' Belîngor put away his own viewing glass. *'The Scaley One can fly through the mountains and destroy the black-eyes, too. Just like Kràg Tahuum.'*

'Of course,' Gata muttered.

'Will you look at that!' Brûgar enthused. 'It's as if the whole fortress were made out of a child's building blocks. Ones made of paper, at that. It's burning like tinder!' He reclaimed his pipe. 'That dragon can give me a light, but I'll ask him to be careful.'

Gata looked at the scout who had ridden after them. He was

pale and visibly shaken. And struck dumb. 'Go back to the army,' she ordered. 'Give them this message: the vanguard is to attack the dispersing orcs. Cavalry to take up the forward position. Tell them to make sure not to let any of the monsters escape. Main part of the army to stay put.'

'But ... what about ...' The scout hesitated, pointing at Szmajro, flying past and breathing fire. 'Won't he . . .?'

'No, he won't,' Gata promised. 'Hoist your banners, putting the dwarf-tribe flags at the front. That will show Goïmron who's coming to help him.'

'As if that dragon needs any help.' Belîngor pulled his long-handled war-axe out of its holder at the side of his saddle.

'Well, I'll take anything I can.' Grinning away, Brûgar waved his war flail and stowed his pipe safely. 'Forward!' He rode out of the shelter of the giant ferns and charged down across the plain, where a few orcs were running for their lives, unaware that they were heading straight into mortal danger. 'Don't try to get past me! You'll be sorry!'

Belîngor followed at his heels.

They are such children. Almost at once the vanguard of the army came galloping up. Gata rode with them on to the flat ground in front of the remains of Kràg Tahuum. They formed a long line to capture all the orcs trying to get away.

In the winter sunshine the standards of the dwarf tribes and the various Girdlegard realms fluttered aloft next to one another on the warriors' lances. The air was filled with the overwhelming noise of battle: the thunder of hoofbeats, the clanking of armour, the bugle calls of the alarm signals, the triumphant roars of Szmajro and the horrified shrieks of the last of the orcs.

Goïmron crossed the snow-covered ground on foot over to the reception party of delegates who had come to meet him. He was grinning broadly, reacting to the astonished expressions of those gathered there: humans, dwarves, elves and meldriths. He had caught sight of their faces while he was still on the back of the dragon. *By Vraccas! What a homecoming!*

After the attack was over, he had instructed Szmajro to come in to land further away from the levelled remains of Kràg Tahuum, to keep to a minimum the disturbance that the appearance of a huge two-headed dragon would undoubtedly cause in the army ranks.

Brûgar, Gata, Hargorina and Belîngor rode over to him, bringing him a horse so he would not have to walk any further.

'Ho! Look what we've got here! Our gem-cutting magician is now a fully-fledged dragon-rider,' laughed Brûgar, hailing him from afar. 'Girdlegard's poets won't be able to keep up with celebrating all your heroic exploits.'

'Not necessary.' Goïmron climbed up into the saddle and embraced all his friends in turn. Gata held him noticeably longer than the others had. 'It's wonderful to see you all alive. And I'm sorry I didn't turn up in Brigantia.'

'*I expect you were quite busy training your dragon*,' was Belîngor's guess.

'Can he fetch a stick if you throw it?' joked Brûgar. 'Does he do everything you tell him to? I've a little famulus in mind he might want to have a nibble of. Just a little toasted snack? Tiny little flame or two?'

The dwarves roared with laughter as they rode slowly back to where the delegates were waiting. The main army was taking up its position in the plain now that it was no longer needed in battle. The advance party and the cavalry had had an easy enough time butchering the remaining frightened orcs. The wagons with the dismantled war-wolves and other siege weapons had become superfluous – all in the space of a single orbit.

All the warriors cheered and rejoiced to see the Fourthling, calling his name and hammering on their shields and stamping their feet in noisy welcome.

'And there again, it's been a dwarf doing the miracles,' said Telìnâs with a smile. 'But I can say I've known you ever since you were still a youngster carving gemstones, well before you became a magus or a dragon-rider.'

'There's lots to talk about. For all of us,' Gata began. 'But first, tell me: is Szmajro likely to present any kind of danger to us or is he a faithful servant to you?'

However happy he was feeling, it was hard for Goïmron not to blurt out a question as to the fate of Rodana and Chòldunja. 'He has joined forces with me and carries out my instructions,' he replied. 'As with any wild beast, a dragon might occasionally misbehave, but I should be able to quieten him down with my magic.'

YOU ARE UNDERSTATING THE SITUATION. YOU HAVE HIM TOTALLY UNDER CONTROL. It was the sea sapphire speaking inside his head. SZMAJRO MIGHT SEE IT DIFFERENTLY BUT HE FEARS YOU AND IS AFRAID OF YOUR POWER, SO DON'T UNDERSELL YOURSELF. SPECIALLY NOT WHEN THAT RIDICULOUS FAMULUS IS ANYWHERE AROUND. IT'S IMPORTANT HE FEARS YOU AS WELL.

Goïmron did not react to this silent and secret piece of advice. 'I think you'll probably want to know where I've been all this time?'

'And how!' Brûgar yelled. He handed Belîngor four gold coins. 'Damn fool wager that, about the seven orbits.'

'And I want to know, Master Chiselcut, how you do the magic.' It was Mostro, directing his horse into the middle of their group. 'I must say I am more than impressed.'

HE IS ENVIOUS AND FULL OF MALICE. MAKE SURE YOU SHOW NO WEAKNESS.

'We can talk about it over a glass of wine later, perhaps,

Master Mostro.' Goïmron had not missed the hidden signal Gata was giving him. *I shan't be disclosing my secret to you as easy as that, Famulus.*

'Don't we have more urgent matters to discuss?'

'We do indeed.' Hargorina pointed to the ruins of Kràg Tahuum. 'But first we must have a good look round to check if there are any survivors. Or maybe you know about that symbol that was on the battlement flags. Before you and your pet dragon burned them?'

'Quite a few women come to mind when I hear the name pet dragon,' Brûgar commented, but Belîngor silenced him with a dig in the ribs. He grinned and took out a pipe.

'No. I had thought it was that älf Mòrdacai's device. But I must have got it wrong.' Goïmron stole a glance over at the rest of the column of soldiers. He could not see either Rodana or Chòldunja. 'Right, let's try and find out.'

Gata gave an order and a blast on the horn sent a good thousand troops in over the northern drawbridge into the smouldering ruins of the fortress, together with the reconnaissance scouts and those soldiers who were specialists at tracking. Then she turned to Goïmron, lowering her voice, as she followed the troops. 'Rodana is well. She is free and has been exonerated of any wrongdoing. She rides with our forces.'

He would dearly have liked to embrace Gata at this news but he managed to restrain his delight. 'Thank you,' he blurted out in relief. 'And what about Chòldunja?'

'She has died. She was attempting to save us all from danger.'

The sense of relief that Goïmron had been experiencing suffered a setback. News of the death of this young woman threw a shadow over the joy he had been feeling. He swiftly changed the subject. 'What's with Mostro now? Why did you warn me about him?'

'Can't talk about it here. We'll speak later, when we are

alone. But don't give him the slightest hint of how you got Szmajro to obey you,' she said darkly. 'It would be utterly irresponsible if ever this jumped-up idiot got control of the dragon and used him for his own purposes.'

Goïmron raised his eyebrows questioningly. 'I seem to have missed quite a lot?'

'Indeed you have. Some good. Some bad.' The queen gestured towards the smoking ruins with the fallen columns and heaps of rubble. 'But you have done something brilliant. Your actions have relieved the troops of a difficult and dangerous task. There was much fear and apprehension among the soldiers about laying siege to this fortress.'

'In spite of your having the magus?'

'Nobody could predict whether or not his powers would work against the defences. There was a nasty rumour doing the rounds that there was orc magic in the stone blocks, runes set in the stones that would send any spells flashing straight back to where they came from.' Gata pointed towards the plain. 'A horrible prospect if it's a fireball of pure energy you're sending at the walls.'

'Understood.' Goïmron reined in his joy at realising he could soon be meeting with Rodana again. Even if Chòldunja's death upset him. His heart beat wildly at the thought of seeing the puppet mistress once more, but first of all the remains of the Kràg Tahuum citadel needed to be thoroughly searched.

The troops spread out, investigating the interiors of collapsed buildings and checking inside partly demolished towers. The soldiers' progress could be monitored by watching where their pennant-topped lances were visible, in case they should need assistance.

The dwarf warriors reached the North Gate and dismounted. The destruction that Szmajro had inflicted in such a short period of time appeared even more devastating in scope when

viewed from the ground. The blackened stones were still glowing with the heat of the flames.

'What a destructive force the dragon has turned into,' he
muttered to himself.

'You can say that again.' Gata looked similarly impressed by
the effects of the dragon's attack. 'It looks as if it was very easy
for Szmajro to destroy this fortress.'

'It was. He enjoyed it. He was able to let himself go and do his
damnedest. It didn't seem to tire him at all.' Goïmron clambered over the piles of broken stones that had once been a
tower. Half of one storey remained intact. You could still see
laundry hanging, a picture on the wall, shattered furniture and
personal objects that had belonged to the inhabitants. A couple
of books. *Just like in any citadel anywhere in Girdlegard.*

'Forget about feeling pity. Just remember all the people who
had been compelled to pay tribute to the pig-faces. Or the people
that ended up in the orc cooking pots,' Brûgar counselled him.
He was about to light his pipe using a piece of wood that was
still smouldering. His pipe gave off a smell of cedarwood. 'They
really don't deserve any sympathy, you know.'

'I suppose not.' Goïmron had noticed some children's toys.
But somehow, they still do . . .

As they walked about through the ruins, far from watchful
eyes and ears, Gata was able to bring him up to date with events.
What had happened with Brigantia, the battle, the Omuthan
and his rhamak ally, Rodana and Chòldunja, the Berengart who
had escaped and the magus, too, who had extracted a loyalty
pledge from Hantu without informing anyone else.

'That Mostro is committing treason puts him in a terrible
light,' Goïmron summed up when Gata had finished telling
him everything. 'He's a really bad person.'

'Vanéra made a pretty unsound choice there. It's even likely he also caused his mistress's death. The evidence did not tally with the story he told us about how she died,' she added.

DIDN'T I ALWAYS SAY SO? I WARNED YOU ABOUT THAT YOUNG MAN. I TOLD YOU HE WOULD BE TROUBLE.

'What do you propose doing about him?'

'How could I consider acting against a magus of such power? I'd have to think about that.' Gata placed her forefinger against her chin, pretending to be deep in thought. Then she looked at Goïmron. 'If only I knew someone who could match him in magic strength. Someone, maybe, in charge of a dragon.'

'You mean me?' he said, rather more loudly than he had intended.

'You're a magus, just like he is. You are powerful. If our little wand-fiddler goes a step too far, we'll be needing your services,' Brûgar chipped in. He was checking carefully under piles of rubble that no orcs had escaped the dragon's fiery onslaught. 'Why not get Szmajro to simply devour him?'

'It's not as easy as all that, you know,' Goïmron declared.

'*You have reduced the battlements of Kràg Tahuum to a burning heap of stones,*' Belîngor gesticulated his objection. '*What's going to hold you back?*'

'Right. If I tell you you've got to promise to keep it secret.' Goïmron looked at the circle of his friends with a conspiratorial air. 'I think the night-dragon, as I call Szmajro, only obeys me because of the sea sapphire in my possession. The gemstone's aura affects me and works like Elmo's fire.' He had been thinking about his interactions with the dragon and could come to no other conclusion. 'That's the reason Szmajro thinks I'm a powerful magus he wouldn't want to risk challenging.'

'By Lorimbur! That means the Scaley One remains a real danger for us,' Brûgar reasoned.

'And he can't be finished off with a simple blow from a sword. Or with any kind of spell. I saw how the magic force detonated inside him back in the Wonder Zone, giving him extra powers rather than harming him,' Goïmron reported. At the same time, at the back of his mind a thought occurred to him that he could not quite grasp hold of. *What is it I am overlooking?*

'It's far too soon to consider Szmajro's death. We still need him. We need him to help us attack the black-eyes on Arima and to lay waste to their ships. They are well prepared for dragon attacks,' Gata objected. 'If the Scaley One is killed in the attempt, all the better.'

'*But we wanted to campaign against the salt sea orcs,*' Belîngor threw in. '*How are we going to manage that without the two-headed creature?*'

'And what about Dsôn Khamateion?' Goïmron wanted to know. When he saw the expression in the face of the black-bearded dwarf, he realised that Gata must have forgotten to tell him something.

'Oh, yes.' Gata seemed to have just thought of it. 'My report to you was incomplete.' She quickly summarised the plans that had been agreed by the leaders of all the Girdlegard realms. 'But I still don't think the Ganyeios is our most formidable foe. Not a priority. Let's sort out Girdlegard first.'

'You are right, of course,' said Goïmron. 'Save the most difficult opponent till last. And then the dragon ...' Then the thought re-occurred that he had not been able to investigate just now, when they had been discussing the death of Szmajro. *The flame flyers! They can attack the horn plates!* The creatures used their sharp beaks to free the scaled dragon of parasites under the armoured scales. *We could use their beaks to kill a dragon!*

'Have you looked after my stuff for me?' Goïmron's question came as a surprise, as he saw from the expressions on his friends' faces. He would not dare to take on the challenge by himself. He was no Brûgar or Belîngor. Not a warrior of the calibre of Hargorina, whose upper arms were twice the thickness of his own puny thighs. But on the other hand no one else could approach the two-headed Szmajro in the way that he could. A dilemma indeed.

'Over here!' came a call from the ruins. 'There's a survivor!'

'There'll be trouble if the pig-face won't talk.' Brûgar set off and ran over to where he saw the pennant being waved from between the charred beams and rubble. The smell of cedarwood had been replaced now by that of rosemary.

'Why would it talk? Knowing that death awaits?' Goïmron moved to join the others.

'Haven't you got a trick to make it tell the truth?' Gata drew her dagger. 'It would make things easier.'

NO. THAT'S NOT NECESSARILY THE KIND OF THING I CAN DO.

'I'll . . . give it a try.' Goïmron made a mental note of the idea of using the flame-flyer beaks. He would have to do a few covert experiments to see if the bony beak material would really be able to penetrate dragon scales. It might, of course, just shatter on contact, like steel and iron would. If it did work he would have to fashion himself a weapon made out of the beaks, and then he would have to disguise it and always carry it with him without Szmajro getting suspicious. If the dragon were to get wind of the danger, that would be the end of the dwarf. *I'd make a nice snack for him. I'm pretty sure he's thought about it more than once.*

The group assembled by a huge wooden beam threatening to crush an orc, preventing the creature from moving. There was blackish-green blood and lots of dust on the dark-green skin and dented armour. The orc bared its long teeth, its eyes rolling wildly, as it tried to keep the enemy from approaching. In its right hand it wielded a long club, spiked at the business end, the metal presumably coated with poison.

Burned on to a leather amulet round its neck Goïmron saw the symbol Gata had described from the flags. He recognised the runes and the star design. *Perhaps some new divinity?* He drew the other dwarves' attention to the device.

'If you tell us what we want to know we'll get you out of there and set you free,' Mostro promised, pushing his way through to the front.

'Oh, no, we won't!' shouted Brûgar, swiping his war flail and stamping his foot. 'Who do you think you are, interfering like that, you wand- fi—powerful fam—I mean magus?'

The imprisoned orc laughed out loud. 'Like a load of vultures squabbling among yourselves. Are you fighting for your share of the carcass even before it's dead?' He spat a gobbet of bloody spittle to land at their feet. 'You will die!'

'Says who? Do you mean the god whose sign you wear round your neck?' Goïmron goaded.

With his free hand the orc touched the pendant protectively and gave a furious roar. 'So you want me to betray him to you? Never! I'm not telling you anything about him and the prophecies!'

Before anyone could stop it the beast slammed its club against the end of the broken beam and forced it loose, sending a lethal shower of stones and rubble crashing down, burying the orc underneath. Its blood sprayed out under the masonry before the pile of debris covered it totally. The dwarves sprang back in horror.

That was a surprise. Goïmron looked at Gata. 'More questions than ever, now. We need a living orc.'

Even Brûgar nodded. 'Shame, that.'

The Gålran Zhadar.

What a beast! You would think at first it was a dwarf. Squat figure, muscular build, forearms strong from repeated heavy work, but the hands are smooth and well cared for as if they belonged to a scribe rather than someone capable of strangling an ogre. Sinister-sounding voice, deeper in tone than the growling of a troll.

Excerpt from
The Adventures of Tungdil Goldhand,
as experienced in the Black Abyss
and written by himself.
First draft.

XV

Girdlegard

United Great Kingdom of Gauragon
Province of Grasslands
1024 P.Q. (7515th solar cycle in old reckoning), late winter

Klaey crouched down close to the cliff, wanting to escape the worst of the vicious night wind. He did not dare chuck another handful of twigs on to the flames to warm himself or the fire's glow would be visible from too far afield. The pointed sandstone outcrop, five paces long and broad and maybe fifteen paces in height, kept him and his troops safely out of sight as they slept. The area in general was flat and offered little in the way of cover otherwise from the icy blasts that froze any water within the blink of an eye. There were sharp edges and projections in the porous rock round which the cold draughts of air whistled and moaned as if in terrible pain.

Taking a piece of bread from the sack of provisions, Klaey gnawed at the crust like a mouse. He and the remaining Brigantians had changed clothing a few times, putting on extra winter-weight garments purloined from washing-lines as they had passed through settlements. Officially they presented as a band of roving labourers in search of casual work. There was little in the way of employment on offer anywhere, which was why it suited them to be able to claim this was the reason they had no fixed abode if stopped and challenged. Klaey had forbidden his men to make easy money by theft and robbery as they went. It was important not to attract the attention of the authorities.

With every orbit that passed they were headed further south, always going away from the Brown Mountains. They made their way mostly on foot, or sometimes they cadged a lift on the backs of carts or sledges or even on timber rafts floating down rivers. It was clear now that there was a reward offered for capturing Klaey and his troop. The authorities were keen to bring the last of the Berengarts to justice after his siblings and their immediate families had been treacherously poisoned. There were rumours of acts of revenge among the Brigantian ranks, given that Orweyn was known to have ordered the deaths of his own warriors.

I knew it was a terrible idea to summon that soul-caller. Klaey utterly refuted the accusation of responsibility for the Brigantian defeat on the grounds that he had failed to carry out his elder brother's express commands. On the contrary: rather than having caused deaths, he had in fact saved many lives. *All it would have done would have been to prolong Brigantia's final days, but it wouldn't have prevented the country's downfall. No one will thank me for it.*

Fragments crumbled off the sandstone boulder and left rusty stains on the dirty, trampled snow. Klaey raised his head. *Was that an owl?* The outcrop they were sheltering behind was the ideal observation perch for predators to watch for unsuspecting prey to swoop down on. *Or maybe a moon sparrow hawk?* These rare birds of prey with their silvery plumage, white beaks and light eyes were nocturnal hunters that competed with the local owls. *I'd like to catch sight of one.*

But when he looked up at the top of the column of stone he saw no avian outline, and he heard no rustle of outstretched wings or the typical call of such a creature. *That's a shame. It would have made a nice change. A different sound for once, not this eternal concert the wind is keeping up.* Klaey looked down and was suddenly aware of a sharp blade at his throat.

At the end of a tionium shaft he saw the hooded face of his attacker, who was dressed in a cloak the colour of night.

'Strange,' came the familiar voice from the depths of the dark fabric, giving Klaey goosebumps. 'Every time we meet it seems there are major events in the offing. Back in Dsôn Khamateion and now here in the middle of nowhere.' The runes took on a threatening greenish-gold glow. 'Is it me or you causing our paths to cross like this, like the streaming tails of fate's comets?'

The scars on his own chest reminded Klaey of how this sinister älf had tried to kill him and leave his body in that temple. *Mòndarcai.* 'To Tion with you!'

'I can understand you might feel resentment.' The älf did not remove the tip of the spear from Klaey's throat. 'But you may count yourself fortunate. I shall let you live.'

Klaey had neither heard nor seen the älf approach. *Cursed shadow-creeper.* 'That's the least you owe me, given that you've only got that armour and the spear because of me,' he said defiantly.

'You have, of course, guessed that I am here for a purpose.' Mòndarcai turned his head, as could be seen by the way the hood moved to one side. His countenance remained concealed. 'Which one is it?'

Klaey frowned. 'Who?'

'The rhumak. The soul-caller. The summoner of the hidden world, as he is named.'

That swine Hantu is still alive? Klaey felt sick to the stomach with fear, and the old scars tightened painfully. His heart was pounding in his chest. The älf exerted more pressure, trying to intimidate his victim. 'He is not with me.'

'But everyone says that Hantu could not be found anywhere in Brigantia. They say you took him with you, to plan your revenge.' Mòndarcai turned to face him. 'This soul-caller is just what I need for my project, since some of my plans have encountered a few unforeseen hitches. I need his arts more urgently than you do.' The spear tip pushed against his skin in exactly the same place where the initial cut had occurred. 'So? Which one of them is it?'

Klaey tried not to swallow. 'I swear by Cadengis and Samusin that I haven't got Hantu here with my men. Wherever he's got to, he's not here with me.'

'I can just kill your sleeping men one by one till you tell me the truth, Berengart. And then I'll kill you.'

Having to stare death literally in the face gave Klaey a certain calm and confidence. There was nothing else he could do. Not against an älf. Even the intimidating powers of an opponent such as this could not alter the fact that he had nothing to lose. *It is over.* 'Kill me first. I don't want to have to watch my followers being senselessly butchered.' When Mòndarcai did not react to this, Klaey threw himself forward to force his own neck on to the rune spear.

But Klaey felt he was falling into the void, then caught by an armoured hand and pressed back against the rock wall. 'Impressive, Berengart. You would really have gone ahead and killed yourself.'

'What difference would it make?'

'It proves that you were not lying.' Mòndarcai studied the group of sleepers, who were quite unaware of their impending deaths. 'Where are you heading?'

'Away from the Brown Mountains.'

Mòndarcai gave a quiet laugh. 'I see what you're up to. You have a plan.'

'It doesn't matter. You are going to kill me. I'm no use to you.'

'That's not necessarily the case.' The älf released the pressure on his throat and planted the spear on the ground by his foot, revealing the glowing runes. 'What were you and your people going to be doing before I got hold of you?'

'Attacking Rhuta.' Klaey had been expecting this to be greeted with a scornful laugh but the inside of the hood was silent. 'It's an ideal opportunity,' he explained. 'Vanéra is dead, Mostro is off campaigning against the orcs in Kràg Tahuum. And famula Adelia is on her way back from the Brown Mountains, I understand. So it will be easy to pick the low-hanging fruit.' All he was missing was that Mòndarcai should join him, or steal his idea and carry out the plan before he could do so himself.

'You have a plan. Let me hear it.'

Klaey sniffed and chucked a handful of twigs into the fire before the flames died. 'The Chamber of Wonders is the key to the campaign. We'll find a way in secretly. We can collect some useful artefacts with suitable magic effects and then we'll send the lazy guards packing. They'll be out of practice by now and won't stand a chance against us. Then we plunder the treasure stores.' He shrugged. 'What's to stop us?'

Now Mòndarcai did laugh. 'Brazen. Fresh. Slightly on the thoughtless and impetuous side. But bold. Plunder the magic realm. The first step of your plan might work,' he conceded. 'But as soon as Mostro and Adelia learn of what you have done they'll descend on you like a thunderstorm. Have you considered that?'

'Adelia is a famula with no idea how to cast spells. All she knows about is using magic artefacts. She'll be no problem. And by the time Mostro gets to Rhuta we'll already have helped ourselves to all the valuable items out of the Chamber of Wonders. We'll have sackloads of gold and jewels and we'll be over the horizon by then.'

Mòndarcai nodded in agreement. 'I expect you will. That kind of adventurous spirit you have could have garnered you many precious diamonds and rubies from the Dsôn Khamateion temple. If it hadn't been for me. And we know how that worked out.'

Klaey said nothing.

'I've got a proposition for you, Berengart,' said the älf, circling and ready to pounce. 'A deal: the lives of yourself and your people here. In exchange for three artefacts from the Chamber of Wonders.'

Klaey looked baffled. 'You want me to steal them for you?'

'Exactly. I heard they've got something in the store that is effective against any älf or monster, stopping them getting in,' he explained. 'You and your troops, on the other hand, might manage it if Samusin is on your side.'

'What do you want me to get for you?'

'The chamber is stuffed full of objects. You might need time to locate the right ones. I'll grant you a full cycle,' Mòndarcai suggested. 'Then I'll come and find you, wherever you are by then. By that time I'll have completed my preparations.'

Klaey listened attentively. 'What kind of preparations?'

'I'll have to think about it. Some of my projects have gone slightly awry lately. You know what that's like, don't you?'

Of course I do. Klaey assumed the älf would be intending to retire to a place of safety in order to see how things in Girdlegard developed. *He'll want to wait till things have quietened down a bit. Then he'll seize his chance.* 'So tell me – what are the three things you want me to get for you?'

'Got a piece of paper? I'll show you what I mean.'

From his rucksack Klaey retrieved a Wanted poster about himself that he had torn down in passing. He found a stick of charcoal to write with.

Mòndarcai thrust his spear into the ice-hardened ground. It went in as easily as if the earth had been soft as a moorland swamp. Taking the paper and charcoal, he made detailed sketches of three separate items, adding information about the relative measurements, colouring and the materials they were made of. 'You're not to use them yourself and you're not to mention them to anyone at all,' he insisted, looking Klaey sternly in the eye.

'What if I can't find them?'

'In that case I would not be looking forward to our next meeting if I were you.' The älf handed him back the paper and the writing implement. 'It's possible you may not see them. But we Originals have our spies everywhere. You will find you are being watched.' The älf got to his feet and yanked his tionium spear out of the ground. 'Try putting some dried bark on that fire to get it going again.'

'But it's still burning . . .' Klaey objected, and then he saw how the flames suddenly died and impenetrable darkness swept back over the campsite. Total obscurity remained for at least ten heartbeats. The älf had invoked his special powers once more.

By the time the moonlight's strength had returned to the scene, Mòndarcai had vanished. Klaey cursed under his breath and knelt down to blow gently into the smouldering ashes. He crumbled bits of bark into the remains of the campfire. The ashes started giving off smoke again and a little warmth returned.

'That was a near thing,' Klaey heard one of his people say. The man had kept very still during that exchange between Klaey and Mòndarcai. Klaey indicated with a nod that he agreed.

Girdlegard

Empire of Gautaya
Salt Sea
1024 P.Q. (7515th solar cycle in old reckoning), late winter

Barbandor was sitting in his familiar wooden cage, which had been suspended from the end of a beam at the end of one of the block houses. The highest-ranking of the orc tribes from the Salt Sea region had assembled here to witness the marriage ceremony of the princess Akrosha the Beheader and Borkon Gràc Hâl. The festivities were scheduled to last fourteen orbits.

The eighth evening of the celebrations had just started.

Even for Barbandor, accustomed as he was to the noises of hammer on anvil, the loud music, the drumming, the whoops and roars of the wedding guests presented quite a challenge. There were very few periods during which all the beasts slumped down in a drunken stupor, leaving only the sound of their snoring, which could be as loud as the stentorian snorting of a buffalo bear. Other beasts were indulging their inclinations and desires to the fullest extent possible. This was accompanied by other noises at an equally overwhelming volume. *I'll never be able to forget what I'm hearing now.* Barbandor had been informed that the marriage of an orc princess represented a significant event. This union between Akrosha and the One Who Had Been Foretold was a unique occasion. In consequence the prevailing atmosphere was extravagant, not to say excessive. Every so often a wrestling bout would be announced, or a challenge to armed combat between two rivals. These events would end only in the surrender of one of the contestants. Or death, of course. Copious amounts of alcohol were readily available. Feasts were provided at tables groaning with enough food to feed an entire army for a month.

The orcs were cruel in their treatment of their slaves and the captives they had made during their recent campaign in the salt desert. Humans were forced to fight each other, with the victor in each case then having to face an onslaught from drunken beasts, or their hunting dogs as large as small horses.

These duels were never won by a human. Much of the meat on the monsters' plates was of Gauragon origin.

To Tion with Akrosha and Borkon! Barbandor had been pretty sure he was going to be on the menu himself, maybe as dessert, or forming the centrepiece of the offer of culinary delights, but nobody touched him. He hung there in his cage, exhibited like some trophy. People came to stare at him, to laugh at him, to chuck beer or brandy over him. Some even drenched him in piss. But nobody attempted to stab at him or to actually do him any physical harm. *What do they want with me?* Barbandor leaned forward, grabbing hold of the bars of the wooden cage, as he watched the riotous behaviour. *What is it about me? Am I seen as some kind of lucky charm?*

On this eighth evening a drinking contest was taking place. There was a competition going on outside, with the aim being to see who could chuck a limb the furthest. Prisoners thought to be too weak to fight in the ring had their arms or legs wrenched off to be thrown as far as possible along a marked track.

Barbandor did not try to understand the scoring system. It was the cruellest sport imaginable.

They ought to have the same thing done to them so they'd find out what it's really like. Barbandor was given a gnawed-off piece of ox bone and half a roast chicken, thrust through the bars. A drunken red-skinned orc tried to hand him a full tankard of beer through the gaps but gave up in frustration. The jug broke against the wood.

There were musicians providing squeaking fanfares on horns and trombones. The noise encouraged the drunkenness. Drummers kept up a steady rhythm and the participants all joined in the general shouting. Tobacco smoke mixed with the smells of sweat and roast food and spilt beer.

Barbandor consumed the roast chicken. It was surprisingly

good. Then he sat down with his back to the partying, rocking slightly if someone knocked against his cage. He stared at the welcomely bare, quiet wall. From time to time he would nod off and then come awake with a start, hitting his face on the bars of his cage contraption.

The fourth time he woke up like that he noticed things had quietened down somewhat and most of the lights had been doused. The combined stink of sweat, food and pipe smoke was overwhelming, and the sound of snoring echoed like a hundred lumberjacks sawing timber in an enclosed ravine.

'You should have something to drink.' Barbandor was given two mugs: one with water and the other with wine. 'I think they've forgotten about you.'

He turned to the unfamiliar brown-skinned orc, who had a glassy stare. The effects of beer and brandy were clearly preventing him from focusing properly on the prisoner. Sometimes he squinted.

'Very kind of you.' Barbandor sniffed the water carefully to make sure he wasn't being tricked into drinking urine. As he drank he looked round the hall. 'So, who won?'

'Shrugg the Barrel,' the orc replied with a hiccup. His scruffy clothing was stained and the garments hung off him oddly. 'I only came second.'

'Then you must be the little Firkin?'

'No! My name is Mortog the Butcher. The brother of Princess Akrosha – the bride, don't you know?' he announced loudly, slapping himself on the chest, making his chains rattle. 'One day I'll be a prince and I'll be Lord of the West.'

'You mean the West of the Desert?' Barbandor was keen to hear more. A drunken orc was just what he needed. *And he's Akrosha's brother, at that.* 'That's not much of a title.'

'No! The West of the whole of Girdlegard!' the outraged orc shouted. 'The others want to get back the old Toboribor region but I like the idea of having the west. Near the sea and all. Nice beach . . . nice water.'

With a sigh Mortog drank the wine he had given to Barbandor. 'It'll be amazing. Absholutely amazing.'

'Ah, so you want to win the whole of Girdlegard, all of you?'

'Borkon's going to lead ush when the time is right. When What is Forgotten rises again. Borkon is itsh precursor – harbinger of victory, you know,' Mortog burbled happily, wiping the dribble from his chin. 'You see, it's all about us. We're the ones in the know. We Never Forgot. We're dead clever, we are.' He tried to touch his nose but kept missing. His eyes were definitely looking in two different directions. 'Oh yesh, we are clever, we are, and don't you forget it, groundling.'

'What's the plan till that happens?'

'We'll be nice and peaceful and we won't upshet anyone.' Mortog grinned suggestively, licking his lips and then shaking the cage, sending Barbandor off balance. 'But then we'll do *that!* We'll multiply. There'll be lots of ush. More and more, till we've got enough of us for Borkon to lead into battle. Unbeatable army. Borkon and my shister, Akrosha. Both of them together.'

'Stop that. Stop fucking around!' Barbandor called to him as he continued, to rattle the crate.

'No, Yeah, no fucking, you're right. We don't need any little orcsh with ugly beardsh,' Mortog said, grunting and bashing the top of the cage. 'But we need big ones. Big and tall and strong!' He stood up and yelled, flexing his arm muscles. 'For Borkon!'

Barbandor got up on his feet. 'What is it that's going to rise up?'

'The Forgotten One, that gave everything its shape. And it will give the present times a new shape, too, and we'll be lordsh of everything,' Mortog murmured, his tone full of awe. 'The prophecy will come true. First Borkon Gràc Hâl. The Horn of Gorshnok. The tune of Heshbaar. And then: you.'

'Me?' Barbandor made a face. 'Of course, I'm your lucky mascot.'

Mortog grinned drunkenly and looked around, swaying, in search of another jug of beer. He grabbed a drink off a slumbering orc and pushed the other beast off his seat with a laugh. 'You are part of the prophecy of Noshruk the Ripper, groundling. If Borkon hadn't had *you* with him he'd just be some weird blue-skinned bastard, wouldn't he, with a load of random tattoos. My sishter would just have flayed him and nailed his pretty patterns to the wall.' He pushed the cage and made it swing to and fro. 'But with you: that's different. The One Who Was Foretold. All thanks to you, of course.'

So I'm part of the whole spectacle? Barbandor finally gathered what it was that had made Borkon get him carried everywhere to show off. 'Aha. It's good to have it explained. So what's to happen to me?'

Mortog shrugged his shoulders and belched. 'Nothing.'

'So I stay a captive?'

'Like a little pet bird, my pretty groundling. Why don't you give ush a little shong?'

'Maybe later on.' Barbandor gave praise to Vraccas for sending him this drunkard. 'Then you'd better look after me very well indeed, don't you think? You don't want me dying on you.'

Mortog clapped his hand over his mouth, aghast. 'No, we certainly don't want that, by Tion! No. Oh no. Never. We can't have that,' he whimpered, horrified at the thought. 'That would put the whole prophecy in danger. We need you, rock maggot.'

'Oh, come on. If I were to die, you could just find someone else,' Barbandor said, trying to provoke a reaction.

'No. No. it's got to be *you*. You are the shpecial little bugger. For some peculiar reason. I don't know why. Only Tornasuk knows.' Mortog finished off the beer and chucked the empty jug to one side at one of the sleeping forms. His target tumbled from the bench. 'Otherwise I'd have torn you to pieces ages ago, wouldn't I? We could have used you in the limb-tosshing contesht. Dwarves are easy to throw. They kind of fly if you aim them properly. You pull the arms and legs off firsht, of course.'

No. I didn't know that. Barbandor realised that the drunken orc was starting to become bored with their conversation and was looking for a spot to lie down. 'I feel very honoured.' *I wonder who Tornasuk is. Another prince, maybe.*

'And so you should, you little squirt.' Mortog tipped up one of the trestle boards, sending food, plates, mugs and pitchers crashing to the ground. Then he crawled up on to the emptied table. 'I'm going to have a little kip now. I can wait here for Tornasuk's shignal. Sho The Forgotten One can rise up, of course,' he muttered as he stretched out. 'But before that happens I'll make lots of little Mortogs, won't I? I'll make so many of them the desert will be heaving with them.' The orc's swollen eyelids closed. 'Shing me to shleep, why don't you? Come on, funny little songbird in your cage. But mind you . . .' The very next moment the orc was fast asleep and snoring away.

Barbandor waited a while before sitting down and pushing aside the straw that formed a cushion at the base of the cage. He had had his eye on the one particular cage bar that looked a bit rusty, as if the wires holding it were coming loose. Every time the beasts had brought him beer, water, piss or other liquids the corrosion had grown. And the salt-laden air had helped things along further.

The evening of competitive wine-drinking had proved to offer the ideal opportunity, not just to think about escaping from his prison but to actually put a plan into action. The drinkers had emptied every barrel. They would be sleeping it off till late afternoon, for sure. The guards had not been holding back, either. By the time they woke up he would have got far enough to find a way out of the salt flats.

It was Mortog himself who had just handed him on a plate his chance to escape.

Drunks and small children tended, it was thought, to blurt out the truth. Barbandor had to get back to his own people and to warn them and the whole of Girdlegard about Borkon and his intentions. *They have no idea about any of it.* News about Brigantia had taken over all the communications with the other realms. Nobody was wasting any time thinking about what the orcs might do; orcs were generally considered semi-idiotic low-lifes.

Barbandor had briefly considered remaining in his cage to try to glean more details, but he was never going to get a better opportunity than this one. Once the wedding festivities were over he would always be closely supervised, given his import-ance because of the prophecy.

Then it's now or never. Barbandor took the ox bone, tied a strip of blanket round two of the bars and twisted the material, winding it as if spanning a catapult.

The iron wires had become fragile and they broke with a clicking sound.

By Vraccas! Nearly done! Barbandor used a jagged fragment of broken pottery to cut through the ropes holding the cage-construction together, sweating and panting with the effort. He had to keep stopping to check none of the sleepers had been disturbed.

But nothing stirred. They were all heavily intoxicated still.

He had soon severed the strong fibres and managed to wrench the wooden bars apart, leaving a gap at the bottom through which he could slide out. Barbandor stretched his limbs and back in relief at being out of the confined space.

Right, now, orcs. You've seen the last of me.

Despite the urge to behead the lot of them in order to avenge Gyndala's death, he restrained himself. Instead, he pinched some warm clothing off a couple of the comatose orcs and used the combined garments to make a passable winter coat. He grabbed some provisions, stuffing things in a bag. He then picked his way carefully over a veritable carpet of snoring monsters to reach the hallway of the large log-cabin building. He stopped a few times, trying to locate the orc with the black-and-white patterned skin. He really wanted to eliminate that one, the one with the specialist knowledge of herbs. It would rob Borkon of one of his prime assets. However, neither that orc nor the bridal couple were in the hall.

Outside it was an icy-cold clear starlit night. The moon was shining down on a world that appeared to Barbandor tranquil and at peace. No sign of any guards. Deep in the salt desert miles away from Brigantia, the beasts were obviously not worried about being attacked. No army was going to try to invade this inhospitable landscape.

Barbandor noticed his own breath forming a white cloud in front of the scarf covering his mouth. He thought it looked as if he was on fire with fury. *Let's get to the stables first of all. Then I'll head north-west. To Platinshine.* That would be the safest port of call.

Girdlegard

United Great Kingdom of Gauragon
Province of Fire
1024 P.Q. (7515th solar cycle in old reckoning), late winter

Since getting back, Goïmron had not had a chance to speak to Rodana. They had waved to each other from a distance and had exchanged smiles and shouted greetings. But whenever they tried to approach each other, someone would turn up with an urgent request or an important message or a summons to attend a strategy meeting or an invitation to go and see Tungdil Goldhand.

Now that they had left Kràg Tahuum, he finally got the private moment he had so desired. He would be able to speak to her. He cleaned himself up, had his curly dark hair cut short, had a shave and had his sideburns trimmed. Dressed once more in his familiar shirt and tunic from the old days under a warm winter mantle, he walked along next to Rodana's new caravan. She had been given this vehicle as restitution for past ill-treatment. His heart was hammering in his chest, so great was his excitement at being close to her. He had intentionally not brought her a gift, thinking it would seem too pushy.

'May I wish you a wonderful orbit,' he said gallantly, greeting her as if they had just bumped into each other outside the baker's in Malleniagard rather than in the middle of an armed column marching towards Waveline in Sinterich where they would be preparing to set sail in order to destroy the älfar fleet.

Wrapped up warm against the cold, Rodana sat on the coachman's seat, reins in hand. 'Oh, it's you. Lovely to see you.' She slid to one side along the bench and patted the seat next to her. 'Can I give you a lift?'

'Yes, that'd be grand.' Goïmron climbed on board neatly. 'Much nicer than walking.'

'They won't have given you a horse because you're so used to riding on your dragon, I expect,' she teased him.

Under the scarf covering his face, Goïmron was grinning. 'Szmajro isn't *my* dragon, you know. He acknowledges me. As someone who . . . Ah, no matter. But tell me how you are. That's much more important.'

Rodana gestured to the rear and then she moved her scarf

down from her face so that she could be heard more clearly. 'As you see, thanks to Gata and Goldhand I've been given a new vehicle after the other one was burned out. The puppets and the props and all the theatre scenery, of course – that's all gone. It'll be some time before I manage to replace everything.'

'Have you started carving your new set of puppets?' He removed his own scarf. How he had missed seeing her, even if now her face showed the hardships she had gone through since he had seen her last. Her fine-featured countenance with the high cheekbones reflected all that had happened.

She shook her head in answer and moved a stray blonde lock of hair away from her eyes. 'I've had no time, if I'm honest. And I can't seem to find the motivation.' A sigh escaped her dark lips, the breath vanishing into a white cloud. 'I'm worried, to tell the truth. And I'm not sleeping properly.'

Goïmron nodded, placing a hand on her shoulder in commiseration. 'Belîngor's told me what you had to go through. At the wall. And in Brigantia, too.'

'Did Brûgar tell you about the episode at Mostro's tent?'

He nodded again. 'It's so difficult for me, having to keep silent. Having to try so hard not to give anything away. Not to reach out and drag the mask off that monstrosity.' She smiled at him, relief on her features. 'But now you're back, it'll soon be time to do just that.'

'What do you mean?' He moved his hand from her shoulder again, not wanting to appear intrusive.

'Time to restore Hantu's real appearance and time to make sure Mostro is taken to task for his treachery – treason against the people of Girdlegard. You can challenge him. You, with all your magic – and with Szmajro.' She looked up, searching the horizon. 'Where is the dragon? I've only seen it from a long way off.'

'Szmajro is nearby and will come when I give the signal.'

Goïmron felt ill at ease, because he was going to have to disappoint her. He had already discussed the situation about Mostro and Hantu with the others – Gata, Brûgar, Belîngor and Goldhand. They had agreed to wait until after they had destroyed the älfar ships on Arima before exposing the rhamak and the magus. Goldhand reckoned the two were not posing any immediate danger. It was important not to open up a second front. However, Goïmron was not at liberty to divulge this to the puppeteer. 'Give me a bit more leeway, I need a bit more time before I confront Mostro.'

'Why on earth?' Rodana stared at him, surprise and indignation in her voice. 'His slanderous allegations were the reason Chòldunja and I had to flee from the camp. So he is responsible for her death! I want him punished. If not for her death then at least for his treachery. I want satisfaction. And justice.' She frowned, obviously thinking. 'So . . . I'm beginning to wonder about something.'

'Meaning?'

'About you and her.' Rodana felt along for a double-walled flask on the bench next to her, poured out a mug of hot tea and offered it to Goïmron.

'Is it about her teaching me?' He assumed Chòldunja had probably admitted to her mentor that she had had a part in his magic training. And that Rodana knew he must have realised about the young girl's being a ragana but had kept quiet about it. 'It was me asking her for her help. Don't think badly of her.' He accepted the hot drink gladly and breathed in the scented aroma of the tea.

But to his surprise Rodana shook her head. 'Before she sent me away so I could warn the besieging troops – she was going to try to hold the rhamak up – she spoke of a debt she had to settle. I've been trying to work out for ages now what she could have been referring to. I absolutely believe that she never harmed a child. She would never have killed and eaten an infant. But what was this guilt she carried with her? A debt she needed to settle by sacrificing her own life?' She placed the flask down at her side. 'Then I remembered what happened back in Malleniagard and a terrible suspicion struck me. Could she have had something to do with your friend's death? Remember?'

Remember? Of course I remember. Goïmron remembered the onyx beard clips that had belonged to Gandelin. He had not wanted to mention finding them after hearing that the young ragana had lost her life. 'Maybe because Gandelin realised she was wearing a moor diamond round her neck. And she was afraid perhaps he would inform the city guard,' he surmised, continuing her train of thought.

'The night it happened I'd sent her off to sleep at the back of the carriage while I tried to find the right road to take us out of the town. I kept going the wrong way. At one time I heard a loud bump coming from inside the caravan,' Rodana told him. 'And when I asked Chòldunja about it she claimed to have fallen out of bed.' Rodana adjusted her hold on the reins, 'I can't be sure she was even in the back of the caravan at all. She could have left, secretly, and gone off to kill your friend. For fear of being exposed as a moor-witch. And captured.'

For fear you would be involved, too. And that is exactly what did, in the end, occur. Goïmron felt the decorative beard clips heavy in his pocket. He always kept them with him in memory of his friend. 'No, I don't think she did that,' he said. But it was a lie. It was no longer relevant. Chòldunja was dead and it would be less upsetting for Rodana to continue to think well of her aprendisa. 'She liked Gandelin, she told me so. I'm sure she would have confessed to the killing.'

Rodana sighed with relief. 'I was hoping you'd say that.' She turned to face Goïmron. 'Forgive me.'

'You've done nothing wrong.'

'I have been very slow on the uptake.'

Goïmron was embarrassed. 'I think it's me being slow now.' He had certainly noticed how this petite creature's tone altered. *What's coming, I wonder?*

'Gata had a word with me. While I was in prison. She told me that she had a soft spot for you but that you were keen on somebody else entirely.'

'Oh.' Goïmron knew he had gone bright red. He could feel the heat in his face. He imagined the clumps of ice and snow melting on his clothes and dripping from his cap. 'Oh dear.'

Rodana flashed her light-green eyes at him. 'I think that other person can count herself very lucky. Considering that a dwarf as fine as yourself might want to offer her his heart.'

'Oh, yes. Absolutely,' he stammered. He wanted to jump off the wagon and disappear.

'I think you should give that other person a little more time to examine her feelings. She is certainly fond of you.' Rodana bent her face to his and bestowed a long, thoughtful kiss on his cheek. 'I think you would make a lovely couple.'

Goïmron would never have believed for a moment that there could be a wave of emotion that was greater than the one he had just experienced. Excitement and joy made him want to leap up and down. He felt so exuberant that he wanted to climb up on to the top of the caravan and start to sing love songs at the top of his voice.

Calm down, he told himself. *Don't make a complete fool of yourself for love.* 'And the other person shall have as much time as she could possibly want.' A happy sigh escaped him. Heart pounding, he felt brave enough to edge nearer to Rodana. She mirrored his movement and they sat pressed close side by side on the coachman's seat, enjoying the moment.

Suddenly Mostro trotted up. He was wearing an extravagantly

tailored robe with an overcoat and a fur hood. A very young soldier rode at his side, in light armour and a woollen mantle and with a cloth armband displaying the Rhuta coat of arms. The two of them kept pace with Rodana's vehicle.

'That youth is actually Hantu,' whispered Rodana. 'He's joined Mostro.'

'Greetings, Master Chiselcut.' Mostro's tone was friendly. 'I don't want to give you the title of *Magus*. That would imply a great deal of something special that is lacking in you.'

'And may I wish you a pleasant orbit, yourself,' Goïmron returned, not rising to the bait. 'I don't care about titles. It's results that count, don't you agree?'

'But you ought to be addressing *me* as Magus, of course. Because I am one.' Mostro laughed. 'You have been leading us a merry dance with all your trickery. It seems you never could find any spare time, these past few orbits, to pay me a visit. We really must get together and have a good long talk about your magical applications. I'm awfully keen to hear about all of it. You, a dwarf. No education at all, and yet you're capable of these wonders! What interesting times we all live in!' He indicated the military figure accompanying him. 'May I present Darislaff? He is my personal bodyguard and a founder member of my new magic contingent. The soldiers in this unit will be equipped with the most dangerously effective of artefacts from the Chamber of Wonders.'

'So you won't be relying on your own powers?' Goïmron was courteous diplomacy personified.

'I do not trust the subversive element. Which can be found everywhere.' Mostro was wearing the ragana's moor diamond pendant over his clothing to be sure that it could be seen by the dwarf and by the puppet woman.

Obviously intended as a challenge to us. A declaration of war? 'But you didn't come here to give Rodana her young aprendisa's gemstone as a memento?' said Goïmron as an opening shot. 'And as compensation, of course. She suffered considerable material losses on your account. Not to mention other forms of harm.'

'However dearly I would have wished to be able to do that . . .' – at this point Mostro clutched the diamond protectively – 'Unfortunately I am not at liberty to make that gesture. It would be far too dangerous. A sister ragana might turn up and demand its return, esteemed Madam Doria Rodana de Psalí. That would lead surely to your death.'

He's not intending to provide any kind of apology or to make any offer of restitution, is he? Where all along he has been the cause of all her distress. He, that is, and . . . also . . . to a certain extent, myself. Goïmron forced a smile on to his face. 'As you seem not to want to compensate Rodana for the wrong you have done to her, do tell us what it is that brings you here.'

'It is *yourself* I sought, Master Chiselcut. I was told I might find you in the puppeteer's company.' He stuck out his right hand in a demanding gesture. 'And if we are talking about wrongs: on the previous occasion you were taken off by a dragon before you were able to restore the stolen sea sapphire to the rightful owner.' His smile was full of malice, but the frost covering his pointed beard gave him a comical aspect. 'Now you have an excellent opportunity to put right your criminal act.'

'You find me overcome with regret on that issue.' Goïmron gave a sigh full of pretended remorse. 'I would so gladly have returned it to Vanéra while she was still with us. However –'

'Since I am her successor, Master Chiselcut, all her possessions now fall to me,' Mostro cut in greedily. 'And particularly an artefact holding such dangerous power should not remain in the hands of a beginner in the profession of magic. But should you want to apply to be taken on as a trainee, I might perhaps consider appointing you as my famulus.'

Goïmron put his hand slowly into his pocket and drew out a

violet-hued amethyst. 'But I fear I must disappoint you, esteemed Magus Mostro. *This* is what I use for my magic.'

'Never! I clearly identified the sea sapphire in your keeping,' Mostro hissed, wagging his finger. 'Hand it over.'

'That is correct. I had been in possession of that unlucky stone. But when Szmajro carried me off I was unconscious for some time. The gemstone must have slipped out of my pocket, I expect,' Goïmron lied. 'Szmajro and I spent ages searching for it. But all in vain. If you want to have it I can tell you roughly whereabouts the artefact might have fallen. I mean I can tell you more or less the regions we would have flown over.' Making a contrite face, he added, 'I'm most awfully sorry about this. I would have liked to make my apologies to Vanéra. We lost her far too soon. Despite your heroic efforts.'

Mostro retracted his outstretched hand. 'You are sure you lost it?' he asked, his voice sharp as a paper-cut.

'How could I be mistaken about something like that?' Goïmron pretended to be offended. 'What are you implying, Magus Mostro? That is not—'

'All right. Let's forget it for now. But if the sea sapphire were to be found – found, I say, and not somewhere deep in the wilderness of Gautaya – then . . .'

'Then what?' Goïmron put the amethyst back in his pocket. 'In that case I expect you would attribute the finding to some divine miracle. Or were you hinting at something else?'

'Just that, Master Chiselcut. Just that. And nothing else.'

How could Vanéra ever have taken him on as her famulus? Goïmron felt an almost overwhelming urge to expose the magic disguise of the ostensible bodyguard, to reveal his true identity and thus take the wind out of the sails of the boastful and deeply unpleasant would-be magus.

In his pockets he felt for the sapphire and exchanged it for the amethyst.

NO. REALLY DON'T DO THAT.

'Why ever not?' he asked inside his head. *I could summon Szma-jro. Mostro would have to capitulate.*

IT'S NOT A MATTER OF DEALING WITH THIS OVER-WEENING MAGUS. IT'S THE BODYGUARD WE NEED TO CONFRONT.

We turn him straight back into being Hantu and ...

HE IS ACCOMPANIED BY TWO BEINGS FROM ANOTHER SPHERE, warned the sea sapphire. I CAN VAGUELY MAKE OUT THEIR SHAPES. THEY DON'T SEEM VERY BIG OR POWERFUL BUT THEY CERTAINLY PRESENT A THREAT BECAUSE THEY'LL BE DIFFICULT TO LAY HOLD OF AND OVERCOME. DIFFICULT FOR US, THAT IS.

So, maybe only a rhamak could beat them. Understood. Goïmron looked at Darislaff and nodded at him. 'Then I'd advise you to take good care of your master. There's no way of knowing whether the älfar might send out assassins to target him in particular.'

'Thank you. I shall bear that in mind, Master Chiselcut,' the soldier replied, not showing any hint of suspicion.

WE DO THE THING WITH THE ÄLFAR SHIPS IN ARIMA FIRST. AFTER THAT WE'LL HAVE TIME TO WORK OUT HOW TO GET RID OF THE RHAMAK AND HIS COMPANIONS.

'We'll meet again at the next rest stop,' said Mostro, a sour note to his voice. 'My invitation stands, of course, Master Chiselcut. I would like to have a good chat with you about magic.' With an angry kick of his spurs to its flanks he sent his alarmed horse shooting off in pain. Darislaff followed in his wake.

'That was very cruel, what he just did,' Rodana murmured. 'No good person treats a horse so badly.'

Goïmron whirled round and stared at her eagerly. He had had an idea. 'You could do me a huge favour.'

'Go on.'

'Reckon you'd be any good at carving a piece of bone?'

'Of course.'

'Then help me with this plan. But it's got to stay secret. Keep it just between the two of us. *Absolutely* no one else must hear about it.'

To his delight Rodana nodded in agreement.

The Children of the Smith occasionally banish some of their own kind.

It's not nice, but it happens. These outcast dwarves will form roving bands of plundering outlaws, laying waste to particular regions. Other groups might even join forces with the Brigantians. These dwarves believe that Vraccas has abandoned Girdlegard and his own children.

More worrying still, they think the mountains have been taken over by some unknown deity.

Dar Whjenn, academic expert in the fields
of flora, fauna and the laws of nature

XVI

Girdlegard

Sinterich
Waveline
1024 P.Q. (7515th solar cycle in old reckoning), late winter

As he stepped out of the harbourmaster's office on to the quay-side accompanied by the assembled leaders, Goïmron kept a good grip on his padded cap to stop the icy blasts blowing it off his head.

A couple of dozen largish ships were bobbing up and down at anchor in Waveline's harbour. Most were two-masters but there were a few with four masts, too. Goïmron did not know any-thing much about the different kinds of sea-going vessels but it did not strike him that any of them looked particularly warlike. *They don't even have ramming spars.*

'So is this our combined fleet for taking on the älfar?' he asked Joros Gunmarr, a long-serving Sinterian naval com-mander, to whom he had been introduced on arrival.

The man nodded. He resembled a walrus to some extent, with a heavy moustache covering his top lip. 'But it's not all the ships, yet. There was quite a storm that came up, holding the others back.'

'Oh, for the sake of Tion's wretched little sister! Those are never proper fighting ships,' Brûgar complained. It was unusual for him not to be smoking his pipe, but the strong wind coming off the sea would have scattered all the tobacco, or at the very least would have put out the flame.

'Whatever. A ridiculously easy target for the black-eyes to pick out,' Gata agreed. 'Even I can see that and I know next to nothing about naval warfare.'

No way am I setting foot on one of those boats. I wouldn't have done it in the past and I'm certainly not going to now. I'm not going to give Elria the satisfaction.' This was the decision that Belîngor delivered in a string of gestures. '*Dwarves are land creatures. On dry land and inside mountains, that's where we belong.*'

Or up in the air, of course. Goïmron observed the others all deep in discussions – the commanders of the various groups: humans, dwarves, meldriths and elves. They were all grim-faced and voices were raised as they argued. The sight of this unconvincing collection of ships had been a shock. *We were expecting at least fifty.* 'What was that you just said about a storm?'

'The fleet is supposed to gather here in Waveline so the ships can set out together,' Joros explained. Fighting with the wind, he tried to retain control of his beard. 'But we got news – sent by carrier pigeon – to say over half the ships from Litusien and Palusien had encountered bad weather and were running late. Plus, the ship from the Seahold fortress in the Red Mountains won't make it on time, either. The storm has forced them to find an anchorage or to turn back.' The veteran seafarer pointed at how the flags on the vessels' masts were straining horizontally in the constant wind. 'The squalls we're having now are the back end of the appalling weather conditions. It's comparatively quiet at the moment. We've had breakers coming in, topping the harbour walls. Many of the ships have sustained damage.'

Well, well. So the Firstlings have got their own ships. 'So the storm has passed?'

'Yes. Towards the west.' Joros gave up on his attempt to keep his beard looking dignified. 'I can only assume the älfar ships will be in bad shape as well. An isolated island in mid-ocean is very exposed. Nothing to absorb the power of the wind. It's different on a landmass.'

The älfar fleet will be having trouble, just like us. A bold idea occurred to Goïmron. 'How far is it to Arima?'

'One hundred and fifty sea miles. If we could hold course in this wind we'd be flying there. But the rigging would have got damaged and the sails ripped to pieces and the shrouds would have snapped.'

Goïmron went over to the commanding officers and bade them enter the office to get out of the wind. 'Listen. I'm going to set off on Szmajro and try a pre-emptive strike on Arima,' he announced. People reacted with dismay to his risky suggestion. He went on: 'I appreciate that you are concerned but it seems an ideal opportunity. The älfar fleet will be confined to harbour to avoid the risk of losing ships in the storm. So they'll be an easy target for me and the dragon. Even if we don't manage to set all of them all alight, we can still inflict enough damage to reduce their effectiveness, making them less of a threat to us. And once our ships have finally all turned up, together with the efforts of the magus, we'll then be well placed to defeat the älfar navy.' *Even if we've only got a couple of dozen ships at our disposal.*

'Have I understood you aright? You're intending to take off in this weather?' Joros could not believe his ears.

Telìnâs was obviously worried. 'Brave of you, Goïmron. But do you think Szmajro will be able to fly in this?'

'Sure to. And the älfar won't be expecting an attack. We can take them unawares,' he explained, even though his heart was beating wildly at the prospect of having to ride through wind, rain and lightning strikes on the back of the dragon before launching an attack on eight heavily armed vessels. 'And you know I've got my gemstone magic to help me.' He looked each of the commanders firmly in the eyes. 'It will work. Vraccas will be with me.'

'And so will Lorimbur,' Gata added.

Although Goïmron did not actually require the others' approval for his scheme, he was keen to get their agreement. One by one they nodded, accepting his plan. They all shook hands with him, slapping him on the shoulder encouragingly. He knew they respected the gesture he was making and acknowledged his leadership in this matter. He had never experienced this type of acclaim before in his life.

'Come back safe,' Gata insisted, embracing him. 'As you know, we've a lot of plans. Lots to do about the magic and dealing with the treason affair.'

'I know.' He hugged her, then turned to Brûgar and Belîngor. 'I'll be back really soon. May Vraccas be my witness: I shall return.'

'But don't keep us waiting as long as last time,' Brûgar warned him with a laugh. 'If we end up thinking you're dead again, we'll never forgive you.'

Goïmron said his farewells and hurried away from the port, heading back to the military camp that had been set up outside Waveline. The plan had been to assemble as many soldiers as possible, ready to send them over to Arimar, to fight the Undarimar forces and their älfar allies. Combat on land and at sea. Exactly how many troops would be transported depended on the number of ships they could acquire in the meantime. At least fifty vessels would be needed to land a respectably-sized army on the island. Given how experienced their adversary was, this remained a daring proposition. This was why Goïmron felt it was crucial for him and Szmajro to carry out the pre-emptive strike. He did not care about personal glory. His entire purpose was the avoidance of pointless and unnecessary deaths. *I didn't join the fighting in Brigantia. Now is my chance to do my bit on Arima.*

He quickly reached Rodana's caravan and knocked at the door. She invited him in. 'Have you finished it?' he asked, closing the door behind himself and pulling off his headgear to release his short curls.

'You sweep in here like the storm wind itself.' Wearing a leather apron over her simple brown dress, Rodana was seated at the table, where something the length of an arm was covered in a yellow cloth. She flicked a few white fragments off the table. 'But of course. It's ready for you.' She pulled the cloth aside with a dramatic flourish. 'There you are.'

What she revealed was a long, slender and beautifully crafted bladed weapon. It had once been the beak of a flame flyer. Rodana had fashioned an elegant carrying-sheath for it out of ironthorn wood, disguising the whole thing as a walking stick. Nobody would suspect it had a sword-blade concealed inside it. *Not even Szmajro.*

'Excellent!' Goïmron lifted the dagger-like implement. 'It lies in the hand nicely.'

'I didn't have to do very much. The shape practically offered itself and with a couple of clever tricks the bone was easy to work with. Making the carrying-case was much more time-consuming a task.' Rodana raised her mug of tea to toast the dwarf. 'Do you really think the dragon will be scared of it?'

'I don't want him to be scared. I want to be able to kill him with it if he ever turns against me, or against Girdlegard.'

Rodana laughed. 'But you remember how big your dragon pet is?'

'Yes. I'll have to have a think about how best I can use the beak-dagger most effectively.' Goïmron cast his eye over the length of the carved bone blade. 'If I need to. Only if I need to.'

'Then I would suggest you fasten it to a long pole and use it like a harpoon. Otherwise the tip won't reach all the way to the heart. Unless you're going to hack away with it and dig deep inside Szmajro's body.' She made a face. 'But if you did that you'd get scalded with red-hot dragon blood, wouldn't you?'

'I'll come up with something,' said Goïmron, determinedly. 'Don't forget I am a magus.'

'Oh. Understood. You'll send the blade floating through the air by magic to cut the creature's throat. Good idea!' Rodana watched him slide the weapon into its holding-case and then cross the room with a halting gait. 'What are you doing?'

'Practising.'

'The limp?'

'It's vital Szmajro doesn't get suspicious when I start to use a walking stick when we set off.'

At this the young woman's expression changed. 'Has the fleet arrived, then?'

'No. It'll be just me and the dragon.' He quickly outlined his plan. 'With Vraccas on our side we'll take the älfar by surprise and set all their ships on fire. I feel it's my duty,' he added. 'Because of what happened in Brigantia.'

Rodana stared at him aghast. 'That's far too dangerous.'

'Szmajro is well armoured. It'll be child's play for him to ward off any missiles.'

'But those missiles brought Ardin down, didn't they?'

'Ardin was much smaller,' Goïmron countered.

'How do you know?'

'Szmajro told me.' Secretly he was thrilled that Rodana was so worried about him. She was extremely concerned. This must mean he meant a great deal to her. 'It'll all work out, you'll see.'

Getting up and taking off her apron, she came over and put her arms round him. 'Do you promise?'

Goïmron returned the embrace, revelling in the affection

she was showing him. He breathed in her scent and nuzzled his face against her soft neck.

'There aren't many left that I care for,' she murmured into his ear. Her delicate body quivered slightly. 'Don't leave me by myself.'

'I shan't.' Goïmron hugged her tightly for a few more moments before releasing her. Both of them had tears in their eyes. 'I've got to go,' he said huskily. 'I have to set off while the storm is still raging on Arima. Otherwise they'll see us coming.'

Rodana gave him a kiss on the forehead and walked out with him, remaining in the doorway as he made his way through the maze of big and small tents in the camp.

He had felt love in her embrace. And for that reason alone he must survive this next dangerous flight. *Then we can be happy together.* In great good humour, he found himself twirling his new walking stick gaily – until he remembered about the need to walk with a pronounced limp. *Concentrate.* He crossed the open fields to the place where he intended to summon the dragon. His heart was beating wildly and his face felt hot. He could not have said with certainty whether this was nerves or emotion.

Girdlegard

Inland Sea
1024 P.Q. (7515th solar cycle in old reckoning), late winter

Xanomir looked up at the star-strewn sky to check his position by the constellations for the fourth time, using his night mirror sextant. *No way. This can't be right.*

The as yet un-named diving vessel bobbed up and down on the gentle waves. The sea looked incapable of ever being angry.

Whereas it had recently swallowed up the *Seablade* together with her whole crew. Plus the saboteur. The loss of so many brave souls weighed heavily on Xanomir's mind.

But for now he had a more urgent preoccupation. It was inexplicable. 'Buvendil,' he called down the companionway, and then he went out on to the flat top of his specially built craft. 'Are you sure you checked our compass properly before we left?'

'Of course. Why?'

'Because we've sailed entirely the wrong way.' Xanomir picked up the night mirror sextant again, noting the position of the stars against the instrument and taking the readings. *Same results.* 'We're far too far south of Arima.'

'Have you maybe got your measurements wrong?'

'Five times in a row? Hardly.' Xanomir pivoted carefully round. There were no lights showing anywhere on the black surface of the sea. No red and green port and starboard lamps of other ships and nothing from the lighthouse they were expecting to see, which would have shown the location of the island of Arima. 'Can you check whether the compass needle is stuck?'

'Just a moment.'

Xanomir was enjoying the fresh air up here. Several orbits ago they had seen the last of the terrible storm that had sealed the *Seablade*'s fate. As they travelled they took it in turns on watch, whether on the surface or under it. If the sea was too rough, they would send their diving craft well below the huge swell. To navigate underwater they used an improved version of the instrument devised for seeing round corners. It was made up of a staggered mirrored tube extending up about three paces in height. This meant the diving craft could stay safely submerged while still allowing them to see where they were heading. Three times every orbit they would surface to vent the stale air from the cabin. Then they could catch fish, have a wash or do their laundry.

The dwarves were not bothered by the cramped conditions, being as a race used to working in narrow underground tunnels. *It makes sense for us Children of the Smith to use undersea craft to travel. Who else is going to understand all the technology needed?* Xanomir took his seeing-tube and let his gaze sweep the horizon. *Nothing. Nothing but water.*

Suddenly he caught sight of something glittering on the surface.

What's that? He adjusted the focus and was able to make out a shoal of fish whose lateral fins were powerful enough to let them leap over the surface of the water for thirty or forty paces. *Flying armour fish!*

At first he watched them, fascinated, but then he realised they could pose a danger to the diving boat. The fish were the size of large dogs and had sharp pointed muzzles. They were heavy enough to dent and damage the thin shell of the craft, given the momentum they could create. Moonfish were a similar species and had been known to sink a sailing ship in a collision.

We can't get away from them up here. Better dive down and head past them underneath the shoal. To be quite sure of avoiding them Xanomir thought he would have to dive deeper than thirty paces. Quite a major challenge for their experimental vessel. He had only yesterday completed the running repairs following the damage incurred when the boat was so hurriedly launched.

'We have to get out of here,' he called out.

'Why is that?' Buvendil shouted back.

'Flying armour fish. A huge shoal of them. Too dangerous.'

'Understood. But I've just found something.' There was a clang and then Buvendil's fair head appeared. He held out a tiny dark object. 'It's a magnet stone. It was well hidden and had been attached to the compass casing.'

Xanomir cursed. *No wonder we've gone the wrong way.* 'That will have been our confounded saboteur! May Fridgatt's soul never find peace!'

'We had told the crew not to come near the diving craft and we had our eyes on it the whole voyage,' said his friend, contradicting him. 'It can't have been him.' Xanomir focused the seeing-tube on the school of flying fish. There was not much time. 'So maybe you just missed the magnet when you were doing the initial check, back in the dock?'

'Come on! You know how meticulous I am about things like that.' Buvendil was indignant. 'It's always been thanks to my punctiliousness that all our complicated experiments have worked, if you remember rightly.'

'What do you mean?'

'That there was a second saboteur on board the *Sea Blade*.'

Well, of course. Xanomir recalled Fridgatt saying to him in the wheelhouse that he was about to go down to the hold to kill Buvendil, just like Alreth and the crew. *Up to that point Fridgatt had not been down to the hold.* Xanomir quickly put down his scope. *That means it wasn't Fridgatt who made those holes in the sides of the ship.* 'When was the last time you checked the diving boat over?'

'Before we—' Buvendil stopped short. 'By Vraccas!' he muttered, clambering up the rungs of the companionway ladder. 'You think he could still be on board with us?' he whispered. 'But where? There's so little room. Surely we'd have noticed.'

'Think about it. Which race is very slim and able to hide in the dark?' Xanomir's question was purely rhetorical. It sent shivers down their spines. They must have spent orbit after orbit living cheek by jowl with an älf without realising it.

The two dwarves looked at the top of the diving craft

without saying a word, knowing they would have to be back inside if they wanted to survive the current threat from the armour fish shoal. But somewhere inside the vessel at their feet the enemy was waiting.

'The black-eyes will have noticed that I've located his magnet stone,' Buvendil whispered.

'Sure.' Xanomir checked his sextant. *What else has our black-eyes been up to?* Feeling carefully with his fingertips, he discovered how the markings on the metal device had been altered. This meant that not only had the compass led them astray, but his navigation calculations from the stars had been faulty. *What else has he sabotaged?*

'Why hasn't he killed us?'

'He probably wants to find out as much as he can about our invention. He wants to know how it works. How it's manoeuvred. He's spying on us. Watching what we do, since there aren't any blueprints for him to study. He needs our knowledge and skill,' Xanomir ventured. 'That's what's kept us alive. So far.'

'Then it won't be long before he does away with us. Then he'll sail our boat over to his folk and that'll give the black-eyes a mighty advantage. They'll take it apart and work out how it functions.' Buvendil took the tiny magnet out again. 'Do you reckon we stand a chance against an älf in the cramped conditions of the submersible? Or shall we lure him out?'

It's vital the älfar don't capture my diving craft. Or our technical know-how. Xanomir shrugged his shoulders. 'Worst-case scenario: we scuttle it.' *With us inside.*

Goïmron watched the troubled sea moving hundreds of paces below him. White foam crested the waves and the wind sent the froth flying through the air. In spite of his scarf and hood, his face was so cold he could hardly feel it. The speed they were doing increased the wind-chill factor.

'I can't work out how long it'll take us to get there.' He had never been bothered before about travelling on the dragon, but this time he was nervous he might slip off Szmajro's back and plunge into the water, only to succumb to the curse of Elria. Although, come to think of it, falling on to rocks or earth or treetops would probably be even more unambiguously fatal. *I do not want to find out.*

'We'll get to Arima very soon. Samusin has sent us a following wind,' Szmajro explained. 'How's your leg doing?'

At first Goïmron did not know what the dragon meant. 'Oh, it's fine. Riding on your back is better than I thought it would be,' he replied, adjusting the position of his stick with the concealed weapon. He had thrust it through his belt to carry it like a sword.

He had made use of the flight time to identify a spot on the creature's backbone, just next to where the dragon's two necks joined. This would be where he could ram his weapon in between the gaps in the spinal column. And Szmajro would die. It would be easier than trying to locate the heart. *This is the only practical solution.*

The rust-coloured dragon went into a gentle curve and entered a cloud formation, which was warmer and damper. 'We'll be over the island very soon. I'm going to use this cloud so they don't see us coming.'

Goïmron had noticed the storm was abating. 'Did you say we had a following wind?'

'The direction of the wind has changed.' Szmajro made a careful descent, leaving their cloud cover behind. 'This is Arima.'

Goïmron took a quick look past the dragon's right neck. He could see the sheltered harbour on Undarimar's main island. The port walls steadfastly held out the angry swell of the storm tide. But all he could see in the way of ships was one eight-master and two escort vessels. 'Where is the rest of the fleet?'

'I can't see it. Maybe it has foundered? Or they've gone another way?' Szmajro flew back up to enter the cloud. 'If I try to fly around looking for the rest of the ships we'll be seen. We ought to attack fast and then worry about where the other ships have got to.'

Goïmron was worried. *Maybe spies from Undarimar have told the black-eyes that there's a fleet assembling in Waveline.* So then the älfar will have set out in their superior numbers to confront our cobbled-together naval contingent, who won't be prepared at all. They'll be easily sunk before they ever reach Arima. *No one has any idea about the danger! We are the only hope.* 'Then let's get going.'

'I'll try a direct flight path. They won't be expecting us,' Szmajro suggested, explaining his plan. He folded his wings back against his huge body. 'Child's play. Hold tight, groundling!' There was a violent jerk and the dragon sped down, swift as an arrow.

They swooped down out of the clouds and saw Arima's harbour at one side.

But the guards on watch had their wits about them. Alarm bells and horn signals were set off as the dragon made its approach. There was frantic commotion on the decks of all three ships.

Before the älfar sailors could drag the large catapults into position Szmajro whirred over their heads, sending powerful jets of fire from both gullets. The flames hissed across the decks, caught the red silk sails and went up the rigging. Soon even the pennants at the top of the mast were on fire.

Goïmron surveyed the damage caused on the first fly-by. The sailors were tackling the blaze with sand from their fire buckets and the crew used boathooks to pull away the charred bodies and replace the artillerists. The älfar did not slow down in their efforts, despite the fact that their ships were ablaze under them. *They know they have to defeat us or they'll be utterly done for.*

'Don't risk another pass.' Goïmron drew the dragon's attention to the palace on the hill. 'Go over there and break some stones off the tower or the walls. Whichever seems easier.'

'Excellent suggestion, groundling. You're bright, aren't you?' Szmajro changed course. As he flew over the battlements his claws grabbed hold of great blocks of stone and carried them off.

In the meantime one of the smaller companion vessels had sunk and the other one was listing badly. Burning shrouds had spread the fire, making holes in the wooden planks, so that water was entering the hull.

But the main ship was sending off its first shots. There was no let-up now. Firing was continuous.

One missile grazed Szmajro's hind leg and he shrieked out his pain through both of his throats. 'They've got dragon bone in those bolts they're shooting,' he screeched furiously. 'They know our weak points.'

Goïmron congratulated himself on his decision to get himself a weapon fashioned from the beak of a flame flyer. 'Drop your stone blocks quickly and fly up out of range.'

'No. I'm not going to let myself be hustled out of the sky like Ardin,' Szmajro fumed. The superficial wound on his hind leg had made him angry. 'I'll show them.'

Goïmron was worried he wouldn't be able to keep his seat if the dragon continued with these swiftly changing manoeuvres. 'But what about me?'

Szmajro did not answer. He plunged out of the sky like a bird of prey, claws open wide. He dropped his blocks from the palace ramparts directly through a hatch in the enemy ship's main deck, resulting in screams from below. White clouds emerged out of the opening. They were definitely not clouds of ordinary smoke.

Pivoting on his own axis, Szmajro wheeled round, crossing the trajectory paths from three shots – again he screeched with pain. With the teeth of one of his mouths he removed a bone-spear and spat it out. 'Oh, they'll pay for that! Those accursed black-eyes! How I hate the lot of them!'

Before Goïmron could hold him back, Szmajro had executed an abrupt turn and half a backflip, had turned again and was loosing fire at the eight-master. The red flames turned white and took on the form of flame-lances, deadly as scalpel cuts. The hull started to give way, the wooden spars and ribs snapping and the decks opening up like a sewing box that had been roughly handled.

'I want to destroy them all,' Szmajro shrieked, beside himself with anger. 'I want them to go down in flames to the bottom of the sea.'

'Not so wild!' said Goïmron, trying to calm the dragon down.

'My work on Arima is done. I'm going to start searching for the rest of the fleet.' Szmajro turned and began to do exploratory loops, going wider each time. 'I want them all to burn. I want all the black-eyes to go down in flames!'

'Szmajro! You accepted my authority. Listen to me,' Goïmron said firmly. He knew he was losing control over the dragon in its anger. Szmajro was following his own instincts. *This won't end well. He is heading for destruction. And he'll take me down with him.*

'I acknowledged your authority, yes. But I can see now that it was a mistake,' Szmajro snarled. 'I can see where I went wrong.'

Goïmron grabbed hold of the rust-coloured, black-veined scales in desperation, determined not to fall off. *What does he mean by that?*

Xanomir looked down at the entry shaft into the submersible. 'We'll be at a disadvantage once we're down there.'

'So what shall we do?' Buvendil chucked the magnet away. It rebounded to attach itself to the metal sides.

'Play along.' Xanomir took his hammer from his toolbelt. 'When I give the signal, you try to make the boat rock.'

He went to the opening. 'By Vraccas, it's armour fish!' he shouted. 'They'll tear great holes in our hull.' Using the blunt head of the hammer, he banged the craft's outermost covering several times, creating a loud noise on the inside. 'Curses! They're heading straight for us. Hold tight, Buvendil!'

He made a nicely judged incision in the metal with the sharp end of the hammerhead, giving his friend the signal. The diving craft wobbled wildly, letting sea water in through the small hole.

'We've sprung a leak,' Xanomir yelled, pretending to panic. 'There's more of them coming.' Another blow to the superstructure, a second incision. 'Accursed fish! It's Elria's doing. She's sent them to sink us. Quick! Abandon ship!'

Buvendil stomped towards the stern, making heavy footfalls. He made to jump in the air as if he were leaping overboard. He landed with great care, pulling out his knife, which had a protective ring on it he could use like a knuckleduster.

Xanomir slipped over to the opening and took off his belt to make a loop. He waited.

From inside the submersible they could hear the incoming water splashing and dripping. But nothing else happened.

Have we got it wrong? He looked at the holes he had made. *By Vraccas, then I've . . .*

A head of brown hair appeared in the opening. And next to it they saw the glitter of a drawn dagger.

Got you! Quick as a flash, Xanomir caught the älf's neck in the improvised leather sling. He pulled the belt tight with both hands, and placed his feet firmly on the enemy's shoulders, keeping him down in the shaft. 'Buvendil! Over here! I've got him.'

The älf struggled against the constricting leather strap. The dwarf's booted feet were preventing him leaving the diving craft. His face showed angry lines and flushed bright red, then turned blue.

All of a sudden Xanomir was overcome with fear seizing and compressing his heart. The älf used all his strength to free himself, taking advantage of the very instant when the dwarf's hands started to slacken. Gasping for air, the älf pushed himself up off the rungs of the ladder, lunging out with his knife as he did so.

The blade went through Xanomir's calf, making him cry out and stumble. The belt slipped out of his fingers. 'Buvendil! Quick! He's getting away!'

The älf dragged the belt away from his throat in a fury, kicking out wildly and felling Buvendil as he ran up. Buvendil dropped his weapon. 'He's got free,' he hissed. A second kick to the skull and the blond dwarf was swept off into the icy black waters.

Xanomir struggled to his feet. 'You will never get my boat!' He hurled his hammer at the älf, striking him on the shoulder. The sharp claw of the hammer lodged in the shoulder joint, making the hand open to release the dagger, which clanged down on to the diving boat's metal side.

'Oh, yes, I shall! And then we will rule over the seas like no one else.' The black lines on his visage remained and his eyes were black holes of fury. It was almost as if pitch-black swathes of shadow were streaming out of his eye sockets, wiping out the starlight. 'Filthy groundlings! Who would have thought you capable of thinking up something like this?' Using his uninjured arm, he drew a second knife.

Xanomir grabbed up the belt that was lying on the deck. He swerved to avoid the stabbing blade. He put the leather sling round his hammer, which was still stuck in the älf's shoulder. He pulled hard, turning swiftly to one side.

The momentum as he swivelled round forced the älf to be flung against the edge of the entrance shaft to the diving boat, before he skidded across the deck to plunge overboard, sinking through the waves.

Xanomir slid over to where he could extend a hand to Buvendil, who was struggling to keep himself afloat. 'Out of that water! I'm not having you freeze to death.'

Shaking with the cold, the blond dwarf pulled himself up back on board. 'We've got to dive. Those armour fish. They—'

Water dripping next to his head warned Xanomir of an imminent attack. He just managed to avoid a blow from his own hammer. Its sharp claw embedded itself in the boat's metal plating. The third such hole. The kick that followed sent him scuttling over to join his friend. Xanomir stumbled and fell, but laid his hands on Buvendil's knife. He stabbed upwards with it as soon as he could turn on to his back.

The älf was kneeling next to Buvendil, having slammed the hammer into the dwarf's face. Buvendil wheezed and groaned, struggling on the brink of death. 'At least I've got one of you.' He shoved the dying dwarf back over the side, where he immediately sank. 'The name of your death is Èthoras.'

Xanomir got to his feet and limped over to his adversary. 'I'll go to the bottom together with my boat before I'll let the älfar have it.'

Suddenly the night air was filled with silvery fish. Their lateral fins shivered and sparked. Water splashed from their bodies. The shoal was in flight. Xanomir was struck on his side by their flying bodies. He tripped and fell. All he could see were these quivering, flashing fish. He cradled his head in his arms protectively, holding his breath as he did so. As swiftly as the shoal had flown in, so swiftly had it vanished again.

Where is that älf? Xanomir slowly raised his eyes and looked around.

On the top of the diving craft there were patches of blood to be seen, some dark strands of hair. And half a finger. There was nothing else left of their deadly attacker.

Buvendil! Xanomir pushed himself up and looked around in dismay, noting how the swathes of black were turning dark blue. The sun was about to rise.

But his friend was gone.

May Vraccas give him grace. He has earned his place in the Eternal Forge. What a bitter irony it was that he had been killed not by Elria but by an älf. *And the water goddess sent her creatures to save a groundling.* Xanomir was overcome with sadness at his loss. And he was full of anger. *Accursed black-eyes. I shall sink them all to avenge you, Buvendil! I shall not let a single one survive!*

He quickly bandaged the wound on his leg with a strip of cloth he ripped off his tunic. Then he repaired the three holes in the hull of the diving craft. The craft that was still without a proper name. He looked at his repairs with satisfaction.

'I hereby give you the name of *Buvendil*!' he announced, placing his hand on the repaired metal side. *That is the least I can do.*

When he glimpsed a movement on the lightening horizon he took out his spyglass. A grim expression stole over his grey-bearded face. What he had seen had been blood-red sails. Four small boats and one huge vessel. Heading straight for him.

Elria is on my side. Xanomir went swiftly below, closing the hatch after him. The *Buvendil* dived, heading for the älfar fleet. It was time to try out the new weapons.

The increasingly-sized concentric circles he was flying took Szmajro far enough out over the sea for him finally to catch sight of the blood-red sails on the horizon. Their course was set due east, so they were heading directly towards Waveline. The älfar had mastered the art of tacking against the wind to get up an impressive speed.

'There they are,' the dragon muttered crossly, accelerating his flight and wheeling round in a curve. 'The last of the eight-masters. And four escort ships.'

'Too many. They'll have seen us coming.' Goïmron attempted to talk Szmajro out of his planned attack. He had absolutely no wish to succumb to älfar artillery miles out at sea. Or, worse still, to be attacked by their acid bombardments and dissolve in mid-air. 'Turn round,' he said. 'And collect some more blocks of stone from the island. Then you can attack them from much higher up–'

Szmajro did not agree. 'Arima's too far away now. It would cost me too much energy and effort to fly there and back. The älfar are travelling at speed. I want to give them a taste of my fire!'

Cowering on the dragon's back to keep out of the wind and avoid being shot at, Goïmron was condemned to watch, as it were, from the sidelines, but he gripped the sea sapphire tightly in his fist all the while, hoping he might be able to save himself in the worst-case scenario with some kind of magic. At that moment projectiles started whizzing past him. The älfar were using conventional weaponry: crossbow bolts and metal balls were harmlessly deflected by the dragon's toughened scales. But an angry screaming made itself heard when Szmajro felt some of the projectiles hitting home painfully. The next sound was the steady hiss of long tongues of flame directed down on to the ships.

Unable to see clearly because the cold air stream was making his eyes water, Goïmron felt the heat from the dragon's flames pass over his head. The warmth might have been almost pleasant, had it not been for the atrocious screeching and the stink of charred flesh from below.

The dwarf was hurled one way and then the other as Szmajro ducked, dived and weaved through the air, but he always managed to hold on securely to the dragon's rust-coloured scales. At one point he nearly lost both the sapphire and the special walking-stick implement as the dragon raged and roared while attacking the escort boats.

At last the dragon slowed down.

Wiping the tears out of his eyes, Goïmron was now able to see the overall effect of Szmajro's onslaught. One of the escort boats had obviously sustained damage, but the eight-master seemed completely unscathed. The other vessels had been destroyed. *Szmajro is a primal force of nature.*

The dragon had paid for this success with several wounds caused by projectiles fashioned out of bone. A missile containing acid had caught one of his wings, making holes in it, but this was not interfering with his ability to fly. Hot dragon blood dripped over the scales.

'You are injured. Let's turn back,' Goïmron urged. 'Leave the rest for our navy to deal with.'

'No!' Szmajro raged. 'These black-eyed bastards are the ones that altered my shape. They manipulated me, changing everything. What happened to the Szmajro I used to be?' he thundered, yelling down at the enemy beneath him. 'The zhussa thought I would be subservient to her if she cut off my horns. But I never surrendered my will. Or lost my hatred.' He made a new swift descent, pulling out of the dive and zigzagging to avoid incoming shots. 'The black-eyes are all going to meet their death today.'

Goïmron ducked behind the creature's necks again. 'Come on! Turn back! It's an order!' He resorted to calling on the power of the sapphire. 'Listen to my words and do what I say: cut short your attack.'

A faint shimmering was observable on the dragon's body, but he showed no signs of obeying the instruction.

'So that's the way of it, is it? Sits back there like a parasitic louse and thinks he can order me about. I'll deal with you later.'

Why is the magic not working? Goïmron tried again. But the only result was a faint glow on Szmajro's scales.

The gemstone imparted some unwelcome news. I FEAR THE DRAGON WAS MADE IMMUNE AGAINST ANY FORM OF MAGIC WHEN THE WONDER ZONE CHANGED ITS SIZE.

Goïmron recalled how the ball of lightning fire had emerged from the ground to cover the zhussa, and the dragon siblings, Szmajro and Slibina. *So maybe all three of them were made resistant.* The thought was frightening. *What do we do now?*

THERE IS *ONE* OTHER SPELL WE COULD TRY. I MEAN THAT YOU COULD TRY. I MEAN YOU MUST TRY. OTHER-WISE WE'LL NEVER BE ABLE TO STOP HIM. NOBODY WILL. NOT YOU. NOT MOSTRO. AND NONE OF THE ARTEFACTS WILL WORK, EITHER.

The älfar had Szmajro in their sights by now and they were fighting back with skill. A glass container filled with acid cracked open on striking the dragon's tail, releasing corrosive liquid on to the carapace, burning holes in the scales and then seeping through to attack flesh and bone underneath.

Szmajro emitted a spine-chilling scream and hurled him-self about before approaching the eight-master. 'You wretched black-eyes!' he raged, drawing back from the two ships on whose decks the cannons were being reloaded. Fully loaded, the two vessels were keeping a steady course due east towards Waveline.

Goïmron noticed a longish cigar-shaped contraption rising out of the waters to one side of the eight-master. Water pearled off the grey metal plating. Then a hatch opened up and a cata-pult appeared, operated by a dwarf.

'What the blazes?' he murmured in surprise.

'It's groundlings! At sea! Despite Elria's curse!' Szmajro laughed out loud. 'What have they built themselves there? It looks like a cork bobbing about on the water.'

The steel sling contraption on the submersible was spraying out its missiles in a steady flow as the long-haired grey-bearded dwarf swept the muzzle from side to side. The flat discs danced from wave to wave, striking the eight-master's hull either just above or just below the waterline, making holes in the wooden planking. But before the älfar had managed to train their own fire on this unexpected enemy, the foe disappeared back under the surface.

'Oh, that was very neat,' Szmajro chortled.

'Just look! The ship's starting to list!' Goïmron forgot for a few moments that he and the dragon were in a state of extreme disagreement with each other.

All of a sudden the strange metal barrel boat surfaced again on the port side of the sailing vessel. The dwarf on board was letting the bouncing disc shots off, targeting the ship's stern, punching new holes in the wooden structure, then diving down again under the waves before the älfar could return fire.

The hollow spaces in the huge sea-going craft started to fill up with sea water and the enormous ship began to sink, sending up great fountains of water as it went down. Älfar were struggling in the waves. Many were picked up by the escort boats until there was no more room. Not all were saved.

'They're mine.' Szmajro was delighted at the prospect. 'And then, my little dwarf-louse, we'll have a word about what you and the Waveline army are going to do for me.'

'For you?' Goïmron felt for his weapon stick for reassurance.

'I am Ûra's heir and have thus inherited the right to rule over the whole of Girdlegard,' declared Szmajro smugly. 'First thing is to get rid of the black-eyes in Dsôn Khamateion. I'll free my sister from the zhussa's hold on her. And you will all help me. Humans, dwarves, elves and meldriths. You are my army. All of you.'

'No! No, you can't make us do that!' Goïmron envisaged thousands dying in the attempt to defeat the älfar. And just as many losing their lives offering resistance to the demands of this dragon. *By Vraccas! It's disaster either way if I can't restrain him.*

'Of course I can. If you don't follow my orders I'll make you all pay. It'll be the worst thing you've ever experienced.' Szmajro circled the last of the sinking warships.

'You agreed to accept my authority,' said Goïmron, trying again to talk Szmajro out of his plan. All the while he was cautiously drawing the bone blade out of its walking stick sheath. *I need to place this exactly between the vertebrae at the joint with the two necks.* He was seated in the optimum position for this.

'I told you before: I was mistaken. I felt the aura from the gemstone and attributed it to you,' the dragon argued back. 'That's the only reason you're still alive, dwarf-louse. If you behave yourself and win your friends round for me I might even make you their commander.'

He'd make me his Voice. Like Stémna was Ûra's. I'm not having that! Goïmron had retrieved the sharp slim blade fashioned out of the beak of a flame flyer.

DON'T DO IT! YOU'D NEVER SURVIVE!

'I've got to! Get ready. I'll need your magic strength in order to thrust the dagger right through his spinal column.'

IF YOU KILL HIM THE SCALDING HOT BLOOD WILL COVER YOU. YOU'LL BE BOILED ALIVE. OR OTHERWISE YOU'LL BE KILLED BY THE FALL.

I HAVE TO DO THIS. May Vraccas be by my side. I'll do it for the sake of Girdlegard. And for Rodana.

Girdlegard

Magic Realm of Rhuta
Western Frontier
1024 P.Q. (7515th solar cycle in old reckoning), late winter

Klaey looked at the big mirror over the shelf and the heavy studded metal box into which visitors were expected to post their permits. In normal times, that is.

But on this orbit the reflecting screen was displaying the following message in large letters:

**NO VISITS
TO THE MAGIC REALM OF RHUTA
ARE POSSIBLE
AT THE PRESENT TIME**

Damn and blast! No matter what they tried, Klaey and his people were unable to cross the threshold. A magic barrier prevented them from entering Rhuta. They had made numerous attempts: at a run, sidling up slowly, walking forwards, sideways or even backwards. Klaey tried kissing his new poppy-flower-shaped lapis lazuli amulet for luck. Nothing worked. There was a powerful spell blocking the approach to the border.

'So near and yet so far!' Iowna complained. She was famed as one of the best and brightest of the Brigantian army: an excellent shot and highly experienced in reconnaissance. The thirty-year-old was held to be merciless and purposeful in action. 'We've worn holes in our boots and thoroughly exhausted ourselves on the march to get here. And now what?' She directed an accusing look at Klaey.

He pushed his fingers through his long black hair and adjusted his cap so it concealed the family-brand mark on his brow. 'I confess I find myself at a loss here.' *To Cadengis with the lot of them – every single stupid Rhuta magician.*

'So what do we do now? Wait here till the border opens up? But by that time Mostro will have got back. We can't take him on.' Furiously, Iowna kicked at a stone. 'A thousand and one demons! All that effort for nothing! There's sackfuls of treasure over there, bloody laughing at us.'

'We might just as well have held up the coaches we saw on the way or plundered the farms we passed,' another mumbled crossly.

'Or we could have set us up a nice comfortable camp. We could have made a name for ourselves as formidable highway-men,' a third joined in the chorus of the malcontents.

'Just settle down, you lot. We'll find a way round this.' Klaey looked into the distance. 'Let's try again another—'

'You want to send us on another forced march? You must be joking,' spat Iowna. 'How far? The border is sealed. Vanéra or one of her predecessors made sure of that. The magicians would hardly have chosen to leave their realm open to invasion while they were away, would they? This invisible wall is intended to keep out monsters and invading armies. We'll have no earthly chance of breaking through. We're just a miserable handful of Brigantians.'

'You won't have to break in,' came a throaty voice behind them. 'Klaey Berengart, I demand you surrender. You and your troop find yourselves in my power. Don't put up any resistance. It wouldn't go well for you.'

Klaey turned to face the speaker. It was a srgāláh in an aggressive stance. Pointed ears were pricked upright, and the nostrils at the end of the long muzzle quivered in excitement. In his hands he carried an extra-long spear with a hooked blade. The badges and medals on his leather armour and on his cloak clearly demonstrated the identity of the figure confronting Klaey here. There were not many srgāláh in Girdlegard who were so distinguished. 'You must be Sònuk?'

'Yes, I am. I've been following you the whole way. You could not shake me off but we were travelling very fast, I must admit.' Sònuk motioned with the spear tip for them all to get down on their knees. 'I'll be tying you all up. And then we'll make our way to the nearest sizeable village. That's a couple of orbits' march away. I know you're well used to walking.'

The Brigantians did not move. They looked questioningly to their leader. Srgāláh were feared adversaries in battle. Agile and nimble on their feet, they could attack with a range of weapons as well as using their strong teeth and sharp claws. They also had special skills enabling them instinctively to sense what moves their enemies might be about to make.

Klaey cleared his throat. *There's a dozen of us. We might have three or four casualties and maybe one fatality. Shouldn't be worse than that.*

'Why not take us in to Rhuta? It's much closer,' he suggested slyly.

'Because no one can get in.'

'Not even you?'

Sònuk shook his head. 'Down on your knees.'

Klaey took a deep breath. 'I'm afraid you'll have to make us.' At this his own people drew their swords, sabres and daggers. 'We shan't be submitting voluntarily. There's so many more of us—'

Without warning Sònuk leaped forward, slamming the flat side of his long blade into Iowna's face, knocking the female Brigantian senseless. She lay in the mud, apparently unharmed apart from the bruising.

'My final warning,' he growled. 'On. Your. Knees.'

Three of Klaey's men backed away from the srgāláh, who was now baring his teeth. The others looked more determined than ever, their weapons raised in the air.

'So, try your luck, why don't you?' Klaey drew his rapier and kissed his lucky amulet. 'We shan't surrender!'

'Your choice. I'll keep asking. When you've had enough, just let me know.' Sònuk went on the attack, whirling his spear with incredible dexterity to meet the sword thrusts made by the Brigantians. He delivered blows on his opponents, causing superficial wounds. Klaey kept to the sidelines and waited until there was a short pause in the fighting. *I think I've got my calculations wrong. It's going to be a near thing for us.* Four more of his soldiers were down in the mud, bewildered and clutching their injuries. *Oh, well.* Glancing reproachfully at his talisman, Klaey pulled out his dagger and went in, rapier and knife in hand. *Here goes . . .*

A sudden whirring sound like a flock of birds, coupled with loud furious neighing – and a dark shadow smashed into Sònuk's chest. Lightning flashes sparked as hooves struck the metal-studded leather armour. Losing his grip on his spear, the srgāláh was hurled backwards by a sudden burst of explosive energy.

'Deathwing!' Klaey exclaimed in delighted amazement. 'Good boy! Finish the bastard off for me!'

Before Sònuk could retaliate, the flight-mare had grabbed him in its teeth and was hauling him off into the sky, to then drop him from a great height. The srgāláh fell like a stone. Klaey could not see where he landed. The winged stallion set off in pursuit. As soon as he saw the flight-mare Klaey knew what to do. *Of course! That's the way!*

'Deathwing! Here, boy!' he called, putting his weapons away. 'Look to the injured,' he ordered his band, seeing the stallion approaching him again, neighing loudly. 'I'll make sure of the Chamber of Wonders and then I'll come back for you all.'

'What are you planning?' Iowna struggled up to sitting, a hand to her swollen cheek.

'I'll be flying *over* the confounded barrier. It must end somewhere up there. Vanéra used to pay tribute to Ûra. So it must have been possible for the dragon to fly into Rhuta despite the magic barricade,' he explained swiftly before swinging himself up on to the creature's back. He caressed the stallion's neck, noting how the flight-mare's mouth was dripping with the srgáláh's blood. 'How I've missed you. You and your lovely sharp teeth.'

'Don't you dare abandon us, Klaey. I swear, I'll find you if you try to leave us in the lurch,' Iowna threatened. 'Remember my archery skills.'

'Have a bit more faith, Iowna. And don't worry about Sònuk. He won't be coming back. What do you reckon? Shall we be Rhuta's next rulers?' he called down exuberantly as he flew off on Deathwing. 'How about I make you the Minister for Lost Faith?'

'You can do one, Klaey Berengart!' Iowna laughed. 'You'll be the Minister for Empty Promises, then!'

He flew higher and higher on the flight-mare, leaving the ground far below. Klaey kept testing to see if the barrier had stopped. The air was getting thinner. Just when he thought he would have to give up, Deathwing flew over the invisible barrier and they were swooping down into the interior of the land, heading south.

I knew it! Let's go and plunder the Chamber of Wonders. We'll take all the treasure we can find. Klaey directed the flight-mare towards Vanélia, the capital city, which they reached quickly just as dusk was falling. The maga's palace was easy to spot. He got Deathwing to land on the roof. They had not been observed and they had the cover of darkness now.

'You wait here for me,' he said to the snorting stallion. He rubbed the blaze on Deathwing's head. 'Eat anything you like. Except for me, of course.' The stallion whinnied and swished its tail. 'Hey! Keep quiet, though!' He slipped away silently, hurrying off.

Klaey found a way down inside the building, and went along corridors, up and down steps and across halls, avoiding palace guards and servants who were going about their duties, putting lighted candles in place to illuminate the rooms. The statues and paintings portraying the maga had been draped with mourning out of respect. Klaey found it easy to make his way through the palace. Nobody had been expecting any kind of intruder. After a long time he reached the entrance to the Chamber of Wonders. *There you are, you very special thing!*

He was not dismayed at finding the gold-studded double portal of highly polished light grey liguster wood closed. Discarding his heavy mantle and his cap, he took out his lock-breaking equipment and stepped forward. *I just hope there isn't a spell on the entrance door. Or I'm done for.* Ready for anything, after kissing his lucky charm, and with his lips firmly pressed together in concentration, he started to insert the various tools into the lock – only to see that it was already open. Vanéra had obviously trusted her subjects implicitly.

Or could it be there's someone inside? Someone on the make, wanting to help himself, like me? Klaey pushed the door a little way open and slipped inside without making a sound.

Inside he found the cavernous hall fully illuminated. Shelves and cupboards on all sides went right up to the ceiling. An unfeasibly large number of artefacts met his gaze, piled high in random heaps. Candelabras and lanterns floated through the room by magic.

By the mother of Cadengis! Klaey stepped up to the balustrade and looked down at a thirty-pace-high forest of shelves and magic objects. *How am I supposed to find anything in here?* His plan had worked well so far but now the whole project was in danger of collapsing. He scratched his head in confusion – and out of the corner of his eye saw a figure moving. It was a woman, dressed in deep mourning. She had stepped on to the landing out of a small chamber. He recognised her face from paintings he had seen in the hall. *Adelia? Damn!* The famula had managed to cross Girdlegard to return to Rhuta quicker than he and his Brigantians had. *She mustn't see me. I'm done for if she raises the alarm. Or hell and blast, what if she attacks me with one of her confounded artefacts?*

He had to do something. He crept closer, grabbing Adelia from behind and jabbing at her throat with the point of his dagger. 'Don't make a sound!'

She froze. Then she turned her head towards him and laughed. 'I know you. It's Klaey Berengart, the Croaker, isn't it? That voice is unique. And I can see your face and the brand on your forehead. You're on all the Wanted posters.'

'The Whisperer. Not The Croaker.' Klaey pushed her towards the wooden guard rail. 'Keep your eyes front, famula. I want no trouble from you. Tell me which the most valuable and effective artefacts are for me to take. Then show me to the treasure store and after a brief visit there I'll be gone.'

'So this is a robbery campaign, far away from the army of your enemies? It's always a good idea to do the unexpected,' she said, nodding in approval.

'Exactly.' Klaey increased the pressure on her throat, though he regretted having to do that. Her long blonde hair was tickling his nose. 'Right? I'm all ears.'

But the famula did not move. 'How about we do a deal, Klaey Berengart?'

'You what?'

'A business deal to our mutual advantage.'

Klaey could not resist. 'How do you mean?'

'You pretend you've captured Rhuta and that I'm your hostage. I'll make sure no one comes in to harm you,' Adelia suggested. 'No soldiers. No other beings, either.'

Klaey was not for one heartbeat taken in by the sincerity of the proposal. It sounded far too good to be true. And it did not make any sense. 'Your friend Mostro will chuck us out pretty sharpish. Or is this a trick of yours, so he can catch us and then play the conquering hero?'

The famula gave a loud laugh full of contempt. It echoed from the walls. 'On the contrary! I hate him. It would be a delight if I could bar him from the place.'

Have a think. Why would she even do that? Klaey recalled that it was really Adelia, as the senior famula, who should have taken over in Rhuta on the death of her mistress, Vanéra. Mostro had flouted tradition and the maga's wishes. *Right. So she has every reason to want to go along with this little game.* 'And you're sure you can do that?'

'Of course I can. I'm the only one with any idea about the artefacts. Vanéra never knew what was in here and Mostro did not show any inclination to use artefacts to make spells. He wanted to be known as a genuine magus,' she said. 'We've got everything we need to keep the fellow away.'

'And you could say we'd forced you to go along with my demands,' said Klaey with a laugh. 'You'd be able to talk your way out of it if there were a coup.'

'You've got it. You would have your own realm and I would administer it for you. The people trust me and they like me. They don't trust Mostro. And you wouldn't have to keep wandering around Girdlegard all the time with enemies in hot pursuit because of the price on your head.' Adelia turned round slowly and looked at the blade in his hand. 'Now, why don't you put the question I can see in your eyes?'

Klaey was taking a liking to the famula. She was devious, unscrupulous and very amiable. *Suits me down to the ground.* 'How do I know you won't use your artefacts against me and my people as soon as I remove my knife from your throat?'

'Because I could have done it a dozen times over by now.' Adelia lifted her left hand to reveal a fan she was holding. 'With this. I can use it to make a draught strong enough to blow you straight off this platform and send you over the balustrade. All the way,' she said, pointing thirty paces down.

With a grin Klaey removed the dagger and stowed it away in his belt. 'We seem to have ourselves a very workable agreement, Adelia.' He proffered his hand. 'You'll soon find I am the nicest rogue imaginable.'

She shook hands without hesitation. 'I succumb to my fate at once, cruel Brigantian. But don't think of trying to double-cross me. Rhuta has many, many secrets that only *I* know about. Without those secrets Mostro would make short work of you.'

'Then it seems I should marry you without delay.'

Adelia smiled at him. 'I know where your people are waiting. I can bring them in through the barrier. I'll send a wagon so they don't have to walk here. They were making quite a fuss about how far you'd insisted they march.'

'You heard all that?'

'The mirrors can do more than just show us who's looking at them, Klaey Berengart.' Adelia went over to the entrance. 'Have yourself a good look around. After all, you've just taken over the whole magic realm, haven't you? Then I'll meet you and your people in the dining hall. They'll be quite hungry by now.'

Klaey watched the young woman in her mourning robes leave the Chamber. He couldn't suppress the grin on his face. *A bold plan.* He moved down the steps, gave his pendant a grateful kiss, and then had a stroll through the archive of Wonders piled high on every side. *Best game ever.* Laughter escaped his lips. *Ruler of Rhuta, eh?* In name only, of course, but the outside world did not need to know that.

Klaey nearly got lost in the labyrinth. Looking up at the landing with its balustrade gave him his bearings again. As he was walking around he came across a note on the floor in one of the corridors that seemed to be unusually tidy and carefully ordered. He picked it up and read the inventory listing for that section:

Artefact No. 7862

THE STONE OF MISFORTUNE

A flawless sea sapphire mounted in a dragon-shaped setting.

Origin of the gemstone: the Brown Mountains

Quality: fully charged with magic energy.

ATTENTION: FOR ADORNMENT ONLY

IT MUST NEVER be taken to the Wonder Zone

&

NEVER come into contact with sea water.

Or the disaster inherent in the jewel cannot be averted.

Stone of Misfortune? By the mother of Cadengis – I don't want that one. Klaey put the label back on the floor where he had found it. The description jogged something in his memory. *I hope I can find some better artefacts.* He wondered what other treasures the blonde-haired famula could show him. And he found himself greatly looking forward to seeing Adelia's smile again.

Other dwarves are considering a dangerous notion, namely whether the Children of the Smith should rule over the whole of Girdlegard. Is this the new intention of Vraccas and is this why the god has created the new ranges of mountains deep inside the land? Was his plan to shake the dwarves out of the mountains in order that they seize the opportunity and become the true protectors, governing the whole of Girdlegard?

This is also being discussed in secret assemblies, it is said.

Dar Whjenn, academic expert in the fields of flora, fauna and the laws of nature

XVII

Girdlegard

Inland Sea
1024 P.Q. (7515th solar cycle in old reckoning), late winter

Goïmron inserted the tip of the bone blade carefully in between the hard carapace scales, impossible to pierce, given their magic protective power. *I do this in Rodana's name! This is for her sake!*

He made a decisive stabbing motion, needing the help of the sea sapphire to give extra strength – but before the blade had gone in by half a finger length Szmajro shrieked and bucked, somersaulting in the air. The centrifugal force sent the dwarf flying and the weapon slipped out of the dragon's body, leaving a mere scratch. Hot blood dripped from between the scales, dropping on to Goïmron's clothing and directly on to his neck and face. The liquid hissed and fizzed as it burned his flesh, making him yell out with pain.

It was utterly impossible for Goïmron to hang on. Screaming, he plunged down towards the sea. The surface of the water grew larger by the second, and the foam-topped waves seemed to swell in size.

Szmajro appeared at his side, one muzzle open wide. 'Traitor!' the dragon roared. 'You'll be sorry for what you've done! I'm going to devour you even as you fall!'

'Get away!' Goïmron slashed out with the bone weapon,

striking the dragon's snout. The blade left a gaping wound and the dragon's head recoiled in fury.

ARMS BY YOUR SIDE! QUICK! the gemstone instructed. CHIN ON CHEST. TOO LATE TO TURN ROUND.

Goïmron followed the order just in time before splashing down. The violent impact robbed him of his senses for several heartbeats. Totally bemused, he struggled in the black water, having no idea which way was up. He was short of breath and the extreme chill was making movement increasingly difficult. His limbs were beginning to seize up. He imagined Elria was holding him fast in her arms and dragging him down to the depths.

HEAD FOR THE LIGHT. PULL YOURSELF TOGETHER. SWIM TOWARDS THE LIGHT!

Making a huge effort, Goïmron managed to re-orient himself and head towards the sunlight. He resorted to doggy-paddling. By now his teeth were chattering with the cold and his muscles were weakened by the immersion in icy water.

Gasping for air, he surfaced. Luckily, he located some floating wreckage he could cling to and eventually climb out on to. *I am alive!* There was blood running out of his nose. It had a metallic taste.

BUT YOU WON'T STAY THAT WAY FOR LONG UNLESS YOU DO EXACTLY AS I SAY.

Goïmron saw Szmajro flying around overhead. The dragon was searching for him. *And he'll find me pretty soon.* 'What can I do against this beast? It's immune against magic.' Shivering, he raised himself up on his elbows and noticed that he had somehow kept hold of the bone-bladed weapon. 'You jolly well let me down just now!'

I TOLD YOU I KNEW A BETTER SPELL.

Goïmron had a vague recollection of this. 'Will it work?'

IT'S A SPELL I ONCE OVERHEARD A GREAT MAGICIAN CAST. I NEVER THOUGHT I'D EVER HAVE OCCASION TO

USE IT. HOLD ME UNDER THE WATER AND REPEAT THE
WORDS I'M GOING TO TELL YOU.

Letting out a long screech of triumph from both mouths,
Szmajro swooped back towards the dwarf in a wide curve.
Goïmron's whereabouts had been discovered.

I have no choice. Shaking, he inched his way forward on the
wreckage, held the gem in its dragon-shaped setting under the
water and repeated word for word what the stone whispered
into his mind. A hot stabbing sensation pierced his hand. The
sapphire glowed as bright as a small blue sun. At the same time
the dragon-mount frame fell away from the jewel and slipped
out of the dwarf's trembling fingers. Finally, the sapphire lost
its glow – and it shattered.

'Oh, no!' Goïmron pulled his hand back. The fragments fell
on to the makeshift raft and shrank in size until they were
washed away by the waves. *I've made a terrible mistake here! I must
have said the spell wrong!* He looked on horrified as the last of the
tiny shards disappeared. *The last chance to defeat Szmajro and, idiot
that I am, I've scuppered it.*

There was strong gust of wind. 'So there you are!' Hovering
by means of powerful wing-strokes, the double-headed dragon
was directly above Goïmron's floating wreckage. The creature's
blood-red eyes gazed down in contempt. 'You have just got rid
of your own special quality, haven't you? Without the gemstone
all you are now is a tasty morsel for me.'

Using the very last of his strength, Goïmron raised himself
up and pointed his weapon at the beast. 'You'll find me very
indigestible,' he promised in a shaky voice. 'I'll do my best to
make sure of that!'

Szmajro descended slowly, snorting with disdain. Anticipa-
tory drool dripped out of both mouths. 'I'll find someone
sensible to put my demands to Girdlegard. I'll tell them what
I've done with you. I'll tell them what you tasted like.'

All of a sudden a powerful jet of sea water gushed up next to the wreckage with explosive force. A spout ten paces high drenched Goïmron in ice-cold water. Spray went everywhere. In the middle of these geyser-like eruptions a slim body shot up, grabbed the loudly shrieking dragon and dragged it down below the surface. High waves rocked the wreckage, toppling Goïmron back into the sea. This time he was quicker off the mark at reacting to his circumstances. He fought his way up through the bubbles and managed to grasp hold of a wooden spar once more.

About thirty paces away from his wreckage-raft the waters seethed and churned, with foam and moisture vapour droplets obscuring the dwarf's view. From time to time Szmajro's tail jerked convulsively in the water, and a head with fire horns emerged, while the rust-coloured dragon hollered and screamed so loud that Goïmron was forced to stop his own ears so as not to be deafened. White and red tongues of flame appeared, only to be hissingly extinguished.

So it worked! The spell had created a magic creature working to drown Szmajro. *I only hope it's powerful enough.*

The dragon's resistance soon weakened. The splashing, spattering and bubbling died away. Apart from pungent clouds of salty vapour that stung in the eyes, the sea was calm.

What's happened to Szmajro? Goïmron, soaked to the skin, could hardly feel his own body anymore. Had it not been for the sturdy plank of wood he was draped over, he would have gone to the bottom. *Just like the dragon.*

HANG ON IN THERE, said the sapphire, astonishingly. YOU'LL BE PICKED UP IN A SHORT TIME BY AN UNDER-WATER BOAT.

'What just happened?' Shivering, Goïmron looked around, but could see nobody.

YOU HAVE BROKEN THE SPELL THAT HAD ME BOUND

TO THE SAPPHIRE. I HAD THOUGHT I SHOULD NEVER BE FREE OF IT.

'Free?' Goïmron stuttered, coughing up some of the salt water he had swallowed. 'I thought you were the gemstone?'

NO. I WAS THE FIGURE THE JEWEL WAS SET IN. IT WAS NEVER THE STONE SPEAKING TO YOU. FORGIVE THE DECEPTION. I THOUGHT OTHERWISE YOU WOULD NOT TAKE ME ALONG.

'So . . . you were a real dragon all that time?' It was all starting to make sense.

A VERY LONG TIME AGO, FAR AWAY FROM HERE I WAS CAPTURED AND A SPELL WAS PUT ON ME. BUT YOU GAVE ME A GLIMMER OF HOPE. AND NOW YOU HAVE GIVEN ME MY FREEDOM. I SHALL BE ETERNALLY IN YOUR DEBT.

Goïmron had so many questions but he was so tired, so incredibly tired. The teeth-chattering and the bouts of shivering were lessening, however. 'What is your name?'

WHENEVER YOU NEED ME JUST HEAD FOR THE SEA, PLACE YOUR FACE IN THE WATER AND CALL THREE TIMES. TALLAS. AND I'LL APPEAR.

Goïmron did not want this new dragon to disappear. 'Don't go away! We're going to need you against . . .'

I AM A SEA DRAGON, GOÏMRON. AWAY FROM MY OWN ELEMENT THERE IS NOT MUCH I CAN DO. BUT I WILL HELP YOU WHEREVER, WHENEVER I CAN.

Goïmron saw bubbles rising up next to his wooden spar. They heralded the surfacing of the submersible craft he had previously espied from up in the air. A hatch opened and a grey-bearded dwarf clambered out. Walking with a pronounced limp, he came closer, bearing a boathook. 'I seem to have arrived just in time to thumb my nose at Elria,' he said, relief in his voice. 'Right, lad. On board with you and welcome. Let's get you warmed up.'

I SHOULD PREFER IT IF YOU KEPT ME SECRET. I GIVE YOU MY WORD NEVER TO HARM GIRDLEGARD'S PEOPLE.

'Agreed,' Goïmron murmured.

'I'd have been extremely surprised, in the circumstances, had you not agreed,' the dwarf responded, yanking the floating plank closer. He heaved Goïmron out of the water. 'I'm Xanomir. Welcome on board the good ship *Buvendil*.'

ONE MORE THING. YOU ARE NOT A MAGUS. ANYTHING MAGIC THAT HAPPENED WAS DOWN TO ME. MIND YOU DON'T TRY YOUR HAND IN BATTLE THINKING YOU ARE ANY KIND OF MAGICIAN.

'That would indeed be better,' Goïmron whispered.

'Yes, very much better. You're right. It's nice and warm down here.' Xanomir led him to the hatch.

I WILL GO AND DEAL WITH THE LAST OF THE ÄLFAR WARSHIPS. STAY SAFE, GOÏMRON CHISELCUT. MY THANKS TO YOU.

As the sea dragon's voice faded away and Goïmron felt his own senses failing, he knew for certain: *I am going to miss him.*

Girdlegard

Sinterich
1024 P.Q. (7515th solar cycle in old reckoning), late winter

Gata was rocking gently backwards and forwards in her comfortable chair. The sunshine was inviting her outside to take a little walk round Waveline's roads and lanes with their brightly coloured houses and painted wooden shutters.

But she resisted the call to go exploring. It would not be polite to leave the meeting, even if she had nothing to contribute to the current topic under discussion, namely the future of Undarimar.

Gata liked it here in the little coastal town, though she found the extreme proximity of the sea to the inn where she was staying a little unnerving. It was disturbing, rather than relaxing, as others had commented, to behold nothing but an endless expanse of water on looking out of her window in the mornings. She was keen to get back to the familiar landscape of the Brown Mountains.

There is so much I have to do, back at home, now that the greatest dangers have been removed. Gata looked round at the others. They were meeting in a large room that normally functioned as the local dance hall. Tables and chairs had been brought in. The various delegations – humans, dwarves, elves and meldriths – were considering how matters should best be progressed. The powerful leaders were accustomed to discussions on this level. They knew and respected the rules of debate, well aware that if everyone tried to speak at once in a meeting it would take that much longer to reach any agreement.

With Goïmron at his side, Tungdil Goldhand sat in the centre, chairing the discussion, which sometimes was in danger of becoming heated. He attempted to steer the meeting towards solutions that ensured no one would feel disadvantaged. At the start of the meeting the dwarf tribes had appointed the venerable figure as their Honorary High King in acknowledgement of his decisive contribution to making Girdlegard safe from enemy attack.

Gata's attitude was not quite so positive.

Her own realm had suffered losses when the tunnels had collapsed. A valuable fortress out in the east would undoubtedly soon be overrun by mobs of marauding beasts. She had, however, voted with the others when it came to awarding Goldhand's honorary title. Goldhand was a Thirdling. This gave her own folk great prestige. The actual throne of an official High King, as opposed to the honorary one, remained empty for the present.

Speaking on behalf of an obviously tired Tungdil Goldhand, Goïmron announced, 'Good, we are agreed.' His face and neck still showed the burn marks received in the encounter with Szmajro. Gata thought the scars rather suited the slightly built Fourthling, who had matured during the past semi-cycle, giving him a new air of self-confidence and assurance. She thought he would have looked good at her side. *But he has chosen another.*

'The motion before the meeting: Following the älfar defeat Undarimar has surrendered and has declared itself ready to sign peace treaties with all the neighbouring states. In the light of this the coastal realms will eschew any demands for compensation payments for damage sustained. Are we so resolved?'

Hands went up to signify agreement.

But what will such a treaty actually be worth by the end of this cycle? Let's wait and see. Gata voted with the rest.

'Motion carried,' said Goïmron. 'Next item on the agenda: the matter of the salt sea orcs and the mysterious figure of Borkon. Has everyone had sight of the notes I sent round?'

Gata nodded and recalled the paper Barbandor had shown her: pages of notes giving details of encounters with Mòndarcai and Borkon, explaining the unfamiliar flags seen in Kràg Tahuum, the puzzling words uttered by the orc found under the rubble, saying he would rather die than be a prisoner and a traitor. The paper went on to note the inexplicable immortality enjoyed by Borkon and his kind.

'To emphasise the seriousness of the situation he has reported on, Barbandor has made the effort to come to Waveline to address us in person.' Goïmron gave a signal to the guard on the door. 'Let us welcome the hero!'

The doors of the converted ballroom opened. Applause greeted the entrance of the dark-haired councillor from Platinshine. Gata could see at once that the dwarf had lost a considerable amount of weight. Her friend's features had become harder as result of what he had gone through. The first silver threads were showing in the dark beard. They went well with the beard clips of white gold.

'What a wonderful surprise!' She could not resist getting up and going over to embrace him. 'You are the bravest of all of us.'

Barbandor returned the warm greeting, while Belîngor and Brûgar clapped him on the shoulders. Then Hargorina came up to give him a hug. In his armour and with the white sash of office he had the air of a king.

'Compared to Gyndala and the others I got off lightly.' Barbandor stood beside Goïmron. 'I have made the long journey from Platinshine in order to warn you all about the danger Borkon poses. I wanted to address you in person, in case my letters have not been able to convince you.'

'They have, friend Barbandor,' Telinâs assured him, interrupting his usual crafting activities. This time it had been a dragon he had been making from folded paper. 'Absolutely and completely.'

'I know you have read my report. I swear by Vraccas that every word is true and I have not exaggerated.' Barbandor's words were heartfelt. 'Whatever that blue-skinned bastard is planning – we have to stop him, now that Undarimar and the älfar allies have been defeated. Or he and his brood will go on multiplying until the orbit comes when he discards his apparently peaceable nature and turns on us all. What are they waiting for? What will happen to Girdlegard then? We have to act. All of us. Humans, dwarves, elves and meldriths.'

The meeting applauded, addressing his words and acknowledging his achievements.

Gata returned to her seat. 'I suggest we—'

'One moment, please.' Goïmron broke in with a smile. 'A messenger arrived this morning with news.' He waved the letter. 'It is from Borkon.'

People started to whisper.

'I'm afraid there was no time to make copies for everyone. The letter is written in Old Dwarfish. So I will do my best to translate as I go.' Goïmron cleared his throat and began. 'My greetings to the elves, dwarves, humans and meldriths of Girdlegard. As I presume Barbandor Steelgold will have told you about his time with us I should like to assure you that I have no evil intentions.' Goïmron stifled a laugh. 'We do not want war. Not with any of you. To back up my assertions I am always ready to provide hostages from our highest-placed families. Signed: Borkon.' He lowered the paper. 'No mention of the prophecy.'

'Well, of course not! They're going to wait till they get the sign they were promised,' Barbandor broke in excitedly. 'And then they'll attack. Borkon's little note wants to persuade us not to undertake anything against him and his pig-faces. But can we afford to stand idly by?'

'Our people are very unlikely to be in a position to conquer their territories and certainly would never be able to hang on to them,' the Gauragon representative objected. 'The Fire Fields and the Salt Sea are lethal places. For us, that is.'

'Borkon is well aware of that. That's why it's easy for him to claim to be peaceable. He knows we can't attack,' countered Barbandor. 'This scribbled note shows his disdain and contempt. And it's the height of mockery to have composed it in Old Dwarfish! How can he have dared do that?'

You have a point. Gata looked over at Mostro. 'What do you say, Magus? Are you able to solve the problem, seeing as Goïmron has unfortunately lost his amethyst while fighting Szmajro?'

The arrogant young man was delighted. For the meeting he

had draped himself in the most expensive of royal-looking robes, in the hope of getting a chance to speak. With a friendly but patronising air he arranged his flowing locks and touched his pointed beard. 'I shall come up with something to put this blue-skinned monster out of action. And I'll do it before it can carry out its plan.'

His bodyguard Darislaff stood behind him. In reality this was Hantu, transformed. As Sònuk was still somewhere in Girdlegard hunting down the last of the Berengarts, there was nothing to prevent the rhamak appearing in the midst of all the delegates. Only a fine sense of smell would reveal him for what he was.

Gata still wanted to slit Hantu's throat to remove the danger he posed. She wanted to do it this very instant. Right here. Right now. But she had not forgotten Goïmron's warning. Surrounded as he was by beings from another sphere, he would be immune from any attack on his person. *I'll wager Mostro has absolutely no idea what steps Hantu has taken to ensure his own safety. To protect himself from Mostro, as well.*

'So can I take it you are in favour of our attacking Borkon, esteemed Magus?' she asked

'Give me a little time to reflect, Queen Regnorgata. I expect I shall find a spell or an artefact that will eliminate him. I'm sure it won't be necessary to send in our troops,' Mostro replied boastfully. 'There will be something in my Chamber of Wonders that can give him a deadly shock.'

'Fine. Then we will leave you in peace to get on with your research in the matter,' Goïmron said decisively, turning to the assembled delegates. 'Had it not been for our friend Barbandor's report we might well have been content to sue for peace. But we are aware now of the true intentions from that quarter. We are thus forced to take arms against Borkon. Are we agreed on that score?'

Gata was the first to raise her hand in agreement. She could not take her eyes off Mostro's bodyguard. She would have to think of how best he was to be dealt with. *Perhaps it can be done in conjunction with the zhussa? She might collaborate to thank me for arranging Dsôn is not attacked, perhaps.* The rhamak would not know anything about älfar magic. *He won't notice Ascatoîa until it's too late.*

Realising that his speech and his report had indeed had the required effect, Barbandor heaved a sigh of relief. 'The sooner we go ahead, the better. Just imagine what would happen if we were faced with vast armies of more or less indestructible orcs!' He turned to Goïmron and Goldhand. 'I hope the assembly will forgive me. I must send out some messages. On the morrow I shall be travelling back up north to arrange, with Gautaya and Gauragon, to keep an eye on the pig-faces. Continuous surveillance.' The delegates of the two realms he had named nodded. 'May Vraccas send you his blessings and help you make wise decisions.' He left the hall to a fresh round of applause. 'And this evening I would like to drink a toast with all of you. A toast to life and to the future of Girdlegard.'

After Barbandor had withdrawn from the meeting the next item for discussion was about the north-eastern region of Girdlegard. It was almost as if Goldhand had read Gata's mind. Bendoïn was keen to draw attention to the fact that Dsôn Khamateion was situated deep in the Brown Mountains and thus in Fourthling land. This should not be tolerated, he stressed. At the same time, he said, there was much too much to do in their newly liberated territory with all the work involved in removing every trace of Brigantian influence. It would take many cycles before the accustomed state of defences was restored.

This is the notch where I'll set my next axe thrust. Gata raised her hand and was given leave to speak. 'We Thirdlings are ready and willing to act against the black-eyes,' she told the assembly. 'But the recent fighting has taken its toll on all of us. It would also be strategically unsound to start a new war before the Fourthling kingdom is properly secured. I'm sure you are aware of that, King Bendoïn, given how long you were in command of your tribe's border fortresses.' Feinunz gave a slightly hesitant nod. 'Who knows what mines and tunnels the Brigantians may have dug that are marked on none of our maps. If such tunnels exist it would be possible, using them, for black-eyes to reach the Fourthlings before we can get there to defend them. And the black-eyes have a witch and two dragons.'

'Don't worry about all of that. Leave it to me,' Mostro butted in, patronisingly. 'I'll find a solution very soon to deal with that problem as well.'

'Don't forget we know about the älfar fleet, honoured queen. Xanomir's submersible vessel was able to retrieve some of the flasks of acid from the seabed. A proven remedy against the dragons,' Goïmron added in a friendly tone. 'As soon as we have analysed the acid Girdlegard's alchemical specialists can set about producing sufficient stores of it. We should never have to fear dragons again.'

This news was greeted with expressions of great relief. The delegates banged their tankards on the table in approval.

I'm going to talk them out of marching on Dsôn. 'That's great,' Gata called, then she waited for the hubbub to die down so she could continue. 'How would it be if we thoroughly explore the Fourthling territory and do a technical survey with accurate measurements? That wouldn't take longer than ten cycles, I would say.'

'It'll be done much quicker than that.' Goldhand raised his croaky voice. 'My people, the ones who prepared the tunnels for the planned demolition, have noted every recent alteration.

They can send their maps over to the Brown Mountains whenever the Fourthlings are ready. That will make things simpler for you, King Bendoïn.'

Curses. Gata restrained herself, not wanting to let her face show how disappointed she was. 'All the better,' she managed to say with a smile. 'But I should still allow five cycles for the work. There will be repairs needing doing on the fortress after all the bombardments during the siege.'

'I agree with Queen Regnorgata,' said Telìnâs. The paper dragon he had been making had now morphed into the figure of an älf. 'The campaign against Dsôn Khamateion should wait until we have sufficient acid-flask ammunition, our esteemed Magus Mostro has found us the right artefacts, and the Fourthlings have sorted out their defences. We do not want to risk heavy losses by pressing ahead recklessly.'

The elf's contribution was welcomed, much to Gata's relief. This meant she was not the only one present to be advising caution. *Just as well, or it would make my objections too obvious.*

'If Mòndarcai were to turn up and offer us another pact,' Goldhand went on, 'I am of the opinion that we should accept it.' All eyes in the room were suddenly on him. Goïmron was as surprised as anyone. 'By Vraccas, why do you all look so astonished? He has lost all his orcs and he never stopped detesting the älfar. He has the rune spear in his possession and he has incredible magical powers we would be well served with if we had them on our side in any battle.'

Gata had to bite her tongue not to blurt out a warning and not to tell everyone what she knew about Mòndarcai. She contented herself with giving a general rejection of the idea. 'We should never accept black-eyes in our ranks.'

'I disagree. He would be a weapon we could use against Dsôn Khamateion. Against the zhussa. If you will permit me, esteemed Magus Mostro – with two dragons against us I'll be happy to have him on my side,' Goldhand added. 'Once Dsôn is eradicated we can always see about dealing with Mòndarcai if he seems untrustworthy.'

The suggestion was greeted with deafening silence.

'What about the Originals Ascatoîa was going on about?' Bendoïn stared at the silent delegates.

'They're sat tight in their holes,' Telìnâs answered, touching the paper älf on the table in front of him. 'We may not like it, but we'd find it very difficult to track them down.'

'One thing at a time,' said Goldhand, nodding at Bendoïn. 'Vraccas will help us. The time of the dwarves is at hand. Let us occupy the new passageways and keep Girdlegard safe in the way it deserves.

'True. It is the Return of the Dwarves,' replied Bendoïn emotionally. 'The Brown Mountains will welcome us back with open arms.'

So Dsôn is safe for now. That means we are all safe. All of a sudden Gata felt a slight vibration under her feet. For a few moments the jugs on the tables rattled, bits of dirt fell down off the ceiling and participants' drinks sloshed over the side of the goblets. A further shaking, like an earthquake, was running through Girdlegard and giving the lie to Bendoïn's words.

The door to the conference chamber flew open.

A travel-stained messenger in a long brown leather mantle came storming in, pulling the filthy hat off his head. He looked utterly exhausted, and very agitated. 'You nobles all! Forgive the interruption.' He went down on one knee. 'I bring news that brooks no delay.' From his shoulder bag he pulled out a heavy box the size of a book and placed it on the table in front of Goïmron and Goldhand. 'Rhuta has fallen.'

'What?' came Mostro's shrill exclamation. He leaped up from his seat as if he had been bitten by a spindle spider. 'That's ridiculous! Who could have got in through the barrier?'

The room was full of excited voices shouting and speculation was rife.

'Those wretched pig-faces,' Bendoïn exclaimed. 'They've tricked us!'

'It'll be the zhussa and her dragons!' someone yelled through the tumult.

'Mòndarcai, I bet,' said another. 'He must have—'

'Can we have calm, please?' This from Goldhand. The room fell quiet. 'And you. Carry on with what you have come to tell us,' he said to the messenger, who had brought a strong smell of sweat, leather and horse into the room with him. The venerable, white-haired dwarf pointed to the box the messenger had brought. 'What is it?'

'You are to open it, they told me. Then you need to touch the blue stone. Klaey Berengart will explain everything else himself, sir.'

'Berengart? To Tion with him!' yelled Mostro, beside himself with fury. 'How does that cut-throat dare to march on Rhuta? He could never have got through the magic barrier! This is a trick.'

'Let's find out.' Goïmron opened the small box and folded up the mirror, which was decorated with floral patterns etched into the glass. He had hardly touched the blue gemstone before the reflective surface showed the view from the high landing within the Chamber of Wonders. Three men and a woman were walking around in the corridors, wearing brand new Brigantian uniforms. They were pulling artefacts out of the cupboards and off the shelves to inspect.

'No!' whispered Mostro, horrified. 'How could . . .? Get out of my palace, the lot of you. Off with you! At once! This instant! Oh, just you wait. I'll come to Rhuta and I'll skin you alive!'

Then the screen showed a different view.

All the delegates crowded round to watch the grinning

visage of Klaey Berengart. He had thrown one of the magus's cloaks over his shoulders and had set a cap far forward on his decorated forehead to cover his black curls. 'My greetings to you all,' he said, speaking in a friendly manner with his croaky raven's voice. 'Surprised?' He waved at them. 'One of the ground rules of warfare. If the enemy is all gathered in one place, go elsewhere.' He pointed behind himself. 'I chose to go to Rhuta, as you can see. Lovely little spot. We've got everything me and my people need.'

Gata had to suppress a laugh. She in no way approved of what Berengart had done but she had to admire his brazen cheek and his courage in swiftly crossing Girdlegard to invade the domain of the highly unpopular magus. That showed class.

'You know you won't be able to keep it,' she said to Klaey's image. 'Don't get too comfortable.'

'How on earth did you get through my barrier?' Mostro demanded. His red face had now turned deadly white.

'Didn't go *through* it. *Over* it. On my flight-mare, you see. The creature is fond of me. Just imagine! It followed me and sought me out. And beforehand it must have devoured poor old Sònuk, I'm afraid,' Berengart elucidated. 'Then I entered the Chamber of Wonders in Vanélia, taking Adelia hostage and seizing power.' All at once he became serious. 'It would not be advisable to come to Rhuta, Mostro. We have what it takes to keep you out. So many artefacts! So many possibilities.'

'I'll nail you and your people to the highest tree and I'll get—' hissed Mostro, splattering those around him with saliva.

'We shall be staying here,' Berengart curtailed Mostro's threat. 'And the funny thing is, Mostro, your subjects are really happy about it. They detest you. Did you know that?'

'That's an outright lie!' exclaimed Mostro, his complexion changing from white to red to white again.

Gata was secretly enjoying the spectacle. Berengart remained an outlaw and the last member of a murderous family – but he was still descended from a ruling dynasty. And he had returned to his ruling destiny.

'The people loved Vanéra. But nobody likes you,' the Brigantian croaked. 'Rutha and Vanélia are now mine. Definitely for the next twenty or thirty cycles. Nobody misses you. Find yourself another realm.'

'I am a magus! You don't have any means of stopping me!'

'Oh, I'd say we had. We've found so many cool things. If you do come we can show you, of course, what we are capable of,' Berengart challenged him. 'Did you know there was a sword that I can use to strike a target miles and miles away?'

'We have got your message. Do you have anything else you want to tell us?' Goldhand looked steadily at Berengart. 'You are aware that your seizing of power has no legitimacy?'

'My message is that I and my people will consider that Rhuta is ours in rightful recompense for the loss of Brigantia. We will treat the people well. I promise,' he croaked. 'No one can throw us out. You know how many magic articles there are in the Chamber of Wonders. Don't think of sending in an army. Or assassins. We only wish to exist here in peace. And who knows? Perhaps we'll move on in two or three cycles, if we find it too boring here.' He leaned forward, his face bigger now on the screen. 'But if you are really intent on war, we will use all the means at our disposal. So my recommendation would be: go and deal with the orcs and the älfar. Or that rhamak. We do not represent any kind of threat to you unless you force us into armed opposition.' He tapped the brim of his hat in a gesture of dismissal.

The smooth surface turned back into a conventional mirror.

'Berengart will pay for this,' Mostro muttered, his face white as chalk. 'Let us take the army to Rhuta and throw the scum out of my palace! I'll work out how to get round the barrier problem. Then we march right in.'

Nobody spoke in the ensuing silence.

Gata looked to the right and to the left. *Nobody's going to support him on this.*

'You have nothing to say?' Mostro had got the message. 'That's the way you thank me for everything I've done?' His voice failed. 'You . . . You . . . you won't lift a finger to help me? You're content to leave Rhuta and all those artefacts in the hand of that upstart of a Berengart?'

'Esteemed magus, see here, we . . .' Goldhand began.

But at this attempt at a diplomatic approach Mostro had heard more than enough. He thrust his hand up. 'I see, Goldhand. I can see very well what is happening here in this room. I am being refused the very support that I gave you all so often myself.' He turned away abruptly. 'This will have consequences for you. For you all. Whatever you have planned for the next few cycles, don't count on me and my arts.' He moved off.

'Where are you going?' Telìnâs was trying to stop him. 'Do stay here. What Master Goldhand meant was: we must find a better way to liberate Rhuta from the outlaw who has taken over. A better way than a military campaign.'

'If anyone wants to offer me support once you have all come to see reason, you'll find me in the Wonder Zone,' Mostro announced contemptuously. 'That will be my transitional realm. Anyone thinking of setting foot there should know that I shall prevent them from so doing. Until I can get back into my own land I intend to stop anyone else charging up their energy from the magic source.'

Paying no heed to the calls for him to take things more calmly, he left the hall, pushing two servants roughly out of his path. They had come in with trays of refreshments. Carafes, beakers and glasses shattered. Wine, beer and warm tea spread out in huge puddles on the floor.

Mostro's bodyguard, Darislaff, followed him out, casting a grim look of pure hatred over the assembled delegates.

It being impossible to continue the meeting after that, Gold-hand called for a break of one full sandglass to give everyone time to order their thoughts.

Mostro, Mostro. That's what I call a dramatic exit. And quite a threat to leave the room on. Gata did not know if she should welcome this turn of events. *Berengart is quite the demon fellow. Brave and cocky with it.* At least the little interlude diverted immediate attention from the matter of Dsòn Khamateion. So it was a success, if a questionable one.

Goïmron sat at the window of the small quayside inn in Waveline, far removed from the intense disputes, debates and urgent negotiations of Girdlegard's powerful leaders. He was dressed in the fashion of humans, in his favourite doublet, with a white shirt, light-brown hose and buckled boots. The wounds on his face and neck were healing but still painful. The medicus said they would leave scars. He would carry the marks with pride.

Goïmron had withdrawn from all the commotion on purpose. He no longer considered he was part of it. Now the sea sapphire had shattered, he had relinquished his role in the drama; the stage belonged to others now. For him the discussions were over. After a quick celebratory drink with Barbandor, he had found himself a quiet corner.

On the table in front of him he had started to record his initial notes for a book he wanted to write. There was a potential, bitter title: *How I Went on a Quest to Be a Fool.*

That was how he felt at present.

He had never made it to magus status. He had not acquired the magic arts associated with gemstones. Everything Chòl-donja had taught him had been a complete waste of effort.

Wasted time. *I am nothing but a gem cutter who was given a tiny sliver of fame by fate.*

He had ordered a cup of tea, raising a few eyebrows. At this time of day people were normally having a beer or a glass of wine. The aroma of warm spiced drinks floated through the room. There was a dartboard on the wall he fancied having a go at. He could challenge one of the locals to a game, perhaps.

'Ah, so there you are,' came Rodana's voice. She sat herself down at his table and requested a herbal infusion. Eyebrows were raised again at this. The blue and white elf dress given her by Telìnâs had been altered to fit and was very fetching. Her unusually dark fingertips and lips did not seem out of place. There were so many outsiders in the fishing community at the moment. 'They're looking for you, you know.'

Goïmron heaved a sigh. 'Who are?'

'All of them.'

'Am I needed to interpret for Goldhand again? Has he nodded off?' He had absolutely no desire to continue in that role. 'They'll just have to wait till he wakes up. I don't want to do that anymore.'

'I get that you're a bit downcast. You've lost the artefact. But your last spell did for Szmajro brilliantly. Girdlegard is safe from that dragon.' Her tea arrived. She thanked the waitress. 'Xanomir was telling us how you got the sea to rise up and seize hold of the dragon. Really good idea, that.' She tapped her mug against Goïmron's beaker, waiting for a response. Then she drank, alone. 'You'll find a new gemstone that suits your talents.'

Goïmron gave her a twisted smile. He had kept the existence of Tallas the sea dragon secret. Xanomir's eyewitness account supported the explanation he had invented. Nobody doubted the truth of it. 'No. I shan't.'

'You're a jewel magus. Of course you will.'

'You're wrong. I'm not. It was all down to the artefact,' he insisted, averting his eyes to gaze out at the harbour, so she would not notice his awkwardness. 'I may be good at evaluating the qualities of jewels. Possibly I can instinctively recognise jewels with certain magic properties. But that's it. That's all I can do.'

'But . . . but didn't you tell me Chòldunja had been giving you lessons?' Looking confused, Rodana pushed back a long strand of blonde hair.

'The theory. Yes. Whatever happened was due to the artefact. I was mistaken.' Goïmron scanned the waves. Tallas was swimming out there somewhere. He had been carrying Tallas around with him in the form of the carved figure on the jewel's setting. Thanks to Goïmron the figure had metamorphosed back into its original shape as a sea dragon. 'I am nothing special, Rodana. Just a dwarf, a scrawny Fourthling and a pretty untalented gem cutter, at that.'

'Don't say that.'

'But it's the truth.'

'It isn't. If it hadn't been for you the dwarves, humans, elves and meldriths would never have joined forces and marched on Brigantia. The Brown Mountains would not have been liberated. Kràg Tahuum would not have fallen.' She took hold of his hand. Her fingers next to his own looked like slender twigs. 'But for what you've done Girdlegard would never have achieved this unity.'

'Then someone else would have done it.' Goïmron turned towards her, thoroughly dejected. All the stress of the recent orbits was weighing on his shoulders. 'Had it not been for finding that book and my quest to locate Goldhand, my best friend would still be alive. So would hundreds or maybe thousands of warriors who fell in battle. I have all their deaths on my conscience.'

'Those soldiers were fighting for what they believed in. They fought against injustice. They knew what they were doing,' Rodana insisted. 'Don't do yourself down. You're putting a really dark perspective on your achievements.' She pressed his hand. 'Please, Goïmron! Think about all the good that has arisen because of you. Girdlegard will soon be flourishing.'

'Will it? What about the älfar in Dsòn Khamateion? And Berengart? And Mostro? And that blue-skinned orc and the prophecies of a new era? And Hantu? Doesn't sound like much of a success rate to me.'

Rodana took a deep breath. 'You are really depressed, aren't you?'

'Worse than that. I wish I had never had anything to do with any of it.' Goïmron drained his tea and rubbed the side of his face. 'No, I wish I could turn back time.'

'And if you could? What then?'

'Then I'd have gone to join Gandelin to watch your performance. I would have seen you and fallen in love with you. Gandelin would have arranged for us to meet and we would have got married. He and Chòldunja would have been our witnesses at the wedding.' Goïmron gulped. 'I know. It's ridiculous. But it's a much better version of events. Don't laugh at me.'

Rodana gave him an enchanting smile and leaned in. Before he realised what was happening, she had kissed him carefully on the mouth. Her darkened lips were soft and tasted of tea.

'We can't turn back time. But we can make good use of it.' She sat down again, not letting go of his hand. 'What have you got planned for the remaining cycles of your life?'

Goïmron was trying to regain some composure. That kiss had given him a certain sensation. It had started in the centre of his body and then shot out to every fibre of his being. 'I . . . I'll go back to Malleniagard and ask Master Sparklestone for a job. He did say I could come back any time.'

'Well, he'll be glad to have you back. A hero in his workshop. Quite a prize. You could make copies of the special artefact and sell them,' Rodana suggested. 'A sapphire in a dragon setting. People will go wild to have one.'

'Good idea.'

'They'll want to have even more if there's a theatre play telling your whole story,' she went on.

'Oh, fantastic!'

'Perhaps in a small theatre in Malleniagard? A permanent theatre. I've had enough of being constantly on the road. It only brings back horrid memories of the time I was forced to spy for Stémna.' Rodana took both of his hands. 'I'm not going to make you any promises, Goïmron. But how would it be if I moved to the same town as you? We could see how things went?'

Goïmron could hardly believe his luck. What a chance for happiness had emerged from the depths of his despair! 'I think that sounds like a marvellous plan. We'll find a house for you that's got its own little theatre! And with a bar! I know all the best breweries!' It all came tumbling out. 'People will come from all over Girdlegard to be in your audience. Dwarves, humans, elves and meldriths! And maybe even älfar if they want. I shan't mind!'

'Mostro will be furious. I'll make sure of that. He can be the wicked magus in the play. The opportunist at Evil's side,' Rodana said, stone-cold earnest in tone.

Goïmron was shocked, guessing her intentions. *She's going to use the play to campaign with. Against the magus and Darislaff.* Of course Rodana could not reveal the secret about Hantu, so she would work against him in a different way. *I shall have to keep my eye on things. Or we'll have a catastrophe on our hands.*

'Always remember the proper term is spectators, not audience.' She covered her seriousness with a smile. 'I've already got a name for the marionette and shadow puppet theatre.'

'Tell me!' Goïmron delved in his pocket for the gift he had been intending to give her.

'Curiosum. One of my forebears was an actor, my mother said. I want to revive the tradition.' Rodana beamed at him. 'I'm so looking forward to everything.'

'May it all be good things.' Goïmron pulled out the moor diamond that used to belong to Chòldunja. He saw the colours, the shadows, the powerful magic within, gathered from the lives of innocent souls. But for Rodana it would represent a reminder of her aprendisa, who had selflessly confronted the rhamak. 'You should have this. Decide what you would like to do with it.' He opened his hand and gave her the small, inconspicuous pale-pink gemstone.

She looked at the jewel in surprise. 'Where did you get it?'

'Mostro dropped it on his way out of the meeting. He knocked over a couple of the servants and the pendant chain broke in the scuffle. It seems the moor diamond did not want to stay with him.'

Rodana touched the stone, tears in her light-green eyes. 'Something to remind me,' she whispered, emotionally. 'We both understand where its terrible power comes from. It must never, ever, be put to use.' Without anyone in the tavern noticing what she was doing, she opened the stove door and threw the stone on to the glowing coals. 'This is what Chòldunja would have wanted.'

They watched together, hand in hand, as the pink moor diamond discoloured and lost its brilliance. Goïmron saw the ragana magic struggling to escape its destruction. The jewel shattered with an audible crack, its pieces falling into the flames and burning up, turning for an instant bright red. A faint chorus of children's sighs could be heard and a cold wind blew through the room, making all the patrons shiver.

'Well, I never.' The inn keeper poked the fire and put on another few briquettes of coal. 'Did you all hear what I heard?'

Rodana wiped away her tears and smiled, pressing the dwarf's hand firmly 'How about it? Shall we have a game of darts?'

And Goïmron was happy.

How does a ragana go on a slimming diet?
She only eats dwarf children.

Dwarf joke

EPILOGUE

Girdlegard

United Great Kingdom of Gauragon
Province of Grasslands
1024 P.Q. (7515th solar cycle in old reckoning), spring

'This is the best testimonial I have ever seen in my long career as a doulia trainer.' Seated at her desk, Gubnara looked at Stémna, visibly impressed. 'Judging from their report, you must have been reading your Widestone employers' wishes from their eyes.'

'Thank you, Mistress. I think I read their wishes from their very souls,' Stémna said, adding, 'I found it easy to adapt to them. I'm quick on the uptake when it comes to sensing others' priorities.'

'Exactly what Helka of Widestone has written here about you. Her report is full of respect and admiration. I get the impression it's more than mere gratitude.' Gubnara placed the report down on the desk and folded her hands. 'She also says you have been a great support to her in her bereavement.'

'I know what it is to suffer loss. It is never difficult for me to put myself into others' positions, Mistress.'

'How did it happen?'

'You want to hear about my own personal loss?' Stémna deliberately misunderstood Gubnara's meaning.

'Perhaps another time. For now I need to learn more about the death of Tithmar of Widestone. As far as I know the pitiless tyrant enjoyed excellent health. It appeared the cruellest divinities had taken him under their wing.' The sixty-year-old Gubnara narrowed her eyes. 'Exactly how did he come to die?'

'A rebel ambush. A group of resistance fighters targeting members of the nobility in the province. There was a message left scrawled in blood on the snow,' Stémna summed up the events. The lies came easily to her. 'They kidnapped and then killed him.'

'Quite a relief for the whole region. Now Hekla, her family and the Wideholm villagers, too, of course – they're all free of his cruel yoke.'

'That is true. But the funeral procession was just what he would have wished for.' Stémna continued her fluent string of lies, so as not to let any suspicion arise. She did not want to be interrogated on the matter. She was sure Gubnara already had an inkling she might have been involved in the death of her employer. Without direct evidence it was all speculation. Hekla would say nothing, she knew.

'You realise that you were originally intended for a completely different family?'

'Oh, really? No, I had no idea.' One lie followed dutifully on the heels of the next. *I'm getting quite good at this.*

'Someone must have muddled up the assignments.' Gubnara indicated the testimony. 'But it seems that in the end it was the right person who was sent to Widestone.'

'I did what I could.'

'If Helka was so pleased with your work, you must have been almost a member of the family. So why did she dismiss you?'

'There were changes in the household after Tithmar's death. Helka and the children decided they wanted to manage without servants or serfs. So I was sent away. But Helka told me I could come to her at any time if I encountered any problems. No matter what kind of trouble.'

Gubnara raised her eyebrows. 'The Widestone family are going to run the estate by themselves?'

'Yes, with help from the villagers. I think it's a bit risky. But it's a very progressive attitude. Well, it's a new idea in this region of Gautaya, that's for sure.' Stémna certainly did not regret what she had done. She would do it all again without hesitation. Killing the despot Tithmar had given her a deep satisfaction she had never known in her previous existence.

'That is one way to see it, I agree.' Gubnara tapped the desk decisively with both palms. 'Whatever. You are now available for different duties. I think we'll have a new vacancy to fill tomorrow. Go and rest, for now, do your laundry and enjoy the spring sunshine.' She got to her feet and leaned over to give Stémna a hug. 'Everyone will be told about your splendid record of achievement. You will be receiving a vote of praise from the highest authority.'

'Too kind of you. I was only doing my duty as a doulia.' She returned the embrace and then left the room. 'My thanks to you for accepting me as a candidate.'

'Never forget it. I would not like to have to remind you,' came Gubnara's warning as Stémna was closing the door behind herself.

Stémna analysed how the interview had gone. She was lucky that the situation in Wideholm had changed to her advantage, although she had now lost her direct access to the noble family as their doulia. She did, however, still have a certain influence on Hekla and the Widestone household.

Her dirty linen was quickly washed and hung out to dry in the fresh air. The sunshine was doing its best to dispel the last of the winter. The first insects were buzzing around in their search for blossom.

Stémna turned to cast her eyes over the extensive grounds of the estate where doulia were trained for placements in the households of the highest noble families. Not only to serve them and to make their lives as easy as possible – there was a hidden reason, too. A greater purpose. Stémna was determined to find out more about this.

At nightfall she slipped across the landing to the secret staircase down to the archive. Manipulating the special mechanism, she quickly had the door open. This time no light had been left burning. She had to make her way down the steep steps in the dark. She did not dare light her lamp until she was at the foot of the stairs.

Little had changed since her last visit. The vaulted cellar was full of cupboards and shelves for storing documents holding details about the rich and the mighty, together with information about their localities. She noted that a few new marks had been added on the large wall map. There were now more doulia than ever, scattered throughout Girdlegard, except for in the dwarf realms and some areas in the elf lands of Tî Silândur. These untouched regions had been marked with different symbols whose significance Stémna could not work out. She took a step back in order to see the map better. *The doulia have got pretty much everywhere.* They were now safely installed near the seats of power and knowledge. *But none near the new passages that have recently formed.*

She was curious to find her own personal file so she could see what evaluation had been recorded for her. In the register she found the positive comments about her work record. Nearby there was a sealed flask with a clear liquid in it. The top was fastened with black wax.

What can that be? Stémna lifted up the phial and held it against the light, shaking the flask gently. A viscous liquid moved slowly inside the bottle. The flask could not be opened without breaking the seal, so she could not test its odour. *Poison?* She replaced the phial with the utmost care. She found a note referring to the small flask.

> Not yet ready. Not a natural born doulia. Effectiveness
> not guaranteed or not desirable. More evidence needed.
> To be excluded from awakening programme.

So what, by all the demons, is the awakening programme? Rather than finding out answers to riddles, Stémna realised she had found herself an even more complicated problem to solve. She would only find out more when she had achieved the next level. *Am I an obedient doulia or do I try to find the answers on my own?*

She cast a glance at the sealed phial that she was not to be granted access to. If she were to break the seal and try the contents she would be found out. And perhaps she would be dead. Nobody with a trace of common sense would taste a substance of completely unknown composition and especially if there were an explicit warning attached to it.

I'm afraid I'm going to have to be patient and wait. Stémna closed the drawer.

She could, on the other hand, use one or two of her special orange feathers and send the cellar and the whole place up in a fireball. The doulia conspirators would lose their commander, their archive and all the valuable knowledge they had acquired.

Whatever it is they're using all this information for, it won't be for the good of Girdlegard, I suspect. Stémna used her lantern to shed light on the shelves and cupboards. *If I set fire to it all I might well be doing my next good deed.*

But that would not bring her any closer to her goal of revenge for the murder of her dragon mistress. *The bonfire had better wait till later.* Stémna extinguished the light and left the secret archive. *I'll find a way to discover what is really happening. For now patience is the name of the game.*

Almost as soon as she had got back into bed and closed her eyes the night seemed to be over. She was up with the first cock-crow, busy helping with making breakfast, although no one had told her to. Some of the other doulia acknowledged her with a new-found respect. News had obviously got around of the praises she had received.

The whole community took the first meal of the orbit together in the big hall. While they were eating, Gubnara got up from her seat on the raised dais where the supervisors sat. She moved over to the desk with solemn steps and rang a small bell for everyone's attention.

'May this orbit start very well and spur you on to higher attainment,' Gubnara said, addressing the doulia in the hall. 'I take great pleasure in announcing a commendation for one of your number.' She pointed at Stémna, gesturing for her to stand up. 'In recognition of her accomplishments in the Widestone household, and in the light of the outstanding testimonial, I hereby confer on our sister Elora the honour of the Golden Hand. Elora, please come forward to receive the insignia.'

While all those present applauded, Flora moved over to the desk to accept the button-sized badge in the shape of a hand. It was fashioned from real gold.

'The Golden Hand stands for meticulous attention to our standards of behaviour, and for pride in total devotion to our duty of service. Wear it with dignity. And ensure you are always worthy of it,' Gubnara said solemnly, while she pinned the emblem to the material of Stémna's tunic. 'Until the time of the Awakening.'

'Until the time of the Awakening,' came the echoed chorus from the other doulia. Another round of applause was heard.

After an embrace from the leader of the doulia, Stémna was

sent back to her place, where she was congratulated by those sitting close to her. 'I shall try to be like you,' one of them whispered to her.

'Elora will be setting off this very orbit to take up her new post at the royal court in Khalteran,' Gubnara went on. 'Nobody could be better qualified for the position.'

There was a further burst of thunderous applause.

Stémna put on a show of being delighted, but on the inside she was disappointed. Khalteran was in the extreme south-west and thus a long way away from Dsôn Khamateion, where she suspected the treacherous murderer of her own former mistress would be found.

It was illusory to assume she would be able to get into the älfar realm to seek Mòndarcai out. And it was even more illusory to presume that she would manage to be in the city on the very orbit that Mòndarcai was there. It was, however, dismaying to be sent so far away.

'Now I should like to announce another honour,' Gubnara said. 'Isbilla, top of this cycle's whole training group will be going to Rhuta. Klaey Berengart wrote to me personally from the Magic Realm, to request that we send him the best of our doulia to serve him. I assume he is tired of artefacts and wants some proper company.'

There was a ripple of laughter in the hall.

That's the last place I'd want to be sent. Stémna took a drink from her herbal tea. *And to have to cope with the demands of that dodgy Brigantian.* She grinned, remembering their last encounter. *But, of course, he's got his flying horsey thing back now. Nasty vicious creature. I should have killed it.*

'Oh, how exciting,' a doulia near her was heard to whisper. 'How I envy her.'

'Rhuta is probably just like any other place,' said Stémna, hiding the fact that she had ever been there. 'Apart from its magical properties, that is.' She replaced her cup quietly on the table. 'And Berengart is an idiot. Wouldn't be any fun, serving him.'

'No, that's not what I meant.' The other doulia was acting as if she was privy to secret information. 'I mean because of his friend.'

'Berengart doesn't have any friends. He has subjects. They'll follow him until his fortunes change. Mostro won't leave him in peace for long. Believe me.' Stémna asked for the platter to be passed and helped herself to some cheese. 'It's going to get uncomfortable in Rhuta. Death is on its way.'

'But there might be an opportunity to catch sight of the älf.'

'Did Vanéra have one in her dungeon, ready to experiment on?' To go with the cheese, she had her eye on the gooseberry jam. Excellent combination of tastes. 'How unwise.'

The other doulia gave a polite laugh, hand held in front of her mouth. 'No, she didn't. But I saw in the written records that one of Berengart's men mentioned that Mòndarcai had come back.'

As if electrified, Stémna sat up straight in her chair, the desire for jam forgotten. 'He's in Rhuta?'

'You see? So you *would* want to go there after all, wouldn't you?' The doulia sighed. 'How I'd love to see him with my own eyes. His tionium armour, you know. Pieces of it anchored directly into his flesh. And his magical spear, with the rune—'

'I expect Berengart's fellow was just saying that for effect. Probably not true at all. Why on earth would Mòndarcai be meeting the Brigantian?' Stémna pretended to be astonished at the idea. 'It makes no sense.'

'I'm only telling you what I saw in the reports. Daleris, one of the junior sisters, vouches for the man. She was listening in when a group of Brigantians were talking together. It seems Mòndarcai paid Berengart a visit at night and demanded one of the artefacts from the Rhuta Chamber of Wonders. He was going to come and collect it. And he had said if he got it he would, in exchange, spare the Brigantians' lives.'

'Oh, in that case. Yes, you're right. That is exciting.' So now it was starting to make sense. *The älf is looking for new possibilities. And I shall be there when he turns up.* She would have to make sure of taking over Isbilla's assignment, even if she would have to practise deception. She would have to wear a mask to prevent Berengart recognising her.

Of course, Isbilla would not surrender the job voluntarily. The position carried prestige.

And so it happened that Isbilla, the best doulia of her group, fell down two flights of steps. And broke her neck. By the time anyone found the young doulia, she was past help.

By the afternoon of the same orbit Stémna was on her way to Rhuta, armed with a dazzling testimonial from the noble Helka Widestone, together with any number of orange feathers, and a seething determination to meet the hated target of her revenge – the murderer of her former mistress. *But I can be patient. I will wait. However many cycles it takes.*

AFTERWORD

The latest episode of the saga of the dwarves has taken slightly longer than usual to arrive but it is a double volume. I hope you will find it has been worth the wait.

I realised that the previous stories had all been told in books one to five.

There are, of course, flashbacks and references to the past, but, as with the Uldart chronicles, a new approach had to be found – an approach that would allow the characters and the landscape itself to move forward, making room for innovation and providing new sources of surprise. An approach that would satisfy loyal readers and catch the imagination of newcomers.

While making the first outlines I noted the influence of ideas that seemed to arrive of their own accord. Such a wealth of potential material demanded two books for itself.

And opened up possibilities for further novels in the sequence.

The end of this double volume hints at the challenges to be faced by the heroes and heroines. I am looking forward to all of them! And I can reliably inform you that things will soon be under way. Very soon!

My thanks are due to the publishers, Knaur Verlag, for their unstinting support for our 'Little People'. And to my initial test reader Yvonne Schöneck, who has cast her expert eye over the text, unfailingly checking phrases, sentences, descriptions, dialogues, and details of various types of weaponry.

Markus Heitz
Late spring, 2021

DRAMATIS PERSONAE

DWARF TRIBES

Firstling Kingdom

Buvendil Shellgrasp, of the clan of the Hot Smiths, tribe of
the Firstlings, engineer and constructor

Xanomir Waveheart, of the clan of the Steel Makers, tribe of
the Firstlings, inventor and engineer

Thirdling Kingdom

Belîngor Blade-eater, of the clan of the Steel Fists, tribe of
the Thirdlings, warrior

Brûgar Sparkbreather, of the clan of the Fire Swallowers,
tribe of the Thirdlings, warrior

Hargorina Deathbringer, of the clan of the Stone Crushers,
tribe of the Thirdlings, female warrior

Regnorgata Mortalblow, of the clan of the Orc Slayers, tribe
of the Thirdlings, queen of the Thirdlings

Fourthling Kingdom

Bendoïn Feinunz, of the clan of the Arrow Seekers, tribe of
the Fourthlings, commander of the Fourthling troops

Goïmron Chiselcut, of the clan of the Silver Beards, tribe of
the Fourthings, gem specialist

Fifthling Kingdom

Barbandor Steelgold, of the clan of the Royal Water Drinkers, tribe of the Fifthlings, city councillor in Platinshine

Gyndala Tenderfist, of the clan of the Gold Finders, tribe of the Fifthlings, female blacksmith and mason

HUMANS

Adelia, Vanéra's famula

Chòldunja, Doria Rodana's female apprentice

Doria Rodana de Psalí, female puppeteer

Emaro (of) Staine, obrist in Fortgard

Enes, one of the Doulia

Fridgatt, sailor on the *Seablade*

Gubnara, trainer of the Doulia

Hantu, a rhamak

Helka of Widestone, Tithmar's wife

Ilenis Berengart, Kawutan's wife

Joros Gunmarr, admiral of the Sinterian naval forces

Kawutan Berengart, younger brother of Orweyn

Kiil, Irmon, Jowna; Brigantians

Klaey Berengart, Orweyn's youngest brother, a zabatay

Mostro, Vanéra's famulus

Ólstrum, ship's cook of the *Seablade*

Orweyn Berengart, Omuthan of Brigantia

Stémna, envoy of Ûra

Tithmar of Widestone, member of landed gentry in Gautaya

Vanéra, maga

ELVES

Randûlas, leader of the delegation from Tî Silândur
Telinâs, elf warrior

ÄLFAR

Ascatoîa, zhussa
Cintalôr, reconnaissance scout
Èthoras, assassin
Mòndarcai, warrior
Ophîras, warrior

ORCS

Akrosha the Beheader, female leader of the salt sea orcs
Borkon Gràc Hâl
Mortog the Murderous, Akrosha's brother
Shashka, priestess in Kràg Tahuum
Torsuk, healer

OTHERS

Grasstooth, smallest dragon in Girdlegard
Nebtad Sònuk, srgāláh
Slibina and Szmajro, flying dragon siblings

PLACES

Arima, main island of Undarimar
Dsôn Khamateion, älfar empire in the Brown Mountains
Enaiko, city of knowledge in the south of Girdlegard
Gautaya, empire in Gauragon
Kràg Tahuum, orc fortress in the centre of Girdlegard
Landbolt, a mountain, eleven thousand paces in height
Platinshine, a fortified dwarf settlement at the foot of the
    Grey Mountains
Smallwater, humans' village near Platinshine
Tî Silândur, elf realm
Towan, river in the north of Girdlegard
Undarimar, marine empire in the west of Girdlegard

RACES AND SPECIES

acront, huge warrior creature that hunts down beasts
armoured fish, large fish found in the Inland Sea
bastard-horse, mounts that orcs ride on
by Cadengis, a common oath
Cadengi, a group of divinities widely worshipped in Brigantia
Cadengis, the most dangerous of the Cadengi gods
Cadengis' mother, the most dangerous of the Cadengi
    goddesses
doulia, immigrants from the Outer Lands who volunteer to
    serve as slaves
drinx, a mythical creature
fire eaters, beasts in the lava fields in the north of Girdlegard
flame flyers, flying snake-like creatures, related to dragons
meldriths, people of mixed elf and älfar parentage

narshân beast, a wolf-like predator
Phlavaros, the älfar name of the first flight-mare
ragana, moor witches
rhamak, summoner of souls
salt sea orcs, beasts living in the salt deserts of the empire
    of Gautaya
srgāláh, humanoid with head of a dog
visok horse, a large type of horse
ygota, flying insects sensitive to magic forces

TITLES AND DESCRIPTORS

aprendisa, female apprentice
banner officer cadet, junior soldier in the supply corps
famula/famulus, human with a talent for magic, in training
fîndaii, elite elf regiment in the service of the Kisâri
Ganyeios, title of the ruler of Dsôn Khamateion
Kisâri, title of the empress of the elves
magus/maga, sorcerer/ sorceress
Omuthan, title of the prince of Brigantia
zabitay (m) or **zabitaya (f)**: rank of general in Brigantia
zhussa, female älfar magician

MISCELLANEOUS TERMS

Consortio, governing assembly in Safegard
Elriahaube: name of diving bell, *Elria Bonnet*
P.Q., post quake
quid, chewing tobacco
suihhi, name of a deadly plague in Gauragon
war wolf, a catapult of extremely large dimensions